THE PRICE OF
FREEDOM

MICHAEL C. BLAND

This is a work of fiction. Names, characters, places, and incidents are products of the author's imagination or are used fictitiously and are not to be construed as real. Any resemblance to actual events, locations, organizations, or persons, living or dead, is entirely coincidental.

World Castle Publishing, LLC
Pensacola, Florida
Copyright © 2025 Michael C. Bland
Hardback ISBN: 9798891263390
Paperback ISBN: 9798891263406
eBook ISBN: 9798891263413
First Edition World Castle Publishing, LLC, April 8, 2025
http://www.worldcastlepublishing.com
Licensing Notes
Cover: Dorothy Mason
Editor: Karen Fuller

DEDICATION

To Gary. The best brother-in-law a guy could've asked for.

My name is Dray Quintero. I'm not the monster they claim.

I've been labeled the most treasonous person in history. Supposedly responsible for the deaths of hundreds of people trying to overthrow the U.S. government.

We were trying to rescue it.

I used to be an engineer responsible for many of our country's innovations—including a surveillance network that linked every camera across the nation. The software was meant to keep you safe. They'd twisted that as well.

I tried to warn you. Our government has been hijacked, those pretending to be our elected Congresspeople hiding behind the technology implanted in our heads. We needed to take our country back. Yet my plan failed.

Now, my family has been imprisoned, held by the true traitor, a man who'd once been my friend. My older daughter and I have been tortured, my younger daughter hooked to machines. Barely alive.

I've failed everyone.

Timeline to Rebellion

Year

2030   The OCB1 virus escapes the thawing permafrost. Highly contagious, the virus attacks humans by crystalizing the lenses in their eyes before consuming their brain tissue over a nine-week period. The infection rate is 97.7%. Within months, over 1 billion are blind worldwide, and 40 million are dead. Although human travel, commerce, and interaction virtually cease globally, infections continue to rise.

2030   Unable to create a vaccine in time to save humanity, scientists discover that OCB1 is affected by medical-grade steel. They propose a radical plan to world leaders: replace every citizen's lenses using the same procedure as cataract surgery and install a permanent steel rod into citizens' brains to neutralize the virus.

2031   In the greatest mobilization of resources and healthcare providers in history, countries across the planet follow their scientists' advice. Billions are saved. The United States, however, becomes mired in political posturing and lawsuits. Though a percentage of Americans opt for the procedure, most refuse. Millions needlessly die. Sensing America's expanding weakness, foreign terrorists begin to attack U.S. cities, killing thousands. During this time, American innovators begin to modify their implants.

2033   As U.S. deaths reach 32 million, more Americans decide to adopt the OCB1 procedure. The country starts to emerge from its darkest days but finds itself left behind by the rest of the world as China, Russia, India and others expand their influence and eliminate their reliance on the West.

2034   Following the success of those early American innovators, Congress passes the Personal Integration of Vital Organized Technology (PIVOT) Act, which mandates that instead of simple silicone lenses, each citizen be implanted with lenses that have clear computer screens—and the implanted rods expanded to contain neural nets, offering a way to save lives, as well as make the U.S. competitive and innovative again. After some resistance, the law is embraced by tens of millions.

2035   Adoption reaches 85% of the population, but PIVOT mandates every citizen receive the modified lenses and neural nets. The law includes severe penalties for noncompliance, including forced implantation. Even so, the U.S. government struggles to achieve 100% adoption and enlists the National Security Agency (NSA) to help.

2037   The U.S. once again becomes the dominant country on the planet. The NSA grows in size, as many still refuse to get the new implant, though terrorist attacks in Chicago, Miami, and Los Angeles strain resources. The attacks culminate in the Daisy Chain Massacre when multiple bombs explode in cities from Los Angeles to Atlanta. 4,300 people are killed, and 21,000 are injured. Dozens of separate security cameras capture video of the terrorists responsible, but by the time the footage is compiled, they fled the country.

2037   Dray Quintero's company is commissioned to link the country's security camera systems into a unified whole. Dray oversees the project, completing it in under 10 months. Crime plummets, and terrorist attacks stop.

2038   The NSA morphs into The Agency, the government's domestic enforcement body. Under new leadership, The Agency unleashes drones and other surveillance equipment, begins physically enhancing its Agents — and starts using everyone's implants to spy on people, further tightening its grip. Within six months, virtually every citizen is implanted.

2038   When Congress reconvenes, a group of Congresspeople implements a coup d'état. No one outside the Capitol witnesses it, as The Agency uses people's lenses to hide their takeover.

2040   Kai Spencer, a former NSA/Agency employee, claims the government was overthrown. He posts a shaky video to support his accusation and agrees to do a live interview but is murdered fourteen seconds before his feed links with CNN's network. His killer is never found, even though five separate surveillance cameras guard his apartment building.

2042   Two women claiming to be Agency employees post statements supporting Spencer's claim and upload documents — schematics, computer code, and other information — to prove their assertions. News agencies pick up the story, but the women disappear. Though The Agency quickly erases the documents, the story strikes a chord in those who have felt something's off. Individuals from Schenectady to Eugene locate copies of the documents — nothing is ever completely deleted online — and as they decode the data, they realize they have to fight back against a ruthless enemy. The rebellion is born.

2047   Dray Quintero illegally accesses the network that controls the implants of everyone in the Los Angeles/San Diego area. He broadcasts a claim that people are being lied to, that their implants are being used to manipulate and trick citizens. Riots break out in both cities, and Quintero is labeled a federal criminal.

2047 Two months after Quintero's broadcast, five hundred self-proclaimed freedom fighters attack numerous locations across the country. The attacks result in dozens of innocent citizens dead, state and federal property damaged, and most of the freedom fighters killed or captured. Quintero is identified as the mastermind of the coordinated attacks. Declared the most heinous traitor in the nation's history, his whereabouts are unknown.

CHAPTER ONE

I no longer trusted my mind.

The Agency, the nearly all-powerful federal organization that controlled the country, had not only imprisoned my body, they'd hijacked my brain, repeatedly warping it. Mapping it.

I was imprisoned in a cell in west-central Texas, that much I was sure of, but the setting projected onto the lenses in my eyes was so clear, rendered so deep, I felt my control slipping.

My senses told me I stood on a rocky ledge that jutted out over a turbulent sea. Saltwater sprayed up as waves crashed against it, the droplets so cold they stung my skin. Inland, a massive, funnel-like structure stood, its top at least two hundred feet wide, the bottom a fifth of that. Men in mechanics' jumpsuits worked on the structure, assembling the final pieces. As I watched, some attached a rippling metal panel to the hull while others ran diagnostics on the primary engine.

Drones flew past the structure toward a thermal energy generator a quarter-mile away, its distinctive bulge and angry red glow a giveaway. One seemed linked to the other.

I risked losing my grip on reality.

The men seemed to ignore me as I approached the structure. I could hear their voices, though the crashing waves drowned their words. I could smell the saltwater in the air, felt the fitful breeze.

The breeze was what scared me.

A man appeared beside me. "This is just the first of dozens we'll set up," he said. He was my height but thin, tanned, his hair swept back with a touch of grey at the temples, jaw solid in a way that magnified an underlying cruelness. He wore a mechanic's jumpsuit like the others, though it looked wrong on him, like he should be wearing a business suit instead. "They'll clean the air in months, powered by your fusion reactors when you fix them. Then we can start reintroducing species."

"The reactors still don't work?" I asked. I'd managed

to ignite Gen Omega's first reactor, though I'd heard my old company had failed to light any others.

"That's why we need you."

Something felt wrong. I didn't remember walking to this spot.

"This unit will clean thousands of cubic feet of air per minute," the man continued. He pointed toward the middle of the structure, which had its panels removed to reveal an empty interior. "We'll have rows of Olishaly-coated filters to capture carbon monoxide and dioxide."

He continued, but I tuned him out. The design had been tried and abandoned. They should have gone with nature's most efficient design, a lung, though modified —

I cut off my thought. People were watching my brain activity, searching for knowledge, thought patterns.

I could feel my grasp on my mind crumbling.

At first, I'd easily been able to shake off their efforts as I'd had a tiny hole burned into one of the clear computer screens that coated my lenses. Anya, the brilliant surgeon I'd fallen for, had burned the hole in my lens — the same kind of lenses the entire population had — months ago when my enemies had used them to blind me. But The Agency's scientists had found it. Every lens had a camera attached to it that rested in a person's blind spot. The scientists had probably found it that way, though how didn't matter. I'd fought them as they replaced my lens; now, I had to fight to retain my grip on reality and resist giving them what they wanted.

With an effort that made me sweat, I struggled to imagine my small, dark cell rather than the scene my senses told me was real. Yet, it was nearly impossible to ignore the signals that filled my mind.

Then I caught something, a rhythmic sound that was out of place. I clung to it in desperation.

The cruel man grabbed me, the feel of his hands so real I struggled.

The sound grew louder. A helicopter.

The man yelled over the sound, "We have company."

An image of a helicopter appeared though it looked wrong, superimposed on the cloudy skies overhead. I could have shouted in relief. The hasty addition of the helicopter ruined the scene.

The projected world broke down around me, and I returned to reality, first seeing only blackness, then my cell as the overhead lights brightened: cot, sink, toilet, and a TV encased in Plexiglass. The sounds disappeared — except for the helicopter.

I scanned the windowless room to see if someone had actually touched me, but I was alone.

I'd been injected with a device I thought of as a burrower that tapped into my brain, allowing The Agency to read my every thought. I'd been tortured, manipulated, and experimented on, the latest of which were these damn simulations. I'd been able to retain a toehold on reality, but each projection was a fight to what felt like the depths of my soul.

The touch I'd felt in that simulation was disorienting — and alarming. Whoever ran the simulation must have projected it through the implant in my head, along with the sights, sounds, and smells. My implant, an inch-long computing device in my head, was just like the one every other citizen had, though an Agent, Kieran, had made sure I could never remove mine by anchoring it in place. An implant allowed a person to access the internet, store libraries' worth of data, interact with others, and enhance their skillset as it connected to the clear computer-screen lenses in people's eyes. Yet, it had never been able to mimic other senses before.

Not unless the burrower they'd injected, which now resided in my brain, was responsible.

I cupped my implant with calloused fingers as the fake world faded, though they could use it, or the burrower, against me any time they wished.

I could go mad in this place. I couldn't escape. There were fifty or more Agents of varying degrees in this prison. There was no chance for freedom.

The helicopter seemed to land directly overhead with a jarring thump, then quieted as its engine revved down. I knew who'd arrived. Zion Calloway. Head of The Agency and, by extension, the true leader of the country. Even if he hadn't initiated the secret coup d'état that had overthrown Washington, my former friend controlled everyone's implants. That power enabled him to hide the true identities of the men and women serving in Congress and possibly the White House.

I thought about that sense of moving in the simulation. If they developed that more fully, it had terrifying implications. Future prisoners wouldn't know what was real.

This wasn't the first time my enemies had tried to trick me. Their scenes were usually in motion when I woke, complete with sounds and smells. I'd been disoriented the first time until I'd focused on the hole in my lens and realized what The Agency's scientists were doing, though after they'd replaced my lens, I'd struggled every waking moment to discern what was real.

Zion's arrival was concerning. I wondered why he was here.

I noticed a small rod lying by the door—which was ajar. That was new. It stirred an old hunger. However, it could be fake. I remembered the day I'd woken to what I'd thought was a patient room at a rebel camp, and Kieran had nearly tricked me into stepping off the roof of a half-constructed high-rise, the danger around me masked by the false image of the room displayed on my lenses.

The rod and open door could be false as well.

I'd been imprisoned for over a month. It was a nightmare how I'd gotten here. When my nineteen-year-old daughter Raven had ripped her then-boyfriend's implant out of his head, I'd covered up her crime. Then she'd told me about her hope to join the rebels and free the country.

I'd thought she had been fooled by conspiracy nuts who had taken advantage of her desire to do something profound with her life.

When I realized the threat she'd described was real, I took her, her twelve-year-old sister Talia, their mother Mina, and fled to the rebels. Then Talia was shot, a victim of Mina's betrayal, and died in my arms. Or so I'd thought.

I was caught, blinded, and stabbed. When I regained my

sight, my stab wound patched up by Anya, I did something desperate to save Raven: I blasted a challenge to the citizens on the West Coast to rise up and fight for their country. Raven had been more correct than she'd known, as our enemies didn't just use our lenses to mask the damage done to the air we breathed, they masked the coup.

My broadcast had saved her — and thrust us into the effort to take down The Agency and everyone behind the coup.

I hadn't learned Talia survived that gunshot until two months ago, after I devised a plan I thought would take down The Agency. Once Mina announced Talia was alive, though I didn't trust Mina, I couldn't ignore her claims. I had to search for my daughter.

Raven and I managed to break into this complex to save Talia, but it had been a trap. Talia was alive — but only so Zion's men could experiment on her, violating her by reading her thoughts to finetune the systems they planned to use on the rest of the population. Zion wanted to access and interpret people's thoughts to find any threats to his power, and her mind served as an exceptional test case.

Now Raven and I were captured, and Talia was on the verge of death, hooked up, a shell of herself. I hadn't seen her or Raven since that day, no matter how I begged, though I'd heard Raven screaming in pain night after night, her room somewhere close. I'd pounded on my door and shouted to stop their torture, to no avail.

Her screams told me she was alive, but her suffering gutted me.

I didn't know if Talia was still here, if she was OK, or if Zion continued to use her. Given the wires hooked to her brain, I suspected he kept her alive to continue his experiments. I feared the day she would no longer be useful.

I'd planned the attack on the nodes that enabled The Agency to hide their coup but abandoned the fight, abandoned my friends, to rescue her. Yet I'd been caught and the rebellion destroyed, gunfire and explosions wiping out those who'd fought for freedom. My friends, our hope, gone.

I wanted to bust out of my cell and hurt every Agent I could get my hands on, but I didn't go for the rod. I wasn't going to fight. I wouldn't give Zion the knowledge of how my mind mapped when I did. Besides, one rod wouldn't let me do the one thing I yearned to do with every fiber of my being: get my daughters out of this hellhole. Give them a chance at life.

The door opened the rest of the way, and two Agents walked in, both of whom had inflicted innumerable pain on me. Pierce was an inch taller than me at six feet, broad-shouldered, close-set eyes, his full head of silver hair swept up and styled, wearing lined slacks and a dark-navy Oxford shirt. Wraith's silver hair was shorter, nearly a buzz cut, though Agents had to keep their hair long enough to cover their many implants — which was why their hair was silver, to hide them. Wraith had a square face, two scars along his jawline, and a wide mouth, his black slacks and off-white shirt not as nice as Pierce's, though his shoes were made of premium leather. Steel tipped, I suspected.

Pierce strode toward me and slammed his fist into my face, the force throwing me back against the wall. "You should've done your job."

They came at me, fists connecting, then feet when I found myself on the ground. I'd lost weight over the past month and felt it as they attacked. I tried to deflect their assault, but they'd learned my weak points, back of my head, kidneys, groin, the foot I'd injured when I'd cut open a sphere containing dark matter. I couldn't do more than protect my face.

"Get off him," a deep voice commanded.

Zion stood just inside the room, looking disgusted and frustrated. He had similar features to the man in the simulation, cruel jaw, hair touched with grey — though it was tousled, no doubt from the helicopter ride — brown-eyed and tan, coated in a $5,000 suit that fit perfectly.

My former friend, college roommate, and business partner, the one behind all of this. Earth had nearly run out of oil. Panicked, world leaders had extended their supplies by including additives, though that had polluted the skies and caused terrible breathing issues. They'd invented lung diseases to blame for the rise in deaths and used everyone's implants to mask the brown skies. Some learned the truth, of course. Nothing that big could be completely hidden. So Zion used my own network to find those who discovered the truth—and squashed them.

He motioned to the TV. "Why isn't it on?" It used to run constantly, showing various scenes and events. After I stopped reacting, they stopped. Now when it was on, it only played C-Span, which showed the fake Senators and Representatives he had installed. More mind games.

He turned to Wraith. "He's in better shape than he should be."

Wraith swiveled and kicked me.

"Not the point. You're not getting the data needed." Both Agents hesitated, their annoyance poorly hidden. "A solution takes many approaches. Didn't your military training teach you that? Or were you not listening?"

They stiffened and began to reply, but he waved them back and faced me. "I'm past being impressed by your fortitude. What I do is ugly, but I have to do it. If you saw, you'd agree, though I'm not sure you'd have the stomach."

I saw the toll whatever he was talking about had taken on him. I wondered if the man I knew in college was still in there at all.

As if reading my mind—which he could—he leaned forward. "Remember we talked about making the world better? To enhance people's lives while saving the planet? Help me do that."

I got off the floor and sat on my bed, pain flaring from where the two Agents had beat me. "What do you want?"

"We're taking steps but need to do more. This is where you come in."

He seemed sincere, but I didn't believe it.

His expression changed, and I again feared he'd read my mind. I had to confuse him. "By doing 'more,' you mean shackles and torture for everyone?"

Zion's nostrils flared. "Don't you care about the fate of the planet?"

"I tried that."

Yet my thoughts betrayed me. I recalled the attack I'd orchestrated, rebels blowing up the locations where Zion's Agency had hidden node structures that broadcast their lies onto people's lenses. He had known of our plans. His men slaughtered our people. Memories flashed of Anya and Raven's boyfriend Jex disappearing in an explosion, others shot down, the bodies and the later claims, proclamations as a result of the attacks, all blaming me, ignoring the fact I'd lost many I cared for. I told myself I couldn't have stopped what had happened. I probably would've died as well.

With our failure, The Agency and those who stole the country would lock in their power for generations. He no longer had his nodes, but he'd switched his network to a drone grid before we'd attacked, so we hadn't hurt him. He retained his control.

"Companies have read people's minds for years, but not at this level," Zion told me. "Now, with the implants and our research, I can root out those who would rise against us. I just need the last bit of data from you to pinpoint the worst threat."

I didn't know what he was talking about and didn't have the strength to find out. I'd fought out of necessity to protect my family. And, over time, I'd believed I had a moral obligation to fight for everyone.

Look where that got me.

"You're so noble," I said dryly. "The country should thank you."

"Stop making me the monster," Zion said. "I've protected this country from rogue AI systems, country-wide riots, and dozens of foreign attacks. You have no idea. Work with me."

My body tensed, causing another flare of pain, as Kieran suddenly entered the room. "You *are* here. I didn't expect you."

The athletically-built, angular-jawed Agent I'd fought numerous times, who'd stabbed me, manipulated me, led the team that had shot Talia, and slaughtered an entire room of rebel hackers. My vision narrowed as I clenched the mattress. Kieran sported a streak of sandy-blonde hair now, his hair having grown back naturally where Raven had blasted him the day we'd invaded this godforsaken place, the blonde dark compared to his silver hair. His foot, a casualty of a previous fight with me and Raven, was no longer in a cast, but I detected a slight limp.

Like the other Agents, he had multiple implants in his head. His primary one, which I'd removed, had been replaced with one that stuck out an inch from his skull.

"This is the leading edge of our efforts," Zion said.

Kieran didn't look convinced. "I know you have other demands on your time—"

"You're not doing a good enough job." Kieran started to protest, but Zion cut him off again. "You're fully operational. Act like it. I'm running out of patience. You're better served elsewhere."

Wraith leaned toward Zion. "If we had more specific direction—"

Zion glared. "Here? With him listening?"

The room felt claustrophobic. I wasn't used to so many people in here, and I'd only glimpsed Kieran once over the past month. Yet I'd been a focus of his.

Kieran said, "We make progress daily."

"I gave you a chance to achieve our goal, but it's time to take the next step."

I dropped my head. I was done looking at them. I was done, period. I'd reached my end. A month of beatings. A month of not seeing my girls, of Zion's psychological games and constant battle to protect my every thought without end. I wanted to save my family, wanted to strangle Zion for what he'd put us through, but couldn't find a way. I'd barely seen them, barely seen much of this place—and I questioned what I did see. Zion had made sure of that.

I might go insane.

"We both know he won't just fight. He needs a reason," Kieran said. "The motivation we talked about. It'll enable my team to map the missing parts."

Against my better judgment, I looked up. Zion was gazing at me thoughtfully. "I'm going to show you a kindness."

I said, "You gonna let me drive a tank over you? It's been my dream."

"I'll let you see Talia. I expect you to cooperate."

"And put her in more danger?" Even as I said that, I ached to see her.

Kieran gave an inscrutable look. "She doesn't have long."

* * *

As Kieran clamped my arm and pulled me to my feet, I tried to temper the fear his words evoked. Talia had been so vibrant before they shot her.

I nearly tripped as he led me to the door, but he slowed, holding onto my arm so I could regain my balance. He then straightened my shirt before leading me out of the room.

His acts of civility confused me. We were enemies. I was his captive.

We stepped into the hallway where men dressed in grey passed by, either orderlies or guards, I wasn't sure. This section of the hallway was utilitarian, an area of the building that was part of the hospital section but unrenovated, light fixtures yellowed and walls blank; the only decoration was the plaques that displayed door numbers. I wondered which room Raven was in, the solid doors masking the contents of the rooms we passed. I'd heard her screams over the past month, each one shredding me, coming from what sounded like the next row over, but I didn't know where exactly.

Kieran and I walked for a minute, my injuries making my limp worse than his, this section of the Facility cold and forlorn, then through a pair of security doors—what I assumed was a monitored checkpoint—and into a nicer, hospital-like area that was familiar from the day we'd invaded. We passed a larger room with a long window that revealed a research lab where a 3D holograph of a brain filled much of the space. Men and women in white coats walked around and through the image, pointing to different sections and the data that hovered throughout the image. I wondered if that was Talia's brain, mine, or someone else's.

I started to get excited, even as I tried to prepare myself

for the worst.

We passed a nurse's station with staff also dressed in grey; the doors here had windows in them, though many had coverings over them. The sounds of medical equipment operating and soft voices caressed the air, almost foreign to me.

I glanced at Kieran, who seemed even more menacing with the blonde streak in his hair. I couldn't trust him, but I couldn't stop myself. "What is Zion planning?"

His bio-enhanced jaw flexed. "Focus on this time. You'll thank me. Remember, I didn't put her in this condition."

Maybe my fear of how I'd find Talia made me reckless. "But you did. You aren't a hero, no matter what you tell yourself."

His eyes narrowed, then he forced me forward. Seconds later, he stopped and opened a door.

Talia's room.

My heart hammered in my chest as I stepped inside, Kieran no longer beside me. He backed away and let the door close between us.

The room was as I remembered, with a scattering of equipment—next-gen holograph interfaces, satellite rapid uplinks, multi-phase communicators—to the right side of the room, and a lone hospital bed to the left, partly hidden by a curtain. The body in the bed was so small. I forgot how small my younger child was.

I stepped closer, saw her face, and tears formed.

Unlike last time, she laid on her back though her head was to the side, a lump laying on her chest, the wires attached to her head curving away toward various machines nearby. She seemed catatonic, though her cheeks were fuller than I remembered, her brown hair a tangled mess. A small hand rested on the lump, her breathing shallow, a shell of who she'd been. I feared if she woke, she'd be as distant as when we'd broken in to save her.

I dropped to my knees beside the bed, not bothering to look for a chair, and took her other hand. After a moment, I dropped my head, my worst fear imagined: my daughters imprisoned and in pain, me helpless to change it.

She wouldn't want to live like this, fragile and confined.

I felt movement and heard a rustle.

I raised my head. Talia was staring at me. She then looked past me to the door—and swiftly sat up, one hand holding the thing on her chest, the cords attached to her skull rising up with her, her auburn eyes sparkling.

Full of life.

She smiled. "Abouts time."

CHAPTER TWO

I stared at Talia in disbelief as I knelt beside her hospital bed. She was supposed to be near death, a ghost sustained by Zion's beeping medical machines after he'd "cracked" her. I wanted to scan those machines but couldn't look away. She smiled at me with secrets and amusement.

"I had to wait for Stripe to scoot. He was snooping," she said.

The contrast from the barely-alive waif I'd expected was so jarring I struggled to keep up. "'Stripe'?"

"Kieran," she whispered. I realized she was referring to the sandy-blonde streak in his hair.

She brought her knees up, drawing the blanket up with her, and rested the object she'd been holding on her knees. The gleaming cords draped against her spine as they hung from the back of her head.

Other than the cords sticking out of her and the ominous device on her knees, she looked vibrant, her skin healthy and pink.

My joy sparked and swelled so intensely it hurt. I hugged her, not caring how awkward it was with her knees up, the cables from her head brushing against my arm.

"Shmaltzy," she said but hugged me back.

I didn't want to let go but had so many questions. "OK talk," I said as I pulled away, noting her hug had been shaky. "What happened? You looked weaker a month ago."

"I wasn't that bad—well, kinda bad—but I couldn't squawk with those gooners around. I've been getting stronger for a whits but been hiding that from them. It took oodles to locate my bio readouts in their system, and they knew at first I was healing, but once I found the right reads, I fiddled with the data, so they think I'm still weak."

"What do you mean locate your readout?" She couldn't leave the bed, not with those wires.

She leaned forward, the sparkle in her eyes growing. "They totally whiffed things. They plugged me into their system." She giggled. "I know they scanned my noggin and used me as a wheel rodent, but they gave me something they never should've: access. I'm plugged into this place."

She was an excellent hacker. She'd broken into the LAPD's system, my company's database, government websites, and who knew how many other systems. Zion's men had hooked her into his network—and she was claiming she'd taken advantage without their knowledge.

I'd feared Zion would turn her into an Agent. I never dreamed she'd turn the tables.

With a start, I scanned the room and spotted what I'd feared. A camera in the far corner capturing all of this. "Talia, it's too late."

She followed my gaze. "Posh. I flipped that ages ago. I had to, to stealth my abilities. It's on a loop. We need to hush-like, though."

"Are you saying you took control of that camera?"

"Not just that one. I'm hooked into the whole Agency system." She wiggled excitedly as she struggled to keep her voice low. "I can open doors, mask cameras, change data. I've got fingers in the whole soup. It's *huge.*"

"Do they know you have access? Have you changed things?"

"Not that they would've noticed. Like my bio bits. I changed the info mouse-like over time to be sneaky. They think I just lie here, which I do, but while my limbs lay all floppy, my mind explored their system. I created whole pathways with my mind, like a snake in their maze. Or a worm."

I was stunned. These idiots hadn't had a clue about her abilities—or thought she was too weak.

"Don't you see?" she asked with big eyes. "I'll help you escape."

My mouth dropped open. "You...how?"

"First time I woke up in this creepy room, I was so confused. When I tried to move, I was tied down. Took bits to realize what they'd done. They saved me. Brought me back. Didn't they?" Before I could answer, she hurried on. "I figged they were using me, felt an interface-presence that didn't just read my head whispers, it tried to change them. At first, I let it, but then I noodled how to slip under the scientists' noses, let them play with randoms. I was too late to stop them from buffering me, but I wanted them to pay. At first, I only did it at night, but after I sunk my claws in, I found my feeds, ghosted my movements, and went exploring.

"I found you once," she went on, "trying to jimmy an Agency office. I hid your implant codes before it could trip alarms and helped you."

The memory struck me: crouched in the stairwell of that office building in Los Angeles' New Downtown, trying to use my implant to hack the door lock into The Agency's office. I'd failed — but it had unlocked on its own. She'd done it.

"I couldn't find you after that, not until your broadcast at the football stadium. I slowed Agents so you could skedaddle. Did other stuff, too, like that blinking light at the farm. You needed an exit. Coppers almost had you, but their scanners told me where you were. I hid you two other times and blocked a feed that would've blabbed your face."

"I had no idea."

"When you busted in to snatch me, I knew it was a trap. I wanted to help, locked doors to block some of the silver creeps from reaching you, but it wasn't enough."

I was stunned by what she'd accomplished and could do, but I was also afraid. "Agents may know you're faking, that your weakness is a sham. They could be toying with you."

"Only Kieran comes to see me."

"Then he knows."

"He acts odd. He gave me a teddy bear," she indicated a small, white-haired bear that laid next to her pillow, "and moved two of the louder machines away so I could snooze better."

I glanced at the machines. In addition to the equipment I'd noticed before, there were four machines that monitored biometric data, including a heart monitor and blood oxidation.

"You control these, too?"

"They were trickier, but yeah."

As she talked, I touched her, assuring myself she wasn't a projection, that she was alert. "I'm so sorry I left you at Free Isle."

"Dad, they tried to make me a robot. They had no right." Her face clouded. "I couldn't shield you from what they've done to you. I looked in a few times but couldn't watch. They kept hurting you, then flooding you with visions. I had to be super careful not to interfere."

A thought struck me. "Are you looking through my eyes? Can you?"

"Looking through eyes would make me queasy. Not sure I could warg that. I mean, yeah, maybe, but so icky." She brightened. "I can trick Agents, though. They have screens over their peepers, too. I've used that to make them think I'm ghost-like when an Agent nurse checks on me."

"Do you know what Zion is up to? Does he want to reconfigure everyone's mind?"

"Not reconfigure them. His peeps have learned how to scan people's thought bubbles, tracking attitudes, feelings, and other bits to see if they'll rise against him."

This was what Zion had been talking about. He'd eradicate threats before they had a chance to blossom.

"I can erase The Agency's data when it's time, but if I do it now, they'll discover my access."

I was thrilled by her ability, even awed, but until she acted, Zion could read my mind, which meant I had to be careful. Somehow, I had to shield my thoughts. Not only could I screw up and reveal her secret, Zion could use her against me. Now that I knew she was healthy, I had to get my family out of here. I'd longed for it since Zion trapped us, but now, for the first time, I let myself consider it.

I felt cautiously excited. "What do you have in mind for an escape?"

She rubbed her hands together in a way that almost made me laugh. Even with being in Hell, with her being hooked up, she could bring that out of me. "I'll trick them, use their tech and locks against them. You warn Raven and Mom."

I hadn't been allowed near them, but as I opened my mouth to admit that, she wavered, her cheeks paling. For all of her claims, she was still a young girl who had been through a tremendous amount—and I feared she was weaker than she acted.

At my insistence, she laid down and rested her cheek against her pillow. She looked at me sadly. "I couldn't stop your hurts. I'm sorry, Daddy."

I assured her she had no reason to apologize and convinced her to let me examine her. The three cords disappeared into the base of her skull via some kind of bio-interface ports. The fourth went under her hospital gown.

With her assistance, I shifted her gown to inspect the device attached to her chest without exposing her. The cable that disappeared under her gown went to a box with a digital readout. Two wires exited the box and plunged into her body, one going into her ribcage down to the right and the other to the upper left, both close to her heart. I also saw the top section of a scar that ran vertically down her chest.

I realized the device did two things: tracked her heartbeat and sent signals to whatever The Agency had surgically implanted, probably within her heart. The scar indicated as such.

"My heart can't beat on its own," she said in a small voice. "I have holes in it. Moms told me."

I struggled to maintain a positive expression, but if I tried to take her out of here, she could die in minutes. Maybe seconds. A hurt as strong as the day I'd thought she'd died—that she *had* died—gripped me.

I brushed strands of hair from her face. "My lioness. I'm so sorry for how you've suffered. You're so strong. I'm proud of you."

Her eyelids dropped, but she forced them open. "Raven's tried to run away, but you haven't. Whys not?"

"I wouldn't leave you."

"You have to. Take Moms. She cries most nights."

"You realize she's why you're hurt." Mina had betrayed

us back on Free Isle, after we'd hid with the rebels, by contacting Kieran and making a deal. In exchange for us, she'd get her data files that synched with an app that allowed her to pretend our son Adem — who'd died as an infant — was still alive. Her betrayal had led to the firefight that had taken Talia from me.

I could never trust Mina again.

"I remember," Talia said softly.

Rallying herself, she said, "I've hidden your implant codes and will corrupt all your data bits, so after you three scoots, you'll become invisible from The Agency's systems. I think Zion already knows how your noggins work, but his software will misread your faces. He won't find your codes anywhere, and any searches for any of you, names and stuff, will come back empty. You'll be able to hide, maybe have a chance.

"I have the programs ready, but the only way it works is if I protect you so you can run away," she added.

I realized the implication of what she was saying. "No. I won't do it. Leaving you behind will wreck me."

"You have to. I'll help you three escape. But I'm staying."

CHAPTER THREE

Worry and anxiety gripped me as I left Talia's room. I needed to stop my tumbling thoughts, but I was overwhelmed. I couldn't ignore what I'd learned — or the sacrifice she planned.

Kieran approached from where he'd waited down the hall. "Were you strong for her?"

The oppressiveness of this place crashed back in as I imagined leaving her behind.

Kieran steered me back through the complex, though I only half paid attention to our route, more focused on the Agents we passed, each one a threat, each one an accomplice to our enslavement.

What Talia suggested was highly questionable. Multiple systems ran this place with dozens of cameras and even more men and women, each stationed here to undergo the metamorphosis from patriotic soldier to brainwashed, biologically-augmented Agent.

Breaking out was impossible.

Though she had done impossible things in the past.

Even if she could get us out, I wouldn't leave her.

Kieran and I entered the two-door checkpoint. The first door had to close and lock before the second one would unlock, possibly a security addition after Raven and I had invaded this place — though we hadn't reached this back part of the building.

Raven.

I could destroy Raven's best chance to escape, to have a life, by trying to take Talia with us. She needed to be free, but I could doom both of us by simply trying.

As the first door locked, Kieran clamped a hand around my neck and leaned close. "There's no way your little band of rebels could've won. Zion's control can't be broken."

I stiffened when he clamped my neck, but his words made my muscles ache. I was terrified I would reveal Talia's secret. I let myself look distraught. Maybe Kieran would think I was too focused on Talia's condition to pay attention.

The second door opened, and we entered the prisoner section, the cold walls, bare light fixtures, and metal doors too familiar, as was the smell, a mix of cheap paint, bleach, and mildew.

Pierce walked toward us, his styled hair bobbing slightly, patent leather shoes reflecting the harsh light. "You coddle him, Kieran. Clout him in the kidneys." He pantomimed a low punch as he passed.

Kieran paused, stopping my forward progress with the hand gripping my neck. Worry flared, that he'd read my mind or that he'd follow Pierce's advice. A number shot through my mind. Seventy-six. I wasn't sure what it meant.

After a moment, Kieran continued down the corridor, which had smaller hallways to one side. "Talia is well cared for," he said almost conversationally. "If she starts to hurt, we'll give her pain meds. Zion will allow that now. I don't want her to hurt, Dray. When it starts to get bad, I'll insist she doesn't suffer."

We turned down the hallway to my room, though I only tangentially noticed, his words more painful than any blows from his steel-like fists.

He opened the door to my room, the burnished metal adorned with the label C-12, and pushed me inside. "Play your role. For your daughter's sake." He then added under his breath, as if weighed down by some thought, "We all have roles."

He closed the door.

I stood rigid, warring with myself, my mind too active, which threatened both her and me. I hadn't thought of escaping before, hadn't had a reason unless I knew I could somehow take her and Raven with me.

Ninety-seven, my mind whispered. I didn't know what it meant. Didn't know if Talia could actually do what she claimed. Didn't know if Raven was healthy enough to run, if they'd broken her.

I was being watched, maybe more at the moment than normal. There wasn't a mirror in my room, but I wasn't fooled. Cameras watched the room, one obvious — the one hanging in the corner—but certainly, others that were hidden, additional systems against us.

I had to guard my thoughts, hide my reactions. But Talia was not only healthier than I'd thought, she planned to sacrifice herself for our family. The thought nearly broke me.

Movement caught my eye. A swarmbot crawled out from a crack where the wall met the concrete floor and angled to look up at me. A handful of the black, five-legged robots, each about the size of a keyring, had survived and now hid in the facility, though they weren't enough to do anything, not like the tens of thousands Garly had sent when we invaded this place. As I looked at the tiny 'bot, a second crawled out, both concerned about me, their sensors tuned to my emotional state.

I was at a loss, not sure how to absorb what I'd learned.

I didn't want Talia to risk herself, but she'd do it whether I agreed or not. She'd do it for the ones she loved. She was too much like me in that regard. She would throw her life away for us.

Then I understood the number. Ninety-seven steps between my cell and Talia's room. I'd counted. Which meant I'd already made my decision.

Besides, the alternative was whatever Zion planned for us once we stopped serving a purpose.

I needed to figure out a way to use Talia's access to get us out of here. It wouldn't be a matter of just unlocking some doors.

Yet I was apprehensive. I'd made mistakes before, not listened, taken the hard way out of pride or protectiveness for my daughters, which had led us here. I'd actively opposed my government, had plotted against it, hurt people, and caused so many to die. But the alternative was to be complacent, which would have led to a different form of imprisonment for myself and my family. I'd had to fight.

And I had to fight now. Each piece of data we surrendered to Zion was a tool he could use to control others.

While I hadn't considered escaping before, Raven certainly would have, so they had a baseline. That's why I'd resisted making plans, as I would've shown Zion's team how my brain worked. I would've revealed too much.

I needed to mask my racing thoughts. I could feel my synapses firing like crazy.

To distract myself, I focused on the door, not to figure out how to escape but how it was constructed. The hinges were on the outside, of course, the metal solid. The door was controlled by biometrics, as were most things here, with a four-inch square device in the wall near the door, though as I looked closer, I noticed a tiny hole where the thumb was placed. I'd first assumed the device scanned the fingerprint, but I could see the tip of a needle inside the hole. It drew blood instead, every time an Agent used it to unlock the door.

In addition to the keypad, the door's handle had a key lock. OSHA must have an influence even here, with the key lock able to open the door in the case of a power outage. Yet this carried a separate risk. If Zion discovered Talia's access, he could cut all power here, severing her influence, yet still reach his prisoners with the right key.

Stepping back from the door, I scanned the pockmarked walls of my dingy room, cameras and other monitoring devices hidden in those miniscule craters.

I thought briefly of the network I'd created that linked every public and private surveillance camera across the country. Another mistake I needed to fix, somehow. I was certain Zion had used a version of the software's architecture to create his web of lies.

The door unlocked, and Wraith entered, close-cropped hair like a forest of tiny silver spears. I tried to wipe my mind of all thought.

"How was it seeing your girl?" he asked, his voice educated but barbed. When I didn't answer, he added, "She's in bad shape. How long do you think she has?"

We locked eyes and one of his lit up with data projected on his lens. Tracking my response.

I couldn't slip. I wouldn't be able to protect her if I failed. Forced my thoughts on him instead. Most Agents dressed well. Surrendering their souls to The Agency must've paid handsomely.

Yet Wraith didn't spend his money on his wardrobe.

"Time for your walk," he said.

It felt as if we were a few minutes early from our daily routine, but I didn't argue. I followed him out of the cell, though he paused to face me. "You're acting different. What're you hiding?"

I forced a derisive laugh. "I can't hide anything, remember?"

He frowned and pushed me forward.

I carefully tried to keep my mind blank as I took in my surroundings, really took everything in.

My cell was in the last row of the prisoner area.

Most of the rooms in this area were cells, though some were occupied by Agents to more closely monitor some of the prisoners. I'd briefly glimpsed a few during lunch shifts and trips to the yard, though some days Zion kept me trapped in my room.

The hallway with my cell was connected to the corridor Kieran had used earlier. Now, Wraith and I passed three other cell-lined hallways. Those other cells could be occupied, or none could be—though I'd heard other sounds of torture in the night, not just Raven's.

Right now, the area was quiet.

Beyond the cells, the main corridor branched in two directions. The path to the right led to Talia, but Wraith steered me to the left.

We approached a set of fireproof doors which unlocked as we neared, and we passed the main cafeteria as we continued down the hallway. A dozen Agents of various degrees were scattered about the poured-plastic tables; they were eating and talking as if they were factory workers on break.

He led me to an intersection with a larger hallway. Doors lined the hallway in both directions, another blast door nearby. As we stepped into the larger hallway, I spotted two more Agents, women with the grace of natural athletes. Past them was a supply closet.

The closet inspired me. I'd need a battery for the device on Talia's chest.

Another Agent passed, an older one with a ring of scars on his throat, and I shoved my thoughts of Talia aside. I couldn't slip like that again. Focused again on the Agents.

There were probably more here than any other location outside of their D.C. headquarters. Of course. This was where they were made.

Agents were soldiers who'd failed Special Forces training. Somehow, they were convinced to subject themselves to the modifications, enhancements, and indoctrination that twisted them into silver-haired Agents who did Zion's bidding.

I scanned Wraith's head, his multiple implants poorly hidden. One implant protruded higher than the others, possibly a transmitter. Another was grid-like, its wavy pattern expanding the implant's surface area, probably so it could receive terabytes of information, tactical data, and whatever else oppressors needed to quell the populous.

I suspected their implants included cognitive boosters, along with communication systems that spanned the spectrum in order to hook into so many networks besides their own: other governments', private companies', and so on.

Even if my family and I could escape, I thought as Wraith led me toward the far door, I didn't know how to avoid recapture. The Agency controlled every surveillance system — and had been scanning my brain for weeks. Yet I felt Talia was sending us on a crash course.

Brilliant sunlight briefly filled the hallway as the far door that led to the prison yard opened, and someone was directed back inside the building.

When the door closed and my eyes adjusted, I stopped. The person led inside was Raven. It was the first time I'd seen her since we'd invaded this place. Old bruises were visible on her face, and her golden-brown hair was ragged, but her body was leaner. Stronger somehow. She'd lost the index and middle fingers of her right hand to a gunshot from Sari Britt, a female Agent with a bob of silver hair and an athlete's body. Raven had been given metal replacements with plasma cores, in order to use them as weapons, but those replacements were gone, the bioconnectors in her stumps visible. She wore the same prison garb I did, olive shirt and tan slacks. It was a stark contrast from the day in Free Isle when she'd been happy, believing she was starting the life she was destined for, strong and unscarred and full of life.

Her jade-colored eyes flashed with anger when she saw me — not surprising, given how we'd left things between us. Then, still locked on me, she scratched the edge of her chin. It was the signal Mina and I had devised in college, a secret code to indicate one of us wanted to leave a party.

Wraith pushed me past her before I could respond.

She was still fighting.

I realized he had done this on purpose, to make me falter. I cast my thoughts aside and stepped through the door into the yard.

The Facility occupied a huge swath of land. Two rows of barbed-wire-topped fence ringed the property, keeping everyone where Zion wanted them. The prison yard was a smaller fenced off area inside the compound, twenty square yards of brittle grass to serve as a semblance of exercise.

I was the only prisoner in the yard. They never allowed prisoners out here together. It was always just myself and an Agent.

I began to pace the outer edge, pushing through aches to regain even a sliver of strength. The sun was intense, the wind nonexistent. I tracked a cluster of eight Agents as they jogged past, most with at least two additional implants. Not full terrors yet, though they would be.

Zion wanted to show his grip. That's why his Agents didn't blend in. Their silver hair was only partly to hide their implants. The other part was to display his control. They were designed for enforcement, not espionage.

I would not leave Talia here.

The heart-shaped face of my wife, Mina, flickered in my mind. It triggered a thought that would be risky. I shifted my gaze outward to mask my struggle.

Farms occupied the lands around the Facility. A road cut

to the west, two others to the north at different spots. We were far from the eyes and concerns of the world. I tried not to dwell on that either and began to run number sequences in my head.

Sometime later, Wraith returned me to my room.

He stared at me, one eye bright with data, though I sat on my bed and tried to ignore him.

An Agent-in-training entered with my lunch, shredded beef, corn in a brown sauce, and lumpy mashed potatoes served on a rectangular tray.

I began to eat, using the plastic fork that served as my only utensil. I slowed, then forced myself to continue. I needed to get stronger. And I needed to do something I never thought I'd do.

Wraith sat next to me. "What are you thinking? You're hiding something."

I set the edge of my fork down on an empty section of the tray. Kept my mind blank.

"You can't win this. You might last a couple of days, but your thoughts will slip through. It's inevitable."

The next thought that shot through my head would be recorded and analyzed.

I risked a glance at him, realized I'd been holding my fork at that angle for a reason. I pushed down, and the fork's handle snapped diagonally, creating a shank about five inches long.

I raised my arm, cocked it back, and jabbed the shank toward my jugular.

Because of where he sat, Wraith couldn't stop me from finishing my jab, but he reacted faster than a normal person. He shoved my elbow forward so the shank would miss my neck— which is why I steered the shank downward. And plunged it into my body.

CHAPTER FOUR

The shank's rough point pierced my skin under my clavicle, nearly three inches deep, the momentum from Wraith's blow forcing it an inch to the left, which widened the wound.

Blood soaked my shirt.

Wraith leapt to his feet. "What the?"

I kept still so I didn't increase the damage and focused on the pain.

He left my cell and described what I'd done to an Agent in the hallway, a woman who was just visible from where I sat. "Maybe he couldn't take it," she told him.

I gripped my shoulder and hoped he wasn't the only one confused.

As they talked, I gazed at the camera. Talia might be watching. I wanted to assure her, but others watched as well.

Wraith returned, grabbed my good arm, and pulled me out of the cell. Passing stunned stares, we returned to the large corridor and turned left. The third door down was the infirmary.

I was deposited in an exam room and left under the watchful eye of yet another camera, privacy laws disregarded in this hellhole.

As I started to feel lightheaded, the door opened, and my wife entered.

Mina wore a floral shirt I didn't recognize and black pants, a stethoscope around her neck, her black hair pulled into a bun. Her brown eyes were wide as she took in my blood-spattered shirt and the shank sticking out of my upper shoulder, her Mediterranean skin pale. I noticed a faint frown line that hadn't existed before, and her cheekbones were more prominent, which indicated she'd lost weight, though her outfit hid her body.

She turned around, and that's when I noticed Wraith holding the door open. "What did you do?"

"He tried to hurt himself. I stopped him from something worse."

Her eyes returned to me, this time searching my own. I knew that look. My actions weren't like me, and she was searching for an explanation. More than two decades of marriage would do that.

I would've thought the same applied to her, though she'd caught me by surprise when she betrayed us, her grief over the loss of Adem deeper than she'd let on. I hadn't known she'd made a digital version of our baby son using InMemorium software, which grew into a little boy before her augmented eyes until the day she betrayed us.

Wraith shut the door, leaving me with her as if it would be another form of torture. Under different circumstances, it would've been.

She gathered supplies from various cabinets and set them on a nearby tray. "I've hoped to see you," she said softly. "Though not like this."

"I didn't know you worked here," I lied. I'd spotted her twice over the past month, each time with a stethoscope around her neck.

"I want to help where I can." She rolled a stool over, sat, then paused. She would have to get close to work on my injury. In one flicker of her eyes, I read fear, longing, and uncertainty.

I remembered the day I fell in love with her. We'd been college students, two months into dating and already spending more time together than apart. Her car had developed an odd rattle, and I'd offered to fix it. She'd helped, though she didn't know much about engines. She got greasy with me, acting as my assistant and learning my tools as we worked. We fixed the noise, a water pump that we replaced, and she'd been proud of having assisted. As for me, she'd shown her smarts, ability to learn quickly, and lack of pretention. When I pointed out the grease in her hair and the streak on her nose, she laughed, then kissed me.

That had been the start of what I'd felt was my life. Until her betrayal.

After Talia died, Raven and I had fought for our lives, eventually joining the rebels. Then Kieran had put Mina on TV to reveal Talia was alive. I'd been torn, not sure I could believe her, not wanting to risk the hope and hurt it brought. But I had. I'd searched for Talia, sacrificing everything to get to her, and found her alive, though the announcement had been a trap.

Raven and I had been prisoners since then.

Now, I had to do something I'd never planned to do again. I had to trust my wife.

I flickered my eyes up at the camera. I hoped Talia had figured out my purpose—and had the access she claimed.

"I'm going to start working on you now," Mina said, her conflicting emotions audible. Watching me as she neared my injury, she leaned in, face inches from mine. She raised gauze pads to clean the wound. After soaking those, she replaced them with a fresh set and motioned to the shank. "I'm going to have to remove this."

And I had to confide in her. It's why I'd stabbed myself, to talk to her.

Talia wouldn't be able to block the video in the exam room, so I lowered my head to hide my face and began to scratch at the paper covering the examination table I sat on to interfere with their microphones. I said, "Don't react to what I'm going to say."

Mina nodded as she leaned in and took a hold of the shank's handle.

"Talia is going to break us out."

Mina jerked back, triggering a burst of pain as she yanked out the shank too fast. She gave me a wide-eyed look, then jammed the gauze pads into my bleeding wound.

I let my face show pain and displeasure, then lowered it again from the camera's view. Scratched at the paper. "She's been faking. She's alert, and she's tapped into Zion's systems. She's going to get us out—but she plans to sacrifice herself to do it."

"Oh god," Mina whispered as she pressed the gauze against my wound. "No. She can't."

"It's going to happen." I wished Valor was waiting for us past the fence, but she would've been long gone. She had traveled to this area with Raven and me, but I'd forbidden her from invading it with us. When we hadn't escaped, she would've moved on. If she hadn't, she would've risked capture herself.

"You know the extent of Talia's injuries?"

Mina hesitated, then nodded. She pulled back, busying herself with changing the soaked pad for another one, and dabbed at my wound instead of pressing into it.

"Don't you want to save our daughters?"

"It's all I want to do. The gunshot from that day," she hesitated, struggling, "pierced Talia's heart both entering and exiting. The Agency's team put her on a blood bypass machine as they surgically patched the holes. One patch covers an entire side of one of her heart's chambers, and a second one covers a portion of another chamber. Both have to flex in perfect harmony with her heart, or she'll go into arrhythmia. If either patch loses power, they stop completely. The box on her chest coordinates the beats."

I continued to scratch the paper, crinkling it as well. "Does the device have a battery backup?"

"Not that I know of."

I thought about the plug that ran into the wall. It had an A/C to D/C converter, which meant I could rig one.

"She also has the holes in her head, which might need to be sealed."

I felt a flash of anger. "You caused her to be hooked up."

She cut away part of my shirt, then took a needle, gave me a hard look, and jabbed my chest near the wound. As she injected the clear fluid, she said, "I'll probably be reprimanded for numbing the area, but I thought you'd appreciate it."

I almost snapped as threads of old fights resurfaced, arguments long since inconsequential. She knew what she'd done. She'd lived with it for months. Talia's condition, their lives, had to have been a nightmare.

I reached up and scratched at my implant, purposefully looking at the camera. Maybe Talia would get the message and somehow interfere with whatever readings Zion would get from this conversation, which was also risky.

I refocused on Mina. "I was selfish to leave the rebels. I abandoned the fight, abandoned those who needed me, for my family. Talia plans to make the same sacrifice."

"She's suffered enough."

"She wants you to go with us."

Mina's hand began to tremble as she reached toward my injury, a threaded needle in one hand. I caught her wrist, squeezed it, then let go. She took a breath, then with a steadier grip, began to suture the wound closed.

Her voice dropped to a whisper. "Zion isn't military, not like the Agents. I've heard them complaining. They think he's using The Agency for his own benefit. They're bothered by having kids here, too. Talia wasn't the only one. We could foster that—"

"We don't have time. She'll try to free us regardless of what we tell her. I need your help to get a large battery, at least eighteen volts, along with wire, a sling or tape, and tools to unhook her. And a weapon, knife, scissors, something."

She pulled back to look at me. Her emotions were clear: guilt, wariness, anxiety.

"I need it fast. I don't know when we're leaving."

Understanding dawned on her, and she looked at my wound, then my face. I nodded. She pursed her lips, then refocused on my shoulder to complete the last sutures.

"Even if we get outside, we'll need a way to get away, a car or something," she said, then paused. "Wait, a battery? I don't know of any. I've never seen one in a supply closet."

We had to keep Talia's heart beating.

I couldn't risk looking at the camera again, so my eyes wandered the room. I spotted a medical device, an old-style monitor. There had been a similar one in Talia's room. After Mina finished her work by spraying the injury with a foam sealer, I stood, then pretended to stagger as I stepped forward and fell into the device, taking it with me as I fell to the floor. Pain flashed but I ignored it as I did a quick check. The monitor had a battery backup, which easily popped out. It would work, though I would need wires and a way to splice them.

Mina helped me back to the table and checked the injury. "You need to make sure the same device in Talia's room is plugged in."

"I'm not sure I can do any of this," she said.

"You have to. For wires, you could rip ones out of a device. We need two sets."

She looked at me uncertainly.

"You also need to tell Raven. She has to be forewarned."

"She won't talk to me. I've tried."

"Make her."

Mina turned away to busy herself with cleaning up the used gauze pads and medical tools. "Britt tortured her after you two were first captured. It was one of Zion's mind games, making the woman Kieran cares about do something she hates doing. Yet she did it. She scarred Raven."

"All the more reason to get Raven out. Both of them."

"As soon as Zion thinks I'm up to something, I'll be restricted or kicked out."

I tore the wrinkled paper as I clenched my fist. "Help me save them — whatever the cost."

CHAPTER FIVE

Two days later, the door burst open, and Wraith and Pierce stormed into my room.

"What—?" I started. Before I could say more, they punched me in the stomach and threw me against the wall.

Something had changed. They weren't holding back. Pierce stomped on my ankle, and Wraith kicked me in the groin.

In the past, I'd lain there. No reason to fight. This time, I forced myself up. That surprised them. Before they adjusted, I launched myself at Pierce, landing a shot to his jaw, before Wraith pulled me off and threw me to the ground.

The cameras in the room took on a new meaning. Talia. I pushed myself to my knees, then raised my head.

Wraith punched me hard, his fist like a piston. I caught myself before I fell back to the ground. Straightened. "You made your point," I said, my voice not as firm as I wanted.

Zion entered the room wearing another expensive shirt, indigo this time, with tailored slacks, his tie and jacket abandoned. "Your readouts have changed. Why?"

I hadn't heard from Mina and didn't know what she'd accomplished. I hoped she'd remained under his radar.

"I want to see Raven." It would give me a chance to warn her myself.

I scrambled to my feet as if I was going to run out of the room, but Pierce shoved me back against the wall. Pain flared across my back as I collapsed, my sutures mostly holding, though I felt blood.

Zion smiled. "Something's altered your thinking. You're not suicidal. Why did you injure yourself?"

I knew he didn't expect me to answer his questions out loud. He looked to my brain activity for the truth. If I ever got out of here, I would send a bolt of electricity into my frontal lobe to fry the electronic device he'd buried there.

As I stared at him, I thought of how much pleasure I'd feel

pushing him off a building.

"To attempt an escape," Pierce said.

"Readings are similar, but it's more," Zion said as he scanned me. "To sacrifice yourself? Obtain nanobots to get stronger?" When I didn't respond — and pictured in my mind one of those toy monkeys that banged symbols together — he grew angry. "Talia has been a boon to us. We've plotted hundreds of minds and millions of thoughts, but we needed to make sure our mapping was accurate, which is where she came in. Once we cracked her, we learned how to read the creatives and geniuses."

I wanted to strangle him.

"You were the final piece. We needed to find the markers of thought people follow when they're going to rebel. We got some data from Raven, but her desires are wrapped in ideology, a level that's unique to the young and extreme. Ideology will always be a difficult source of threats to track, but I need the reluctant fight that spawned *your* rebellious thoughts."

He came closer, clearly comfortable that his men would save me from choking the life out of him. If I'd been stronger, I would've tried. "Kieran was right," he said. "Your kids are your weakness. How much more do you want them to suffer? I'll stop as soon as you give me what I need — I don't like hurting them — but until then, you'll hear their screams."

I felt the walls closing in as my mind flickered to Talia, to Raven, to a month of torture and seclusion that broke down my resistance.

I heard a crunch as Pierce stepped on something. One of my remaining swarmbots, which had emerged from its hiding spot to try to help.

The broken remains were a gut-check. I had to give up something. Mina? Raven? No, myself. I lifted my chin. "I've been figuring out a way to escape. Steal your helicopter, get reinforcements, and take this place down."

"I don't buy it."

"Do you even know how to fly a helicopter?" Wraith asked.

My head was throbbing from trying not to think about

Talia or escaping.

They must've caught at least some of my thoughts, for Zion said, "We know it has to do with your family. You've talked to two already and seen the third. Your behavior changed —"

An alarm suddenly blared, a brief blast. It was the alarm system I'd used against the Agents when Raven and I invaded the place. The speakers, which Agents had ripped down, had been replaced with ones that couldn't broadcast as intently. The memory of that audial assault lingered, though, which set Wraith and Pierce on edge.

"Check it out," Zion told them.

They left, leaving the door open — and me alone with Zion.

He lifted me off the floor and placed me on the bed, as if showing a kindness, though I knew better. "I'm tired of you thwarting me," he said almost casually, leaning in close enough I could see data scrolling across his lenses. "I need your cooperation. Ah, there it is, your sub layer. It's off the charts."

Jesus, he could access my subconscious layer. I tamped down my desperation. "It's been a fantasy, that's all."

"Of escaping?"

"Of killing you. My favorite is where I hook you up to machines like you hooked up Talia."

"No, you're scheming to break out. How are you planning to do it?"

I noted the way he stood, remembered the training Cole, the gruff rebel commander I'd fought with, had given me. "Wrong scheming. You were my target."

I grabbed his hands to keep them on me, hooked a leg behind his, and threw my body weight forward. Zion hit the back of his head on the concrete floor as I took him down, his grip loosening. I raised a fist and hit him in the face, raised my fist again —

And was thrown off.

I landed and found Pierce standing between us.

Zion picked himself up, clearly hurt but smug. "Good. You rebelled. I've mapped the last of you." As my heart sank, he said, "You *were* going to escape. Or, try to."

"More games," I said, trying to grasp at something, create doubt, make them recheck their figures.

He shook his head in that condescending manner I'd loathed since college. "You're an open book now. I see what you thought—and how you planned. You've failed, old friend. But really, an admirable effort. I'd expected you to give me what I needed weeks ago."

He waved Pierce and Wraith back. "No more beatings," he told them. "I want him to regain his strength for the next stage." He headed for the door, though paused and smiled at me. "Rest up. You'll need it."

CHAPTER SIX

My throbbing injuries added to the helplessness I felt as I sat on my narrow bed. I feared to think anything, worried it was too late, the game already lost, my family and I doomed to die here.

Yet Zion wasn't done with me.

After graduation from UC-Berkley, he and I had formed Gen Omega with Nikolai, Tevin, and Brocco, each a genius in their respective field. After our company's first success, a product that detected dark matter, we were tasked with creating a way to harvest and store it. While Zion's area of expertise was biometrics, he'd also been our computer whiz. We figured out how to harvest dark matter, but we needed to do it economically and efficiently. That meant coordinating the collection pods, accounting for asteroids, fluctuation levels, and the resulting different storage levels in the pods. Zion was good, but he couldn't write a program that worked. The first effort resulted in over half of the pods floating out of communication range and the other pods only collecting ten percent of their capacity before returning to the spacecraft. The second effort had every pod trying to collect the same thousand-foot grid. Nothing could get them to change course.

I picked up enough of his programming from weeks of trying to help that I discovered his errors. He first gave the pods too much autonomy, then too much control. Instead, I allowed for variances, gave the pods a general goal and then a list of solutions for their AI to utilize in response to the challenges they encountered.

My adjustments were such a success that not only did Gen Omega become the leading collector of dark matter — along with other products — when the federal government decided to link the country's security cameras in response to the Daisy Chain Massacre, they asked me to write the software. Not Zion.

He became apoplectic.

A year later, he tried to mortgage our company to build a

multi-million-dollar facility for a product that hadn't been tested yet. We stopped him before it was too late.

I was the deciding vote.

He resigned soon after. That meeting was the last time we spoke until Raven and I invaded this place.

He may have forgotten those memories, so may have forgotten why he held a grudge against me. He was the type that, after a while, the reason no longer mattered. He had long forgotten how he'd craved his father's approval. After our first big success at Gen Omega, I'd asked if he'd called his dad to tell him. With a mystified look, Zion told me he hadn't talked to the man in years. It was more armor the vastly intelligent, fragile kid had donned to protect himself.

Now, he'd become a warped version of the rude but talented undergrad I'd known, the one who could've succeeded at anything.

Pierce's voice cut through my thoughts. "What do you think you're doing?" he asked from outside my door.

"I'm here to check his injuries," I heard Mina say.

"How do you know he has injuries?"

"Were you trying to be quiet?"

"Don't bother," I heard Pierce say.

"Your superiors are going to publicly try Dray, aren't they? It would solidify your position and would be good politically. Don't you want him looking strong for the cameras? The stronger your opponent, the stronger you look when you defeat him."

When he didn't respond, she added, like the political expert she'd been, "I would hold the trial soon, while it's fresh. The victims have been buried, but it's a raw subject."

The door opened, and Pierce waved her inside. "Don't take long."

Mina entered with a medical bag and closed the door behind her.

I felt relief seeing her—then realized I needed to act as before, so pretended to be standoffish.

I didn't have to fake my poor mood.

She noticed my change. She slowed as she approached,

uncertainty marring her expression as she placed the bag on the bed.

"I need to inspect your wound."

Now it was my time to hesitate, not sure if I could trust her, if she had been the reason for the torture.

I pulled my bloody shirt over my head so she could access my injury. When I did, she caught her breath. Bruises of varying severity decorated my torso, and my weight loss was evident. Yet my stab wound had improved, the cut half the width it had been.

If she'd been allowed to give me medical nanobots, the wound would've healed by now.

She glanced at my hand, which rested on the thin blanket crumpled beside me, then made eye contact. Message received, I began to scratch at the cloth, shuffling my feet on the concrete for good measure to interfere with their microphones.

"I've heard Denver still has pockets of resistance," she said in a low voice as she opened her bag. "There have been a lot of arrests, but people are fighting The Agency."

"What else have you heard?"

She pulled out antiseptic wipes and gauze pads. "More Agents are being deployed from here. Two of the doctors got into a heated argument with Zion. He told them to accelerate their process, and they weren't happy."

Now that he'd recorded the brainwave readings he'd wanted from me, he was pivoting toward…something. I feared what that might be. He'd extracted information from my head about the rebels I knew. His teams could use that to accelerate their hunt for those who'd escaped his traps on the day of the node attacks.

Or he could be planning worse. Much worse.

Mina cleaned dried blood from my wound. "Kieran is packing his things as if he's leaving. Zion has started holding meetings as if he's leaving as well."

"What are his meetings about?" When she gave a tiny shrug, I sighed in exasperation.

She straightened and put her bag on her lap as if to search

for something, though she angled it so I could see inside. Among the gauze and sutures, I spotted scissors and a small tool. Quietly, she said, "Talia unlocked a supply closet for me. It's amazing what she can do."

"You grabbed electrical tape, too," I said, impressed.

"After being married to you for so long, I had an idea what you'd need."

"What about wire?"

"Still need to find some, maybe some food if I can." Two of my sutures had torn, so instead of resewing them, she used medical glue to seal the wound. As she finished, she said, "What about using the wire already attached to the thing on her chest?"

"Even one second without power would tear her heart. It would continue to beat, but the panels wouldn't."

Mina paled. "I'll keep looking."

"I need to talk to her, figure out the logistics, where to meet up, how we're going to get away —"

"I already did. She said she's handling it."

"Did you tell her she's coming with us?"

"She didn't believe me."

"What about the machine? Did you plug it in?"

Mina nodded as she cut medical tape into strips and placed a square gauze against my injury. I knew she was stalling for time.

"What about Raven?"

"I'm working on it."

"You have to talk to her. She has to be ready."

"I can do this."

"What about guards? Routines? Contingency plans?"

Mina's shrug was uncertain. "Talia's taking care of everything."

"We'll only have one shot at this." We'd be taking a huge risk even with Talia's connections. As soon as she interfered with something, Zion would know she'd penetrated their network. Their response would be swift.

Mina taped the gauze into place, then returned her supplies to her bag. She had run out of reasons to stay. As she gathered her used gauze pads, she whispered, "What if we get a battery and escape, but it runs out before we can get a replacement?"

It's one of the things that kept me up at night. "We don't have a choice."

Mina's gaze lingered, filled with apprehension.

After she left, I laid down in the hopes that whoever monitored me would become disinterested. When I felt enough time had passed, I slipped my hand between the bed and the wall. There was a hole in the bottom of the mattress. A moment after I slipped my hand down, a swarmbot crawled onto my palm. I cupped the 'bot and slipped my hand to my temple, where I placed it over my implant's exposed end. I felt its tiny legs curl around as the swarmbot's belly connected with my implant. My neural net flickered, and I synched with the tiny machine. Using the emotion-based communication system Garly had created, I instructed the 'bot and any others in range to find thick-gauge wire, at least two of them. Then I detached the swarmbot and slipped it between my mattress and the wall.

I wasn't sure if they would have any success, but without the wire, I wouldn't leave.

* * *

Kieran's grip was looser than normal as he led me through the Facility to the yard for my daily exercise.

I'd been surprised he was the one leading me, as one of the others usually did it, and it was later in the day than normal, thunderstorms having interfered with the daily routine.

"Be thankful we were able to squeeze this in," he said, his face more guarded than normal. "Another hour, and we would've scrapped it. You'll only have twenty minutes today, but consider it a nostalgic pass."

"What are you talking about?" I asked.

"You're leaving with Zion. He has an assignment for you."

"Where?"

He pushed me forward. "Does it matter?"

My swarmbots had only had a day to search for the wire I needed. I hadn't talked to Talia again or Mina. I needed to warn them both.

As we entered the wide corridor that led to the yard, I spotted Raven up ahead.

I knew I shouldn't, but I pulled from Kieran's grasp and rushed toward her. Before I could close the distance, Zion appeared from a nearby room. "I'm sure Kieran has shared the news. He likes to do that," he said. "You're going to D.C. with me. There's work to do."

Raven's eyes widened as the female Agent escorting her pulled her away. She tried to resist but was no match for the woman's strength.

Zion watched the Agent drag her around the corner, then added, "Raven is staying. If you do well, I may transfer her to you."

That was bullshit. "And Talia?"

"I'll make her comfortable. I've come to admire that girl."

"Let them both go."

"You have projects to complete first."

Zion walked off, seemingly untouchable in his Brioni designer suit.

Kieran forced me down the hallway and outside.

I paced the grounds. I yearned to free Talia and Raven, but I pretended to think about anything other than the catastrophe that was unfolding.

By the time Kieran signaled me to leave the yard, the sun was near the horizon, and sweat traced my face. Our one chance was slipping away.

I spotted Mina as we approached the mess hall. I risked going to her.

I took her into my arms, which made her stammer. I leaned close and whispered, "I'm being shipped off."

"Talia heard."

Before I could ask more, Kieran pulled me away. I risked a glance back, but Mina shrugged helplessly.

Kieran gripped my arm as he dragged me to my cell, his jaw rigid. He shoved me inside, pointed a finger at me, and seemed about to shout. Instead, he sighed and dropped his arm. "You're playing into Zion's hand."

"Are you going wherever he's shipping me?"

He shook his head. "Different assignment."

He closed the door, and I was alone.

I tried to hide my thoughts. Associated Raven with my first car, a maroon 2025 Suzuki, associated my fears with a birthday party I'd attended in middle school, not sure if any of it mattered. I didn't know if Mina had obtained the wire, if I could trust her, if Talia could pull this off. I called the swarmbots to me. Over the course of twenty minutes, four of the six came, but none had wire.

I sent them off again.

As the Facility quieted for the night, an image suddenly appeared on my clear lenses: a map of the Facility with a blinking yellow line.

A moment later, the door clicked open.

Shit. Talia had set her plan in motion.

CHAPTER SEVEN

I flung open the door to attack the guard stationed in the corridor outside my prison room.

The hallway was empty.

Somehow, Talia had lured him away, but she'd exposed her access. I had to get to her.

I hurried to the adjoining corridor. It was clear, so I started forward and passed the next group of prison rooms. When I reached the last grouping, a door partway down opened — and Raven appeared. We went to each other and hugged tight. "You OK?" I whispered.

She stiffened, and I spun around. A brief shadow moved in the hallway, then the person appeared: Mina, carrying her medical bag. Gone were the scrubs she'd worn, replaced with jeans, running shoes, and a black zip-up.

"How did Talia get rid of the Agents?" I whispered.

"I don't know."

"You're working with her?" Raven asked, indicating Mina.

I shot Mina a questioning look, who said, "I didn't get a chance to tell her."

A yellow arrow appeared in my field of vision. Talia. Broadcasting directions to my lenses. From the expressions on Raven's and Mina's faces, they'd received it as well.

"We're getting out," I told Raven. "Talia set it up. We need to hurry."

I returned to the corridor and headed in the direction the arrow indicated. But instead of turning left past the prison area, I turned to the right. The way Kieran had taken me.

"*Turn around*," flashed in my vision, the arrow directing me the other way. After a few steps, another message flashed. "*What are you doing?*"

"Dad, what *are* you doing?" Raven asked.

The hallway was empty, so I led her and Mina down to the corner, made sure the next hallway was clear, and approached the double checkpoint that led to the medical portion of the building. I looked up at the camera in the corner and raised my eyebrows.

When Raven saw where I looked, she threw herself into the corner to try to get out of the camera's sight.

Mina said, "Is this a good idea?"

"No it's not," Raven said.

I continued to stare at the camera. Then, words appeared on my lenses. *"You don't listen!"*

The door unlocked.

Raven leapt out from the corner and faced the door, her fear evident.

I pulled it open, waved the two into the checkpoint passage, followed them, and closed the door.

"What's going on?" Raven hissed.

The other door unlocked.

"It's your sister." I pulled the door open just enough to make sure the coast was clear, then entered the medical area. Raven and Mina followed.

If we encountered even one person, we would lose our chance to escape.

The sounds of the medical ward caressed the air: monitors beeping, low voices, and soft footsteps. The linoleum floors and cold walls didn't muffle our movements, which worked against us as we proceeded forward.

A red "X" flashed in my vision as an arrow pointed to the left. I followed her directions this time, which led down a different hallway, one that snaked past multiple rooms. I paused as footsteps grew louder. Instead of following the new hallway, I slipped into a room and closed the door after Raven and Mina joined me. We'd entered the hologram room, the rendition of someone's brain nearly filling the space. I led Raven and Mina through the projection and past medical equipment to the door on the far side.

I made sure the hallway was empty, then led them toward the nurses' station that stood in our path, though I stopped before we reached it.

No cameras were visible, so I inched forward to peer

around the corner. As I watched, the two nurses at the station shifted to focus on a monitor behind them.

Signaling to Raven and Mina, I stepped into the hallway, completely exposed.

I walked as fast as I dared, balancing speed with my need for stealth, the nurses sounding mildly alarmed as they stared at their monitor, their backs to us. God knew what Talia was showing them.

My footsteps sounded too loud. Behind me, something shifted in Mina's bag. Raven's breath caught. She'd heard it, too. The adjoining hallway seemed so far away.

"Should we call the attending?" one nurse asked the other.

I reached the hallway, but we were still visible. Our destination was two doors away.

Raven, Mina, and I hurried to Talia's room, and I ushered them inside.

"What're you doing here?" Talia whisper-yelled as I closed the door. She sat up in bed with an exasperated look.

Raven gasped and pushed past me, her warriorlike focus supplanted by the hope of a big sister. "You're awake?"

Then she noticed the cords that draped from Talia's skull. She'd seen them when we'd invaded this place, but that didn't diminish the horror and outrage that clouded her face.

"I'm tough, like you," Talia said.

Raven squeezed her tight.

When she stepped back, Talia asked, "What happened to your digits?"

"Britt shot them off."

Mina said, "We need to go."

"Talia, program everything you need because you're going with us," I said.

Talia looked panicked. "*Nozer*. It's too risky."

"Don't care," both Raven and I said.

"I'd need to be severed, and it's so unsafe—"

"Set timers, estimate distances, and map a way out. You got this," I said.

"I won't be able to protect you."

"You have until I can unhook you."

Talia's eyes grew huge, flickered toward Raven, then swallowed and shifted her focus.

As she muttered how this was "such bad mojo," I waved Mina over, who began pulling supplies from her bag.

"Did you get the wires?" I asked her.

"Couldn't find any. Could we take some from one of the machines?"

I swore as I scanned the room.

"This isn't what I modded," Talia grumbled as her lenses shone bright. Her fingers weren't moving, in so deep she didn't need to key in commands. "I was gonna track and shield you."

As Raven searched the machines for wire, I popped the battery from the blood pressure machine I'd targeted. If I'd had an ion blade, I could've sliced open the white plastic that encased the machine to get to its wires, but without it, I'd need a screwdriver. I tried the cover's integrity, but the plastic was solid. It would take time to break it, time we didn't have.

Something tapped my leg. When I looked down, four swarmbots held up coiled wire. I snatched it. The wire was shorter than I would've chosen, but it would work.

With a surge of relief, I held up the wire to Talia. She briefly switched her focus from The Agency's systems to the wire before diving back into the system, her cheeks pale. "Why don't you ever listen?"

I told Raven to guard the door.

As Talia concentrated on her plan, I used Mina's scissors to shave the coverings off the wires, then attached them to the battery. While I worked, Mina inspected the cords that ran from her daughter's head.

"I have programs to blank you three," Talia said as she worked. "You'll be invisible to the silver goons. They won't find you."

"Good. Run those," I said. "Add yourself."

"Can't just throw a switch."

I hooked the modified wires to the battery, then to the device on Talia's chest. She was so focused on The Agency's system, she didn't flinch when I lifted her hospital gown, Mina working with me to keep Talia's modesty as I worked. With the battery attached, the device regulating her heart should continue. Before I cut the main power, I instructed Mina to make a sling to hold the device and battery. We couldn't risk anything ripping loose.

"I erased their mountains of blips," Talia said in a distant voice, eyes glowing. "The brain scans, memory taps, recordings, all poof. I then wrote over the data with videos of Dad lighting his reactor and hid which server they'd used. Did it for you, and you," she said, her gaze shifting long enough to look at me and Raven. Then she looked at Mina. "There weren't any blips on you."

"Did they ever inject you with a tracking-like device?" I asked Mina. She shook her head.

Raven and I exchanged a glance as Talia slipped back into the systems.

"Can you deactivate the device they plugged into my and Raven's head?"

Talia nodded. "Already done. You'll pee it out in a day or two. Heh."

I checked the back of her head. The cords were attached to biolinks implanted into her skull. The Agency doctors had left her hair undisturbed other than those spots, which might hide the links once we unhooked her.

Mina looped a bedsheet around Talia's head and shoulder, then settled the battery and device inside the sling she'd fashioned, the device's power cable sticking out. "It's time," I told Talia.

"I need more."

"Thirty seconds. Then I'm unhooking you."

The frown on her face deepened, then her lenses decreased in illumination, though not completely, and she looked at me. "OK, it's finagled. I think."

"Ready to initiate?"

"Take the head snakes out first." Her eyes flashed bright, then cleared completely. "I've started the program."

I cradled her head and gently pulled the first cord from

the back of her skull. The biolink slid out of the small, implanted interface, the other two sliding out with only minor resistance.

"Oh knarl," Talia whispered.

I lowered her head, then focused on the device. She started to shake as I reached for the power cable.

"You got this," I told her.

She nodded, her fear palpable.

Mina and I shared the same fear. We knew the stakes.

I gripped the cable running from the wall to the heart device, checked to make sure the wires to the battery were securely attached to it, then unplugged the cable from the device. The machine remained operational, its readout normal. Her heart continued to beat.

Talia released a shaky sigh. "Let's skedaddle."

I scooped her up, blanket and all — triggering a flash of pain from where I'd shanked myself — wrapped the blanket around her as she only wore a hospital gown, and started for the door. "Tell me where to go."

Her tremors remained but changed from fear to nervousness. "Out to the left. The nurses should be hoodwinkered." As she talked, Raven grabbed the scissors I'd used and held it like a weapon. Our only one.

I exchanged glances with her. Mina. "Go."

We entered the hallway and went left — back the way we came.

The sounds from the medical wing seemed identical, though the voices sounded more ominous. We reached the nurses' station.

Having taken the lead, Raven stopped at the intersection to make sure the coast was clear, then waved us forward.

Talia nodded her head to the right.

We followed her direction, passing the nurses' station — which showed multiple medical codes flashing — and entered an unfamiliar hallway. We passed an operating room similar to the surgical rooms I'd noticed when we'd invaded this place, with oversized surgical robots and cutting-edge enhancement machines, along with post-op rooms that contained Agents in various stages of recovery.

A security door blocked our path, but Talia motioned Raven to open it. "It's unlocked," she whispered. It was, and we took a left, then a right. We seemed to backtrack at one point, and we closed a set of fire doors at her direction. "Agents anchor different spots," she whispered. "We're mice in a shifty maze. I hope I tinkered right."

Talia's voice sounded weaker. For all her bravado, she was losing stamina.

At her direction, we headed toward the rear section of the complex, which contained the prison cells. We took a left and hurried down a passageway lined with unlabeled offices to a checkpoint. But the large door was locked.

Mina looked at her.

"It'll click. My timing is off."

We heard voices. From the tone, I suspected they were Agents.

"We need to hide," Raven whispered. We each tried one of the unmarked doors, none of which budged except for Mina's. We hurried inside the small office she'd found and shut the door.

The voices grew louder, and a door nearby opened. We heard Agents arguing.

"My zippy attack should hit soon," Talia said, looking anxious.

I heard a soft click. "The door unlocked."

The three of us exchanged glances. "I'll do it," Mina whispered. She opened our door, which made the voices easier to hear, dashed to the checkpoint, and tested the handle. It turned, and she waved us forward as she pushed the door open.

We rushed over, my stab wound burning, slipped through the checkpoint, and closed the door behind us, which auto-locked.

We found ourselves in a hallway that contained a suite of exam rooms. We moved as quickly as we dared. The longer we took, the worse our odds.

We approached what I realized was the double checkpoint, having previously come at it from a different direction.

The door was locked, so Raven and Mina searched for

a place to hide while I pressed against the door. "The attack should've hit," Talia whispered.

"How will we know?"

Before she could answer, a voice shouted. "Don't move."

Pierce emerged from a side hallway and stopped, stunned by our presence — and Talia being unplugged.

The door unlocked behind me.

I wasn't sure if it was from Talia's programming or if someone was coming. No choice. I pushed the door open by shoving backwards and barked Raven's name. I stumbled back into the small checkpoint area, Raven and Mina racing after me.

Pierce started as well, still stunned but stepping forward and picking up speed.

I backed up to give them room, unable to help as I held Talia.

Raven hurried inside and grabbed the door that had swung wide. Mina joined us and helped her close the door just as Pierce reached it. He crashed into it but the latch held, then locked.

"He has a pass," Raven said. "He'll open it."

"It won't work anymore," Talia said.

Pierce slammed into the door.

The other door was already unlocked.

We hurried out, passing the prison area and continuing straight.

The mess hall appeared on the right, the series of windows revealing four Agents tiredly eating late night food. As a faint boom from Pierce's efforts echoed behind us, a female Agent lifted her head — and her eyes widened as she spotted us.

We ran to the next checkpoint door. It was already unlocked. We dashed through it and headed past the entrance to the mess hall, where shouts rose. Another checkpoint was also unlocked, and we busted through. As we closed and locked the door, alarms erupted.

"Oh no," Mina said.

"We're close, right?" Raven shouted to Talia over the sound of the alarms.

"Not yet."

I jogged down the hallway, arms burning, stab wound screaming, and entered the large corridor that ran the width of the Facility, the door at the far right the exit to the fenced-in area. Multiple doors lined the corridor in both directions, and Talia shouted to go to the right.

We started that way when doors at the opposite end opened, and three Agents appeared, unaffected by the alarms, with Wraith in front.

Goddamn buzzcut Wraith.

His face twisted in anger as he started for us, an unstoppable force. Raven raised her scissors, but they were useless.

The other Agents stayed in step with him as he picked up speed.

Wraith's eyes suddenly turned a brilliant, intense white, the others as well, their lenses glowing with light. The Agents stumbled, one falling down, another hitting an open door.

The light reminded me of when Kieran had blinded me with my own lenses.

I looked down at Talia, who smiled.

"The zippy attack," she said over the alarms.

Wraith raised his gaze and cocked his head as he ran his blazing-white gaze over our group.

"He's using his other sensors," I said. "*Move.*"

Raven hurried the few feet forward to the door I'd suspected was the checkpoint that led to the rear exit. She looked back at Talia, whipping her head so fast her hair arced. "Is this right?"

"Yes."

She tried the door, but it was locked.

Wraith headed for us, one hand gripping the side of his head, the other clenched in a fist. Behind him, shouts of surprise and anger rose from the rooms they'd come from, what I suspected were the barracks in this nightmare prison.

Raven continued to yank on the door, but the lock held.

The other Agents honed in on us and started forward, their caution turning to assuredness as they adjusted. They looked furious. I would have empathized — the light was unescapable —

if they weren't trying to stop us.

Wraith was fifteen feet away. Ten.

The door unlocked.

Mina nearly shoved me into the hallway Raven accessed as the Agent neared and ducked in after me. Raven closed it — and the door locked.

The alarm was quieter here, though we could still hear it.

She led the way down a hallway that pierced the last section of the Facility, past branching hallways with offices and conference rooms. There were shouts and a crash as blind Agents raged. They'd rip us apart.

We reached the last checkpoint door.

Raven pulled on it, but it was locked. She tried it a half-dozen times, then looked at Talia. "Seriously?"

"I gave us bad odds."

The alarm continued to blare.

We huddled close as Raven kept trying the door.

A shadow moved in a nearby hallway.

Before anyone emerged, the door unlocked.

Raven opened it to reveal the last section of hallway, the exit doors twenty feet away — where a familiar figure stood in our way. Kieran.

CHAPTER EIGHT

Kieran's blue eyes were clear. Unlike the other Agents, his eyes weren't glowing bright white. Then I noticed the cap, the knit material stretched tight as it encircled his head. It was too small for him — and I realized why. It was the cap Talia used to wear, the one I'd placed over his head when we'd beaten him in his home. I'd wanted to interfere with his ability to reach out for help. I left it on him when we sent him away, before he appeared at Zion's side the day we'd invaded this place. Now, he was using it to block her program.

Authority seeped from his bio-enhanced skin, his muscles tight in augmented strength, a dangerous foe against whom I'd nearly died fighting.

I jerked back in surprise as Mina cried out. Raven took a fighting stance, her scissors in her good hand.

Kieran pointed at the cap. "Learned from you," he told me.

His gaze dropped to Talia in my arms.

"Is this what you envisioned when you joined The Agency? Torturing little kids?" I asked.

"She," he croaked, then started again. "She wasn't tortured."

"The food was torture," Talia said in a weedy voice.

No one moved as the alarm blared.

His gaze swiveled to her. "You did all this?"

She didn't respond.

I felt blood trick down my chest. I'd torn open my wound.

He looked back at me. "You can go. I won't interfere with anyone going after you, but I won't stop you. You'll at least get a head's start."

I wondered if this was a trick.

"Thank you," Talia said, her words sincere.

His face twisted in emotion, which surprised me, and he reached for the cap. He hesitated, then took it off. His lenses instantly went white. He grimaced from their intensity and held out the cap.

She took it, her hand so small compared to his.

"This was my one kindness. We're even, Dray. When I find you — and I will — I won't hold back. We're enemies."

"Only because you choose to be. And we're far from even."

Raven and Mina followed my lead and stepped past him, the two exchanging disbelieving glances. I felt the same.

We'd nearly reached the glass doors when Kieran called out. "You won't get far."

Raven opened one of the rear doors and Mina the other. I followed, carrying Talia out of the building and into the night.

We hurried down three steps into a parking lot that held approximately thirty cars.

"I don't know what that was," Raven said, "but we have to get away."

Mina nodded nervously. "Every Agent will come after us."

"Wait for it," Talia said. "See?"

The lights flickered on a car at the far end of the lot, a red Cadillac, one of those new cars designed like the classic cars of the 1950s but with amenities unfathomable a century earlier. I realized the lights flickered because the car's locks were repeatedly being disengaged.

Talia smiled. "It's Zion's."

"You're brilliant," Raven said. She headed for the car and we followed, passing parked car after parked car as we headed down one of the aisles — though I started to lag from Talia's weight, my muscles trembling from so much use.

The Facility's rear doors crashed open behind us, and Agents poured out.

Raven ducked behind a white SUV, and Mina followed.

I hurried to join them as they opened fire. A bullet whizzed past my face, another clipped the blanket wrapped around Talia's legs. I reached the SUV and nearly dove behind it, bullets piercing the vehicle's side.

Raven tried the passenger door, but it was locked. "Follow

me and stay down." She started past the far end of the SUV—but jerked back as bullets pierced the air before her, adding to those behind us.

We were pinned.

Crouching down, I twisted my neck to look through the SUV's tinted windows. There had to be twenty Agents. As I watched, three more exited the building. Gunfire raked the SUV, one of the windows exploding from the onslaught. I heard an Agent cry out—I suspected the vehicle was his—but it didn't slow the others.

They began to advance. Without a weapon, we wouldn't be able to hold them back.

More gunfire erupted, but this sounded different. It came from another direction. The new gunfire was followed by shouts of surprise. I risked a glance—and spotted Valor racing out of the darkness, past the edge of the fence line and light poles that encircled the property.

I didn't know if I was more stunned by her presence or her outfit. Valor was an ex-artist with a bodybuilder's physique, sporting hatchmark tattoos, long cornrows, and a black eyepatch. Yet she wore coveralls with a pink, checkered shirt that tried to contain her muscular build and a white cowboy hat, her outfit in stark contrast to her dark skin, hair, and eyepatch. She wielded a pistol with an extended clip in one hand and a dusty, cobweb-covered duffel bag in the other.

I wondered if this was a trick, if Zion was manipulating my vision. Could I trust my eyes anymore? Could I trust my mind?

Valor fired three times and hit three Agents, all headshots. She then raced down the parking lot, using the row parallel to ours, her hat falling off as she ran.

Raven half-stood, appearing over the hood of the SUV, as Agents ducked from the sudden barrage.

Valor spotted us and laughed in a strange kind of delight. She sprinted down the far row of vehicles as Agents shot at her, dove to the ground—gunfire striking the cars around her—and landed by the front of a midnight blue Lexus coupe level with us.

She locked eyes with me.

Making sure I watched, she opened her bag and pulled out a remote. There was a chirp a few rows behind me, and the headlights flashed on a brown, extended-cab pickup truck, the light almost dazzling in the darkness. She'd planted the vehicle. I couldn't believe it. Couldn't believe she was here.

I heard its engine start.

Raven noticed the truck as well — which was closer than Zion's car.

Valor extracted a wide-barreled handgun and fired a flare into the air. She reloaded and fired a second flare, that one aimed to the northwest. The flare arched over the Facility as it shot skyward.

The gunfire paused around her, the Agents confused by the flares.

"Raven," I whispered. "The truck. *Go.*"

She ran out from behind the SUV and raced between the vehicles toward the pickup.

"Go," I told Mina, but she motioned for me to go first. I did, forcing my aching body to move and hurrying as fast as I could between the front bumpers of the parked cars, Mina behind me.

Sweat ran down my face as I pushed myself toward the pickup truck.

More gunfire erupted, both at us and from Valor. Then, the pitch changed. Agents had started after us.

Raven reached the truck and opened the driver's door. I headed to the far side of the vehicle, Mina stumbling behind me as she clipped one of the bumpers but stayed on her feet. A distant part of me wondered what all of this jostling was doing to Talia, though I didn't slow until I reached the back door. My biceps screaming, I tried to maintain my hold while I reached for the door handle but nearly dropped her.

Mina opened the door for me, then helped me get into the back of the truck with Talia.

Footsteps approached, and Valor appeared in the open driver's door. "Move."

Raven scrambled to the passenger seat as the gunfire temporarily stopped.

Valor tossed her bag into Raven's lap and got in, while Mina ran to the other side and climbed into the seat beside me. Valor closed her door, then put the car in gear. "I've never been happier to see y'all, but for now, get down."

The truck's engine roared as she gunned it. I cradled Talia's head as Valor steered us out of the space and raced toward the exit.

Gunfire erupted.

Bullets shattered the window behind me, and bits of glass gouged my head and neck. Mina cried out as the glass pelted her, too.

"Told you to get down," Valor said, speaking fast. "I'm not wasting weeks just for you to bite it in the parking lot."

I ducked down, carefully cradling Talia, though Valor's driving tossed us. Talia was still breathing, didn't appear to be in distress—her eyes gleamed with excitement, though there was fear as well—but if anything happened, I didn't know how I'd be able to help her.

"Look out," Raven cried. She pointed toward the road that Valor had turned onto.

Four Agents blocked the road a hundred yards away, three men and one woman, all four muscular and armed. Their silver hair gleaming in the light from the Facility's spotlights, they aimed their weapons at our truck.

"Don't just sit there," Valor snapped. "Shoot them."

Raven dug into the bag on her lap.

I strained to see what it contained. I spotted an assortment of weapons, including pistols, two machetes, and an ion blade.

Raven removed a machine gun, leaned against the window, which Valor had already begun to lower, stuck the gun out as wind burst into the cabin, and began to shoot at the Agents.

As Raven fired—the Agents returning gunfire—Valor held up a remote of some sort and pressed a button, though nothing happened.

Bullets laced the windshield, one of the male Agents went down, and Valor picked up speed.

Our road ran along the western edge of the Facility

property toward a bisecting two-lane road that ran east-west, touching the Facility's northern edge and disappearing in both directions.

I spotted movement by the side of our road up ahead. The next moment, the Gen Omega robot I'd given Valor before invading this godforsaken place, the man-shaped farm model, burst onto the road and tackled the man and woman standing to the left side. Neither saw it coming. The robot, over six feet in height, lifted them off their feet as its momentum threw them across the road. Before the fourth Agent could react, Valor swerved, drove through the gap the robot had made in the Agents' line, and increased speed.

She grinned at me in the rearview mirror. "I found its 'attack' code."

I wanted to touch her shoulder to thank her — and make sure she was real.

"More Agents," Mina warned.

Five raced past the edge of the fence line and onto the road behind us. Two more burst from a side door of the Facility, ran toward us, and leapt over the ten-foot-high, barbed-wire fence as Valor drove toward the intersection.

Agents scrambled for their cars in the Facility's lot, multiple sets of lights blinking as engines started.

The lead Agent running after us, a wiry young man with sunken cheeks, was gaining. He steered wide of Valor's robot as it stood, but the machine leapt at him, closing the fifteen-foot distance too quickly for him to dodge. The two went down, the next Agents — three women in workout gear, leg muscles rippling — dashed past them and gained on us.

"You have any more robots?" Raven asked. I was hoping the same thing.

"No. Hold on." Valor had reached the intersection and swung west, away from the Facility. Four black sedans, then two more, burst from the parking lot we'd left, three of the cars from the first group racing up the road we'd just left, the fourth angling across the half-grown cornfield to try to reach us. A second car followed across the field.

I cradled Talia's head and squinted my eyes from the wind as Valor accelerated on the east-west road, passing dirt driveways nearly hidden by the fields of grown brittle wheat, and Raven fired at the cars behind us. The Agents accelerated, seemingly unfazed by Raven's efforts.

Valor drove faster, but the truck didn't have enough horsepower.

Mina gasped as the first Agent car neared. Gunshots grew loud, followed by popping sounds as bullets pierced our truck's metal frame. "Stay down," I told her, though I couldn't stop from looking back, desperate to help in some way.

The car, a luxury BMW, was twenty feet back.

Raven fired again, though she ran out of ammunition after two shots. As she reached for the weapons bag, I focused on the BMW. It could clip our rear end. With the speeds we were going, we'd spin out of control.

It got closer. Ten feet. Five.

"Why are you slowing down?" Mina shouted over the wind.

We passed a dirt road entrance to one of the farms — where a red, heavy-duty Ram pickup truck burst from the darkness and crashed into the BMW. It drove the Agent clear across the road and into the field on the far side of the road, the BMW flipping sideways from the force of the crash.

"Yes," Valor cried.

"What was that?" Raven yelled.

The driver of the red truck made a U-turn in the field and headed back to the road, but the other three sedans passed him. Then I realized. The truck headed for the Agent racing across the field and hit him head-on. Dust and debris filled the air.

I turned my attention to the Agents gaining on us when all three vehicles flew to either side, spinning as they launched into the air to the sounds of multiple crashes. Trucks had T-boned them from hidden driveways and took them out.

"Area farmers," Valor explained as she accelerated. "I told them about the Facility, and we planned an assault. It would've been ugly, but I couldn't stand you being in there."

The three pickup trucks that had hit the Agents stopped in the road, and as I watched, a John Deere tractor and a truck dragging an empty horse trailer appeared to block the road.

"They got so angry when I told them about The Agency," Valor went on. "Strange metals have gotten in the groundwater and tainted their crops. They complained to authorities but never got anywhere. They'd thought the Facility was a minimum-security prison. After I told them what it was, they wanted to tear it to the ground. I convinced them to wait, but when I heard that alarm yesterday, I knew something was brewing."

I glanced back at the dwindling Facility. Zion's helicopter was visible in the darkness, the ugly gold and silver streaks on its sides making it stand out, though its blades weren't moving.

"Did you lock the door to the roof?" I asked Talia, who nodded. "When does it unlock?"

"Never. I looped the software."

The Facility faded into the distance, though I spotted more vehicles behind us as we crested a hill, both farmers and Agency vehicles. Light from gunfire flickered; I wasn't sure who was firing at who. We started down the other side of the hill, and I lost sight of the battle.

I turned back to find Valor staring at me in the rearview mirror. "I waited days for you to appear. I cried when I left. I felt I'd abandoned you."

"You couldn't have helped," I said as Talia raised herself up in my arms to look around.

"I came back and befriended the owners of the robots you used. I've been staying with them."

"Who are you?" Mina asked.

Raven twisted in her seat. "You have no right to ask her, no right to know anything. Do you have any idea of the misery you caused?"

"I'm sorry I hurt you—"

"*Me*? Have you looked at Talia? At what you've done?"

"Raven," Talia said softly.

Raven's hand shook as she reached over the seat to touch her arm. "I'm never leaving you again."

Valor half-turned in her seat to look at us. "None of you have implant blockers." She hit the brakes.

"I blocked them. It's OK," Talia said.

Valor's eye switched to me. "She serious?" When I nodded, Valor seemed to consider it, then accelerated again. "Kid, you've gotta show me how you pulled that off."

"Kieran let us go. Gave me my cap, too."

Valor switched her gaze between us and the road. "Don't bother claiming he turned over a new leaf. Bad that deep stays bad."

Chapter Nine

The first rays of dawn shot across the flat landscape as Valor parked behind what looked like an abandoned four-story building on the outskirts of a town south of Fort Worth.

The Agency would be looking for us, and the bullet holes in our truck made us stick out. Valor had taken side roads to avoid as many cameras and people as possible, but that made it harder to put distance between us and the Facility.

"Where are we?" Raven asked her.

"A place that's supposed to be safe."

We followed her to an unmarked door.

I carried Talia, and Mina carried blankets and supplies Valor had hidden in the truck. Raven picked the building's front door lock, and we ducked inside, tense for an alarm that didn't come.

None of the switches worked; the place didn't have power, which explained the lack of an alarm.

We slipped past a stairwell, alert for guards, squatters, or anyone else, and into what had probably been a reception area, now empty other than dried leaves that littered the floor, a navy-blue accent wall revealing holes where a sign had previously hung.

A long hallway stretched past the reception area. Doorways extended off of the hall, and the growing sunlight streamed in from those doorways.

"We going to mouse it here?" Talia asked as we passed empty rooms.

"Not for long," I said.

Zion would send every asset he had to find us.

Valor selected a room to settle in. Mina created a makeshift bed from the blankets she carried, and I laid Talia down while Raven scanned the landscape from one of the windows.

As Mina helped Talia get situated, Raven said, "We shouldn't have stopped."

"Our truck's too conspicuous during the day," Valor said.

"Get some rest," I told Talia, trying to keep the concern from my voice. To the others, I said, "She needs a new battery."

"Maybe there's something here you can use," Mina said.

Raven turned from the window. "Since when are you a battery expert?"

Mina straightened as if to scold her, but Raven leaned forward, ready for a fight.

Before either spoke, Talia sighed. "You should've left me. I would've sacrificed myself in an epic, selfless act."

"You can inspire in ways that don't make you a martyr," said Mina.

"Doesn't sound very epic." Exhaustion started to creep into her expression.

As I stepped back, the four swarmbots emerged from her blanket like tiny guardians.

Mina told Talia, "Your father will find something to help. He's good like that." She gave me a quirk of her mouth.

"Keep an eye on her," I said.

Mina rested a hand on Talia's arm. "Of course."

Raven leaned over Talia, essentially pushing Mina back. "You need anything, you let me know."

"A new body?" Talia asked.

"I'd let you have mine, but it's missing some fingers."

"I prefer full fingers, please."

Even weak from not having moved much over the past few weeks, Talia seemed larger than life—though she evoked rage in me toward those who'd used her.

I gazed at her for a moment, joy and love washing through me, then forced myself to leave. Valor and Raven followed, their smiles dropping.

The risks we faced and what I could lose weighed on me. We could be found any second. My desperate dream of freeing my girls would end.

As if reading my mind, two police drones appeared in the distance, visible from a row of windows. The ten-foot-long drones were capable of reporting activity, unlocking doors, disabling vehicles, and immobilizing suspects. I watched them disappear past the building, though there were thousands more out there — using my surveillance system against me and everyone else.

We had few weapons, no destination, and no support.

We spent the next hour searching the property for anything we could use. As we finished, I told Valor, "I can never repay you."

"Never have to." Her one eye dropped. "I spent every night at the farm planning how to bust you out. When I heard that alarm, I got my farmers ready. Used this." She held up the tracking bracelet I'd given her.

When Raven saw it, her eyes widened in surprise — and exasperation. The electronics inside the bracelet were linked to the tracker I'd injected into her arm without her knowledge two months earlier.

Valor handed it to her, but I took it. "It might come in handy again," I said as I put it on.

Raven scowled.

"When you left your room last night, I knew it was time," Valor told her, then looked at me. "You told me to free Raven and Talia, but you were always part of the plan."

"You did that and more."

"I let you two go into that damn place. I knew it was wrong."

She'd named herself Valor because she felt she'd failed to be courageous when she was younger. Another person trying to correct their past. "You couldn't have stopped me."

When Raven and I had prepared to invade the Facility, Valor hated the idea, but I didn't listen. My girls came first.

Valor rubbed her face. "I'll watch the perimeter." Before she left, she stepped close. "Should you have brought Mina? Agents might've let you escape, hoping you'll take her to whoever's survived."

"Has anyone?"

"Some did. Militias rose up after our node attack. They were swiftly destroyed, but they added enough of a distraction that a few rebels got away." She hitched her rifle on her shoulder.

"I gotta make a call."

As she disappeared outside, Raven asked me, "Call who?"

"Don't know." We were alone for the first time since we'd invaded the Facility. I wanted to see how she was, resolve what was broken between us, but Talia came first. "Work on some defenses. I need to look for components."

* * *

I opened the rusted metal door of a maintenance closet and found a broken drill, clusters of wires, and a set of argon detectors. I collected the abandoned items and set them on a dented credenza in a corner office. As I began to take the pieces apart, I heard the faint buzz of a searcher drone in the distance.

I hoped I just imagined the noise or that it wasn't real. Zion had manipulated my senses. Maybe still was. But no, he'd mask the noise, not fake it.

I told myself to focus on what I was creating. Without a battery gauge, I wouldn't know if Talia's heart was in danger. I also needed a replacement battery, but I couldn't find one in this dead place.

It took most of the afternoon and the destruction of three motion-sensor light fixtures, but I completed the gauge using the ion blade and a small set of tools I'd found in Valor's weapons bag. The glowing particles of the ion blade helped guide my cut.

As I maneuvered the components into the former housing of a light fixture, Raven appeared. She held the housing for me, then spoke, her voice low. "I hadn't believed you about Talia being alive. God, I was livid you were trusting Mina. I had a lot of time to think the past month, though."

"Being locked up does that," I said, hoping to lighten her mood. She hadn't just been angry at me. The prospect of Talia being alive meant Raven had abandoned her.

Raven gave me a crooked grin, the quirk closer to her mother's than she would've liked. "I stopped believing in anything but the rebellion. You gave me hope when I didn't think there was any."

"If I'd been wrong, I would've made a huge mistake."

"But you didn't." Raven hugged me as my hands were

buried inside the housing and let go before I could hug her back. "Think that thing will work?"

"If you hold the cover," I joked. When she gripped the housing again, I finished securing the components in place. "It should give us a warning—but we need a better solution."

"This is a bad place to guard. Too big."

I could've used Valor's phone to call the police, report how The Agency had imprisoned us illegally, but I couldn't trust them. Besides, they weren't powerful enough to stop Zion.

She dropped her gaze. "I tried to get a hold of Jex, but he didn't answer."

Of course she would've tried to reach her boyfriend, a rebel fighter from Louisiana who I'd come to think of as a son. "I wouldn't hold out much hope for any of them."

"I'm not mad at you anymore. Well, not as mad. I get why you nearly betrayed me at Kieran's. I was a little out of control—"

"A little? You were so mad it endangered us."

She relented. "I acted foolishly—and if I never saw you again, what I said would've been some of my last words to you. I need to be better."

Her maturity warmed yet saddened me. Zion's torture had forced her to grow up fast, too fast.

"I want you to believe in something again," she said. "You have to."

"What about Mina? You going to work through your anger with her?"

Her smile disappeared. "She's dead to me."

* * *

I returned to find Talia lying on her makeshift bed and using the heart regulator and battery pack as a set of weights. She grimaced as she lifted the pair with both hands, raising them until the wires grew taut, then lowered them to her chest.

"That's not resting," I said, my gaze darting to Mina, who gave a helpless gesture.

"I can't be weak. You needs me."

I sat and put a hand on her 'weights' to stop her. "You need to be smart. Watch those wires. Keep your fingers in place so they stay tight, and don't let go until I've inspected them. How are you feeling?"

"Annoyed."

I explained about the gauge in my hand. "I need to attach it to your battery."

Both Talia's and Mina's eyes reflected their apprehension.

With Mina's help, I made sure the existing wires were still secure, then started to connect the gauge. I had to be careful I didn't interrupt the current running to the regulator.

Whispering, as if to avoid distracting me, Talia said, "Don't let my weakness hold you back."

"I want you to get better."

"I hid your implants. Same with Raven's and Mom's. Agents replaced Raven's modified implant after you guys Normandy'd the hospital, but I hid all of your permanent codes. Agent spiders won't find you."

I made one of the connections, Mina holding the wires to make sure they didn't move. "What about your own?"

"My implant's a ghost. No ways they'll scoop it."

I shifted my focus to the second set of connections. "I'm surprised you aren't tired."

"She slept a couple of hours," Mina said. "After she calmed down."

"I've rested enough," Talia said. She shifted anxiously. "I also messed with their tracking software. Their cameras will never see you. Your face won't register. You can fight and take down the glittery goons."

I completed the connections and checked the gauge. If I'd calibrated it correctly, Talia's battery had sixty percent power. Not as much as I'd hoped. "What about your image? And Raven's? Your mother's?"

"I whizzled theirs. I didn't do mine, though. Didn't expect to dash."

She would be vulnerable.

"Along with disabling your creepy head-things, I altered the records with our DNA and wiped the data Silvers collected," Talia went on. "It doesn't mean snarly suit doesn't know how you think, but I wrecked their program that reads minds. I know they'll figure out how to brain-read again, but not for a while. It gives us time."

To do what, I wanted to ask. Hundreds, if not thousands, of people with nearly unlimited resources were looking for us. I nodded at the gauge. "You have over half power remaining."

She sat up and stared at the tiny readout.

"Get some more rest."

Her voice turned quiet as I stood. "I'm sorry I helped Agents."

Mina gave me a look. Talia must've apologized to her, too. "You couldn't have stopped them."

"I should've been smarter."

Mina and I left the room in the hopes our daughter would sleep.

Mina turned to me, her brown eyes glinting with pride. "That gauge is ingenious."

Her beauty struck me. She was a formidable woman. The last few months had distracted me of that. "Can I trust you?" I asked.

"I learned my mistake. I'll never hurt any of you again."

Valor approached, moving quickly. "We have company."

I reached for my gun.

"It's OK," she said. "I called them."

CHAPTER TEN

From my spot inside the abandoned building, I trained one of Valor's guns on the unmarked gray van, which kicked up dust as it approached.

As I alternated between watching the vehicle and scanning the skies for drones, I tried to accept what I'd done. My decisions had hurt those I loved.

Talia would improve but was scarred. Raven was as well, emotional scars to go with her missing fingers. Anya, the surgeon who'd joined our cause, and I had started a romantic relationship, though I'd ruined it when I left to find Talia. I didn't know if Anya had survived. Cole, a grizzled commander, had probably survived, along with Nipsen, though God knew what had become of them or Jex or any of the others.

All of their efforts and sacrifice had been in vain.

The van neared.

Valor stepped out from the building and waved the driver, a light-brown-haired man with full cheeks and green eyes, into the loading bay. She closed the door behind them, and I slipped from my spot near the side door.

Four men exited the van, all strangers, though the broad-shouldered driver moved in a familiar way. The second man looked younger with tight dark hair, a narrow jaw, and large ears. He had infrared implants on either side of his brow like Agents did, which meant he was military, and his machine gun was specific to the Army. The third man carried a similar weapon. He had broad shoulders, dark red hair, and deep-set eyes that were a piercing blue. A Celtic cross hung around his neck. Like the others, he had a military bearing with battle-hardened muscles and infrared implants. The fourth was Hispanic, tattooed and chiseled.

I trained my gun on them. Raven appeared from the corner and aimed her gun as well.

Valor stepped forward. "It's OK."

Mina led Talia into the loading bay, my daughter holding her battery pack in a wrapped blanket slung over her shoulder.

I wanted to yell at her to get Talia away when two more people exited the SUV. An extremely tall man unfolded himself as he got out and unwrapped a black scarf from his head to reveal the goateed face of my friend, the six-foot-six scientist Garly. A young woman with brown hair, a nose ring, and a falcon tattoo on her neck appeared beside him, the former Agency hacker known as Nataly.

I worried my eyes were deceiving me until Garly rushed over and swept me into a hug. "The only and greatest lives." The twenty-seven-year-old swung me back and forth. He set me down and absorbed my group, though when he saw Talia, he fell to his knees. "My heart shattered when I'd heard you died."

"They battery-packed me," she said.

He took in the devices strapped to her chest, and his brow creased with a mixture of worry and sorrow. Talia saw his expression and became visibly upset.

Before I could reassure her, the light-brown-haired man stepped forward. "We need to go."

I frowned. "I know that voice."

The man hesitated, then touched the side of his face, which began to melt, causing both Talia and Raven to cry out. It wasn't actually melting. He'd been covered in mini-bots, which fell away to reveal Cole's scarred face and disfigured jaw. The rebel colonel was roughly my height but broader, his voice rough, his arms marred with faint scars he'd tried to erase. Small posts stuck up from either side of his mouth. They had to be anchors for the 'bots, which allowed them to move in synchronicity with his mouth when he talked.

He took off his wig. "Dray."

The first time we met, he'd dismissed me. The first time he'd helped me, he'd trained a sniper rifle on me. Yet he'd become a trusted ally.

"I'd hoped you'd survived," I said.

"We'll talk later. For now—" He stopped as Talia came over, her steps wobbly.

"They sizzled you?" she asked. She reached up and touched his jaw, her fingers barely able to reach as they brushed the area disfigured from the gunshot that had nearly killed him. "I'm sorry."

He looked at her in surprise. Then he caught sight of Mina and raised his pistol. "You're not coming."

"She has to," Talia said.

Speaking to Mina, he said, "I lost soldiers on Free Isle because of you. Many were friends. The people you sided with killed them."

Mina said defiantly, "I had my reasons, like I have my reasons now."

The tattooed man frowned. "What's with the family?"

Cole looked at me. "They shouldn't be here. Dray, this is Hernandez. Calls it like he sees it."

"You keep family safe, not—"

Nataly interrupted, her Russian-accented voice sharp. "There's chatter. Agents are heading this way. We need to go."

Cole looked at me, his surprise that I'd let Mina near us evident. "You check her for trackers?"

"She helped us," I said.

Both he and Garly looked unconvinced.

The man with large ears waved us to the van. "Let's go."

I wanted to know who he and the other guy were first, but we didn't have time. Large ears was already behind the wheel. We approached the van, though Cole glared at me as Mina got in. He directed me into the unfinished rear of the van after her. The rear contained a few boxes, two liquicore computers, and bags of supplies. I assumed weapons were stashed everywhere.

Nataly looked at Mina suspiciously as she settled in a corner.

I helped Talia into the van and sat next to her. Hernandez climbed in last, then Cole shut the door and got in the front passenger seat.

"There's a drone out there," I started as the driver took off, but Nataly waved away my concern.

"I blocked its signal and sent it south." She gave me an awkward hug. "It's good to see you."

"How have you been?"

"Being labeled a terrorist wasn't in my five-year plan, but life's not all bad." She glanced at Garly, then looked past me to Talia. "I hear you're a mean hacker."

"Not mean. It's their fault their security is flimso."

As the two began talking shop, Raven scooted over to Garly. She looked thrilled to see him. As they talked, he gently took her damaged hand. "Can you make new fingers for me — and cartridges?" she asked.

"Dray," Valor said, pulling my attention. She motioned to the driver, the one with large ears, and then the other man. "This is Omura, the other is Fritz. They and Hernandez served in the same unit as Monroe. They reached out to Cole after you ditched us in Denver."

"Monroe told us about you," Omura said, referring to the ex-soldier who had joined my quest to find Talia — and who'd given his life protecting Valor, Raven, and me.

Fritz said, "He respected you. Didn't respect many." He spoke with the same military tightness Monroe had.

"How'd you survive?" I asked Cole.

"The shitshow with the nodes you bailed on? Our team was assigned the bell tower in Nashville. We didn't encounter resistance, not a single guard, which gave me a bad feeling. I got them out before Agents sprang their trap, called others to warn them. Don't think many made it, but some did, including Lafontaine and some of his clan. Been on the run since." He leaned toward me. "You have a lot to make up for."

His face hardened as he gauged my expression.

He triggered the bio-coated mini-bots, which reformed his mask. "Every rebel will be hostile toward you. You'll have to decide how to address your actions — and make the sacrifice of those who died worth it."

Raven spoke up. "Have you heard from Jex? Is he OK?"

"He was hit in the back. Doc's been trying to fix him, but I don't think he'll walk again."

My warrior daughter, hardened from weeks of torture, began to cry.

CHAPTER ELEVEN

Cole's comment bothered me the entire journey across Texas and through Arkansas, what normally would've taken seven hours but took twice that due to careful stops and multiple backtracking.

The group caught up during the journey, though many stayed quiet, myself included. I was anxious about what we would find.

It wasn't just Jex, though he was of major concern. Mina was wary — I didn't know what Cole would do about her — Valor was suspicious, and Talia was tired, though she pretended otherwise. It was good to see Garly and Nataly, even Cole, though tension filled the van.

Cole's group described how they'd moved from place to place after the node attack. It had been harrowing, though Nataly announced she and Garly were now a couple — to his embarrassment — saying he'd been sly enough never to find a safe house with enough beds. His face glowed red as he protested, his words drowned out by her giggles.

We arrived in Memphis after sunrise, mist coming off the streets of the downtown neighborhood from a night of rain.

Valor scooted over to me. "See those?" Gray boxes punctured with camera lenses and listening devices hung from telephone poles. "The Agency is blatantly monitoring. People just accept it. And news organizations are telling viewers to report suspicious neighbors or activities."

People walking down the streets were hunched over, skittish and withdrawn. Overhead, drones passed by at least once a minute.

Fritz handed out hoodies, which I immediately put on. Even if Talia had made us invisible to The Agency, I was one of the most infamous people in the country.

Omura drove past a coffee shop and parked next to a gap between two brick buildings. We got out, slipped through the gap, and proceeded along a row of black, unmarked doors. "They were here when we found them," he explained. "He taught her how to set up surveillance. She'll know we're here."

A door opened ahead, though no one was visible. We stepped into a dim hallway, the door closed — and Anya faced us, her platinum-blonde hair and translucent skin nearly glowing in the dim hallway.

I flashed to the first time I'd met her. She'd led the surgical team that saved Raven's life, her assured voice and confident movements the only hope I could cling to that terrible night. She'd helped me weeks later, which had started her involvement — and our relationship, well after Mina had betrayed us.

Without thinking, I went to Anya. Her light-blue eyes teared up, and we hugged.

She pulled away and smiled at Talia, then saw Mina.

"You remember me, Dray's wife?" Mina asked.

Anya's expression hardened. "I know who you are. Everyone here does."

As I stepped between them, Raven asked about Jex.

Anya flashed me a look, then took Raven's hand and led her to the living room.

The hospital bed dominated the center of the modest space.

A thin, tousled-hair figure with broad shoulders laid face down, monitors and a tray with a half-eaten breakfast clustered nearby. Past the bed, six vid screens hung from a makeshift grid, half displaying images from outside the unit, the other half streaming news channels.

Raven cautiously approached the bed. "Jex?"

She revealed old bullet wounds as she carefully slid the sheet from his shoulders.

He shifted, looked up at her, then raised up on all fours, though Anya admonished him, "Don't get up."

Raven twisted her body, slid under Jex, and hugged him.

Everyone gave them a moment, though I was the last to turn away, struggling that another person close to me had been badly wounded.

A well-worn kitchenette occupied a corner of the unit, the

counters covered with packets of ready-made food and medical supplies. There appeared to be a bedroom, though the couch indicated Anya had slept near Jex, ostensibly to keep an eye on him. Two padded chairs and a small table near tinted windows that showed slivers of the waking city occupied the rest of the space.

Anya spoke quietly to Valor, Talia, and me. "I nearly lost him more than once. He was shot multiple times. One of the bullets destroyed his T-5 vertebra and damaged his spinal cord. Nanobots are working to reconstruct his spinal cord, but it's a delicate process. He's had to lie on his stomach as they work. I sealed the wound for now, though infection is always a risk—as is the rebuild failing."

She dropped her voice further. "Cole called during the attack to warn us. We ran, but Agents detonated their explosives before we cleared the building. Only one other survived. He and I moved Jex to a medical clinic, and I operated that night. I removed fragments and shrapnel, replaced three vertebrae with printed bone, and attached four biowoven robo-enhancers to his ribcage with bio-cement to help support his spine."

"Is the support to make him stronger?" I asked.

"So he can walk. The enhancers and corresponding brace he'll need to wear were developed for military veterans. They return the use of limbs and have a feature where the wearer can lock the brace in extreme circumstances. It's complex and not guaranteed, which is why I've had the nanobots working on him. Spines are difficult to reconstruct. He's not out of the woods, though he's shown progress. Two weeks ago, he wouldn't have been able to rise up like he did. Cole found us five days ago. It's been helpful having them, and Nataly helped improve my camera system."

"It's lucky you were with Jex," Valor said.

"I've endangered him by not taking him to a hospital, but he refused no matter how much I argued. I know he would've been arrested, but he would've had a better chance."

"You gave him the best he could have," I said.

Her walk shaky but determined, Talia went to Jex and

Raven, who had disentangled, Jex lying back down with a sigh. He smiled. "Yes, I got shot in the ass."

Talia laughed. "I wanted to blat that."

He hugged her awkwardly. "I'm so happy to see you. You're like a miracle. I'm sorry we left you behind," he said, his Creole accent thick with emotion.

"You gonna be OK?"

As he reassured her, I felt responsible for his suffering, for hers, for the network that tracked us, for Zion being in power.

Anya told us, "Jex keeps pushing his recovery. He's been so worried about everyone, especially Raven." In a whisper, she told me, "I was worried about you, too."

From her expression, I suspected she'd suffered sleepless nights caring for him and fretting about us.

I wanted to hold her again but didn't.

"Any other rebels survive?" I asked Garly and Nataly, who sat nearby.

"We only did because of Nipsen," she said. "He fought an Agent so we could escape. He didn't make it."

"There are others out there. They need to hang low 'til we can reconfig," Garly told me.

"We should switch hideouts. We've been here too long," she added.

"Jex shouldn't move," Anya said. "He could end up paralyzed if we don't give him more time."

"The one thing none of us have," I said. I felt the conflict. There were glances my way. Looking for me to lead—which I didn't want.

I went to Jex, who sat up against everyone's objections. I hugged him carefully, my hand grazing the domed plastic that sealed his injury. "How are you?" I asked as I stepped back. He looked much older than his eighteen years. "You shaved your beard."

"Didn't need it 'nmore. Glad y'all survived. Wasn't sure you did. I shoulda gone with you to get Talia. I feared I'd lost you."

An alert went off on two of the vid screens that were

streaming news. Talia hobbled over to them. "The Agency is splashing your face," she said. Both bulletins were about me, each reiterating their claims that I was a traitor.

"They're putting you on everyone's radar," Cole said.

Valor waved toward another screen. "It's not just that." She found the volume and turned it up.

"...this rollout of an update to everyone's implant will be done in stages, but expect to receive a notice within the next few days," a silver-haired spokesman said. "There's nothing you need to do on your end. It's mandatory and will be run during off-hours."

"They can't just say 'while you're asleep'," Jex muttered.

Garly stood. "I'll start finagling implant covers that broadcast fake signals. That should mask us, unless they spot the codes switching."

As Talia offered to help, Omura said, "We need to fight."

I said, "We need to get away. Nataly said you've been here too long."

Jex whispered to Raven, eyeing Mina with distrust.

"I have a place in Chicago. We could hop there," Garly said.

"Travelling that far north is dangerous," Omura said. "Agents will be watching the roads."

"Especially with a child and someone on a stretcher," Hernandez said.

They were right. With the surveillance network I'd built, roadways were dangerous. So was interacting with people. The more we did, the greater the risk of being spotted, of getting captured. My network aggregated every public and private security, traffic, surveillance, and monitoring camera, tying home doorbell cameras with ATM machines, buildings' private security cameras with traffic cams, and more into a massive system that was nearly unavoidable. That didn't even count what The Agency had for their surveillance.

"You'd like my abode. I have gadgets, weapons, supplies, even foodstuff," Garly said hopefully.

As the group discussed his offer, I focused on the vid

screens that displayed the nearby area. Each one revealed a different street or angle. The monitor on the bottom left showed a view down a street to the docks by the Mississippi. As I watched, a crane swung shrink-wrapped machinery onto a large barge. "We'll go on one of those. It'll keep us off roads."

The group hesitated, unsure.

Mina, who'd watched my and Anya's interactions with increasing displeasure, asked, "Do you think Talia can handle a trip that far?"

Though Talia immediately said she could, I looked to Anya.

"So long as she doesn't overdo it," Anya hedged.

"I don't think—" Mina started.

"You don't get a say in any of this," Raven told her. "Don't like it, stay here."

"I second that," Cole said.

Fritz picked up his machine gun. "Then let's go. Boat's being loaded. It'll leave soon."

"Once we get to Garly's, we can ramp up the war again," Cole said. He looked at me as if daring me to argue.

I knew this had been coming. "I'm taking my girls to Canada. Talia needs to recover, and the Canadians haven't installed the same neural network system the U.S. has. We'll have a chance."

Garly asked, "Aren't we gonna duke it to Agents?"

"No. He's going to run off again," Cole said.

"Even if I wanted to fight, The Agency knows how I think. Besides, we tried and failed," I said. "I need to focus on Talia, give her, Raven, and Jex a chance to survive."

"I wanna fight," Talia said. She approached on unsteady feet. "I wanna get the crushers who brainzapped me."

I knew Raven wanted to fight too, her need to help others driving her. "No."

Talia looked hurt, Garly and Nataly confused, the ex-soldiers angry. Both Raven and Jex looked ready to protest.

"I knew it," Cole said in disgust. "Abandoned the team once, and you're doing it again."

"I just spent a month being absolutely helpless. Now that I have a chance, I'm keeping my girls safe. Besides, the rebellion is over. We lost."

CHAPTER TWELVE

No one spoke as we arrived at the sprawling commercial dock, the sun having burned away the morning fog. Their silence wasn't just to avoid drawing attention. Everyone was upset with me for rejecting the fight. Cole and Hernandez were hostile. Omura and Fritz didn't look at me—seemingly preoccupied by the long wooden box they carried—and even Valor was standoffish as we started through the maze of stacked containers and cargo that filled the place.

Robots and humans worked to transfer hundreds of containers and other large objects onto the barge, the combined weight pushing it deeper into the water. Multi-story cranes swiveled back and forth in the bright sunlight as they added more containers. Along with the items being stacked along its length, the barge held a row of nine fuel tanks near the rear, each roughly the capacity of seven tanker trucks.

The dock smelled of coal, grain, metal, and decay, an occasional rat darting past unfazed by our presence.

We proceeded guardedly through the maze in search of the dock's office to access the freight logs. Crews of robots and men traversed the dock and stopped seemingly at random at various containers for the cranes to hoist. Most of the workers were robotic, the humans there to supervise and resolve issues, though any one of the men could break off and head our way without warning.

I carried Talia as we walked.

After five tense minutes of avoiding discovery while we navigated the area, we located the office but couldn't approach it. Every time we tried, a human appeared.

"Now what?" Valor asked with a bite in her voice.

I glanced at the tablet Talia held. "They wouldn't have Wi-Fi, would they?"

My daughter leaned against my chest as she checked. "Snitz, they do." She typed rapidly, then snickered. She was in.

I flashed a grin, but my team didn't respond.

With the exception of Talia and me, we all carried bags of supplies. No one put anything down in case we had to run.

Faint shouts and the whine of hydraulics laced the air as Talia typed. The closest of the three cranes lifted a pallet of DNA scanners and swung it out over the barge, the machine's movements making the dock vibrate.

Footsteps drew our attention.

Valor and Cole aimed their weapons.

Seconds later, Garly and Nataly appeared with more supplies, including two backup batteries for Talia. Both were new, so they'd get us through the boat ride with capacity to spare.

Garly glanced at Talia with a sad expression as Nataly joined her, and the two hackers worked together to break into the dock's network.

"How's it going?" I whispered after a minute. This was taking too long.

"Holds please," Talia said.

Anya checked on the wooden box, which sported three holes on each side. She spoke quietly, and I heard Jex mutter a response.

Cole moved forward to watch out for workers, and Raven and Valor stationed themselves behind us.

Mina gazed back at me with a mix of longing and frustration.

Before we'd left, she'd pulled me aside. "I never dreamed you would free Talia. Free me." Her smile bloomed.

"She made it possible."

"I saw Kieran's struggle with her getting hurt. It wasn't who he saw himself to be."

She was adept at reading people, which gave her words weight. "Good to know."

She touched my arm. "Glad to help."

I gently removed her hand. "Don't. We'll end up arguing, and a fight won't change what happened. Nor will it change my feelings." Before I could stop myself, I glanced at Anya.

"I'm going to fight for my family."

"You want to fight for the girls, that's between you and them. Don't fight for me. I don't want it."

Shouts from workers pulled me from the memory. They sounded closer.

Talia grinned up at me. "Done. I added a container for us to ride."

"I thought we were taking one already scheduled to go."

"They're stuffed with coal and other junk, so I thumbed our own number."

Nataly added, "We have six minutes." She led us to a green shipping container located at the end of a cluster of containers. Cole made sure the way was clear, then lifted the handle and swung the doors open.

The inside smelled faintly of grease but was clean.

Fritz and Omura entered and set Jex down against one wall. The others followed, dropping their bags in various spots.

Talia was exhausted but happy; she even helped Garly and Nataly spread out blankets after I set her down.

As Anya stopped beside me just outside the container, Mina pushed her way past, pulled more blankets from her bag, and spread them along one side of the interior.

Anya leaned close. "Are we all going in the same container?"

I nodded.

We joined the others, and she added her bags—which held medical supplies and food Cole's team had stocked up over time—to the blankets and warming unit the others had brought.

The three ex-soldiers stepped back outside.

As Hernandez stood guard, Fritz lifted Omura up so he could attach a small camera to the top corner of the container, then Omura pulled a small drone out of his pocket and set it on the roof.

The crane was heading toward us—which meant workers would show up any second.

I extracted the four swarmbots from my pocket and set them on the ground outside as the ex-soldiers entered the container, then stepped back as Fritz and Omura pulled the doors closed. I told them to hold the doors in place; after a few seconds, we heard metallic scurrying, then the handle lifted and moved into place, locking us inside.

Satisfied, I extracted my ion blade and, as voices rose outside, cut a small hole along the bottom edge of the container's side. Seconds later, the four swarmbots crawled inside.

The voices grew to shouts, and our group fell quiet. As hauling straps wrapped around our container, I rejoined the others.

A light flared in the darkness. I found Garly a few feet away, holding an electric lamp. He pointed at the swarmbots. "Can I have one?" he whispered.

I handed one over with a questioning look.

The shouts faded, replaced by a mechanical whine as the crane swiveled over us and dropped its hook.

I spotted Talia near Raven and scooted over to her. Before I could situate myself, we were lifted into the air, the container rotating as the crane hoisted us.

The wooden box slid toward Garly and Mina.

Raven, Nataly, and I arrested it as our ascent slowed — we must've been a hundred feet or more off the ground — then had to nearly jump on top of it as we slid toward the doors, the crane moving us over to the barge. We stopped with no warning, our container swinging wildly — eliciting startled cries from Talia and Nataly — then dropped. Mina, Raven, Fritz, and Garly looked as if they might vomit — who knew if Cole was affected, hidden behind his 'bot mask — and we slowed just before our container landed on the deck with a loud BOOM.

As soon as we did, Omura pulled out a small remote. I heard a faint buzz and realized he'd launched the drone he'd set on the roof. Seconds later, a container slammed on top of us, causing most of us to grab our ears, and a third landed on top of the second one.

Omura steered the drone, then turned off the remote. I suspected he'd landed his device on top of the third container.

As more containers were placed nearby, Anya unlatched the box and opened it. Jex had been clutching the inside, so he looked in one piece. I hoped the ride hadn't inflicted any damage.

"Why do you keep scoping the doctor?" Talia asked. She must have recognized Anya from the hospital back when I'd ripped out Raven's prior implant.

"We'll talk about it when there's more time."

She gave me a weird look.

The banging from containers being loaded faded, and a rumble started. We were leaving.

My unease grew as the team settled, hostility and unspoken issues growing in the cold space.

As Mina wrapped Talia in a blanket and Raven snuggled with Jex, I went to Fritz, Omura, and Hernandez.

The ex-soldiers' stance was standoffish.

"Monroe was a good soldier—" I started.

"We know that," Fritz said.

"We became friends after a time. Raven, Valor, and I probably would've died if not for him."

"What's your point?"

My voice hardened. "Which clan did you come from?"

Omura stepped closer. "We don't have to tell you a thing."

"You didn't come from one, did you? You didn't get involved in the rebellion. You heard my broadcast in L.A., Monroe told me you all did, yet you didn't do a damn thing."

As Omura coiled to attack, Cole stepped between us. "Dray, you looking for a fight?"

"My family is here, people I care about, and you brought men I don't know."

"I vouch for them."

"If you were me, you'd question too."

"You doubt my word? We have a clear enemy. They've scattered our forces—but you want to run. This fight is bigger than any one person. You knew that."

"At least I fought." I switched my gaze to Omura.

The man's lips pressed together, his body rigid. Then he exhaled. "It's not easy accepting the country we've defended has lied to us. We're committed now. We'll fight to the end. Why won't you?"

"I have enough blood on my hands."

"Always keep fighting," Fritz said.

"Just because you were soldiers, that doesn't give you the right to judge me."

"Yes, it does," Hernandez said.

As Fritz and Omura agreed, Cole glared at me. "When we get to Chicago, we're going our separate ways."

Chapter Thirteen

It had been quiet in the container for some time.

I wasn't thrilled about being in one again. The last time I'd traveled in one, I'd been wedged in with a hundred rebels. Then we'd been attacked, and I'd had to leap from the cargo plane to free those trapped inside.

At least now we had room. And weren't falling.

The group had spread out, each claiming a tiny space for themselves.

After we'd started off, I'd replaced Talia's battery. Garly had helped by creating a splinter to ease the switch, though we would need to replace it again in three days.

While I wanted to spend time with her and Raven, having missed so much with them, I followed the others' lead and settled into the routine of the ship. Most of us had gotten little rest the past few days, so we caught up. Valor and the ex-soldiers alternated between resting and taking shifts to watch for dangers via the small camera Omura had attached outside.

The next day, I glimpsed the top of the St. Louis Arch from his camera. It was the only movement visible as the barge picked up speed, the river straighter in this section. I continued to watch, wrestling with my thoughts. Cole's men weren't wrong. But I couldn't imagine fighting again after what we'd escaped.

I spent time with Talia, though she tired quickly. I encouraged her to rest and joined Anya, who ate from a bag of crackers.

She smiled as I sat. "Don't try calling this a date."

"What if I'd brought sparkling water to go with those crackers?"

"More practical than flowers."

"I thought you liked flowers."

"I do. Too bad you didn't stop at a florist."

We spoke softly so the others wouldn't hear.

She offered me the bag. "What's the biggest thing you've

regretted?"

"You mean other than joining a rebellion and endangering my family?"

"How about leaving me at that stadium?"

"That's a close second."

She nodded and put the bag aside, her mood sobering.

I could feel her withdrawal.

"I never discussed going to Canada, and I'm not sure it's what you want, but I want you to come with us," I said.

"And Mina?"

"Regardless of what you decide, she and I are done."

She fell silent.

Her hand rested near mine, but she didn't move it closer. Neither did I.

Raven went to Garly, who sat with Nataly leaning against him. He assured her he would work on her fingers as soon as he could. She had been anxious the entire trip, alternating between Talia and Jex. I suspected she'd slept the least of anyone.

"I want finger weapons, too," Talia said from her spot near them. She held her heart regulator, battery, and gauge, though the three were tightly wrapped in her sling.

"You don't need a weapon," Jex said. "We got your back. No one's leavin' you again."

I could read Raven's guilt as she eyed her sister.

Valor looked away. She'd listened to the conversation, easy to do in the small space, as she etched a pattern on a Smith & Wesson. She rubbed the edge of her eyepatch, which hid the tiny camera installed to replace the eye she'd lost. She didn't have an implant, the only person I knew without one, a fake cover in its place.

Deciding to give Anya space, I went to Valor and sat close. "You OK?"

"I don't like running. It's wrong." She continued to etch. "Don't bother guessing how I lost my eye. Your guesses are never sick enough."

I used to, as a game. Our dynamic had changed. When her one good eye finally looked at me, I said, "OK, I give."

Her triumphant expression bloomed, then faded. "My father was imprisoned when I was a baby. I knew he had demons. My uncle warned me, but I thought I was safe. When Father got released, he saw my neural net and went into a rage. He thought the Feds would use it to keep tabs on him. I thought it gave me a chance at a better life. He got so enraged, he pinned me down and took a crowbar to my implant, crushing the side of my skull and taking my eye. I was twelve. Then he tried to remove his own, which they'd implanted while he was in prison.

"My aunt was a surgeon like Anya. She saved my life and nursed me back to health. She hid the camera she installed in my socket and the fact I no longer had an implant, risking her life not only then but four years later when I was supposed to get my adult implant. She got caught, and Agents came. I saved her son during the attack. We would've gotten away, but he ran back to her, and I didn't go after him. I watched those Agents kill them both.

"I let her down. And him. That's when I changed my name. I wanted something to strive for, to become worthy of my aunt."

I comforted her the best I could, which wasn't much.

Cole waved me over.

"He's furious with you, in case you hadn't noticed," she said with a nod toward him. "Lots of rebels are. You caused the rebellion to be associated with the deaths of hundreds."

As I stood, she said, "Be careful."

Cole, Hernandez, Omura, and Fritz huddled near the camera feed. "Fritz spotted something," Cole said in a tight voice. "It was just a glimmer."

The ex-soldiers alternated between looking at the feed and staring at the container wall. They were using their infrared scopes to look outside. "There's something, but I'm getting interference," Omura said.

"What about the drone?" I asked.

Garly came over, having kept an eye on me, and launched the drone. As it scanned the boat from high above, the camera feed projected on the controller's screen, Nataly joined us. She saw it first. "Look. Four Agents."

One of the figures had a blondish-brown streak in their silver hair. Kieran. They had a robot dog with them.

Cole grabbed me. "Why don't you have an implant cover?"

"Talia masked me—and herself, Raven, and Mina. That's not how they found us."

He weighed my words, his face creased in hostility, as Raven came over.

"Maybe they're just doing a boat inspection," Omura said.

"Way out here?" Fritz asked.

Raven murmured, "Could be standard. Maybe."

"It's not an inspection," I said.

Jex swore. He was looking at a small screen of his own. "I left a drone back in Memphis. Agents are there."

"Everyone be quiet," Cole told us.

On the screen, a dog leapt onto the top of a stack of containers and stared down as it walked the container's length. The Agents fanned out and faced other containers.

"What're they doing?" Raven asked.

"They're not opening anything, which is good."

Kieran led the Agents to another set of containers. Closer in our direction.

I straightened. "They're scanning them. Our body heat will register when they get here. We have to get off the ship." I regretted I'd suggested the barge.

As the group started to get up, Valor asked, "Can Talia get wet with that thing on her chest?"

I exchanged a glance with Garly. "Not the battery."

The tall scientist was already moving, striding down the length of the container. He approached the thick base from Jex's box we'd used to block off the commode and grabbed it.

Raven asked, "What weapons do we have?"

"Four machine guns, a pulse gun, a few remote explosives, and two hand shields," Cole said. We also had Valor's guns, which she'd finished etching.

"The ship's carrying fuel tanks. We get in a gunfight, we could blow us to hell," Hernandez said.

Omura and Fritz disbursed the guns, and Fritz kept the

bag, which I assumed contained the shields and explosives.

Talia was fidgety.

I handed her the ion blade and lifted her up so she could cut the tops of the rods that locked our container. I then set her down and used the blade to sever the bottoms and center brace. As I did, Raven went to Jex, wrapped his torso in a shirt, and, with the ex-soldiers' help, got him onto the wooden board to carry him out, as he wouldn't be able to keep up.

With Mina ready to guide Talia, we cautiously opened the doors.

The sunlight that hit us felt intense after the near darkness of the past two days.

When my eyes adjusted, I stepped out of our hideout into a row of containers stacked three high.

I signaled to Garly, who squinted at the drone controller's screen, weapons bag slung over his shoulder, then waved us east.

Though it was hot and bright, I kept the hoodie on that Fritz had given me and took the lead.

Each of us carried a weapon with the exception of Talia, even Mina with a pistol that she pointed away from our youngest, who pushed herself to keep up.

I reached the end of the row, checked both directions and headed north.

The Agents had started on the southwestern end, having arrived either by boat or hoverbike. They would spread out to cut any escape.

Garly hissed behind me. He frantically waved me back and down a separate corridor, his lanky body bent over.

I joined the others in heading in the new direction. We broke into a run, containers of varying colors blurred.

The thought of facing Agents made my heart pound.

Garly led us diagonally across the barge, steering us around more containers. We passed some large, curved metal cargo, what I realized were sections of my fusion reactor design.

Nikolai was building more reactors.

I spotted a glimmer of the river but was steered away, a frantic but silent Garly directing us to huddle. I didn't understand, then heard a tapping of metal. The sound increased rapidly. It was a robot dog, the same kind that had killed Monroe. Omura, Hernandez, and Fritz became stone-faced; they'd heard how he died.

If the Rottweiler-sized robot found us, Jex and Talia would be the most vulnerable.

The robot slowed as it neared, coming up along the edge of the barge. We tensed, not sure if it would appear from around the corner or leap onto the container we hid behind to attack from above. After a moment, the dog continued on, its footfalls fading.

We hurried out from behind the container and followed its length to the river. Trees lined the west shoreline with tilled farmland beyond, an occasional house or barn glimpsed in the distance.

Sunlight sparkled off the dark waters of the Mississippi as the barge foraged north.

With the amount of weight pushing down on the barge, there was only about a six-foot drop to the water. We'd have to be quiet — and fast.

Omura and Fritz lowered Jex to the deck near the edge.

"I'm staying to fight," Hernandez said.

"No," I said. "All of you, get to shore as fast as possible and out of sight. Once you're in the water, float until you're well past the barge. The less you swim until you're farther away, the better."

Emotions flickered on their faces, but they didn't object.

To Jex, Anya said, "Get in gently."

"How? The boat's cookin'."

Garly waved him to get off the board. When he did, Garly gave me his bag and drone display, then moved the board to the edge of the barge, slid over the side, and held himself up with one hand. With the other, he waved Talia onto the board. Nataly got in on the other side. Talia got on the board, lying on her back. She held her sling with one hand and gripped the side of the board with the other. My heart skipped a beat as Garly and Nataly tilted her, and they went in together, disappearing so fast down the length of the barge I couldn't tell if Talia had gotten wet, if she was OK.

Jex was next. He crawled to the ledge and let his legs dangle over the side.

To Raven, I said, "Get them to safety. I'm relying on you."

She resisted, torn between wanting to protect me and Jex, then hooked her machine gun over her shoulder and went to him. As he lowered the rest of his body over the side, she slipped in front of him, wrapped an arm around his waist, and they dropped into the water. She'd positioned herself to take the brunt of the impact, both temporarily disappearing from view before bobbing to the surface, the current pulling them away.

"We need to distract those Agents," Cole said as Valor and Anya scooted to the barge's edge.

"We need more than that," I said. I went through Garly's bag, removed a hand shield and the three remote explosives, and stashed them in my hoodie's pockets. I stood to find them staring at me. "Get off the ship. I have an idea, but it only works if you're all gone."

Omura squinted at me. "Monroe died believing in you."

"Let's hope he was right." I waved at them, who joined Valor and Anya. They raised their weapons, and the men slipped into the water, Anya following a beat later. Valor hung back, but I said, "Protect them. Please."

Warring with herself, she left.

I'd said I was fleeing to Canada, not fighting. Yet here I was.

As I slid on the glove that contained the hand shield, I glanced upstream and spotted a blockade far to the north. More Agents, positioned to stop the barge.

I needed to blow up the ship, make it so messy Zion might think we were dead.

Soon after I started moving, the controller's screen flashed red. The drone had run out of power and crashed, which meant I couldn't see what the Agents were doing.

Needing to find out, I ran to the front of the ship where the parts of the fusion reactor sat and climbed the back side of a curved piece.

When I reached the top, I gazed the length of the barge. Through the undulating stacks of containers, I spotted Wraith and Pierce, the two Agents glaring back at me, the dog with them. Past them toward the east side, near the back, I spotted Kieran and a fourth Agent. The dog was already gone when I looked for it again. Shit.

The Agents started running.

I jumped from the structure and started down the pathway created by fusion parts on one side and stacked containers on the other, reached the side of the barge, then ran south. Two rows later, I turned east into a wide row and started toward the center of the barge.

Metal footsteps alerted me. I slowed—and the dog appeared from near the far side. It picked up speed as it charged me, its jaws opening to reveal its razor teeth, and jumped.

I'd already crouched and triggered my hand shield, which emitted a faint, dark-violet-tinted energy shield that arched outward in a curved circle about two feet from my fist. Even though I triggered it while the killer dog robot had been twenty yards away, I was familiar with its speed. Before I'd even set myself, I lifted upwards, shoving up and back.

The robot hit the shield as I moved, the beast nearly too fast to see, and flew up and over me.

The impact jarred me, but I got to my feet as the robot landed in the river and sank.

I started forward, my shoulder stinging from the impact. I suspected Wraith and Pierce had split up to try to corner me, Kieran and the other one as well.

I needed to change their focus, so I headed for a row of containers that stretched nearly the width of the barge, separated from another section of containers by a ten-foot gap. When I reached them, I triggered my blade and sliced along the width of one of the containers. Coal poured out from the widening cut as I ran. I leapt out of the way at the end as the container collapsed into the gap, throwing coal across the barge. The container above it smashed into the containers stacked on the other side of the gap.

As I scrambled to my feet, the blow shoved the containers to the side, causing the ones near the edge of the barge to tilt. I started running again as the top container crashed into the river. A second container crashed into the river as well, and I ran faster, the noise from the damage masking my footfalls.

I headed for the rear of the boat.

As the barge began to slow, I reached the southeast corner. The row of fuel tanks became visible, and I dashed to the first one. I secured one of the remote explosives to the curved underbelly and activated it. Feeling emboldened, I hurried to the middle tank, set a second explosive, and looked up at the pusher boat. I glimpsed the bearded captain on the bridge and yelled, "Get off the ship."

I then ran for the far end.

Before I reached the last tank, a metallic growl made me stop. The damn robot dog I'd sent into the river appeared from around the last row of containers, water dripping from its body.

I activated my shield.

The dog, twenty feet away, started toward me.

I began to back up. It followed — and started barking.

I didn't know they made noise. It would bring the Agents.

I darted to the nearest tanker as the dog closed the distance, slapped the explosive to the tanker's belly, then retreated as the dog snapped at me. I deflected it with my shield, and it backed off, though it barked with more urgency.

Locking eyes with it, I extracted the detonator from the pocket of my hoodie.

Over the sounds of the dog's barks, I heard footsteps, then a shout. I glanced behind me. Kieran appeared from between two of the tanks.

I raised the detonator. "Time to go."

His eyes widened — then he disappeared back the way he came.

I squatted, curling into a ball behind my shield, then pivoted to face the tanks. This was goddamn suicide. The robot seemed to sense what I planned, for it leapt at me, jaws wide.

I ducked further behind my shield and triggered the detonator.

Chapter Fourteen

The explosion from the simultaneous detonations blotted out everything. Nothing existed except the deafening roar and blinding light—then the shockwave threw me like a bug flicked off a table. I jetted out over the river, water and land and sky a hazy blur, the water tilting until it was over me before sliding back around. Gravity finally pulled me down. I aimed my shield toward the navy-blue expanse of river as it loomed. My shield made contact—and I flipped, smacking off the water, then slammed into the river, and the waves swallowed me.

Debris splashed into the water around me.

I managed to use the shield to slow my plunge, turned it off, and swam to the surface. Gasping for air hurt. Everything hurt. I was dizzy, nauseous, and half-deaf.

Debris continued to fall.

The barge's rear end had been destroyed, and water poured into the exposed structure. Containers remained on the barge, ones that must've been near the front, but as more water poured in, the containers slid toward the back, which accelerated the sinking. Other containers and machinery littered the water, thrown in every direction. Smoke rose toward the sky, a dark beacon of what I'd done.

The submerged containers and equipment, some of which stuck out of the water, would make navigating the river treacherous for responders. I would've been pleased, but Kieran had seen me. If he'd survived—which I was sure he had, the augmented Agent like a silver-haired cockroach—he would tell Zion I'd blown the tanks. They'd come looking.

Forcing my bruised muscles to operate, I swam toward the western shoreline.

Trees reached for me, some with their branches grazing the water. The river's gurgling grew louder, partly from the current picking up, some from the return of my hearing.

Farther downstream, Garly waved at me from the shore,

Anya beside him. I let the current carry me to them. Within minutes, I climbed out with their help, though my arm ached intently, as did my right leg and the wound where I'd shanked myself.

"How's Talia," I asked. When they reassured me she was fine, I glanced down. While my arm made sense, as it had held the shield, I discovered a six-inch gouge along my thigh. "I guess it could've been worse," I said when Anya squatted to inspect the cut.

I felt off. Maybe it was the blood loss, but that wasn't right.

She and Garly led me into what appeared to be a wooded area with trees clustered in a kind of grid pattern where the others waited, all except Omura, Hernandez, and Fritz, who I assumed were guarding the area. Raven and Talia made sure my injury wasn't serious, frightened by the blast, as Anya patched my leg using the last of her nanobots. I didn't bother mentioning my arm.

"This place is like the last one," Raven said in a strangely excited voice.

I didn't understand until Garly covered my implant with a shield. The wooded area vanished to reveal an abandoned town. It reminded me of the one we'd found in Oklahoma. A cluster of two-story brick buildings huddled near the shoreline, while the main street contained abandoned restaurants, a general store, and a library. Farther from the river, small homes laid empty. Flowerbeds held dead flowers, and worn swings swung gently in the breeze. "What is this place?"

"I don't know, but I want to check it out," Raven said.

I reached for Talia. "You sure you're OK?"

"I held up my battery the whole time. I didn't let it get wet, though my arms got achy."

"What happened with the Agents?" Cole asked.

I told him about Kieran. "Don't know about the others. If they were near the edge, they might've gotten lucky, but if they were in the center of the barge when it blew, they have to be dead."

"We found a couple of old cars. Omura's trying to get

them started. If he does, your group can take one. We'll take the other."

I felt a pull as my desires warred inside me, conflicting needs that could kill us all.

"Dad," Raven said. "There must be other hidden towns. How many are there?"

My voice was harsh. "Right now, we have bigger concerns. How's Jex? Can he move?"

"He's taken some steps."

Memories flashed of what our group had suffered. More would follow. Loss or subjugation. Sacrifice or surrender.

I'd hoped to flee the country with my children before Agents caught our trail. I should've known better. I'd tried to run before.

I took a breath. "Cole, I owe you an apology. All of you. The Agency knew where we were — or where we'd likely be — because they knew my goal: to get Raven and Talia as far from The Agency as possible. Doing that made me act one way. If my goal was to fight the government, I would've acted another way. That's why Agents attacked the barge. They knew my goal."

"What are you saying?" Anya asked.

"Zion knows me and won't stop. He spent weeks studying my mind and yours," I said to Raven and Talia. He'd probably studied Mina's as well. "That upgrade The Agency announced isn't to help anyone. It's to use people's implants to read their thoughts — including plans to overthrow him. Once he's achieved that, no one will ever be able to defeat him. We have to take them all down."

"Wait, you're in?" Raven asked.

"The rebellion isn't over?" Nataly asked.

"Since they won't stop, I can't. I'm already the bad guy, so why not go for broke," I added to try to lighten the moment, though I had a deep unease about Talia and Raven fighting. I searched the group's faces. "I feel responsible for the network tracking us, for Zion being in power. So, I can't run. I have to fight."

Jex said, "I guess you needed to be blown up to change

your mind."

I looked at Raven and Talia. "I'm sorry I'm putting you two in danger."

"We're already in danger," Raven said.

Talia agreed, her face flushed with excitement. "I was gonna fight. 'Least now, I won't have to stealth it."

I didn't intend on her fighting. She was only twelve.

Jex pulled me out of my struggle. "What's the plan?"

"Not sure yet, but it can't be anything they'd predict." I could no longer meet their gaze. Freeing Talia had risked Raven and myself. This would risk the rest of them.

Cole said, "You have a lot to make up for."

"We should camp at my abode," Garly said.

I asked for the address. "I'll meet everyone there. I have to get something. Nataly, you're in charge."

"Why me?"

"The Agency doesn't know you're involved, so won't anticipate your moves."

I didn't have to tell them to hide their faces. Along with the thousands of cameras my network used to search for threats, The Agency used the cameras in each person's eyes. As I'd demonstrated at the Denver stadium, they used those cameras to create an overlapping, unavoidable vision of everything Americans saw. Once their three-dimensional network blanketed the country, there wouldn't be anywhere to hide.

Hernandez, who'd joined us as I spoke, eyed me suspiciously. "Where are you going?"

"I need to get information — and hopefully a weapon."

"Why the secrecy?" Cole asked.

"Until we're safe, we're all vulnerable. You want me to trust your word? Trust mine. I'll join you soon."

Anya touched my arm. "I'd like to examine Talia, see what they did to her."

"Are you going to Chicago with them? OK, check her there. I'd like to know what you find."

She sighed. "I'm sure her mother will, too."

I leaned down to Talia, careful to keep my damaged leg

straight. "Watch your battery level. Have Garly change it when it drops below twenty percent. I'll see you in two days. Stay smart."

"Why wouldn't I?"

As I started off, Raven hurried after me. "You want Mina to come with us?"

"No, but where else would she go?"

"I don't want her."

"If you don't take her, she'll follow you, which could expose everyone."

Raven crossed her arms. "You going to deal with this triangle you have brewing?"

"There's no triangle."

"Tell them. For what it's worth, I like Anya."

I watched her rejoin the others, our small band of hopefuls clustered in the ghost town with smoke coloring the sky behind them. One tiny group against Zion's army. I had no idea how to win.

CHAPTER FIFTEEN

Steering the motorcycle I'd found north of the hidden river town, I slowed as I approached the wooded area north of Marysville, Kansas.

I was exhausted. What should have taken five hours took almost twice that.

After I'd left the others, I felt the world opening up around me — with all of its risks and traps. Even the heavily-agricultural section of the country had monitoring and surveillance, all of which were nearly unavoidable. Drones were everywhere, including ones that followed every police car, ready to veer off to pursue a suspect at a moment's notice. I passed new detention centers, the installation of robotic sentinel stations, and DNA scanners, each a reminder of the dangers my group faced.

Alone with my thoughts, I remembered rebels who had perished: Senn, Monroe, Santo and his hackers, and others. I let my grief embrace me. I didn't want to become hardened, and they deserved every bit of my sorrow.

As the sun touched the horizon, I avoided the road Raven, Valor, Monroe, and I had taken to the house of my former partner, Brocco. Instead, I spotted a dirt path that ran along the edge of a dried creek bed before disappearing into the woods that masked his house from view.

I shut off my engine, hid the bike from the road, and jogged as fast as my healing leg allowed down the path. His house came into view when I crested a small hill, the long upper-level balcony and the window-lined lower level to my left, the shallow lake to my right. The house windows were dark, though he could be watching from that darkness, ready to launch some defense.

Before I could step out of the trees and head to the house, I heard a rustle — and was suddenly tackled.

I fell into a cluster of bushes, my attacker landing on top of me. Adrenaline flooded me as I swung at the guy — but he wore a thick helmet. My fist jolted in pain.

Unfazed by my punch, the guy sat up and motioned for me to be silent. When I nodded, he stood and stepped back. He was about my height but thicker. I got to my feet, thinking I could take him, then saw his taser.

He motioned me deeper into the woods.

My gun was hooked behind my lower back. I wouldn't be able to reach it fast enough. I was still stiff from the barge explosion and long ride here. But I might have to try.

He made me take a faded trail that led away from Brocco's house.

I expected him to grab my gun as I walked, but he didn't. Minutes later, as my limp worsened, a green Jeep came into view. He motioned me into the driver's seat, got in the back, and pantomimed for me to drive out of the area.

My confusion grew. There was something familiar about him.

I started the engine and drove through the grass to a dirt road, then to the street. I was about to ask for directions when he wrapped a headband around my head, settling a curved object against my implant. I realized it was an implant blocker.

Before I could ask, he signaled to head east and glanced out the rear window as I drove. More minutes passed, with nothing but harvested fields around us, before he noticeably relaxed.

I heard snaps as he took off his helmet and revealed his face.

The tan-and-gray stubble appeared first, then the flat nose, sharp gray eyes, and tan hair with swipes of gray. Tevin Shaye, the last member of the Gang of Five as the media had called us, our brilliant astrophysicist—and the cynic in our group, more so than Brocco had been.

I nearly swerved off the road. "What the hell are you doing here?"

"Brocco suspected you'd come. I've been waiting," Tevin said in his guttural voice.

"Wait, why? Where is he?"

Tevin instructed me to drive to an embankment, gesturing with slight jerks, a quirk I'd forgotten. After I stopped near the rise, we got out, and he pointed to the northeast.

A floating platform hovered over the tops of a forested area in the distance.

The ship was one of The Agency's weapons. They'd used one to capture rebels when they'd attacked our headquarters by dropping four-by-eight metal plates to capture targets. The plates pierced the ground around each victim in a box pattern to imprison them. Swift and effective.

"They kept it out of sight. You're lucky I'm semi-retired. Otherwise, I wouldn't have had time to wait around for you to nearly get caught. Brocco's place is a trap. Agents are hidden on his property. I had to guess which way you'd come. If you'd driven up his driveway, I wouldn't have been able to stop you."

They'd read my thoughts. A sickening feeling rose inside me. "How are you involved in all of this?"

"I'm not."

"You're here. You blocked my implant. What have you been doing the last dozen years?"

"Transportation. People need crap, so I deliver it. Less stressful than the world-changing racket."

"That used to matter to you."

"A lot of things 'used to'." He returned to the Jeep.

I followed. "How'd you know to block your implant?"

"Brocco told me. Didn't tell me much, but what he did say was enough. I paid it forward by saving you."

We got into the Jeep, Tevin taking the driver seat this time.

"You didn't need to shield my implant. I have a blocker," I said.

"Why didn't you wear it? It's how you got caught."

"That's not the only way they track us."

"Never wanted an implant in the first place. I resisted to the end. Damn near had the Army show up at my door. A whole team of lawyers, and I still had to accept it. Never trusted it. Both eyes? They're covering something. Barely anyone else objected, so here we are."

"They're doing more than that." I told him about Zion's role and the brain mapping The Agency had done on me, Talia,

Raven, who knew how many others.

"Zion? Figures. His people knew what you would do."

"But this was random."

"You said he's learned how you think. This was within your scope of possible actions, which is why they're here."

"His Agents nearly caught me earlier today."

"You've done what The Agency expected twice. Think you'll escape a third time?"

He started the engine and continued east. The sky grew black ahead of us.

"You taking me to Brocco?" I asked.

"He's dead. Made it look like an accident in that lake of his."

I fell silent, sad about Brocco's death, yet also a little panicked. "He'd figured out a way to hurt Agents — and how to find them. I need to pinpoint where their lies are coming from." I'd been depending on Brocco to locate Zion's base of operations so we could figure out how to defeat him.

"They dismantled his lab. Everything's gone."

I swore under my breath.

"Zion has always been arrogant — and different," he said with a flipping gesture. "Fixated on population levels and master planning back at UC, shit people don't think about. But he's not an idiot. It's easier to just change part of a network's overall design rather than all of it, especially if it's in use."

He pulled into a paved lot in front of a metal building. The place appeared deserted, a fifteen-year-old Ford pickup parked beside it. "You heading east or west?"

"East."

Tevin extracted two envelopes from under his seat with a gloved hand, selected one, and handed it to me. "Take that truck to Des Moines. Jump on a train to wherever you're going, preferably one with a different final destination. Stick to cargo lines. Few cameras. I stuck some cash in there, too. Didn't know how you'd be set."

I was stunned by his offer and impressed by his planning. "Join us."

"A fighter I'm not. Look what happened to Brocco."

"Yeah, look."

Tevin sighed. He took back the envelope, pulled a pen from his pocket, and wrote a phone number. "*One* time you can call for help. That's it. This isn't because Zion saddled Gen Omega with so many losses we couldn't retire rich. He's worse than a shitty businessman. He's a sociopath."

"Fight with me. This is our last chance. The stakes have never been higher."

"The highest. And highest risks. Good luck." He gave a jerky wave of dismissal.

I reluctantly got out.

As I started for the pickup, he said, "Zion needs a central location to house his lies. Your surveillance network doesn't have one because it's unnecessary. It's defense. Zion's is offense. The nodes you attacked have to operate in synchronicity or his lie collapses. That means he needs a place that orchestrates all that data. Take out his nexus, and he's exposed. I don't know where that place is, but wherever he hid it, it'll be impenetrable."

* * *

Two days later, my back sore and my hands stained with black train dust, I walked along Grand Avenue toward my destination. I'd managed to slip a ride on an automated delivery truck from the relay station, which had brought me close. But I had to risk the last few blocks on foot.

I felt the urge to twist Raven's tracker bracelet that I wore or fidget in some other way but forced myself to act calm. Unbothered. It wasn't easy.

I followed the street as it stretched under the interstate, glad for the brief respite. There weren't many people walking about, as the northern November air had a bite, but the drones and cameras and cars around me were threat enough.

I had lost weight and hadn't shaven in days. And Talia had supposedly hidden me. But I kept my head down. There were more drones in the skies than there had been in L.A., commercial, private, and government-owned.

I emerged from under the overpass, once again exposed.

Further ahead, strings of monitoring devices hovered over the center of every street in the downtown area.

An ominous hum filled the air, possibly over the entire city.

Chicago felt insular. Cut off. The few people I spotted seemed more comfortable interacting with computers than employees. In stores I passed, barely anybody went to the manned checkout, just the automated ones. No one seemed to look at one another. I suspected it was a lingering effect of the viruses and bird flus that occasionally ravaged the country, though there was also an increased level of suspicion and wariness. The behavior helped me, but the risk remained. And the oppression, the monitoring, would become worse for Raven and Talia as they grew older — if they were able to have a normal life.

The next intersection was busier than most; along with three intersecting streets, it contained entrances to a submerged subway line, the blue signs glowing in the overcast light. Police clustered on the far side of the intersection.

Wanting to avoid them, I took a right onto the angled intersecting street and headed southeast down Milwaukee Avenue. I had to cross the street but held off until I reached the end of the block, then crossed and approached a narrow, three-story brick building that abutted a larger, two-story building.

There were two entrances, one for the apartments and one for a shuttered business. I pressed the buzzer for the residential units. After a moment, the door unlocked. I stepped inside and, per my instructions, didn't walk up the stairs but pushed against the wall to my left. I heard another click, and a door hidden by a hoverscreen opened.

I walked into the empty shop, closed the door, and made my way to the far corner. As I approached, a portion of the wall opened.

Garly was on the other side, his grin as wide as a tablet. "Our Polaris has arrived."

He gave me a bear hug before allowing me inside the building that had been his home for years. He'd turned a former light-manufacturing property into a comfortable space with a large living area bracketed by a lab at the far end and storage in the rear. The mezzanine level contained a number of bedrooms.

The team seemed to be in better spirits, none more so than Talia.

"I got new zaps." She unsnapped a holster wrapped around her shoulders and showed me a small, hockey-puck-sized battery attached to her heart machine. Gone was the large battery and crude gauge I'd constructed. A small readout appeared when she pressed a button, showing seventy percent power.

"I like it," I said.

"It's *the* primo compact-battery gauge gizmo. I couldn't have crafted it better myself for the royalty," Garly said.

"I'm moving better, too," Talia said. She took four steps, turned with a slight hitch, and returned to me, though she had to put a hand on a nearby chair. Fritz came over, swooped her up — which made her laugh — and carried her toward Cole and Raven.

Jex approached. I was surprised to see him not only on his feet but without the domed plastic protecting his back. "She's charmin' 'em," he said in his drawl.

"How are you?"

"Legs hurt and back's tender, but 'least I'm no longer a lump. Start PT tomorrow."

Raven jogged over, hugged me, then stepped back and slipped an arm around Jex. "You see the surveillance out there? A lot of it's Agency tech."

"I've countered some bits," Garly said, "though I don't know how to crash their mind-reading."

I had the group gather.

They settled in the various couches and chairs that dominated the large living area. My girls sat close, Jex next to Raven, the ex-soldiers on another couch, Anya and Valor — who had changed her appearance, eyepatch and long hair gone, replaced by a fake eye and styled, shoulder-length hair — on a third couch with Nataly and Garly.

Eyes turned expectantly toward me, though Cole was guarded, and Mina stood in a corner with her arms crossed.

I explained how I went to Brocco's and nearly got caught.

"Did you get any intel?" Cole asked. When I shook my head, he said to the group, "Until we develop a plan, we need to accelerate everyone's training and find more fighters."

I said, "I agree we'll need more fighters. Nataly, do you still have those pictures from when we invaded the node in Denver?"

She retrieved her tablet and located the image I wanted. It was of the node network Zion had used to maintain his lies, a spiderweb of white lines that connected bright dots scattered across the country. "This was the network you and the other rebels targeted. The dots are the nodes, and the lines are the cables connecting them. But look here. Remember, Cole? You pointed it out."

I tapped a spot in West Virginia near its border with Virginia that was blank of nodes, lines, and coverage, the only uncovered area in the country. "There used to be a radio blackout area here, a quiet zone established for a scientific complex called the Green Bank Observatory. I'd hoped Brocco could've confirmed it, but I think this is where we need to attack."

"What about the super-bright dot covering D.C.?" Valor asked. "Wouldn't that be a better target?"

"I suspect that reflects overlapping broadcast signals, which is why it's so big. Since they're masking the identities of those in Congress, they need to concentrate their broadcasts there. But for his system to work, he needs a central hub that maintains the petabytes of data they constantly stream to everyone." I tapped the blank spot again. "Every signal across the spectrum was blocked in this area, which Zion could be using to his advantage. No one can just send in a drone to see what's there. You also can't send anything out. The only way to see what's there is to go there. We need to know if this is where he established his hub — and if so, determine its layout, defenses, and how to destroy it."

Omura stood. "I'll go."

I nodded my thanks. "If I'm right, it'll have multiple defenses. Approach carefully."

"Give me a few days." He ascended the stairs to gather his things.

I proceeded to the next point. "Garly, work on a sound machine. Brocco nearly deafened us with a sonic blast, but it was specifically designed to hurt Agents. I don't know the exact frequency, but the one I used when Raven and I attacked the Facility was close. I'll help you."

"On it."

Mina sat up. "You really think twelve adults can overthrow the government?"

"I'm basically an adult," Talia argued.

"We can barely defeat an Agent," Jex said, doubt creeping into his voice.

"He hasn't given us a plan," Cole said. He was still angry with me.

I took them in. This path would redefine our lives. "I believe we have a goal now. But how do we win? I have to change how I think. As an engineer, I look for weaknesses in objects, systems, and processes. It's how I've solved problems and how I tried to break The Agency's hold with the node attack. I have a different goal now: focus on their strengths — and do something that goes against every engineering instinct I have. I have to embrace chaos.

"We'd focused on The Agency's biggest weakness to try to reveal their lie. If we succeeded, we would've taken their power. But we failed.

"Zion holds all the cards, so we need to set them on fire. His organization manipulates the police, national surveillance, and numerous systems. Since he's responsible for keeping the peace, let's break it. Give his people more than they can handle. Create chaos, the bigger, the better." I saw a slow buy-in from my girls, Nataly, and Jex. "What all could we screw up?"

"Stock exchanges," Jex said.

"Electrical grids," Nataly said.

"Traffic networks, media circuits, the internet," Raven said. "Currency markets."

"And anything else we can come up with," I said. "We need to distract them, weaken them, overwhelm them, and shake people's confidence in Washington. Then we'll strike."

Cole said, "This is a horrible idea."

"It's not bad," Fritz said.

"It *is* bad and nearly impossible."

"Seems underhanded," Valor said as Hernandez stared daggers at me.

"We'll only have one chance," I said, but Cole cut me off.

"You'll waste time and resources."

"You've never distracted and weakened an enemy? Never cut supply lines, used psychological warfare?" When he didn't answer, I said, "We can't let the Agency realize what we're doing, or they'll counter our efforts, and we'll never be free."

"It won't work."

"It has to."

The group fell quiet, until Talia spoke up. "All who wants chaos, say 'I'."

CHAPTER SIXTEEN

The sounds of blows, grunts, and shuffling feet laced the air inside Garly's home for the fourth day, the sounds occasionally punctuated by the thud of someone knocked to the ground. Two tablets, four glasses, and a vid screen had become victims of errant swings.

Wiping sweat from my neck, I swept my gaze across the room. The furniture had been pushed to the corners to create an open space for training. Though everyone except Talia, Jex, and Mina now sported bruises, we'd grown closer, sometimes even joking with each other, though our efforts had a grim purpose.

Competitions had arisen, with Nataly trying to best Raven in hand-to-hand combat, and Valor and Fritz out-weightlifting each other. What had helped the comradery was getting Anya to burn a small hole in their left eyes. That way, none could be completely blinded again.

Talia stood to the side, antsy but pale, moving her body to mimic her sister as Raven sparred gently with Jex. He was unsteady, but it was good to see him improving. Past them, Fritz sparred with Valor, who trash-talked him. He was distracted, though, clearly worried about Omura. They all were distracted. My declaration hovered over their heads — and divided them.

As I took in the room, Mina gave me a guarded smile from where she stood near Talia.

Anya approached. "I can work on you now, if you're free."

I set down my dumbbell and followed her to a small room that contained a twin bed and nightstand. The tall lamp on the nightstand illuminated a tray of medical devices. "Lay on the bed."

I did as she instructed, having caught the professional, somewhat guarded tone to her voice. This was the first time we'd been alone since I'd rejoined them, though not by my choice.

Anya perched on the edge of the bed and picked up a laser pen.

She leaned over me, though she kept a space between us. "Stay completely still. Don't shift your gaze in the least."

"I won't." I knew these weren't the best conditions. The pillow shifted slightly as she leaned close, her shoulder-length hair falling down to partially screen us.

The laser would be intensely bright, but that's not what concerned me. Yet I hesitated to broach the subject. Instead, I asked, "What do you think about my chaos idea?"

"It sounds reckless, though it wouldn't be your first time."

As she concentrated on my left eye, I said, "I hurt you when I left Denver. I didn't mean to."

She triggered the laser, the light so intense it took all of my self-control not to jerk away. Tears formed as she moved the beam in a tight circle to burn a hole in the clear computer screen that coated my lens. The intensity grew as she expanded the hole, making it larger than the one she'd burned the first time.

"I know why you did it," she said. She turned off the laser, and my muscles relaxed, though there was a lingering glow to my vision.

She sat back. "I don't do vulnerable." She placed the laser on the nightstand. "I doubt I'll—"

"I missed you. I don't know if I'm being foolish or optimistic to think about life after all of this, but I want that future to be with you."

"You think you can say something sweet, and it'll all be better? That the past few weeks will disappear?"

"I'm telling you what I've wanted to say." I sat up. "How can I make it up to you?"

Her gaze sharpened.

Her beauty struck me, sky blue eyes that shimmered with intelligence and self-worth, flawless skin, her full mouth set in determination.

She said, "You start by not having your ex around."

"Her staying isn't my choice."

"It is to a degree."

"I do regret leaving you. If it had been for any reason other than Talia, I wouldn't have gone."

Her cold look cracked just a fraction. "Hiding behind your daughter?"

"Fighting for her. Which I'll always do. And fighting for us."

"With your ex as part of our clan."

"She's their mother. If they want her, she stays. I can't take her from them."

She dropped her gaze. After a moment, she said, "I don't like it."

"Neither do I." I brushed hair out of her face. "She's not in here."

She gave me an incredulous look. "Nothing's happening. Not with her around."

She was almost smiling, so I took a gamble, leaned in, and kissed her softly.

The corners of her mouth turned upward. She returned my kiss—then pulled back. "Keep those devil lips away."

"Dad?"

Talia hovered in the doorway with a confused expression. Anya stood. "I was burning a hole in his lens."

"You didn't work on me like that."

I asked, "How's your battery?"

Talia exhaled sharply. "I have ideas for your chaos. We could make masks for every citizen so they can hide to trick cops, and we could change the expired dates on food. People won't know if they'll get sickly."

Jex limped up behind her, took us in, and asked Talia, "Wanna spar? I need to build my strength." He wore the brace Anya had obtained to support his spine, the black woven elasti-plastic crisscrossing his chest. "Let these two...talk."

He tried to steer her away, but she continued to stare.

"You should go," Anya murmured.

I reluctantly followed them out. When I reached the doorway, I glanced back.

Anya made an "X" across her lips, though her smile faltered.

I followed Jex and Talia to the training area, then headed

to Cole, who stood over a desk that had been pushed to the side of the room. It was time to hash this out.

"You need to keep training," he said.

"I'm rusty, but I'm getting there." I'd gained a few pounds as well, though I'd need weeks to regain what I'd lost.

"Not good enough."

I understood his anger. I'd left the rebellion.

Maps of the United States covered the table, each with different notations and areas circled. "What are you working on?"

"Something to counter your shit plan."

"What're these notes?"

Cole grimaced, which twisted his damaged face. "Resources, enemy strongholds, areas to attack."

I picked up a map dotted with prominent bases. "Military? You want to open that door?"

"We may have to."

I picked up another and read the notes. "'Satellite comms center.' What's this other one? 'Department of Coerce'?"

"Commerce." He took the map and fussed with the writing, faint remnants of scars visible on his arms.

My eyes drifted to a nearby vid screen. It was turned to C-Span. Four Agents stood in precise spots around the room, which I assumed were signs of support — or control.

Cole had been watching our enemy.

He didn't pitch an alternative strategy, which meant he didn't have one. At least not yet.

I told him, "I want you to take charge of the attack plans for when we've weakened The Agency. We'll need to hit with precision and speed. And we'll need more rebel fighters. Others survived Zion's trap, didn't they?"

"Not as many as I'd hoped. I've talked to some I've found on the dark web. None are revealing much, but I'm building trust."

"Keep on it. We need as many as we can."

"You know your 'chaos' will traumatize people. There could be excessive casualties, not to mention the panic and fear."

"If you can think of another way, tell me." I took a breath. "I'm sorry I left. I won't this time—and I want you to lead our group. I'll oversee the chaos, but the rest is on you."

"I don't want it."

"Few leaders do. You have lists of every rebel group, don't you? Reach out to them. You're respected. You know the players. Get us more fighters." I'd said what I'd wanted. He would either accept my apology or leave.

As I backed away, he stopped me. "This three-way you have going. If you don't choose Mina, will she betray us again?"

I didn't have an answer.

I headed for Garly's windowless lab, which was located just past the double front doors.

Hernandez appeared and blocked my path. "I have a plan that tops yours. We attack The Agency's headquarters."

"That place will be a fortress."

He held up a pad. "I've been calculating. We get enough fighters, attack at night, we'll lay waste to it. But I don't want your family in harm's way."

"I don't, either."

He lifted his shirt to reveal more tattoos and gestured toward five faces. "These are family members I lost. Because of me. After your broadcast, I was reckless, and they paid the price."

My fears resurfaced. I wanted my girls free, not memorialized. "If there's a way to keep them safe, I will."

"So, we'll do my plan?"

"It's too predictable."

I continued to Garly's lab, which was the size of a corner office but felt cramped with its cabinets, 3D printers, test boxes, three-dimensional helix growers, electrostatic dischargers of varying sizes, bio-stunners, and stacks of clothes. Containers lining one wall were overstuffed with datacubes, motherboards, metal parts, and other equipment. In a corner, a machine constructed swarmbots, which sparkled in the sunlight from a small window.

I made sure to knock before entering. Last time, I'd walked in on Garly and Nataly. They'd been sweaty and flushed from kissing but grinned as they tried to act innocent.

This time, I found them watching a vid screen that portrayed the far corner of Milwaukee and Grand, where four cops were clustered.

"They launched a drone," Nataly told Garly. When she spotted me, she said, "See those two guys? They're not on any criminal database, yet the police are tailing them. The only thing they did was look away as they passed them."

The men she referred to were in their early thirties, business types. "Has this happened before?" I asked.

"Yesterday, a woman. It didn't end well."

The drone reached the two men, who stopped, uncertainty reflected on their faces.

"What defenses do we have?"

Garly showed me the sensors he'd embedded in the spotted bricks outside, the door reinforcement arm, and the electro-discharge devices, all of which seemed to be operational. "I got a sealer, too. It expands lightning-fast and hardens like Medusa's glare, sealing the doors whip-fast with supes-strong webbing."

"Can you make a portable version for our team?"

He shrugged, eyes flickering back to the vid screen. In a quieter voice, he said, "The sound machine is stacking. I vibed the harmonics on different metals, unsure if it's their noggin or metal parts waggling that hurts the Silvers the most. The shrieking gadget needs to be bulky to be powerful."

"We need it portable, too."

"I have other gads I'm working on, jefe. I got a noodle for an ice machine."

"Ice?"

"It's impressio, Eureka'd thirty years ago. I think I can crinkle it. I'd thought lasers were the trick but so far, no go."

"Sounds far-fetched, buddy."

"Better than Shifty the robot," Nataly said.

I leaned forward. "You have robots?"

The Santa Monica born, Ivy League prodigy extracted a tiny, square-shaped plastic container from a drawer and placed it in my hand. The container seemed filled with caramel-colored metal. I turned it over. The square slid out — and began to unfold in tiny, rectangular chunks. It flattened out, then curling inward, the inner edges separating to create blocky legs as it fashioned itself into a vague animal shape less than an inch long.

"It's too small to do mucho, though maybe you could wonk it to slip into places or Houdini it in clothes so you aren't snitched carrying recording disks," he said. "It sports a data storage attachment."

"Someone so big made something so little," Nataly said with an affectionate shake of her head as she constructed a collapsible mask, using the prosthetics knowledge she'd gained in college. "You're going to misplace it."

"Nuh-uh. I like Shifty," he said, his sharp features prominent in the overhead light.

"I like the swarmbots more," Nataly told me. "We're enhancing them to be more creative."

On the vid screen, the cops surrounded the two men. A police car pulled up.

I had a thought. "Can you access the 3D network again?"

Kieran had overseen the creation of a network of tiny drones that he had begun to disperse nationwide. The drones, which he first unleashed in Los Angeles, were designed to form a three-dimensional grid and stay airborne for months at a time. The cutting-edge drones could penetrate concrete, wood, and steel to watch citizens and identify threats. Once the network was disbursed nationwide, we'd be found in a day, maybe less.

"I'll check," she said.

As she typed, we watched the police take the two men into custody. It wasn't clear why.

"I'm in," she said. Her screen revealed the 3D network, the state lines creating a clear outline of the country, the drone disbursement displayed as a light green shading — which had spread since I'd last seen it, though not as much as I'd feared. The Rockies must have delayed the expansion, though it had reached western Iowa.

I called out to Cole. He needed to see this.

When he did, I said, "We won't be able to stay in Chicago for long, but we need to use this time to our advantage. Train, recruit, and plan our chaos."

Garly tore at his hair. "I was just starting to cook, my Yoda."

"Nothing's been decided," Cole told me. "The vote wasn't definitive."

I stared at him. If he was going to come up with a different plan, he needed to do it now.

"How long do we have?" he asked Nataly. "Days? Weeks?"

"One week. And no, nothing's settled."

"You're my new favorite person."

Garly frowned. "She is?"

"We need fighters and weapons, enough for twenty or thirty men at least," Cole told me.

I frowned. "How can we arm anyone? We don't have enough for us."

"I contacted an arms dealer I know."

"Where are you getting the money to buy anything?"

"Anya. She got some doctors to donate."

I couldn't hide my surprise.

"We can't stay long, but if you want to pursue this impossible idea of yours, this city has targets," he said. "You should run reconnaissance. And come up with a way to neutralize that drone network."

"Start with the Mercantile Exchange," Nataly said. "It's defended digitally with the latest quantum firewalls. You'll need to install physical killswitches."

"You checked that? I thought it wasn't decided," I said.

"Chicago is a power center. Whatever we agree on, we should set traps before we leave. If nothing else, it could be blackmail."

"There's a massive data facility by McCormick Place. We'll plant killswitches there, too. Let's use Valor and Mina."

"Mina?" Cole asked.

"Makes her useful. They'll both wear masks." Valor had complained about the posts Garly would have to attach to her incisors, but none of us had a choice. And Garly had improved his implant covers with fake codes. It wasn't totally foolish.

"I hate that woman."

Minutes later, he and I gave Valor and Mina their instructions, Valor mystified, and Mina pleased. We made Valor leave her intricately-etched guns — and made sure Mina was unarmed.

As they left, I spotted Fritz hunched over a burner phone.

I put a hand on his shoulder. "Anything?"

He shook his head. "Should've heard something."

Omura could've been killed or captured. Agents could've tracked his movements. If he hadn't been careful, he could be traced back here.

CHAPTER SEVENTEEN

Occasional car horns laced the afternoon wind as I walked with my head down along the downtown street, aware my face was being scanned by door, stoplight, and security cameras, as well as the ones in peoples' eyes. If Talia had done as she'd said, I wouldn't trip any systems. She couldn't do anything about the general public, though.

I expected someone to shout at me, arm pointed, calling me a traitor.

It wasn't lost on me that those I fought to free could be my downfall.

Under gray skies, I traversed New Orleans Street, bag in hand as I passed buildings of various sizes; their storefronts and lobbies carried risks.

Drones flew overheard, including searcher drones. I didn't look up. No reason to make it easy.

This was my first outing in days, and the first time alone since my arrival. A city of this size, the level of surveillance, our talk of fighting seemed foolish. We were a blip compared to The Agency's forces.

Almost half the people I passed wore health masks, a remnant of the last viral outbreak. Garly had thought I needed one, too, but it didn't fit with my utility worker jumpsuit.

Hernandez, Valor, Mina, and Raven were also sneaking around the city, gathering intel and scoping targets. I needed to do this one myself.

As a delivery drone flew overhead, the larger, thicker drone design prevalent in every major city, I approached a bus stop where five people waited. I started to duck away, but every set of eyes glowed. They were oblivious to the world as they watched content on their lenses.

I traversed another block, then stepped onto the pavement and approached a manhole cover. I removed three small orange cones from my bag and placed them in front of the cover, then extracted a crowbar, lifted the cover, and slid it aside as fetid air rose from the sewer below. My non-labeled jumpsuit and orange cones were a flimsy disguise, so I descended the ladder swiftly, though I stopped with my head just below street level.

Agency nodes had been hidden at the Union Power Plant next to the Chicago River and an old Language Academy near Lincoln Park. I'd estimated the line connecting them ran under this street.

Squinting into the dark tunnel, I located a water line and data cables, the varying levels of grime indicating the age of the lines as they disappeared into the darkness ahead and behind me. Ignoring the smell that permeated the sewer, I focused on the water line and brushed away the accumulated crud from its maintenance panel.

We still hadn't heard from Omura.

I removed the panel—and the water line was dark. I removed an emitter from my belt, slid the angled end into the water, and sent a signal, the beam of pure white light stabbing my eyes as it disappeared into the line. The response should've been near instantaneous, though nothing came back. The line was dead. I couldn't connect to the node or hook into The Agency's network, which meant I couldn't find out what had happened to him.

My eyes drifted as I tried to come up with another way. Tiny, cone-shaped objects spaced twenty feet apart in both directions hung from the sewer's apex. Based on their electronics, they had to be listening devices, possibly to listen to streetside conversations. I wondered whether these had been installed in every metropolis. I assumed there would be greater concentrations outside city centers and government buildings, though I'd never seen them before.

I climbed out of the hole, sealed it, and collected my cones.

I felt stymied. I couldn't access Zion's network and couldn't risk breaking into an Agency location. After our one attempt two months ago, each had been fortified. I worried about Omura, worried how much time we had. Once Zion finished installing the 3D drone network and upgrading everyone's implants, there would be nowhere to hide.

I ducked around the corner and noticed a crew taking down a series of posters. They'd been hung from lampposts spaced along the street, and the red and yellow graphic of a robot caught my eye. I scanned the details as the last one was removed. There had been a robotics convention. Today was the last day.

I wondered if Amarjit, my Director of Robotics when I'd been at Gen Omega, had attended.

I hurried to the black Ford that Garly had lent me and drove to McCormick Place Convention Center. Traffic was heavy, so by the time I arrived, the convention had ended, both lanes of traffic blocked with drivers waiting to pick up attendees.

A second, smaller gridlocked cluster of vehicles filled the drive of a hotel on the opposite side of the four-lane road. People stood outside with suitcases as they anxiously waited for their rides. I didn't see Amarjit, but I knew he didn't like leaving things to fate. He would've ordered a car. Taking a chance, I turned on the burner phone I'd been given and sent a text: "Mr. Shah, your car has been changed to a black Fusion. He's arriving now."

This was risky. He might not be there—and I could be recognized.

I pulled out of line and drove across the lanes that headed away from the Center, nearly clipping a white SUV as I made a U-turn and stopped on the road's edge in front of the hotel.

A figure emerged from the crowd and headed toward me. I turned away to hide my face and popped the trunk; after a few seconds, the trunk closed, the rear door opened, and someone climbed in. "Amarjit Shah," he said.

I didn't respond, didn't look back at him, until we were underway. "Where to?"

"Don't you know?"

I turned around to face him, and his eyes widened under his caterpillar-sized eyebrows. "Dray. I cannot believe it." He grabbed my shoulder. "*So* good to see you. You're in terrible danger. You want me to calm down."

I approached the highway. "I'm not sure what you've heard about me."

"Many, many things, few of which are kind." He steered me north, telling me his flight was scheduled out of O'Hare.

I told him about the implants and how I and the other rebels had tried to reveal the truth, but it had been twisted.

"I never believed you were a traitor."

"Zion is behind all of this," I said.

In the rearview mirror, I saw his face darken. "You want me to help."

I nodded. "Find out what you can about him, how much he's gotten involved with Gen Omega again — and see if you can sneak out any tech that won't get you in trouble."

"I'll try, but Nikolai watches me."

"Something happen between you two?"

"He hasn't been able to light other reactor cores. He's not sure what you did."

"Didn't the reactor's software record everything?"

"No. After you severed his tracker, the data became corrupted. He's threatened to fire me, even blamed my robots. He's built eight reactors but none are operational."

As we approached his airport terminal, I told him to contact me via the number I'd used. "Don't do anything unless you think it's safe. I mean it."

He agreed, gave me an awkward handshake that turned into a more awkward hug, then got out. As he hurried inside, I drove away. I hoped I hadn't just exposed him. Or myself.

Before I reached the highway, my burner phone rang. I answered without speaking.

Cole said with excitement, "We found a rebel group."

CHAPTER EIGHTEEN

Cole and Fritz slowed their walk as live music drifted down the residential street toward us. Jex and I slowed as well.

"Are we lost?" Fritz asked.

We were in the northern part of the city where trees, brick townhomes, and corner bars lined the streets.

The block ahead was cordoned off. A banner stretched across the road identified the event as the End of Daylight Street Festival. Portable cement barriers blocked the far intersection, and temporary fencing stretched to the sidewalks where tents covered manned entranceways. Past the entrance, booths offered beer, food, artwork, and other items. The chilly air didn't seem to deter the patrons who gripped beers in gloved hands as they wandered about while a band played "Mr. Brightside" on a raised stage.

The patrons didn't seem bothered by the drones hovering overhead, either.

Cole pretended to consult his phone, though the screen was blank. "The safe house should be close. Damn festival's throwing me."

"What's the address?"

"We should wait until it's over," I said. "Lots of eyeballs."

He considered. "We're masked and can use the distraction. They said to come tonight, but I want to surprise them, test their defenses."

Jex nodded. He'd been determined to come, though the trip drained him. Even with the back support, he was unsteady. Hernandez was across the street, pretending to be a civilian.

"Let's go then," Fritz said.

Cole led us to an alley that ran parallel to the street, clearly anxious to meet the rebels he'd contacted. I felt uneasy recruiting people for such a high-risk mission, but we needed fighters.

Like the others, I wore earpieces and a mask, the minibots wrapped around my neck and over my face with thin rows snaked through my hair for support. They were the size of fleas with a biometric layer that mimicked skin. They even covered my lips, which took some getting used to. I'd already swallowed two of them. They tasted like Tic-Tacs coated in oil.

The alley was deserted, lined with the backs of stores, townhomes, and apartments.

Voices from the festival were drowned out by the music coming from somewhere on the other side, the intro to the song "Runaway Train" echoing off of the wooden decks, garages, and garbage cans we passed.

Talia's voice exploded in my ear. "What's the deets? Pop anyone?"

An electronic squeal from our earpieces made us flinch. Garly's voice got on. "Sorry."

Cole glared at us. "Eyes sharp. They'll have surveillance. Make a good impression." He waved Jex forward and grilled him about how he would recruit the rebels we planned to meet.

As they talked, I spotted a new kind of receiving/broadcasting tower, three feet in height with different-sized antennas. Eight of them dotted the alley. I wondered if they were The Agency's. For the implants to work, they required a massive infrastructure.

The music grew louder as we reached the end of the alley, where on a different stage, a band played "Enter Sandman." As the baseline jabbed at us, we stopped at the edge of the last townhome and glanced around the corner. Barriers blocked off the street from the festival, with two rows of portable restrooms filling the space. I barely looked at them as I scanned for drones and other surveillance.

When I pulled back, Jex had a small drone in his hand, similar to the one he'd had in Memphis. He flew it up to the top of a nearby garage and landed it.

"We're close," Cole said. "Next block up."

We walked across the street, catching a whiff of the restrooms, and entered the next alley at a measured pace to avoid attracting attention.

Our target was a townhome halfway up the block.

As I focused on it, I caught movement too late. An arm wrapped around my neck, and a gun was jammed against my head. Cole and the others spun at the sudden attack, Jex the first to pull his gun. My assailant, thinner than I was but strong with fear, swiveled his gun to aim at Jex. "Down," the man whispered before pressing his gun back against my head. He pulled me into the side door of an attached garage, which was empty other than tools and a small motorcycle. The others followed, ready to strike.

Jex was the last to enter. The man gestured at him to close the door.

I spun and shoved his gun hand upward as I stepped forward, my face buried in his neck, and took him to the ground.

"I'm trying to help you," the man said, his voice muffled as I pinned him.

Fritz trained his gun on the man, and I disarmed him before I stepped back. He was vaguely handsome with graying black hair under a Blackhawks cap, a hint of stubble, and large brown eyes. His clothes were loose, nondescript jeans and a faded black shirt.

His submission turned to confusion. My mask had been knocked askew and reformed as he watched.

"Wow. Never seen a mask that sophisticated," he said.

"Who are you?" I asked.

Seemingly unbothered by Fritz's gun, he led us inside the furnished townhome. "I'm Liam. You were going to the safe house, weren't you? I recognize fellow fighters. Agents raided the place. They're setting a trap."

Cole's mask hid his face, but his eyes reflected his disappointment. "Show us."

Liam led us upstairs to a third-story bedroom. He glanced behind the curtain that covered a large window, then waved us over.

Jex joined me as I looked through the glass. From our angle, we saw down the alley — where Agents dragged four men and two women out of the townhome we'd targeted and into an unmarked, black van. Kieran appeared next, stepping out of the building.

"How did he know you were here?" Jex asked. "You've gotta be why he's in Chicago."

We moved aside so Cole and Fritz could see.

"They're installing DNA scanners and tracker drones and god knows what else," Liam said. "The DNA scanners will identify anyone who gets too close, and the drones will probably chase anyone who tries to run."

Cole asked, "Did they capture everyone stationed there?"

"Not sure. My clan was wiped out last month when we tried to destroy every node in Minnesota and Wisconsin. I joined here a week ago. I was patrolling our perimeter—which we modified for the festival—when I spotted an Agent and tracked her. She led me to Agents positioned to grab anyone who evades their trap." He sat heavily on the bed. "I was too late to save anyone."

Kieran yelled loud enough to be heard through the glass. "You have ten minutes to get in your final position. I want Quintero."

"Are you Quintero?" Liam asked. "I thought your voice sounded familiar."

"You need to fix that," Cole told me.

Hernandez rushed in, gun raised, though he lowered it when he saw we weren't being attacked.

I looked out the window again and saw an Agent lead another rebel out. The man fought to get away even though his hands were bound, but the female Agent easily restrained him. She stuck a skin GPS tracker on his arm, then shoved him into the van.

Kieran directed a half-dozen drones to lift off, part of the trap Liam had described.

"Dammit," Cole said in frustration. We'd come up nearly empty-handed.

As I dropped the curtain, Jex glanced at Liam. "Wanna join us?"

* * *

I scanned the dirty windows of the empty storefront next to Garly's place, then sighed in relief when I didn't see anyone or anything trailing me.

We had split up to reduce the chances we would trigger Kieran's monitors.

I took off my mask, the damn thing sweaty and heavy, and undid the posts anchored to my teeth as I walked across the store and through Garly's hidden entrance. Closing the door behind me, I found that Jex and Hernandez had not only beaten me back, Jex was encouraging Talia as she struggled to finish a set of sit-ups.

"One more rep," Jex said. "And I'll ignore the fact you skipped pushups."

She did one more, then squinted her nose. "How could I with my brick?"

Raven, who sat nearby, said, "You'd find a way. You're good at improvising."

"Trade my brick for your fingers."

"Be happy you have yours. You can open your own jars."

"I don't have jars."

I chuckled, which drew their attention. Raven hurried over. "Jex told me what happened. That was too close."

Cole and Fritz arrived with Liam, which drew Talia's attention. "A newbie. What's your name?"

"Liam Altwall."

She started typing, using a pair of datarings I hadn't seen before. "I'm triple masked, my signal coded to a hut outside Detroit," she assured me. "Ah. Hooked you. Minimal onlines, decent social meds until you went darko ten years ago, History major before flopping to optics sciences, did a couple rallies, handcuffed once, did time in juvie." Her eyes cleared as she turned off her feeds. "He's one of us."

From one of the couches, Hernandez said, "Of 'us'? Be a kid, chica. Go to school."

She squinted at Liam. "Are you a rebel?"

"My parents worked with Spencer," he said, his gaze taking us in. Spencer was the NSA whistleblower who'd disappeared in 2040. "They taught me what they could before they died in a supposed accident. I'd wanted to follow in their footsteps, so

I switched majors to learn how to negate my implant, but after they were killed, I dropped out. I've lived off the grid since."

"I like you. Wanna invade a secret lair? It'll be whack."

He glanced at me. "Secret lair?"

Garly shouted my name.

Raven followed me to his lab, where he and Nataly stared at a vid screen that displayed an old Gen Omega headshot of me.

"...has escaped custody. Every citizen should be on the lookout for the mass murderer and traitor. To repeat, Dray Quintero has escaped. Anyone with information regarding his whereabouts should contact authorities immediately."

Cole joined us. "Dray, we need to go."

"But why?" Garly asked. "You guys just peeped their safe house trap."

Nataly agreed. "We should be fine for a while."

"You know how they operate," I said. "When they realize we didn't fall for their trap, they'll install checkpoints, layer satellite and camera vids, and scrutinize everyone's feeds for a glimmer of us. Cole's right. We should leave."

Garly looked crushed — and seemed to be holding back something.

"What about recruiting other fighters?" Raven asked Cole.

"I have to rethink things. I can't say we're the reason Liam's safe house was attacked, but I can't say we weren't. Everyone needs masks from now on. Like Dray said, The Agency will intensify their surveillance to catch us."

Twisting the tracker bracelet in agitation, I left Garly's lab and found Jex waiting for me. "I heard the powwow. What about my mission? If we're leavin', I better go now."

"Good point. Go to the Mercantile Exchange and plant the switch. You up for it?"

He nodded and walked stiffly to one of the bags Valor had brought down. She somehow already knew we were leaving.

Anya approached, rubbing her fingernail. "We need to talk." She surprised me by retrieving Mina, who had been providing nutrients to our masks' bio-material. She led both of us to the corner of the room. "Talia is dying."

My face turned numb. Beside me, Mina looked panicked.

"The patches The Agency installed in her heart, which synchronize with her heartbeat, don't expand. The material doesn't grow as her body does, and a small tear has started. I confirmed it using Garly's portable CT scanner. We have to replace the patches with new material before the tear widens and her heart seizes."

Mina looked at me to do something.

I recalled how Zion had said Talia would be gone after he took me from the Facility. He'd never planned to keep her alive.

Anya said, "Lurie's Children's Hospital has the equipment and supplies I need except for replacement patches. I found a substance that might work. There's a small sample here in Chicago at a testing site. It's medical grade, designed for gunshot wounds—"

"What do you mean 'might work'?" Mina snapped. "Will it or not?"

"Data indicates it will, but the material is still in beta testing."

"This is my daughter you're risking."

"I'm well aware," Anya said, her medical demeanor slipping before she collected herself. "I think the sample will be enough, but won't know until we get it and Garly shapes it. I gave him the measurements. There's a larger supply, but that's in San Francisco."

I understood what she wasn't saying. Talia wouldn't survive a trip to San Francisco. And even if it was enough of a sample, the surgery would be perilous. There were artificial hearts, but that surgery was just as risky and the technology wasn't developed enough to rely on.

I pushed the words out. "How much time does she have?"

"Days. Maybe hours. Once the tear widens past a certain point, it'll be too late."

"I don't believe you," Mina said, her eyes bright with tears. "It can't be."

Garly approached with a travel bag. "From your faces, she broke the news."

Talia came over. "What's the dealio?"

I put a hand on her shoulder. "We need to get some material for you."

"Don't stop for me. I can't keep being a burden."

Garly squatted before her. "Don't worry, squirt. We're getting magic for your heart."

In a quiet voice, Talia asked, "Will I have this battery thing forever? I want boys to like me. This thing makes me gross."

"We can noodle smaller packs, hide it in a bra or whatnot." He leaned forward as she glanced down at her chest. "The right dude won't care. He'll just see your light."

When he stood, I gave her a hug as Mina and Anya began to argue.

"Why didn't you find it sooner?" Mina demanded.

"Someone with patches on their heart is unique—"

"Do you even know what you're doing?"

Garly pulled a worried and curious Talia away.

"I saved Raven, and I'll do everything in my power to save Talia'" Anya said.

"You want to cut into her without knowing a thing about the material. I won't allow it."

Anya's cheeks flushed. "Do you feel any remorse for what you did to your daughters? To Dray?"

I stepped in. "This isn't the time or place." They were both furious, eyes narrowed and bodies stiff. I'd never seen Anya angry before. "Hear me clearly. I lost Talia once. I can't lose her again."

CHAPTER NINETEEN

Nataly drove the van east onto Kinzie, but a backup pushed us south on Desplaines. The other nearby streets — Lake, Washington, and Monroe — were also impassible. At Monroe, we glimpsed the reason: roadblocks.

At my urging, Nataly gunned the engine and aimed south as every street that led into downtown was blocked. We ducked under the highway, then she took a sharp left, the portable lab's cabinets rattling with objects. The lab Garly had installed also contained centrifuges, 3D printers, and robotic machinery, which meant every turn triggered a disjointed symphony of noises.

Harrison Street looked clear.

She drove us across the river — where Agents dragged concrete barriers into the street to set up another roadblock. Nataly didn't flinch as she passed them, though Garly and I ducked, then turned north onto Upper Wacker.

The city seemed to tighten around us, the monitors and cameras and every other piece of tech poised to expose us.

I caught a glimpse of my face splashed on a seventy-story building.

We passed police cars and too many sensors to count as gleaming buildings towered to either side of us. Nataly passed the Willis Tower, then another building before turning right onto Monroe and pulling over.

We got out — Garly kissing her before exiting — and headed to the high-rise's two-story, glass enclosed lobby, passing the entrance to an attached parking garage.

A riot robot crouched near the sidewalk.

The machine oozed menace with its bristling protrusions and disbursement weapons. During the rebel attack on the nodes, The Agency had unleashed these robots, which killed or maimed hundreds of innocent civilians and dozens of rebels — all of which had been blamed on our rebellion.

Even though the robot was in standby mode, folded

into thirds, it still dominated the sidewalk, its cameras blinking as it scanned its surroundings. I eyed it as we passed, not sure if it would unfold and slice me with its whirling blades and protrusions, though either Talia's efforts had paid off or my mask fooled the metal beast.

We entered the building.

The slanted windows of the geometrically-adorned lobby comprised two of the walls, so as we headed toward the security station, the afternoon sun cut across the floor in bands of light.

Garly removed a six-inch transmitter from a bag slung over his shoulder before he reached the counter, then bent over as if to tie his shoe but instead pressed the transmitter against the underside of the granite slab.

"Help you?" a thick-necked guard asked.

Garly straightened. "Nah. I usually work weekends. What time you got?"

The guard frowned. "5:14."

Garly thanked him and stepped away. His brief chat should have given whatever he'd transmitted time to work.

We followed him as he headed for the turnstile checkpoint. His plain white badge triggered the turnstiles, and we passed through the gate.

Seconds later, we were in an elevator heading to the twenty-third floor.

"Nice job," I told him.

"I didn't get many ticks to scope the research company, but they squat three floors in this building, one for worker bees, one for product tinkering. The third level's got their data tanks, so the second's the best bet."

Cole removed a submachine gun from his bag. I checked my Glock as well as my plasma gun.

Garly extracted a hand shield from his bag and gave it to me, then took one for himself. "I should have a weapon," he said.

Cole handed him a pistol. Garly checked the chamber and thumbed the safety off.

"What? I watch you," he said before his expression darkened. "Zion weakened her. On purpose."

When the doors opened, he took the lead, Cole and I hurrying to keep up with his long stride.

The maze swallowed us.

After navigating a series of corridors filled with the sounds of men and machinery, we entered a suite in the Health Sciences section.

Tables lined the walls of the room, and a large island dominated the center of the first room. Beakers containing various liquid and powder compounds, along with Bunsen burners and scientific equipment, covered every countertop. The second room, which had windows that revealed neighboring skyscrapers, contained organic 3D printers, scanners, a datatank, and three clean-boxes. Cameras hung from the ceiling.

A man wearing glasses and a lab coat looked up from his notes. "Can I help you?"

We hadn't bothered with lab coats, suits, or anything. We wore tactical clothes. Sloppy.

"I'm Bob." Garly thrust out his hand. "Jogracore rep. We're looking for our flexmuscle material."

"These are your clean-boxes. Don't you recognize them?"

I headed toward the farthest clean-box, which sat on the table past the lab tech.

"Big screw-up in shipping," Garly said. "We sent you too much. I'm sorry about this. We'll buy you lunch—"

Before I reached the box, I pulled an implant shield from my pocket, spun, and slapped it over the tech's implant.

"Whew, I was running out of lines," Garly said to me. To the frightened tech, he said, "Don't touch that shield. You'll summon really unpleasant people."

Cole covered the two cameras with paint from a paintball gun.

"My software should've muffled their recorders and conked their alarms," Garly said.

"It's insurance," Cole said. He took the tech's arm and dragged him to a corner of the room.

I focused on the clean-box. Metallic material hung suspended inside, held up by clamps that pulled at it, relaxed, and pulled it again. Then I realized it was the other way around.

"You don't know what that is," the tech said as Cole tied his wrists behind his back.

"Oh we do," Garly said. "This shiny miracle can copycat muscle, like if Terminator had biceps instead of 'draulics. And it can grow." To me, he said, "See those square ridges? They house motors, but they don't crimp, meaning no tearing of muscles as it flexes. Impresso stuff."

Cole gagged and blindfolded the tech, then pressed a hand to his own ear. We each had comms, but Garly and I had kept ours off so we wouldn't get distracted. "They're starting surgery," Cole announced.

A surgery like this needed a team of people. Anya just had Liam, who had med vac training, and Mina, who'd volunteered to help. Anya had surprisingly agreed.

Cole went to the window to monitor the street below.

As I unlatched the clean-box's lid, Garly told me, "We need to snip and shape it. I have drawings."

"You know how?"

"I read their manual."

He instructed me to get the connectors designed specifically for the material from the far clean-box, multiple strings of what looked like exaggerated zipper teeth, each 'tooth' a half-inch tall and a quarter-inch wide. "We'll only need one wire for each gizmo, but we'll have to make sure it responds in the right temp."

Using the gloves inside the box, Garly measured the material, then gripped the lasers.

"Make sure to account for the connectors," I said. He nodded, then began to cut. His lips nearly disappearing inside his goatee as he worked, he shaved the second piece with the laser, then stepped aside so I could connect the second box. Together, we transferred the connectors, and he attached them to the materials' edges.

Cole spoke. "Agents are here."

* * *

After we finalized the piece, Garly retrieved a six-inch-long device. "This provides both juice for the material and the coordination it'll need to beat with Talia's heart. Crazy stuff. But the battery's rechargeable."

"Turn on your comms," Cole said. "No point not to now."

My earpiece clicked as it connected. "We have the material."

"Good," Anya said, her voice muffled. "I've made the initial incision."

"On our way."

Cole suddenly stiffened and raised his machine gun.

I pulled my Glock and kept it low as he stepped into the suite's first room—where an Agent with curly silver hair and black sunglasses appeared in the far doorway. I collapsed my mask so Agents wouldn't know about it, then entered the room.

The Agent smiled. "Zion said you'd come for this stuff."

Cole started toward him, machine gun leveled at his head. I stepped around the beaker-covered island, my gun held below the counter.

The Agent, who I'd glimpsed at the townhome, moved so fast it seemed his hand went from empty to pointing a Rutger at me in an instant.

Cole lowered his machine gun, then swiped a wide-topped beaker that contained clear liquid—the label identifying it as ethylene glycol—at the Agent, the beaker shattering when it struck him.

Fluid covered him.

The Agent tensed as if expecting it to burn. After a few seconds, he smirked, unaffected by the liquid.

I scanned the glass containers, remembering my chemistry classes, and grabbed the one I wanted.

The Agent spun toward me, aiming his gun, but I had already thrown the container filled with purple crystals. The glass struck his chest, shattered—and the potassium permanganate, encountering the ethylene glycol, exploded in purple flames.

The Agent flew backwards.

Garly bounded into the room, gun in one hand and a medical-grade transport box in the other, though he gaped as the Agent collapsed to the floor.

I grabbed him and followed Cole to the elevator.

Once inside, I selected the button P2, the lowest parking level in the attached garage.

As the elevator dropped, Garly slid the box into his bag.

I keyed my mic. "Where's your location?"

"Training OR, subfloor 2," Anya responded, her voice distracted.

Garly's bag caught my eye. Along with the box, it held a white, cube-shaped object, disruptors, ammunition, and other items. I grabbed extra clips for my Glock and a shaped explosive. I also had two zapper grenades along with my plasma gun and hand shield.

The doors opened, and we hurried past the vestibule into the parking garage. Four motorcycles were parked nearby; past them, a ramp led down to the street. We heard idling motors outside — and voices. I suspected they were Agents.

I went to the closest bike. Before I could remove my picking tools, Garly handed me his tiny robot. "For the lock."

I took it, then told Cole, "Get him to Lurie's. I'll distract them. I'm the one Zion wants."

Garly protested as Cole shoved him back into the vestibule.

Two black motorcycles drove up the ramp.

I inserted the 'bot Garly gave me. I felt it shift as it extended into the lock, then I turned it, and the bike's engine started.

I swiped a nearby helmet, made sure the Agents saw my unmasked face, then donned the helmet and gunned the bike. I shot past them, down the ramp, and out onto Monroe.

I turned north onto Wacker and accelerated fast. I knew I was driving like an ass as I whipped from lane to lane, barely making the light at Washington before taking a hard left onto Randolph.

I cut over the river and past cars turning onto the interstate.

A motorcycle appeared in my rearview mirror, then a second. The Agents from the building.

As the street widened, they gained on me.

I floored it, nearing a strip of restaurants, then hit the brakes, cut hard at Halstead, and shot north. The Agents appeared on Halstead seconds later and continued after me.

"She's reached the heart," Mina reported, her voice also muffled. "The robot anesthesiologist is tracking her vitals, but they don't look good."

I wanted to go to her, to my daughter, but the Agents were gaining.

Blocks whipped past, though cars stopped on the cross street ahead due to the Kinzie checkpoint forced me to slow before finding a gap and taking it, slipping between a delivery truck and an old Mazda Tribute. Gunning it, I swerved past a blue Lexus SUV as horns erupted behind me.

"We've set up the bypass, but she's bleeding. We're trying to stop it. We need the material."

Grand Avenue neared.

The cops I'd relied on to be there were missing. I revved the engine, hoping to attract attention, then slammed on the brakes, the light red in front of me. I steered toward the sidewalk, then the light turned green. I floored it, taking a sharp right onto Grand—and three cops near the building stared, mouths open, as I shot past.

I headed east and glimpsed police drones in my side mirror, rising to give chase. One of the Agents appeared as well and pursued me with even more disregard for speed limits than I had.

Before I could search for the other Agent, he appeared at the next block and nearly crashed into me, clipping my back tire.

I struggled to maintain control but overcorrected, swerved, and smashed through a coffee shop's storefront on the south side of the street. Glass shattered, and the door flipped upward as I slammed through it, hitting tables and shelving and ricocheting off the counter, my bike taking out its legs and everything else in its path.

Broken glass and wood and knickknacks pummeled me as I slid to a stop past the counter.

I removed my helmet to catch my breath, frazzled by the sudden crash.

Mina's voice in my ear. "She's stopped the heart and cut

the power to the patches. She says she can see where the primary patch began to pull away. There's blood everywhere. My god, so much."

A figure appeared in the shattered doorway. "Come out, come out."

I wanted to shout in frustration for having to play hide and seek with my daughter possibly dying on an operating table.

The smoke and dust hid me, but only for a moment. His sensors would find me.

The building groaned and shifted from the destruction. There were secondary crashes and shifting; among the noise, I crawled to where my bag had ended up.

Mina spoke again. "An—I mean, she is having difficulty removing the old material." I could tell she was doing everything not to cry.

Anya said, "There's excessive scar tissue. I'm trying not to cause more damage."

Police drones settled in spots on either side of the damaged building.

Part of me wanted to charge my way out, barrel over the Agent and anyone else who got in my way. Instead, I moved to a spot against the wall. Past the Agent, a row of two-story buildings lined the north side of Grand, and a steel bridge angled across the road over them.

The Agent—I couldn't see who it was—used his datarings, and the riot lights in the area flipped on, their unforgiving light illuminating the street behind him.

I removed the shaped explosive from my pocket, set it against the base of a stool screwed into the floor, and aimed the charge at the Agent.

"There you are," the man said.

Before he'd taken two steps, I activated my shield, curled behind it, and detonated the explosive.

The blast shoved me backwards, my ears ringing, but the Agent took the brunt of the explosion. The force threw him across the street and slammed him into a compact car so hard the vehicle collapsed inward.

My body ached, and it felt like I'd cracked my ribcage, but I got to my feet.

"We need the material. We can't wait much longer. Her vitals are slipping," Mina said, no longer trying to hide her sobbing.

A shadow moved into the shattered doorway. "That was *ruthless*." Pierce. My skin grew cold as the Agent chuckled. "Too bad you didn't get me."

I dove to the right as he opened fire.

I raised my hand shield and deflected three shots. I ducked behind a pile of debris, then lunged for my bike, two bullets narrowly missing me. The engine was still running, but I didn't know what kind of condition the bike was in.

Men started to shout outside. Pierce pivoted and fired at a target I couldn't see. A voice yelled while multiple people returned fire. The cops must've arrived.

Keeping my hand shield between myself and Pierce, I lifted my bike, straining from the weight, managed to get it upright, and climbed on. The handlebars were askew, and the engine had an ugly rattle, but I engaged the engine and steered the bike through a side door that had popped open from the damage and into an alley.

I exited onto Grand seconds later, gunned it past the cops and Agent, and raced east.

I'd barely gotten three blocks when two Agents on hoverbikes flew past overhead. They swung around on their Wave Runner-shaped flyers and came after me.

I was running out of time. Talia was running out of time.

Driving one-handed, I reached into my bag and snatched a grenade. A girder bridge was coming up. I could use it.

The two Agents, a man and woman in their twenties, slowed. I did as well. They each pressed a hand to their ear. Receiving instructions. Then they smirked at me and flew off, heading northwest.

Talia.

I keyed my microphone. "Agents are heading your way."

Cole responded back. "They're already here."

CHAPTER TWENTY

I raced past cars, pedestrians, and cyclists, the sharp wind ripping through my clothes.

An overhead section of the "L" appeared.

I banked left to head north and used the tracks as cover for whatever drones or satellites tracked me. I didn't take stock of the area; instead, I reduced everything before me to obstacles.

"The material's been sanitized. We're coating it with mimic DNA to ensure her body doesn't reject it," Mina said, the wind making it hard to hear her.

I reached Chicago Avenue and took a right, past shops and businesses, aggravated by the traffic I had to weave through. "How is she?" I asked.

"Her vitals are getting worse."

There was so much that could go wrong. So much already was.

When I arrived at Lurie Children's Hospital, a high-rise near Lake Shore Drive, I found a troop transport parked haphazardly in front of the building, abandoned near the closed entrance and exit rollup doors labeled AMBULANCE USE ONLY.

Anxious to get inside, I drove to the rear of the building and spotted a drive-in service area, which contained two loading docks, sealed trash dumpsters, a large service elevator, and a keypad-controlled door. There was also a food delivery truck parked near the service entrance, which appeared out of place but might be useful if Talia survived. The thought fed my panic as I parked, removed the small robot from the motorcycle's ignition, and hurried to the keypad door, which had been left ajar. Pulling my gun, I went inside.

The hallway was nondescript, painted in shades of yellow — and had no indication where to go.

I ran until I encountered an intersection, though the next hallway didn't have any signs or maps.

I found a stairwell, which echoed with the sound of

gunshots, and descended two long flights to Subfloor Two. As I reached for the handle, the gunshots rang loud.

I opened the door—and stepped into another yellow-painted hallway, though this one had a gunfight.

Kieran stood over thirty yards away with the two Agents from the hoverbikes and an older female Agent, along with three Agency soldiers, the armed men dressed in black with stylized "A"s on their shoulders. They fired at Valor, Cole, Hernandez, and Fritz, who crouched twenty yards past them, using an adjoining hallway for cover. Blood smeared the wall between them; an Agency soldier laid under it.

Small spikes that emitted potent charges—a Garly design—had been scattered on the ground between the groups.

I raised my Glock but paused. While Kieran's group was closer, I risked shooting my own people.

Bullets whizzed past me, my team's shots wide.

There was a door to my right, which I used.

I found myself in a lab-type classroom. It was empty, the overhead lights dim. A door leading to the adjoining room stood on the far side, what I discovered was a practice room for med students. Tables contained fake body parts to cut and suture. Another door allowed me to continue parallel to the hallway, which reverberated with gunfire.

I entered a wide lecture hall—and found Britt standing over a kneeling Raven, gripping Raven's hair. They stood near double doors that were opened to the hallway.

I ran at them.

Britt forced Raven to face me, then stepped behind her.

I activated my hand shield as Britt pulled her gun to fire at me. Kieran was visible in the hallway past her, directing his forces.

I removed my ion blade as Britt fired, the violet-tinted energy of my shield catching and melting her bullet—and flipped the blade to Raven, tossing it to her right side. Raven reached out and managed to catch it.

The Agent was forced to keep her attention on me as I closed the gap. Ten feet.

Raven activated the blade, grabbed Britt's leg with her free hand, and buried the blade in her leg.

As Britt cried out, Raven sliced up her thigh.

Britt shoved Raven away.

I tackled the Agent, throwing her into the hallway and into Kieran, my momentum carrying me into the hallway as well.

I found myself in the middle of the Agency's forces; while Britt laid on top of Kieran, clutching her bloody leg, the other Agents and the soldiers stood to either side of me.

They — and my team — froze in surprise.

I fired at the hoverbike Agents, close enough to inflict damage with my Glock, then scrambled back into the room and away from the doorway.

Five Agents. We were fighting five of them. Dear God.

I grabbed Raven, who had gotten to her feet, and hurried toward the next connecting door. She ran ahead to where her gun laid, scooped it up, and positioned herself to protect me from attack.

I removed a grenade, tossed it back toward the opening to the hallway, then hooked Raven's arm and pulled her into the next room.

The grenade detonated, the blast heaving us across the classroom and throwing us against the far wall. I crashed to the floor, and Raven landed beside me as smoke billowed toward us. Through the haze, part of the wall between the hallway and lecture hall collapsed, adding to the destruction.

The grenade's digital scrambler would've knocked out the Agents' feeds.

Valor and Hernandez appeared in the smoke and dust, helped us to our feet, and steered us across the hallway to join the others, who looked sweaty and anxious.

Anya's voice issued from my earpiece. "I'm ready to suture, but the second piece is too small. It'll impede her heart's rhythm." If she could get it beating, she didn't add.

Garly triggered his earpiece's microphone. "It's designed to grow. Try massaging it."

Cole read the look on my face. "We have a job to do."

He was right. We needed to give Anya time, which meant keeping Kieran's team at bay as long as we could.

New voices filled the hallway the Agents occupied. "Police. Put down your weapons."

Kieran said, "This is a federal operation. Leave immediately."

I approached the corner. Through the haze, I saw him on the floor, cradling Britt as she writhed in pain. Four police officers stood at the far end, guns drawn. A distraction. Maybe even protection — though they didn't have shields.

"Put them down."

"We don't want to hurt you," Kieran told them. "Be helpful. She's wounded. Get medical help."

"For the last time, drop your weapons."

Britt did look debilitated. They weren't invincible. Still, we faced multiple Agents, three soldiers, and now the police.

Gunfire erupted as the Agency forces cut through the police. Before I could react, all four fell. I raised my gun, but it was too late.

A female officer surprised me by grabbing the mic pinned to her uniform. "Officers shot. Lurie's Hospital — "

The older female Agent killed her with a bullet to the head.

Just like that, Kieran's team had taken out the cops — and would do the same to anyone else who got in their way. I clenched the glove that contained my hand shield as I backed away.

Mina reported, "She's started the robo-stitching, but blood's leaking from somewhere."

My team retreated down the hallway, though we kept our guns on the smoke-filled intersection. "Where's the OR?" I asked.

Valor led me past a nursing station positioned at the intersection with another corridor to a pair of doors that blocked the hallway thirty feet past the station. When we went through them, the hallway ended at a pair of wide glass doors labeled TRAINING OR.

The room was situated between a small, scrub/prep room on the right and doors on the left that opened to a fourteen-bed Pre-OP area, each bed empty. Instructions and training guidelines hovered on screens around the room. Past the beds was another corridor, which would allow Kieran to flank us.

"This floor is used to train med students," Valor explained as we rejoined our team at the nurse's station. "Anya knew it would be empty since it's the weekend. We were quiet, could've slipped out without anyone knowing, until Kieran's team showed."

"Where's Post-OP?" I asked.

"We're standing in it," Nataly said.

The station was the nexus. Post-OP rooms surrounded us.

I keyed my earpiece. "Status?"

Anya's response was clipped. "The patches are in place. We need to fill the heart with blood before we start it, then perfectly synch her beat with the patches. Otherwise, they'll tear away. That means her body won't get any blood flow for at least thirty seconds. Starting now."

I wanted to be in there, my anguish like a physical pain.

"We make our stand here," Cole said.

I reluctantly agreed. "Go to Pre-OP. Make sure no one comes that way," I told Raven and Fritz.

They slipped through the wood doors bifurcating the hallway.

"I'll be point," Hernandez said.

We started to take defensive positions behind the nurses' station—Nataly and Garly heading toward a patient room, Cole taking a room across from them that contained tanks and transport canisters filled with nanobots and synthetic stem cells— when gunfire erupted.

The female hoverbike Agent appeared from out of the smoke, gun flashing as she pressed a hand against the spot where I'd shot her.

Hernandez jerked as bullets pierced his tattooed body, and he collapsed.

Valor shoved me toward Cole.

Bullets sliced the air as I stumbled toward the door, some rat-a-tatting the walls—and Valor cried out behind me.

Though I made it to Cole, Valor laid in the overly-polished

hallway. She activated her shield, but blood leaked from a bullet wound in her thigh. Past her, Nataly and Garly stared at her and Hernandez in shock. It was clear Hernandez was dead, and Valor was hurt.

With rising dread, I glanced down the hallway. The Agent continued to fire at our team as two soldiers emerged from the smoke-filled coordinator behind her.

Nataly collected herself and leaned out of their room, her shield catching bullets meant for her as she fired.

Garly unloaded his machine gun, firing over Nataly's head.

The Agent disappeared into a patient room, Garly's bullets cutting a line across the doorway while the soldiers returned fire.

Beside me, Cole took out one of the soldiers, and Nataly took out the other.

Cole struggled to catch his breath as he reloaded. Blood coated his ear and the side of one leg. On the opposite side of the hallway, Garly fired a few more shots.

I needed to get to Valor.

I made sure Cole was OK, then extracted my last grenade and pulled the pin. I stepped into the hallway, lobbed the grenade toward the Agent's room, and scrambled toward Valor. As I neared, she shouted, "Look out."

The Agent had swatted the grenade back toward us.

I dropped to the ground as it arched through the air, raising my hand shield —

The grenade exploded.

It detonated between us and the nurses' station, destroying the back side of the station, damaging the hallway, and throwing Valor and me back.

Smoke clawed my throat as my ears rang louder. Aches covered my body.

Cole appeared and pulled me into a nearby room. Nataly dragged Valor to a room on the opposite side of the hallway.

I couldn't tell the extent of Valor's injuries, but blood smeared the floor.

I got to my feet.

Leaning into the hallway, Cole and I fired down the hallway as Nataly returned to Garly, then shot at another soldier who appeared out of the smoke, his machine gun firing.

My shield arrested his bullets, each hovering before me: three, then two more, then another before the shield's energy melted them.

A shot from the other side of the hallway took him out.

As the hallway quieted, I caught the rough churn of gunfire from the Pre-OP area. Kieran had split his forces. Boxing us in.

We couldn't try to flee until Anya was done. More than thirty seconds had passed. I keyed my mic. "Status?"

Jex answered instead, his voice issuing from my earpiece. "More cops are here."

I realized he was missing. "Where are you?" I asked.

"Outside. Workin' on a plan."

No response from the OR.

I switched to my plasma gun as Cole reloaded—and Garly used the lull to scramble from his room.

He charged toward the damaged nurses' station, his large bag swinging from his hip. He was focused on his bag, struggling to unzip it, as he scrambled forward.

Kieran emerged from the smoky hallway, his clothes partly shredded from the first grenade blast and his pants coated in blood. Britt's blood.

He must have taken her to the ER for treatment. He wouldn't have left her in the hallway.

Her injury made this personal.

Face hardened, he fired multiple shots as he proceeded forward, joined by the male hoverbike Agent who wielded a plasma rifle, bandages wrapped around his midsection.

I returned fired to give Garly cover, Cole squatting beside me to fire as well.

Kieran shot at us, his bullets caught by my shield flickering from the light of my plasma fire as well as the male Agent's. Then Kieran switched his aim and fired at Garly as the scientist reached the station.

He hit him in his ribcage and side.

Garly collapsed on top of the pulverized section of the nurses' station, the undamaged portion temporarily shielding him.

Nataly cried out in horror. I was horrified, too.

Garly shuttered in pain as blood seeped from his wounds.

Nataly fired as she dashed toward him, her gunshots driving Kieran and the other Agent into rooms near the female Agent's.

Cole and I increased our gunfire to try to push the Agents back, though the female Agent emerged from her room and picked up one of the soldier's dead bodies. As we switched our focus to her, she used the body as a shield.

Nataly dropped beside Garly and pressed her hands against his side.

We kept firing at the female Agent as she neared the nurses' station—the body she carried absorbing our shots—and ducked into a room closest to the station. "Boss knew you'd try to save your girl," she called out.

Garly twisted under Nataly and reached for his bag.

As she tried to stop his bleeding, fear coating her expression, he struggled to open the bag.

Kieran advanced toward the station, the male Agent steps behind, both holding soldiers' bodies as shields with one hand while they fired at us. Their bullets shredded the doorway beside me and embedded themselves in my shield, the energy capturing and melting them.

Though we returned fire, occasionally catching them in exposed areas, Kieran and the Agent kept coming. Our hits made them grimace but didn't slow them.

Kieran reached the station and gazed at Nataly from around his man-shield. "I know you."

She went for her gun with a bloody hand, but he stopped her. "Touch it, I'll shoot."

The female Agent emerged from the hallway and approached them.

Garly reached into his bag and pulled out the white device I'd seen earlier.

Before Kieran could figure out its purpose, Garly set it between them and activated it.

The device exploded outward, the material bursting in a foot-wide band that expanded upward and outward across the open area before smashing into the edges of the hallway. Even as it expanded, the body hardened into the concrete-like, white webbing he'd described to me in his lab. In less than three seconds, it stretched from floor to ceiling and across the thirty-foot space, sealing off the Agents as it emitted a sweet, polyurethane-type smell — but leaving us with access to the hallway to his left, what I hoped was a way out.

I hurried to him and Nataly. "How many more of those do you have?"

His face was a light bluish-gray. "Just one."

"Help me," Nataly said. "He's lost too much blood."

Cole dropped beside her with self-sealing patches. "We can't fix him here."

He was right. I quickly retrieved a wheelchair I'd spotted.

Muted shouts rose from the other side of the webbing, followed by a weird tearing sound. The webbing, which stretched nearly thirty feet across, vibrated.

"Dad," Raven said behind me, her voice raw.

She held the hallway doors open.

Anya wheeled Talia out in a suspension bed designed to eliminate trauma to a patient's body, a domed monitoring panel arched over her small chest. Mina and Liam followed, their scrubs flecked with blood, Talia unmoving, the color of her face the same as Garly's. Their eyes widened when they saw Hernandez's body, Garly's injuries, and the bloody hallway.

Gunfire rose from the Pre-OP room.

There was a snap as Kieran broke off a piece of webbing.

"Grab saline, monitoring cuffs, sedatives, gauze, and as many nanobots as you can find," Anya said.

Liam and Raven ran to different rooms and rifled through cabinets as I guarded the hallway.

Anya checked Garly's injuries, then looked at me. "His injuries could be life-threatening."

"Gotta go," Garly whispered.

"He's right," I said.

She gave me a look as if confirming I knew I was risking his life, then swiped Cole's patches. "Garly, stay with us."

His nod wasn't convincing.

To Mina, I said, "The room behind me has nanobots and stem cells. Grab them."

She went to retrieve them.

Cole and I sat Garly up, causing him to cry out, and lifted him into the wheelchair.

As Cole got him situated, I went to Valor's room. I found her wrapping her leg with blood-coated hands, more blood smeared on the floor. "You'd make a terrible doctor."

"Not the time for jokes," she muttered through gritted teeth.

I helped her up and into the hallway. She leaned on me with an arm clutching my shoulder.

Supplies, including four nanobot and stem cell canisters, had been laid on Talia's bed, as she required little space.

Anya refocused on Talia, her eyes alight with the readouts from her vitals.

Kieran's hand appeared in the newly-formed wall. He grabbed at the super-strong webbing and broke away a fistful of strands to widen his hole.

"Move," Cole said. He keyed his mic. "Pre-OP, we're going."

Liam took the lead, heading down the side hallway with a gun in his hand, Nataly pushing Garly's wheelchair behind him, Cole firing through the hole to drive Kieran and the other Agents back.

I carried Garly's bag as I helped Valor walk. I wanted to take Hernandez with us but couldn't.

Fritz caught up to us. He'd seen Hernandez; though he was stoic, tears were visible.

Without a word, he scooped Valor up and carried her.

"Put me down," she said.

When he didn't, she wrapped her arms around his neck.

We charged down a peach-colored hallway with murals of smiling children that stretched past two sets of wood doors and three intersections. We moved as fast as we dared, checking each intersection before hurrying to the next.

Liam turned the corner to approach what I suspected was a bank of elevators when he suddenly waved us back. We hurried to a side hallway as we heard elevator doors opening — and a voice spoke. "Teams, move. Find who did this."

We slipped into the hallway, first Nataly with Garly, then Talia and her surgical team, then the rest of us.

We pressed against the wall as over a dozen Chicago cops ran past with their weapons drawn.

Our group hurried down the new hallway, Raven last to protect our flank.

Liam steered us past two intersections and into a third, which led to a service elevator.

I hit the button for the elevator.

Talia's face was mostly obscured by a breathing mask. I couldn't tell if she breathed on her own.

Anya checked on Garly, who was visibly in pain. To distract Nataly, I handed her his bag. "Find his other web expander."

Shouts and gunshots echoed down the hallway. The cops had found their coworkers' killers.

The service elevator dinged.

When the doors opened, Anya pushed Talia's bed into the twelve-foot-wide, twenty-foot-long elevator, the rest of us following.

The gunfire was already dropping off — and that's when we heard footsteps.

Raven, Cole, and I activated our shields as the doors began to close.

Kieran appeared from around the corner, firing, bullets catching in our shields as he charged.

Before he reached us, the doors closed, and we began to rise, but the elevator was too slow — and he wouldn't stop.

I knelt in the middle of the elevator, triggered my ion blade, and sliced a hole in the floor, just missing one of the narrow

I-beam supports. "Nataly."

She tossed me Garly's web device.

I shoved it through the hole and made sure it was oriented to expand width-wise. "Hold on."

The group braced themselves, Nataly holding Garly tight.

I triggered it as I let go.

The device expanded—and rocketed our cab upward. More than one of my group cried out as the device heaved us, the top edge pushing up into the hole.

We stopped almost as abruptly as we started.

Alarms flashed on Talia's display as she started to seize.

"Her heartbeat is off," Anya said. She dug through a bag on Talia's bed.

I glanced at Cole. "Get us out of here."

Fritz set Valor against the side of the elevator, then helped Cole pry open the doors to discover the bottom edge of the main floor's hallway four feet up. The webbing had pushed us most of the way to the main floor, about thirty-five feet. Fritz climbed up into the hallway, scanned the area with his weapon, then reached for Valor.

As the team worked to get the wounded out, Anya held up a defibrillator. "Do I shock her? Will it damage the panels?"

"Do it," I said. No choice.

The cab trembled as noises grew from below.

Kieran was climbing the thick web.

Anya shocked Talia. Her little body arched, then collapsed. She stopped seizing, but Anya said, "Something might have torn. The reading's off."

The rest of the team had exited the elevator.

With Cole's help, we lifted Talia's bed out of the elevator. I turned to help Anya up when a hand appeared. Kieran tore at the webbing at the top of the hole.

I lifted her out and climbed up after her.

We hurried into the service bay, the readouts on Talia's bed blinking yellow.

An ambulance was now parked in the bay next to the food delivery truck. Past them, four cop cars, lights flashing, partly blocked the entrance.

Jex exited the ambulance. As sirens rose in the distance, he said, "They're ready to go."

The rear doors of the food truck were opened to reveal the interior of Garly's mobile lab. I later learned Jex had installed camo shields on both it and the ambulance.

Talia's displays turned red, and she seized again.

I wanted to get her back into the OR, but we couldn't. With desperation and a deep foreboding, I helped Cole get her bed into the ambulance. Anya climbed in after and started working on Talia. Others got in the two vehicles, Garly nearly unresponsive, and we took off, alarms beeping as Anya shocked Talia again.

CHAPTER TWENTY-ONE

The area appeared deserted this time of night, a blacktopped side street that led from the town's main boulevard, though as I prepared to move, a car with dark windows appeared. I stayed still and watched the car slow before taking a corner.

I traded a look with Fritz, who looked as tense as I felt.

As he covered me, I approached the dusty, reddish-brown door located in the rear of the small brick building. Squatting down, I picked the lock. The door opened to a narrow staircase. Faint light came from the room at the top of the stairs, which he and I cautiously ascended.

We entered a dark-web server site with blacked-out windows, hardwood floors, servers clustered in the center of the room, and wires running along the ceiling. The place, which was only accessible via the stairwell, was empty other than the servers and a bathroom in the corner that was still functional. These sites wouldn't last long after Zion expanded his 3D tech; the servers' heat signatures would alert them.

We wouldn't last long, either. He had a starting point to search for us.

We'd made it past the border from Indiana into Ohio, reaching the two-story office building where old attorneys on the first floor worked occasionally, located on the outskirts of Toledo. We'd pulled over twice during our escape, each time risking discovery as Anya struggled to stabilize my daughter. She didn't have to say it, but each time, Talia's chances of survival decreased.

From the attack in the hospital, it was evident Zion considered her a threat. Maybe Garly was right. Maybe Zion had hampered her on purpose—and had instructed his men to shoot her in the first place.

I just wanted her alive.

With a nod to Fritz, I returned to the side street and signaled to my team.

They emerged from our two vehicles, which now looked like neighborhood delivery vans. Cole and I removed Talia's bed from the ambulance and maneuvered it up the stairs, struggling to keep her level as we climbed to the second floor, Cole scowling from where a bullet had gouged his leg during the hospital battle.

He wasn't the only one hurt. Everyone was injured to varying degrees and exhausted from our escape, Valor and Garly most of all. My injuries from the motorcycle chase ached, but I didn't complain. I was more worried about Talia. And Garly.

The team took spots along the walls, no one saying much. They didn't have to. They'd fought and nearly sacrificed themselves for my daughter.

"How is she?" I asked Anya as she checked Talia.

"Her heart's bruised. I've had trouble synching the patches to her heartbeat. I rushed the surgery."

"We were out of time."

She avoided my gaze. "The escape traumatized her body. If she suffers another one…"

During the drive, she'd described the surgery. She'd set up the bypass, simultaneously disconnected the battery and stopped Talia's heart, then used surgical tools that slipped under the sternum to drain the heart and remove the bad patches. They were forced to wait precious minutes, but once Garly arrived, she installed the new patches, coating the edges with nanobots to help the "teeth" adhere to Talia's heart muscles. Quicker than Anya wanted, she let the heart refill with blood to restart it.

Even if Talia didn't recover — a thought that wrecked me — Anya had given her a chance.

"How's Garly?" I asked next.

Anya rubbed her fingernail. "The bullet in his side missed his intestines, but the one in his chest shattered a rib. I used half a canister of nanobots to create a lattice to hold the pieces together, as well as remove the fragments. The lattice will provide support as the bone regrows, but he's suffered internal injuries. I can't tell how extensive, not without better equipment. It will take time to heal.

"As far as Valor, she lost over a liter of blood but should

recover. Her bullet made a clear exit. I'm monitoring both of them."

I faced the group. "Thank you for what you did. I owe each one of you."

The team got situated, everyone checking on Talia, Garly, and Valor at one point or another, some using the bathroom, others falling asleep.

I left to gauge how safe the building was. I was surprised to find Jex outside.

"Puttin' a drone in place, like Chicago," he said. "For when we're ready."

The drone was a retail model, available in countless stores, modified with some shielding tech. He'd be able to distribute them wherever we went.

He was also setting up defenses, many of which Garly had created.

When I approached Garly's van, a muffled clicking arose as a large bag rippled, what I realized were my swarmbots.

Jex followed my gaze. "He told me he grabbed thousands but wasn't sure it was enough." He grimaced in pain.

"How's your back?"

"Worry 'bout Talia, not me."

When I returned to the room, Nataly pulled me aside. "Once we establish a new base, we'll continue the groundwork for your plans."

"Does that mean I have your vote?"

"You do now."

My eyes found Talia. "She'll want to help."

"We'll need it." And needed Garly healthy, Nataly didn't have to add.

As she returned to his side, I went to my daughter, where Anya and Mina finished the setup of a monitoring system to keep an eye on her.

Anya gave a tired smile. "How's the pain?"

"Manageable."

"Let me give you some nanobots."

I deflected her concern, but she still injected a syringe's

worth. "I need to close my eyes," she said.

I helped her make a space near the wall.

Mina approached and handed her a blanket. "Thank you for saving our daughter."

Anya hesitated, then gave a weary nod.

Though they were being civil, the tension remained.

As I stepped away, Mina followed. "Get some rest. I'll watch our girls."

When I laid down, a swarmbot crawled out of my pack and into my lap. Garly must've added a rudimentary speaker because the 'bot made a clicking sound like I'd heard outside, though this 'bot clicked in a way that sounded like purring.

We needed to recover, get healthy, and refocus on my plan. Time was running out.

* * *

Late that night, as the moon hid behind a cloudbank, I watched the street. I'd been unable to sleep. I worried whether Talia's heart would heal, whether her body would reject the panels. I wondered what kind of future she would have. Wondered if we had any real chance.

We'd escaped Chicago, but Zion would hunt us—and I didn't know if Talia would live.

Though Valor would recover, Garly was touch and go, his injuries worse than I'd realized. And Hernandez was dead. His murder tore at me. Cole was beside himself.

I feared what we'd face next.

I'd returned outside and relieved Liam, though it hadn't been my shift. At least he could benefit from my insomnia.

The darkness reminded me of when I was a kid, when Mom was between men and left me alone while she worked odd jobs. I hadn't wanted anyone to know I was by myself so kept the lights off even after sunset, the night gradually taking everything away.

A sound disturbed the calm of the street.

I gripped the handle of my Glock, then relaxed. It had been the door to our hiding spot. As I watched, Raven slipped out of our building. A minute later, she appeared beside me.

"I have watch for another hour," I said softly.

"Couldn't sleep. Have you?"

"Liam already chastised me."

This part of town was silent, not even a stray cat on the dark street.

"I understand why you wanted to take us to Canada. I hate Talia being in danger."

"Both of you."

"I'm old enough to choose." She searched my face. "You're trying to figure out how to do this without us."

I didn't meet her gaze. The attack had made me question my decision to fight.

"You need us. All of us. Besides, what kind of chance do you and Anya have if Zion stays in control?" I saw her grin as she needled me.

"Maybe all of your actions are just to impress Jex."

"That man doesn't need impressing. He's got the 'swoons' as Talia says." She took in the area. "I feel like I should be smoking a cigarette, all dramatic in the darkness. Or we should be at a bar, the only ones in the place, as some guy plays piano."

She was so young yet mature in many ways. For one, she'd gotten over her reticence to fight Agents.

The fact this seemed like a normal thought threw me. "I've been a terrible father. How have I let you get exposed to this insanity?"

"I exposed you, remember?"

"Then you've done enough."

"We're not done."

"We've taken a huge step back and exposed ourselves."

"We had to, to save Talia," she said.

"Anya and Liam saved her." Anya looked at me differently now, not in a good way. I wasn't sure if she would stay. If anyone would. "Is the group going to split up?"

"Jex is worried. They all are. We got our asses kicked. But Dad, we did the right thing. Everyone agrees, even Garly. It's Talia."

I wasn't convinced.

She hugged me, then stepped back. "Get some sleep. I'll take watch."

* * *

Sounds filtered through the building the next morning as the law firm's employees arrived to start their day.

We'd stayed in the dark server site to avoid traumatizing Talia's body further. She was paler than I liked; Anya couldn't find any internal bleeding, though the portable CT scanner could've missed it. I studied the Jogracore manual Garly had stolen and fine-tuned the material with Talia's heartbeat, though it wouldn't do any good if she seized again.

Staying carried risks. While our hiding spot was inaccessible from the firm below, the chances of our vehicles being identified, of us being found, rose by the hour.

We maintained a vigil, taking shifts, and used some of my swarmbots to act as tiny sentinels — not that they could stop an Agent if one showed.

"How's the leg?" Fritz asked Valor.

"I'm going to have a great scar."

"That'll be hot."

I wondered if something was happening between them. They sounded suspiciously like they were flirting. She also wasn't shy about taking nanobots. "I need to be stronger," she told me. "So do you."

Garly had taken more nanobots as well, though he was still weak. "My chest aches worse than the time I crashed on a sick half-pipe."

"You were a skater?" Nataly asked.

"Always will be, chi'. At least in my heart."

I frowned. Even that exchange winded him. "Get more sleep."

My concern for Talia was even greater. She only woke to eat a little food. She didn't say a word.

That evening, I stood watch on the roof. Other than when I'd checked on Garly and Valor, this was the first time I'd left Talia's side. I was still shaken from the hospital attack. The fact Zion's people could kill cops and do whatever they wanted would've been unfathomable to me six months ago.

After the millions of deaths and resulting fear and uncertainty of the early 2030s, people changed. Even those who weren't infected became unruly, untamed — and the political and religious leaders ate it up. The resulting riots and lawlessness and economic collapse nearly destroyed the country until we realized the rest of the world no longer needed us.

The U.S. came back from the brink that time. Became civil again. Became strong again.

If we succeeded in defeating Zion, the truth of what he did could shatter everything. But we had to risk it.

CHAPTER TWENTY-TWO

I looked over Liam's shoulder as he scanned the unassuming, two-story Department of Agriculture building that stood like a forgotten mile marker to a distant land. He had multi-wavelength sensors and binoculars, both from his prior rebel clan, who had trained him at recon.

He and I were masked by his camo-shield.

"The place will be a challenge to defend, but it's clear," he said.

We had continued east along northern Ohio before stopping at the government facility, which had been established to study how to save the country's topsoil. Plywood covered spots where two large windows had been, but otherwise, the building appeared solid.

When we pulled into the docking bay, I asked, "Is this the right place to hide? Is it predictable?"

Fritz growled, "Should stay mobile."

"We won't remain long," Cole said as he exited the second van.

After constantly moving for the past two days, we craved a break.

"I'll jockey the holograms to Casper our vehicles. Then I'll keep finagling the sound machine," Garly said with an effort. He'd developed an infection. His bullet wounds were inflamed, and his skin was hot to the touch.

"You should rest, sweets," Nataly said.

"We need to swap our vehicles," Cole said. "Even the lab."

I helped the team carry supplies inside, careful not to overdo it myself. I still wasn't at full strength.

Jex paused long enough to send a drone to the roof before pitching in.

Abandoned rooms greeted us. Most of the first floor consisted of laboratories of varying sizes, some with plots of dirt, others with dried-out hay, wheat, and other stalks I couldn't identify.

"Who picked this pad?" Talia asked. "It's righteous."

Her gait was unsteady, but she walked under her own power, Anya and Mina gently steering her as she took in the labs. She continued forward as she clutched the new, smaller pack strapped to her chest.

Jex and Cole passed us, heading toward the exit. "Swapping vehicles now?" I asked.

Cole shook his head. "We're going to the arms dealer. We need weapons to lure recruits."

He'd ridden in the other vehicle, so I hadn't been aware of his plans. "I thought you were holding off on recruiting to avoid exposing anyone."

"Lafontaine has pulled in dozens, so we need to step up. I'm making progress, messaging with three groups, but we need weapons."

"Recruit as many as you can—and warn them about Chicago."

Jex said to Talia. "We'll train when I get back. Don't worry, I'll be gentle."

"Better not," she said.

As the two men left, her face fell. "Will Garly be OK?"

I helped her sit. She was pale from even that exertion. "He's a strong guy."

"I feel so bad. Valor acts giddy she got shot, but she doesn't snow me. She hurts because of me. They all do."

"Let's do your checkup," Anya said.

"I'm good. You fizzled me straight."

"You're not good. Heart muscles don't naturally grow back from damage this large. But your body has accepted the new panels so far, and they will grow with you *if* you let your body heal. It's also imperative that your battery be charged at all times."

Talia exhaled in irritation.

"We can look at options for a better battery when you're stronger," Mina said, glancing at me for support. I nodded—not only at her comment but Anya's. Talia's eyes were bloodshot, she was short of breath, and she occasionally flinched in pain. Her tough act was just that. An act.

We didn't have much food, but I retrieved a sports drink for her. After she took a swallow, she shuddered.

"I thought you'd like it. It doesn't have sugar," I said.

"Bleh. I'm sorzo you abandoned Garly's domo for me."

"Make it up by going slow as you heal."

"Don't be snarly."

Anya said, "We don't have any more patches if you overdo it."

Talia looked away. "Still gonna fight."

After getting Talia situated, Mina asked for help setting up her room next door. I agreed, though as she fashioned a bed out of blankets and straw, I sensed a shift in her attitude.

"You can take it from here," I said.

Before I reached the door, she stopped me and put a hand on my chest. "I want us back. I'll do whatever it takes."

I gently removed her hand. "I understand why you did what you did — but don't."

"These last few months, I've seen you thrive. Your love for our family has inspired you to do great things. It's made me want you more."

"Don't —"

"We built a beautiful life together."

"Which you destroyed when you betrayed us."

"I couldn't lose my son."

"He was already gone."

She fought to retain her composure.

I stepped around her to leave. As I reached the doorway, she said, "When you're ready. I'll wait."

I felt disgusted by Mina's actions. While I couldn't deny there were residual feelings — we'd been together over two decades — I felt revulsion over what she'd done.

I returned to Talia's room and sat by Anya, who didn't move her gaze from Talia. "She's next door, isn't she?" When I nodded, she shook her head. "This isn't what I signed up for."

A pit grew in my stomach. "If you want to leave, I'll set up a way for you to leave safely. Whatever you decide."

She continued to stare at Talia, then sighed. "Your flirting skills have gotten worse."

I wasn't sure what to say. "I'll work on it."

I returned to the main area.

Valor waved me over. She'd been using a tablet to search online. "Agents are portraying you in the news as a ruthless killer who wants to subvert everyone's belief in our government."

"Sowing doubt if I try to publicize what I know. Smart move, actually."

"When will they start dragging our names through the mud? If I were them, I'd start with your girls."

"They do that, they won't like how I respond."

"They'll hope you do something rash. You'll play into their hands."

She had a point.

I called my team together.

Anya, Liam, Nataly, and Garly joined Valor and me in the main entrance area. I didn't expect Mina or Talia, though Raven should've responded. Before I could ask about her, Fritz appeared from one of the rooms, his eyes as red as his beard. "Omura is dead."

With a strained voice, he explained that Omura—acting like a lost hiker to get close to the Observatory—had recorded a video one town from his destination and uploaded it to a temporary email account. If he didn't check in within a week, the account would send the video to Fritz.

He'd just received it.

While Omura's death was a loss and a tragedy, we still didn't have the information we needed. We had to know if the Observatory was our target, if Zion had used the area's dead zone to house the communications nexus that coordinated his lies. He could've buried it inside a mountain, could've built a fortress, or could've put it in some other place altogether.

As the others consoled Fritz, I used a tablet to access the surveillance network I'd built for the police. I'd held off because if The Agency knew about the fake account I'd established, I could tip our hand, but I had to see what it could give us.

I was sure Nikolai, the head of Gen Omega and part of the Gang of Five, had locked me out of our company's system. He'd fired me, after all. But the network I built was separate.

After digitally masking my location, I logged in, tapping into the thousands of public and private cameras that blanketed the country.

While I searched for cameras in and around the former quiet zone, Fritz said, "They gotta hurt. They're bloody killers."

I couldn't find a single feed.

I faced the group. "The area is a black hole, which means we'll have to do this the hard way. We need to refocus on our plan, preparing our chaos—and find The Agency's nexus."

We quickly set up assignments. Nataly would spearhead our hacking efforts, Garly and I had weapons and tech, Cole and Jex would spearhead the tactical plans—assuming Cole agreed after he returned from his mission—and the others would help. "Raven should be a part," Valor said.

"Where is she?" I asked.

"I saw her step outside," Liam said.

I searched out front, but she was gone—as was one of our remaining vehicles. Swearing under my breath, I turned on my bracelet to track her location.

She was heading west—toward a column of black smoke that rose in the distance.

CHAPTER TWENTY-THREE

I turned off the two-laned state road, the column of thick smoke towering over me, and stopped near a row of sawhorses that blocked the road with "FEMA – KEEP OUT" painted on them. When I got out, I smelled the smoke and heard wood crackling.

I'd spotted at least three Agency drones on my drive here, and from the sudden change Raven made during her journey, I suspected there was a checkpoint. I took a different route to avoid it, but I didn't feel safer. The black smoke billowing into the sky seemed like a beacon. A bad one.

I pulled my pistol and started forward. As I passed the FEMA barrier, Raven emerged from a hiding spot and glowered at me, a drone controller in her hand.

"What are you doing here?" I asked.

"The entire town is on fire, but there aren't any fire engines—"

"Dammit Raven, The Agency is hunting us. Your obsession with these towns—"

"Uncover your implant and look up."

I thought to argue but knew that expression. Her stubbornness gave me fits. I turned away and removed my implant shield. As it connected with Zion's network, the column of smoke disappeared.

"You know what they're hiding," she said as I covered my implant. She stepped past me, flexing her metal fingers hidden inside her black glove, but paused. "Why the hell is Mina still with us?"

"You want to talk about that now?"

"Fine, but we are having that conversation. She needs to go."

She led me to the town, which a sign identified as Green Springs.

It was larger than the one she had found in Oklahoma. Maybe Zion was getting bolder. Like the first town, this one appeared abandoned, probably masked by his network — though fire consumed multiple structures. I could make out a defined retail area through the thick smoke farther up the main street, while closer to us were two industrial buildings, a small car dealership, and a combination post office/government building. Flames consumed many of the retail stores, though everything would burn if left unchecked.

Raven inspected the industrial buildings, then the dealership. Her face reflected her sorrow as she returned emptyhanded. She pointed to the government building. "I'll be in there."

She headed to the structure, pulled her gun, and slipped inside. The flames were six or seven buildings away, so I didn't stop her, though we couldn't stay long. Agents must have just left the area, which meant they'd be close.

I didn't understand how Zion thought he could hide the town's destruction or why he'd done this. There would be connections to other towns, to families and friends living elsewhere.

I wanted to stay close to Raven, but my need to learn his motive forced me to investigate.

I jogged one street over and found houses engulfed in flames.

I traversed another block to gauge the extent of the fire. Some houses had already burned to the ground. Others were just starting. I couldn't determine the pattern but wasn't sure it mattered.

That's when I noticed the burn holes left by plasma shots.

The holes dotted one of the houses, the front door left open. More holes marred other houses, along with a car abandoned in the middle of a yard and a backyard shed that'd had its doors torn off. In fact, every house's front door hung open, some of which reflected forced entry. I wondered if there had been a rebel hideout here.

I coughed from the smoke as I returned to the prior street and confirmed those doors had been left open as well.

We needed to go. But first, I uncovered my implant.

It reconnected with the network, and the smoke and fire disappeared. Everything did: houses, trees, lawns. I looked down—and vertigo powerful enough to clench my stomach hit me, for my lenses projected a massive sinkhole. I appeared to be suspended above it, the hole large enough to have swallowed the entire town.

I reattached my implant shield, closed my eyes to allow my brain to adjust, and opened them as reality returned, the fire and smoke closer. The entire town would be destroyed.

Tread marks from earth-moving equipment marred a nearby park. I didn't have time to investigate.

I returned to the retail/business district and discovered the fire had spread faster than I'd expected. It had reached the government building, flames coating one side of the structure as smoke filled the air.

Coughing again, I ran inside.

The air wasn't as smoky, though that wouldn't last. "Raven," I called. I went to my left, toward the side that was on fire. The area served as the post office. I went behind the counter and searched the back rooms, calling Raven's name more softly to avoid a coughing fit, but it was empty. Smoke and heat rose as I searched, and flames appeared overhead. I backed away, aware that the abandoned mail would make fast kindling.

I returned to the entrance and headed the other way, which was filled with cubicles and offices. Many of the offices showed signs of a hasty exit: some computers were still on, desk chairs laid on their sides, and a half-eaten breakfast burrito congealed in a cubicle.

I caught the sound of a printer running. I searched for it, then heard coughing. "Raven?"

She appeared from a large office with a stack of papers.

"The building's on fire."

"These are tax rolls. They're proof of those who lived here. I have to tell people." She grabbed a folder for her papers as I propelled her toward the entrance.

The walls ahead flickered with orange light as the air grew hot. "Tell them what?" I asked in annoyance.

"Something bad happened here. I don't know what, but we can't let Zion get away with it."

As sweat ran down my chest, I took the last corner.

The building's entrance was just ahead — but flames coated the ceiling.

The intense heat made me flinch. More flames coated the walls, nearly reaching the doors, as smoke filled the space.

We had seconds before the entrance became unreachable.

Gripping Raven's arm tighter, I raced forward and barreled through the scorching hot door. In the process, we let a wave of oxygen into the building, and the fire exploded, throwing us outward.

We landed hard on the road, the rising smoke battling our efforts to get air into our lungs.

I made sure we weren't on fire, then helped her to her feet.

I started leading her away from town, but she stopped me. "There may be others."

I had her turn around and uncover her implant. When she did, I caught her as the vertigo struck her. I helped her recover her implant, then triggered my mask and indicated she do the same. "Everyone's gone. Let's go."

This time, she didn't resist as I led her away, clutching her folder.

The sawhorses came into view, our cars just past it.

As we neared the sawhorses, a man emerged from behind my car. His hat screamed law enforcement. The sheriff's badge on his shirt confirmed it. "What are you doin' out here?"

"We got lost," I said. Raven and I had put our guns away, but I casually placed my hand on my hip, inches from my Glock.

"Didn't see the big damn sign? What happened here is horrific. Been tellin' families one at a time, the ones we can find."

"The sinkhole is a lie. Let me show you."

He scoffed. "I'm not getting near that edge."

Deputies appeared to either side of us, guns drawn.

I was furious with myself. I'd let my guard down — and my own network, which would've tapped into cameras nearby, had caught us.

The sheriff said, "You're under arrest for trespassin'. Got you on car theft, too. Bet if I followed your whereabouts, I'd find a string of stolen cars, wouldn't I?"

The deputies directed us to our knees and cuffed us.

"Those who died in town, did anyone contact their loved ones?" I asked.

"Yeah. The Feds. They took jurisdiction of this mess. They'll decide what to do with you."

CHAPTER TWENTY-FOUR

Raven and I sat in a jail cell at the sheriff's station. We'd been stuck here for hours.

"You should've let me blast them," she said, indicating her fingers. It was the first time she'd spoken since they locked us up.

"You would've murdered three people for doing their job. And if you didn't kill all three immediately, you would've been shot."

The other five jail cells were empty. Most of the station was empty, the sheriff and a deputy the only ones around, though the sheriff kept an eye on us at all times.

"I have to find out how many other towns have been destroyed."

"You need to drop it," I said.

"People are dying."

"The Agency read your mind. Any town they've targeted could become a trap."

Occasional transmissions issued from a broadband radio—which only cops seemed to use anymore—news reports interspersed with information about criminal activity, but the latest caught my attention. "More of that Spencer and Quintero graffiti spotted near the Erwin plant on Route 89," a voice said.

"Artist wannabes or those so-called rebels?" a second voice asked.

"Dunno. Should still notify the big guns."

Raven and I exchanged glances. "Any ideas how to get away?" I asked.

She held up a gloved hand. "I can blow the lock on our cage."

"The sheriff's right over there. Even if we escape without him shooting us, what then?"

"Steal a car?"

"Backup would get us before we got far." Her fingers were

a potent weapon, but we had to use them at the right moment.

The cop had taken our guns along with my burner phone, my bracelet linked to her tracking device, her lock pick kit, and her paper-filled folder.

"I feel terrible for bringing you into this. I opened your eyes but endangered Talia. She's been hurt so badly. I have to be better."

I doubted I kept the surprise off my face. I hadn't expected her admission.

She added, "If we do get away, you'll need to deal with her. She wants to be part of the action."

"I'm well aware."

The radio came to life again. "Notice from Washington. Software upgrades to citizens' implants will start tonight. The upgrades should reach this part of the country in a few days. Public announcements will be issued tomorrow."

Raven stood. "We're running out of time. I'll blow the lock."

I didn't want her to do it in front of the sheriff, but we'd waited long enough. I'd caught his mention of the Feds. "Do you have enough charge?" The locking mechanism was made of steel.

Before she could answer, the sheriff approached. "You with those rebels the TV talked about?"

I forced a smile, more to feel the bots on my face shift, confirming they continued to hide my identity. "Why would you think that?"

"Got a hunch."

Behind him, the front door opened, and an Agent I didn't recognize stepped inside. He moved with a grace that indicated extensive hand-to-hand combat training, his silver hair glinting off the overhead lights, his high-quality, aqua-colored Oxford shirt tailored to his lean frame. "Got a hunch about what?" he asked, gray eyes sharp with intensity.

"Who are you?"

"Your backup." The Agent approached. "More like your replacement, least where these two are concerned."

The sheriff tensed too late. The Agent pulled an HK P30

and shot him in the head.

My ears rang from the gunshot, but I still heard the *thump* as the sheriff's body hit the floor.

The deputy called out from the other room. "Leo? You OK?"

The Agent winked at us before going after the deputy.

"Run," I shouted.

A gunshot rang out.

The Agent returned and shook his head. "Nice try. And nice try with those masks. I can see your real faces. When the sheriff's boss asks what happened, we'll tell them you killed her men. What does it matter, right? You can only be hung once." He rifled through the desks until he found the clear bag that held our personal items. "Ready to go?"

He unlocked our cell, swung open the door, and gave a cocky grin as he aimed at us. "Wanna die here or after we're done with you?" When neither of us moved, he nodded. "What I thought."

He made us cuff ourselves with our hands behind our backs, then took us to his car, what appeared to be a typical sedan with bucket seats in the front. He shoved us into the back, but before he climbed into the driver's seat, he activated an energy field that divided the front from the back. That's when I noticed the transmitting/receiving brackets, which traced the sides and top of each bucket seat as well as the sides and ceiling of the car.

"You that worried about us?" Raven asked as she eyed the brackets.

"Standard procedure." He closed the door. "Good choice back in that cell. I mean, you will die, but you'll help us first."

He kicked up gravel as he left the lot and keyed something with one of his implants. "On my way. Find the rest of their group. They'll be around somewhere, crying with worry over these two."

He threw us a grin in the rearview mirror and turned east onto a two-lane state road.

"So tell me," he said after a minute, "how did you get out?"

"Of where?" I asked.

"The Facility. Everything is keyed to our biometrics. Someone help you?"

He must've been referring to the keypads that controlled nearly every door at the Facility. "There are ways to get fingerprints," I hedged.

"Don't play dumb. You needed blood. Did you cut an Agent somehow? Is that how you popped the doors?"

I remembered the tiny hole in the keypad's sensor. I'd been right about the needles.

I heard a brief sizzle and thought I smelled burnt cloth. "Why did you destroy that town?" Raven asked, her voice sharp with anger.

"Don't know what you're talking about."

"Yes, you do." She had been growing angrier since we were forced into the car.

"Is your sister dead yet? Boss wants to know."

"Go to hell." Raven raised her gloved hand, one half of her now-severed cuffs still locked around her wrist, jammed her metal fingers against the back of his seat, and fired a pent-up bolt of plasma energy.

The blast slammed into the Agent's back with blinding intensity.

Our car swerved off the road and crashed into a tree.

I found myself pressed against the back of the passenger seat, unable to use my hands to protect myself.

"Here," Raven said. She reached around me and used a small bit of energy to cut the links between my cuffs, as she'd done to her own. "You OK?"

I nodded, made sure she was, then eyed the Agent. His back was a mass of charred flesh and muscle. The blast, which had left a fist-sized hole in the driver's seat, would've killed a normal person.

Raven must've clipped the edge of the transmitter because the energy shield winked out.

I dove between the bucket seats, hit the unlock button on the front passenger door, then snatched the clear bag with our possessions. One glance confirmed it didn't contain our guns.

As I pulled back, the Agent moaned. Not dead — though horribly injured.

We exited the car. "You get my papers?" Raven asked.

I grabbed my phone from the bag before handing it over.

We jogged away from the wreck — though I limped from the accident, my body bruised all over — as I called Anya.

She determined where we were. "Nataly's the closest to you. There's a town a mile north. Head there."

* * *

Fifteen minutes later, having cut across fields and two small forested areas, we approached the town. It was more expansive than the one we'd escaped, with a larger downtown and three state roads cutting through it.

My phone rang.

"See the theater up ahead? Go there," Nataly said before disconnecting.

The theater filled an entire block, visible past a line of retail stores. We ran toward it, passing a DNA scanner, the concrete sidewalk around it still curing.

My limp grew pronounced.

I pushed myself, though I couldn't keep up with Raven.

Suddenly, a black SUV raced past and skidded to a stop nearly out of sight as the road curved around the side of the theater. We ran faster before we even saw who was driving.

A voice shouted, "Don't make me come after you." Wraith. Goddamn militant Agent. I'd hoped never to see him again. The Agent Raven blasted must've contacted him.

We sprinted to the theater.

The hundred-year-old building was in disrepair, the three-story-high atrium occupied by a sad scaffolding and a few buckets of paint stacked on the checkered carpet, though there weren't any workers.

We ran past the scaffolding and through a set of doors into the main theater.

The structure had two balcony levels with a domed ceiling overhead painted with clouds to try to give the theater a greater level of grandeur, though that was the only real ornamentation to the large space.

We raced down the center aisle, passing row after row of velvet-covered seats toward a broad stage that tried to evoke Broadway and might have once upon a time but no longer compared, the building materials scattered on the stage further hampering its attempts at opulence.

As we ran, Nataly appeared on stage, descended the stairs on the far side, and dashed over to the main aisle as if to meet us.

The doors crashed open behind us, and Wraith appeared. He immediately started gaining on us.

Nataly stopped at the front of the aisle, swung a backpack off her shoulder, opened it, and yelled, "*Zap attack.*"

Armed drones I didn't recognize, streamlined with sharp angles, launched into the air and headed for the Agent. The first two hit him simultaneously and knocked him back as the next two opened fire.

"Garly made them for me. Let's go," Nataly said as we reached her. More gunfire punctured the air.

We followed her up onto the stage. As we headed to the rear exit, I glanced back. Wraith had managed to grab a drone and was using it to try to fend off the other seven. Blood lined his face and dotted his shirt.

We ran out the back exit and down five steps toward a sedan I assumed was Nataly's — when the rear door of Wraith's SUV, which was just visible, opened to reveal two robot dogs. They started growling when they saw us.

"Back inside," I said.

We hurried back into the theater. I turned to close the door — and found the lead robot leaping for the doorway. I slammed the door into the dog, arresting its forward momentum, though I was thrown back as well. With Nataly's and Raven's help, we kicked the dog's head out of the doorway and shut the door.

I said, "Get somewhere high."

We scattered. Nataly headed to the left while Raven and I ran to the right.

Raven slid to a stop in front of a ladder built into the

theater's brick rear wall that led to the catwalks overhead. She started up, evidence bag in hand, as the door crashed open behind us. The lead robot dog fell to its side as it slid across the hardwood floor. I followed Raven, taking the rungs as fast as I could as the second dog entered the theater.

Both machines raced over and leapt at me. Their razor-sharp teeth just missed my feet as I scrambled out of reach.

In seconds, I reached the nearest catwalk, which hung parallel to the back wall, three feet from the ladder. I stretched across the open space and stepped onto the catwalk — little more than a twenty-foot-long board suspended by ropes — just keeping my balance as it swung back and forth. The walk I stood on led to others hanging at different levels. The group stretched wider than the stage. Unlike normal catwalks, none of these had handrails.

Nataly appeared at the far end of the building, having found a different way up.

Scraping from below drew my attention. The two dogs began to climb the ladder, their metal paws able to adapt to the climb.

I looked for a way to stop them but couldn't.

I was forced to back away as the lead dog leapt onto the catwalk.

Its momentum made the catwalk swing widely and nearly threw me off. I clung to one of the ropes, then took two steps and leapt onto the next catwalk. I stumbled but caught myself by grabbing one of its ropes — my momentum causing this catwalk to start swinging — and moved to the far end as the robot adjusted to the swinging it had caused on its catwalk. It stepped forward, jumped, and landed on my board fifteen feet from me.

I had two choices: jump to one of the two nearby catwalks or fight.

I faced the robot, which crouched as if to launch itself. Behind it, the second robot landed on the first catwalk, though it had to claw at the boards as the catwalk swung even more wildly.

Just as the first robot prepared to launch at me, Raven appeared. She'd hidden by lying on a catwalk two boards over, and as the robot prepared to attack, she rolled to the edge of her board, aimed her right hand, and fired a blinding shot of plasma.

The blast sheared off the robot's head.

It fell from the catwalk, though its angled fall drove the catwalk into the board parallel to Raven's, which knocked hers.

She gripped the side of her catwalk to hang on—but couldn't stay. The second robot had spotted her.

I leapt onto the catwalk between her and me. Pain shot up my leg as I landed. Pushing myself, I reached for her, but she was already on her feet, the catwalk I'd jumped on once more knocking hers, though she stayed erect.

"I'm out of plasma," she said.

"Get behind me. Go."

She hurried onto my catwalk, then stepped onto the one behind me as the second robot landed on the far end of mine.

I thrust a hand behind me, palm open. "Give me the blade."

I eyed the robot as she searched the evidence bag, the robot locked on me as it took a step, then a second. I moved with it, backing away to maintain the dozen-foot distance between us.

Reaching the end of the catwalk, I risked a glance to the next set of boards and stepped onto them.

The next movements happened fast. The robot leapt, Raven slapped the ion blade into my hand, I swung my arm around, ignited the blade, and sliced through the ropes that held the end of the previous catwalk.

The dog robot followed the catwalk as it plummeted to the floor below, the robot's weight and momentum causing it to crash through the floor and into the basement.

Raven and I hurried to Nataly at the catwalk's far end, where steep wooden stairs led down to the main level. When the three of us reached the bottom, we rushed to the door the robot dogs had destroyed, climbed over the broken pieces, and hurried down the five steps.

Along with Nataly's sedan and Wraith's SUV, there was now another SUV, one I didn't recognize. The doors stood open—with Valor on one side and Anya on the other. As Valor's face twisted with alarm, Anya raised a rocket launcher. "*Out of the way."*

I glanced over my shoulder to find Wraith a dozen feet away, covered in blood. He yelled in fury as a loud hissing sound erupted from the rocket launcher. I grabbed Raven, Nataly already dropping to the ground, and hauled her with me as I dove to the side.

The rocket shot past us into the theater and detonated.

CHAPTER TWENTY-FIVE

With the theater collapsing behind us, I struggled to my feet, more pains and a few minor burns adding to my injuries. Raven stood with a grimace, dirty but alive, as was Nataly.

Anya hurried over, made sure we were OK, then threw her arms around my neck and kissed me.

A luxury RV pulled to a stop beside us.

As Anya pulled back, the door opened, and Talia appeared. "Huggy time's over. Hop in."

* * *

I discovered the RV was only partly finished. Other than the bathroom near the rear, the interior had been left gutted, its metal skeleton visible.

"This ride was my idea," Valor said as she pushed a weapons crate against a side wall, using her good leg for leverage, her limp less noticeable.

Other crates had been secured to the metal floor with various supplies and food stacked on top of them, including the medical supplies we'd pilfered at the hospital. Just visible past the bathroom — the only finished part of the RV, other than the front dash — were boxes and the curved shell of Garly's sound machine.

I suspected they'd stolen the RV using one of Nataly's fobs. In Chicago, she and Garly had created a universal car fob that could scan, unlock, and serve as the ignition key for every make and model. A second device blocked the vehicle's GPS. It was faster and more efficient than picking a vehicle lock. I later learned it was how Anya and Valor had stolen the SUV they'd had at the theater.

Anya followed Raven into the RV with the empty launcher. Instead of joining us, Nataly got in her car and trailed us as Liam pulled away. Within minutes, we left the town's limits, a firetruck's wail sounding in the distance.

"That Agent jumped aside before the rocket hit him,"

Valor said as Talia hugged Raven. "But the explosion should've taken him out."

Fritz and Jex scanned the RV's tinted windows to see if we were being chased as Cole and Mina glared at me. I told them and the others about the town, our arrest, and subsequent escape. They all needed to know — though I skimmed over the part with the catwalks.

"How could you let this happen?" Mina asked.

Raven said, "I'm not five years old."

"You acted like it."

Cole said, "You two never should have gone to that town. Our enemies are closer now."

I raised my hands. "Everyone, take a breath."

Garly held up his pad, still weak but looking better. "I don't see any searcher drones."

"Stay on back roads," I called to Liam. "We stick out, but we'll pass fewer people."

"I figure we can use Garly's holograms," Jex said. "Can't change the RV's size, but we can change our look."

"So we're traveling in this thing?" Raven asked.

I smiled. "Are we thinking straight?"

"I guess not," she said as Jex shrugged.

Talia grabbed my hand. "Check it." She took me to the rear, where she and Garly had started to set up a lab. Along with the boxes and sound machine, the space held datatanks, fabricators, 3D printers, and other objects.

"What are those?" I pointed at a trio of harmonizers and some machinery I didn't recognize.

"For my ice weapon," Garly said behind us. "My sound machine is taking longer than I noodled."

"He's kicked its shell a few times," Talia added.

Cupping his damaged ribs, he grinned sheepishly.

As I exited the room, hundreds of swarmbots rose up before me as if realizing I'd been attacked. From their movements and clicking sounds, they seemed anxious.

I assured them I'd take them with me next time, and they reluctantly settled back down, though a few clicked loudly as if admonishing me. I frowned as the rest disappeared in a gap in the floor created by an access hatch that hadn't been closed properly. I opened the hatch to find replication machines running in the storage space underneath us.

"They set it up themselves," Valor said, joining us.

Thousands of copies rippled in the darkness.

I closed the hatch and stood. "Where are we all sleeping?"

"We've got sleeping bags for everyone," Talia said.

Valor's mouth twitched. "Sleep by Anya. I wanna watch Mina squirm."

Talia was listening, so I changed the subject. "Energy level?" I asked her.

She looked. "Seventy-three percent. Anya's rocket was hipcool. Can I launch one?"

"Why don't you help Nataly?" Garly said. "She snookered into two major telecoms. Wanna see if you can sneak into more?"

Talia agreed, and as they set to work, I turned my attention to the rest of the group. While the transportation wasn't ideal — sudden turns made everyone slide, there was nowhere to sit other than the driver or passenger seat, and we seemed overly conspicuous — we were mostly together and could focus on our plans. I helped Jex set up and calibrate the dual camouflage shields for the RV while others hacked, constructed killswitches, and planned targets.

As we passed rolling farms and skirted towns, I finalized the list of targets with Cole and Fritz. "Timing is key," Cole said. "We can't let a single institution discover what we're doing, or they'll circle the wagons."

"Talia and Nataly are being careful with their hacking. Right Talia?" I called out.

"I'm a little mouse, tiptoeing past the grizzly guards as they slurp porridge and bellow show tunes."

"Less metaphor, more focus."

Cole said, "Harder will be installing your damn killswitches."

"Show me what you got from the arms dealer. What's his name?"

"Goes by Alizar. Former Coast Guard. Straight shooter, but if you try to cheat him, he goes after everyone you know."

He and Fritz opened the crates to reveal ten Kevlar vests, thirty-six machine guns, twenty pistols, thousands of rounds, four additional rockets for the launcher, grenades, four plasma rifles, a sniper rifle, and five pounds of C4. "This is my chaos," Cole smirked.

The Kevlar was outdated tech, as there were better options like Dyneema, but old protection was better than none.

"You think we'll recruit enough to use all of that?"

"We need to build an army—before Lafontaine does. I'd rather work with him than compete for fighters, but that blowhard wants to be the next Washington. He'll only listen if we have numbers."

"We still have to find where we need to attack. Otherwise, we're spinning our wheels."

As Cole carefully placed the C4 back in the crates, Fritz leaned toward me. "Think we'll win?"

His doubt surprised me as it was a sharp contrast to his normal cockiness. "We have to."

Cole either didn't hear us or pretended not to. "Anya, come here." When she joined us, he said, "That was an impressive shot with the launcher. You were able to thread that rocket through a narrow doorway. Ever shot one of these?"

He'd left one crate uncovered, the one containing the sniper rifle.

When she shook her head, he started to assemble it. "You should try."

She gave an incredulous grin. "Where exactly?"

He motioned to a side window. "Jex, launch one of your drones. She needs a target."

"While the bus is still moving?" Anya asked.

He ignored her protests. Instead, he instructed her how to operate the rifle as Jex launched a drone to a spot roughly a quarter of a mile away. Shaking her head, Anya stuck the rifle partway out of the window, waited until the road straightened, then fired. The first two shots missed, but after Cole told her to slow down—and Raven gave a couple of pointers—she nailed the drone with her next shot.

Our group cheered except for Mina, who gently took my arm. "We don't want her fighting. What happens if she gets shot and Talia takes another turn?"

"Anya could be a big help," I said, matching her quiet tone.

"Talia has a long recovery ahead of her."

"Mina, we both want the same thing—"

"Do we?" Her eyes pleaded with me to say the right thing, to come back to her.

Raven suddenly spoke up, her voice stunned. "Dad."

She was staring at pictures of us on her pad: herself, Talia, and Mina along with me, the images broadcast by the top national news organization. I didn't need to hear the broadcaster to know. The Agency had released the images. They were accusing my family of horrible crimes, claiming Mina had slipped toxins into Chicago's water supply, Talia had stolen millions by hacking people's bank data, Raven had killed the Sheriff and deputies who'd caught us, and I'd orchestrated it all. Making us threats.

Making it personal.

Just as Valor had predicted.

The image switched to the theater we'd destroyed. A female reporter with thick makeup, bits of hair breaking away from the layer of hairspray she had probably used that morning, spoke of the sudden attack and the damage to the building.

The reporter stepped over to interview someone. The camera followed her—and revealed Kieran. "One of our operatives was injured in the fight, though he'll make a full recovery," he said, his hands dirty as if he'd dug Wraith out himself. "We cannot let the Quinteros continue their reign of terror on our country."

More lies placed on my head—and now the heads of my children.

CHAPTER TWENTY-SIX

As the sound of shuffling feet filled the air, I stared at the Senators on my pad. I'd avoided studying my enemies, the memories of Zion broadcasting C-Span in my cell tainting my desire to ever look at a politician again, but I'd held off long enough.

The pad streamed a live feed of a Budget Committee hearing. Senator Patricia Dixon of California was on the panel. She was the one I'd attempted to meet in San Francisco, who'd made me realize the members of Congress were phonies. She was soft-spoken but influential. Of course, given her true identity.

Senator Dan Malatone had the most powerful position as the Majority Leader, though in reality, he might not have true seniority, and like the others, he answered to Zion. Dixon, Malatone, the House Speaker Melanie Sanchez-Riaz, and every other Senator and Representative were beholden to my former partner — which meant they were controlled by him.

President Holland had broadcast a threat to me over a month ago, which meant he was probably a Zion puppet as well.

My group had less than a month before the entire country was covered with Kieran's 3D network. Nataly had shown me. The tiny drones had been disbursed as far east as Chicago and were moving steadily across Illinois. They would show the actions of over five hundred million people, but their AI would find the anomalies. Would reveal us.

Though the drones were getting closer, we chanced taking a break. We'd been focused the last forty-eight hours on the chaos we needed to unleash, but if we didn't rest, we'd make mistakes we couldn't afford.

Next to me, Raven sorted through the tax rolls to identify who'd lived in Green Springs and search for their next of kin. Nearby, Jex and Talia circled each other, moving in and out of the afternoon sunlight that cut across the bus's interior.

We'd parked by an empty farm in east central Ohio, the owners away, their cameras disabled. Our holograms masked our transport as a rusted dumpster, a fake construction company's name displayed on the side.

I'd gone to the bathroom earlier but couldn't look at myself in the mirror.

"Try to move like I taught you," Jex said. He had grown stronger, confident and patient.

"Can't," Talia said, her excitement evident in her voice.

"Why do you keep eyein' the door? Focus on me."

She squinted as she raised her fists, her battery slung across her chest. She feigned one way and lashed out from the other, connecting with his arm. She followed with a spin that was a little sloppy. Jex didn't go in for the "kill" but blocked her arm instead.

"Take him down," Fritz encouraged her, smiling.

I smiled, too, thrilled to see her getting stronger.

I became aware of Cole watching Talia and Jex. He straightened as if really seeing her for the first time. After a moment, he approached them. Talia involuntarily stepped back, but he stopped her and changed her stance so she faced Jex from the side instead of straight on. "Give your enemy less to hit. When you attack, stay centered and punch through your target. And move faster. Your enemy won't move as slow as he is."

He spoke gruffly. I couldn't tell if that was to scare her or because his instructions evoked the guilt from his past. Either way, she didn't seem fazed.

"Grump," she muttered as he started away.

He turned back. "Say that to my face."

She squared her shoulders. "*Grump.*"

He nodded in satisfaction.

I shared a glance with Anya. We'd taken a walk earlier, after we'd parked the RV and members of our group had gone off to do their own thing. "Talia is progressing well," she'd said. "Her heart muscles are still bruised, but the meds arresting her heart rate have helped her heal."

"I worry she's overdoing it."

"Have you ever been able to curtail her?"

"Only when she's asleep."

"Are you a heavy sleeper?" She sighed before I could answer. "We haven't done normal dating stuff."

"I offered to buy you flowers," I teased.

"Which you still can."

"You have a favorite?"

"Where's the fun in me telling you?"

Talia pulled me from my thoughts. "Whoop, grub's here," she called out.

Valor and Garly entered carrying six large pizzas. "This was Talia's idea," he said as he set out the pizzas, his gangly elbows swinging wildly.

His infection was gone, though he was still weak. His injuries had greatly dampened his production. I'd helped, but we needed better tech to fight The Agency's superiority.

The next few minutes were filled with thanks for Talia and selection of pieces to eat.

We talked and joked as we ate, except for Mina. The RV's radio played some pop band, maybe The Jonas Sons, and the sun crawled toward the horizon, its rays illuminating intricate patterns Valor had etched on the RV's exposed metal support struts.

"I've accessed the last of the major telecom companies," Nataly announced. "With that, we can alter most people's access to the internet. We have the cable companies, too. Satellite is the last group."

"Then our chaos plan can launch. People will piddle like crazy," Talia said.

"That's not the goal," I told her.

Cole leaned toward her. "Make them piddle."

As Talia giggled, I asked, "Anyone find anything on Zion's communication nexus?"

"There's stuff online about that quiet zone from when it was a research lab, but nothing in years, and nothing that would indicate them modifying it from a benign lab to some all-powerful, national-conspiracy broadcast facility," Liam said.

"I dug into the federal archives and searched for contractor bids, appropriations, or anything else that might clue us in,"

Raven said. "The only thing I found was a notice of permit for the installation of high-voltage electrical lines to the area. No reports on the state's site, no news articles, no feasibility studies, nothing."

I mirrored her frustration. If we couldn't confirm Zion's base of operations, we'd lose.

Talia forced a smile and clapped her greasy pizza hands. "How did everyone learn The Agency turned our implants against us?"

"When they tried to recruit me," Garly said. "Silvers wanted me to improve the hardware bits in everyone's implants. I fretted over what might happen if I ruined them, so I finagled how to block my feed. Then I saw the true sky and crinkled the rest."

Nataly, who sat beside him, said, "I learned it from your father's broadcast."

"Me as well," Fritz said with his mouth full.

"I'm here because of that," Cole said.

"Did you learn about it from his broadcast?" Talia asked.

"No. Someone I later failed told me."

Valor spoke up. "I knew the air was bad, had known for years. I didn't know why people weren't freaked out about it. It wasn't until I heard about Dray's broadcast and found it online that I realized the lies everyone was told. What they've done is terrible."

I said, "Raven and Anya helped me figure out the truth."

Talia picked toppings off her piece of pizza. "Why do you all fight? I know my family's reasons, but I don't know Anya's or Valor's or Fritz's or Liam's."

"You know mine?" Cole asked.

"You're sad and want to stop being sad."

He had told me an innocent pregnant woman had died because of him—something I seriously doubted Talia knew about.

If she saw the surprise on his face, she didn't acknowledge it. Instead, her eyes flickered to Mina before asking Fritz.

"We've lost privacy," he said. "Can't stand it. I gotta fight.

It's what matters."

"What matters?"

"Our personal freedom."

Liam said, "As Talia discovered, I spent time in juvie. The way The Agency controls our eyes, it feels like I'm still locked up."

He was meshing well with the team—except for the fortunes. He'd studied philosophy during his years as a rebel, and he'd written horoscope-like predictions or "fortunes" for everyone in the group. He'd only managed to distribute four when Cole found out. The colonel had ripped them up before anyone could read them, much to Talia's disappointment.

Anya said, "I learned from Dray. I didn't know I was installing cameras in my patients' eyes."

Mina got up while she spoke and slipped into the back. A minute later, she left the RV, a stuffed backpack slung over her shoulder.

I followed her outside. "Hey," I said as I closed the door behind us.

She brightened, though her joy faded when she read my face. "You're not trying to stop me."

"So, you *are* leaving."

She nodded toward the door. "I see why you rejected me."

"You started me on that path. Not her."

"I've been trying for weeks to make it up to you."

"I'm not sure you ever could."

"You felt the same crushing grief I went through. I couldn't face Adem being gone."

"Raven and Talia needed you. I needed you."

She twisted away to wipe at her face. Her body language told me she wanted to argue. Then her shoulders dropped. "I know The Agency could spot me. They know who I am. But I'm no fighter. I'll try to help in my own way." Tears welled, though her voice remained level. "I know how much I screwed up. I also know Talia's in danger when she's with you. I asked her, but she wants to stay. Protect her."

"With my life."

She nodded, hesitated, her face creasing with the emotions that battered her, then got in Nataly's SUV, which Valor had used to get the pizzas, and left.

We'd had marital problems since we lost Adem, our issues masked by the challenges of raising our daughters. Her betrayal had been the final straw, but our marriage had already crumbled. Anya had nothing to do with it.

Mina's comment about The Agency stuck with me. She could expose us and ruin our chance, but what choice did I have? I couldn't kill her.

* * *

When I stepped back inside, I found that dinner had ended.

As the leftovers were being consolidated into one of the pizza boxes, Cole stood off to the side with Jex, who watched me with concern. Talia was at her computer; when I looked at her, she ducked her head so I couldn't see her face.

I started toward her, but Raven stopped me. "It needed to happen. No one trusted her."

I searched her eyes but couldn't tell if she'd confronted Mina. I knew Cole and Garly distrusted her. Maybe Raven was right. Maybe they all did.

Raven added, "Mina didn't like that Anya and I got close. She saved my guy. Of course I'd like her." She paused. "It's weird seeing you with her, but I want you happy."

"Does Talia know about Anya?"

"You think she doesn't?"

I went to Valor, who stared out the windshield where Mina had disappeared with the SUV. "How long you think she'll last out there?" she asked.

"Let's hope long enough."

Minutes later, we drove off. Not a single person asked why. It wasn't a comfortable feeling.

Liam approached. "I was thinking. Not everything's online, especially something as sensitive as The Agency's communication nexus. But something would've been filed for a construction project big enough to coordinate their lies to the whole country, blueprints or plans that had to be approved. West

Virginia would've required it to issue permits."

"We've searched every database we could find," I said.

"Then we go where the *physical* paperwork would be stored. I checked. That state requires paper applications. If nothing else, there should be a layout of what had been there before. It'd give us some idea of the compound's design."

Raven, who'd stayed close, nodded. "Let's check it out."

Chapter Twenty-Seven

Hours later, Anya, Raven, Liam, and I descended from the mountains into Charleston, West Virginia. Though the interstate was empty this time of night, we were on edge. We could be heading into a trap.

Anya drove, her body tense as she exited to downtown, the streetlights illuminating us more than I wanted. Raven and Liam sat in the back, their tools hidden in their packs. My pack rested on the floor between my legs, the swarmbots inside shifting periodically. A second, larger pack took up the trunk.

Jex had wanted to come with us, but I'd asked him to remain behind. "Stay with Talia," I'd told him. "Keep working with her."

"Get back before she fixes to come after y'all."

Raven pulled me from my thoughts, "Has Kieran's network reached this far?"

"No, but it's reached Columbus," I said.

"Can you neutralize the drones?"

"We're working on it."

At my signal, we activated our masks. The tiny robots climbed up our faces in an undulating black and pink wave, their bio-constructed outer layer settling into place as the robots locked into their preset positions, which included pushing at my eyelids to subtly change the shape of my eyes. Within seconds, all four of us were cast with specific but plain-looking faces — which we hoped made them unmemorable.

Keeping my pad low, I logged into my national camera network and scanned our destination. The area appeared deserted, though the cameras and multiphase scanners that surrounded the area were a concern. Then I spotted a problem. "There are two DNA scanners within a block of the building."

We tucked the bottom edge of our masks into our shirts and donned gloves, the ends extending up under our shirtsleeves.

Raven ran UV lights over each of us and across the interior

of the car. Half measures that might not be enough.

I zoomed in on another issue: two black obelisks like the ones I'd encountered in L.A. We'd have to walk right past one of them. The obelisk in L.A. had dismantled an eight-foot-tall robot. They'd shred us in seconds if we tripped their sensors.

"Almost there," Anya said.

Raven stowed away the UV light.

Anya pulled to the curve, dropped us off, and left.

I wasn't sure if it was Zion's influence, the proximity to D.C., or some other reason, but the air felt more oppressive and the streets more dangerous. A cop drove past, not slowing, though he could watch us from my network — or initiate one of the obelisks. Of more immediate concern were the DNA scanners. Even with our precautions, we risked being identified.

The Agency's response would be swift.

I took the lead and headed to the next block. The building we wanted was on Virginia. As we walked, light flickered simultaneously from four vid screens in apartments nearby. They were broadcasting the same channel. I didn't know if there was a reason, but I hastened my step.

We turned the corner and traversed a tiny park to the stone-covered building.

The three-story government structure was over two centuries old, but it wasn't immune to modern times. In the shadows cast by nearby streetlights, I could just make out a robotic guard near the building. At least one other would be stationed at the opposite entrance. If we failed to use the right code to enter the building or tried to break in, the guards would come to life.

We approached the side door, which had a small keycard reader.

Liam removed a keycard he'd synched with his implant. He touched the card to the reader and held it in place while he typed with his other hand — trying to hack his way in.

I heard the robotic guard activate. We were taking too long.

The swarmbots shifted in the pack I carried. They felt it,

too.

There was a click, and the door unlocked.

We hurried inside as the guard powered down. Another few seconds and alarms would have triggered.

Liam gave an apologetic grin. "These machines are being converted to DNA scanners. Did you see the slot under the reader? We'll really be screwed then."

"They'll require blood samples to get inside?"

Raven frowned at me as he said, "No, you breathe into them. Results are the same. Both kinds of readers scan and crossmatch forty thousand DNA clusters in less than a second. Can't hack them. You're better off busting through the door."

Raven pushed past him. "Let's get what we need."

A holographic map brightened as we neared.

We located the Archives department and descended a granite staircase to the basement level, choosing to let our eyes adjust to the darkness rather than using flashlights.

At the bottom, we moved cautiously down a dimly lit hallway until we found the door we needed. Finding it locked with a normal key slot, Raven pulled out her pick set, but I motioned her back. I held up Garly's tiny robot. "Remember this?" I stuck it in the lock, waited until it stopped moving, then turned it. The door unlocked, and we entered.

"Neat trick," she said.

The Archive room contained a Formica counter that ran the width of the room, followed by rows of storage, a mix of metal cabinets, shelving, and airtight containers. Bundled cables snaked across the ceiling. The counter held two vid screens; along with a screen for accessing the Archive's database, a screen hung on the wall like a digital poster that switched announcements every few seconds. As I watched, pictures of myself and my family appeared with reward information.

Liam and Raven stepped forward and accessed the database computer as I traversed one of the aisles. I scanned the tags on the drawers. "You'll be looking for a series of letters and numbers," I told them. "First two are letters, then a seven-digit number."

"Found it," Raven called, and the three of us hurried to the spot. I needed the swarmbots' help, as the box we needed was on the top shelf. They swelled as they climbed out of my backpack, up the side of the shelving unit, and around the box. They then lifted the box, working as a combined unit to lower it to me.

I frowned when I felt how light the box was. I set it on a nearby table and opened the lid, but it was empty. Either Zion had instructed someone to clean it out, or the plans had never been stored.

Liam scratched his head. "Now what?"

* * *

I didn't say a word for the next hour. We had no idea what we were facing, which meant we couldn't plan for it. We'd be foolish to blindly invade the old Observatory area — which I still hadn't confirmed was Zion's communication nexus site.

We stopped at an old, two-story motel off of I-64, just past an empty restaurant called Rusty's Roadhouse. We were too tired, too disheartened, to make sure we weren't being followed.

Minutes later, Liam approached with room keys. "The desk clerk's a first-gen service robot, so there's no risk of facial recognition. Here. We're on the second floor."

I frowned. "Anything available on the first?"

"Robot said no."

We followed him to the two rooms, which were in the middle of the building. They were adjoining, with a door that connected the rooms. Both had two queen beds and a bathroom in the rear. I set down both large bags of swarmbots — I hadn't brought every 'bot, just those I could fit in the bags — by the door.

Liam took in the three of us before disappearing into the other room.

Raven eyed me. I knew she was frustrated. I was, too. But it was something else. "What's wrong?" I asked as Anya set her bag on the far bed.

Raven shook her head. "This place is ancient."

"I don't think it's ever been updated," Anya said as she rubbed a fingernail. I agreed. The place had to be a half century old at least.

Raven turned on a prior-generation LED TV, which showed the local news. "...next section of the country will start receiving the software upgrade to their neural nets tomorrow..."

I started for the adjoining room. "Well, goodnight."

"Wait."

I looked back. Raven shook her head. "Can't believe you'd take the other room." As she walked past me, I caught her knowing smile. "Keep the TV on."

She closed the adjoining door.

Anya laid back on her bed and gave a look I couldn't turn away from. "Come here, devil lips."

I went to her.

We'd just reached the clothing-removal stage when Raven yelled. "*Dad.*"

"Are you kidding me?" I muttered, then yelled, "*What?*"

"Listen."

I pulled down my shirt and went to the TV. When I turned it off, I heard what sounded like rain, but it had a metallic edge to it. Then, it turned heavier.

Anya got up, entered the bathroom — and cried out.

Hunter-drones completely covered a small, thick window next to the shower. Sporting insect-like joints and cutting-laser tails, these little nightmares had attacked my family in a swarm on Free Isle. As we watched, lasers flashed, though there were so many, the mass interfered with those trying to cut their way inside.

"Oh god," I said, then looked up as the metal thumping overhead intensified. "They're attacking the roof, too."

I hurried out of the bathroom, Anya right behind me. "*Raven.*"

Frantic clicking rose from the bags of swarmbots.

There was a crash from the front window.

I threw back the curtain. The hunter-drones had broken through the first pane of glass and were scrambling over each other to get to the second pane. The front door vibrated as other drones attacked it, while overhead, the sounds grew louder.

The adjoining door flew open. "We got company," Liam

said.

Anya dropped to her knees and reached for one of the bags I'd brought in. Both were jerking back and forth as the swarmbots inside went crazy, trying to get out. She managed to grab the zipper and wrenched the bag open. The 'bots poured out, a large portion climbing up the wall to the front window and forming a barrier, linking themselves together as they filled the frame — though I didn't know how long it would hold.

Other 'bots scurried to the adjoining room, their clicking sounds fading as they disappeared, while a smaller group headed to the back window.

Bits of ceiling fell down.

Raven pushed past Liam and into our room with her pack slung over her back. "They're almost inside."

"Where do we go?" Anya asked.

The swarmbots in the second bag managed to open their zipper. They poured out and scrambled to join the fight, but they wouldn't be enough.

The ceiling began to sag from the hunter-drones' assault.

I chose a spot near the beds, dropped to my knees, and activated my ion blade.

As the ceiling groaned, adding to the sounds of the hunter-drones eating away at the building and the swarmbots clicking, I pierced the floor with my blade. The cheap brown carpet — matted down from God knew how many years of abuse — caught fire as I began to cut a circle in the floor. Raven stomped at the carpet as I cut, but I waved her back. No time — though the smell was horrendous.

The front window shattered, which caused the shield of swarmbots to collapse. The hunter-drones started to crawl inside, though they were met with resistance from the swarmbots.

I'd cut half the circle I needed. Switching hands, I continued to cut, the blade vibrating as I forced its way through carpet, concrete, wood, and whatever else served as the barrier between this floor and the first. As the others shouted my name, I neared completing the circle. Twenty inches. Ten. Five.

My blade began to spark, the handle heating rapidly, and

then died. Shit. I just needed three more inches. I smacked the handle, but the blade was dead.

"*Dray,*" Anya shouted.

The swarmbots from the bathroom were being driven back into the main room by hunter-drones, while overhead, the ceiling let out another groan as it dropped lower. In seconds, it would collapse.

As Raven and Liam opened fire on some of the drones, I stood and jumped on the circle, but the floor didn't budge. I jumped again to no effect.

A small pack of hunter-drones broke free and scurried toward us.

Raven joined me, and we both jumped, then Liam leapt, landing inside the circle the same time we did — and the floor gave way.

We plummeted into the room below, landing hard, my legs flaring with pain as my knees gave out. I collapsed to the floor, as did Raven, while Liam hit the ground at an angle, flew over us, hit the bed, and bounced into the corner.

The room's occupants, a naked couple, screamed as they scrambled to the bathroom, flashing us with his back hair and her Jessica Rabbit tattoo.

Anya swung down, gripping the edge of the circle, then dropped the last few feet, the pack with our weapons over her shoulder. "Anyone hurt?"

"Yes," we all said.

Raven and I pushed ourselves to our feet. Liam stumbled out of the corner and joined us as I went for the front door. I threw it open, and we hurried outside.

I ran for our car, though sounds behind me drew my attention. Hunter-drones poured out of our unit above and dropped to the ground from the second-floor walkway. I knew they could fly and was surprised they didn't. Then I saw the swarmbots. They were half the size of the hunter-drones but fought them every step of the way. Many were sliced in half by the drones' laser, but the rest fought, blocking their wings and jabbing at them.

Hundreds more drones poured over the railing, landed, and started after us.

We neared our car, Anya hitting the fob to unlock the doors—when a thick metal plate, four feet wide and eight feet tall, dropped from the sky and slammed into the ground before us.

We skidded to a stop, though I immediately pulled Anya and Raven to the side. I recognized the plate. I looked up and spotted a floating platform, a type of flying structure that Agents had used when they'd attacked Lafontaine's rebel headquarters weeks earlier. Then, I caught a flash of silver. I knew that bob. Britt, on a hoverbike two hundred yards away, looking fully recovered—and pissed off.

"Move, now," I barked. I ran back toward the motel, the direction Britt wouldn't expect, nearly reached the leading edge of hunter-drones, then ran along the lengthening edge of robots.

Tiny laser bolts laced the air as I ran.

Raven caught up to me, but Liam and Anya were farther back, forced to veer away from the motel as more hunter-drones appeared.

The motel rooms we'd occupied collapsed. Smoke billowed.

Raven pulled ahead. "I'll distract Britt."

"No, wait," I said. I ran harder and nearly reached her when a plate landed a foot in front of us.

Unable to stop, Raven slammed into it. I then crashed into her.

Two more plates pounded the ground to either side of us, then a fourth behind us.

Britt had trapped us.

The plate we'd slammed into had started to tilt outward from our impact, but it was now frozen in place. As Raven clawed at a wall, I anchored my body on the back panel to push on the front one, but I couldn't budge it.

As Anya shouted my name, Raven said, "They're held together somehow, magnetic fields or something." She held her arm as if she'd hurt it.

I called out to Anya. "Get somewhere safe. Don't stay together."

I inspected the tilted panel. Raven was right. Some sort of energy field held the plates in place. We could touch the metal but couldn't move them.

We heard scratching as hunter-drones tried to climb the panels to get to us. Some of the swarmbots could be as well.

Reasoning that the energy field emitted from the plates themselves, I scanned the angled plate and found a panel that wasn't noticeable. Four screws kept it closed.

I didn't have my ion blade anymore, but when I searched my pockets, I found Garly's tiny shapeshifting robot. I pressed it against the first screwhead, felt the robot shift, and quickly unscrewed the bolts.

Someone fired multiple rounds nearby, followed by a woman cursing and stomping. Anya.

I removed the panel. The electronics inside not only generated the fields that held the plates together, but they probably provided navigation/propulsion to make sure they landed where Britt wanted. I wasn't familiar with these components, but I noticed that two of the motherboards had rubber between them.

"You have a piece of metal?"

Raven whipped out her pick kit and handed me a thin metal post.

I pressed the post to the edges of the two metal-covered boards, connecting them. The boards sparked, jarring me with a flash of electricity, and shorted out.

The panel slowly resumed its tilt.

Moving as one, Raven and I pushed on the panel, which fell to the ground with a thud. Anya was waiting for us, my pistol in her hand, crushed drones at her feet.

We joined her, then started to run. Liam was ahead, firing at Britt, having dodged a couple of panels. My swarmbots were still fighting Britt's swarm, though they were losing, only a few dozen left to fend them off.

I frowned. Britt was firing back at Liam, but she continued to miss. I suspected she was a better shot.

"Let's go," I shouted at him.

He nodded but continued to engage with Britt. He stepped forward as if he was driving her back, but this was all wrong. I spotted a thick, six-foot pole just visible in the darkness past him. It hadn't been here when we arrived. I was sure of it.

The pole stood in the shadows on the far side of the alley that ran just past the property's edge.

Britt was herding him toward it.

"Liam, get back," I shouted too late. The top of the pole rose into the air and broke apart into tiny drones that swarmed him, pinned his arms behind him, and lifted him into the air.

A second hoverbike appeared. Pierce. He aimed a plasma rifle at the graying rebel.

I ran forward but had no hope of getting to Liam in time.

Pierce fired two plasma bolts, killing our companion.

Raven, Anya, and I cried out in horror—and Anya raised my pistol. With remarkable accuracy, she struck the hoverbike's tank, which began to leak. Pierce swung his rifle around, but a second shot ignited his hoverbike. It exploded, the eruption throwing him past a nearby cabin.

A metallic uncoupling sound echoed to our right.

A second pole a dozen feet away, which I hadn't noticed before, began to detach.

The last of my swarmbots, no more than two dozen, scurried up the sides of the pole, clicking desperately, and crawled over the upper portion. They hauled it back down and held it in place—for the moment.

I grabbed Raven and Anya and pulled them away. As I did, Raven fired over my shoulder at Britt, who had come closer, forcing the Agent to veer off.

There were still hundreds of hunter-drones, Britt would be back, and the swarmbots couldn't keep the pole together for long. I heard the buzz of more drones. I wasn't sure if they were more hunter-drones or something else.

But they gave me an idea.

I pulled out my burner phone.

"You're making a *call*?" Anya asked.

I dialed 911. "Multiple gunshots, three people are down. There's blood everywhere. We're at Rusty's Roadhouse." I hung up and looked at them. "Run."

We dashed across the motel's parking lot, passing our car, which Britt had blocked with her first panel. Behind us, Britt fired at us as she swooped down. Raven returned fire, though after two shots, her gun clicked empty.

Anya had my weapon. I didn't even have a knife anymore.

We ran into the street, then onto Rusty's parking lot, Anya and Raven switching clips as they ran.

Britt circled the lot, and the platform overhead rotated as it glided toward us. More plates would rain down. She wanted us alive.

Laserbolts seared the air as the hunter-drones scrambled after us. When I glanced back, I spotted over half of them lifting into the air and heading toward us.

Red and white lights flashed as three ambulance capsules, each the size of a Mini Cooper, descended from the sky. Their massive propellers kicked up every speck of dirt and trash in the lot as two of them landed—and flung the hunter-drones in every direction.

Squinting through the throbbing wind, I saw the doors open on the two capsules.

"Get in," I yelled.

The two women ran to separate capsules.

I knew the ambulance capsules would get reprogrammed, but we had to try. I ran after Raven and half-entered her transport. There was a seat for an EMT, a cushioned bed for a patient, and various supplies to provide triage. I pointed to a large red button near the doorframe. "See this?" I yelled over the noise. "When I get in the other capsule, hit it—and keep an eye on us. Be ready to bail." EMTs used the button to rush back to the drone's hospital, such as when a patient was coding.

I ducked back out and started for Anya's capsule—but Britt fired at me as I moved into the open, forcing me back. Above her, the platform approached.

No time.

I rushed forward, aches flaring, and ducked to the side to put the third ambulance capsule, which hovered thirty feet overhead but twice that distance-wise, between us. The capsule's downdraft battered me as I ran.

There was a deep thump, a shriek of metal, and a loud crash.

Britt had dropped a plate directly onto the capsule.

The capsule and plate crashed to the ground.

One of the capsule's propellers pinwheeled across the lot toward me as shrapnel filled the air. I dove to the side, the propellers missing my leg by less than an inch as it spun past, though smaller bits of shrapnel cut me.

I rolled, forced myself to my feet—and was exposed to Britt.

Gunfire rang from both ambulance capsules to drive her back. Yet she didn't fly away. She was trying to distract us. The leading edge of the platform drifted directly overhead.

Why I didn't bring a hand shield with me, I had no idea.

Forcing myself to move, I ran to Anya's capsule, my bad leg giving out as I lunged for the opening. Anya nearly hauled me inside, and I slapped the emergency button.

Britt fired as the door closed, bullets ricocheting off the metal doorframe.

A flash of silver drew my attention. Pierce, clothes burnt and face smeared with soot, raced across the parking lot toward us.

My capsule lifted just before he could reach us, pivoted, and took off, Raven's capsule moving nearly identically.

While we were going fast, Britt could catch up. She must've been thrown by the arrival of the capsules, not sure if she should follow. But we weren't out of the woods.

"How did they find us?" Anya asked.

"DNA scanners, or maybe Liam's face was captured when he checked in. Even a partial could've been enough. Or the government building was a trap." Either way, Liam had paid with his life.

Britt appeared beside us, twenty feet away, the wind

blowing her silver bob off her face.

Anya pushed me aside, shot a hole in the canopy door, then fired at Britt.

Britt returned fire, a quick succession that shattered the window. The next shot clipped Anya's neck, just missing a more serious injury.

As the wind battered us, Anya steadied her pistol and fired.

Britt's hoverbike dropped, the Agent fighting and failing to stay level.

I snatched gauze from a dispenser to clean the blood from her neck. "You OK?" I asked.

Before she could answer, we slowed. "What's going on?" she asked.

"Kieran. They're changing the drone's destination."

I looked down. We'd reached Huntington, a smaller city on the Ohio River. Buildings ranging from five to twenty stories rose up to meet us.

I waved at Raven, then took Anya's gun, fired at the capsule's door lock, and forced the door open. I caught a flash of plasma from Raven's capsule, and she forced her door open as well.

An eighteen-story building neared, narrower than I would've wanted. We'd have one shot. Grabbing Anya's arm, I scooted to the edge of the open doorway, the wind snatching whatever worry or warning she gave me.

Our capsule suddenly pivoted, the rooftop swiveling under us.

As the autonomous capsules locked onto new coordinates, the three of us dropped and hit the roof, our momentum dragging us toward the ledge. We caught ourselves, then hurried to the rooftop door as the capsules flew off.

CHAPTER TWENTY-EIGHT

I leaned against the RV's exposed-metal interior wall as Valor drove us east.

I'd previously watched the road as we'd woven our way through the backroads of eastern Ohio and western Pennsylvania to make sure we weren't being followed, but there wasn't much to see, and my heart wasn't in it.

A day and a half had passed since our escape in the ambulance capsules, but we were still shellshocked. Liam had died, and Raven, Anya, and I had nearly been captured.

All for nothing.

"That woman is evil," Raven said, not for the first time.

Both Agents were.

Anya sat beside me, her body rigid as if expecting another assault. She hadn't left my side since the motel. "We can't let Liam die in vain."

Him, Omura, Hernandez, and so many others.

Cole and Fritz commandeered the RV's rear to watch for threats. Garly and Nataly sat across from us, Nataly with a pad in her lap and her head on Garly's shoulder, both as affected by Liam's death as the others. Talia sat up front with Valor while Jex hovered near Raven, a gun in his hand.

Through a dummy account, we'd found an empty loft outside Pittsburgh's business district to rent for a week, a nice contrast to the RV. The group would switch to smaller cars, get grounded.

I had a different plan. I wouldn't tell them. It was my path to walk. Besides, they'd try to stop me.

Or maybe they wouldn't. Cole had made so much progress with the rebel groups that they were ready to meet. They'd made demands, but he was confident he would recruit at least three squadrons of fighters.

If they joined, they'd have a say in my chaos proposal. They could vote it down. Even kick me out. They'd be justified.

I had a flash of a memory, Mom's gravestone being installed at the cemetery, a tiny concrete block carved with her name, and the loneliness that had swallowed me.

As Valor softly sang "Jump" by Van Halen, her tapping of the beat on the steering wheel turning the song soulful, I took in my team. I admired them, not only for the skills and backgrounds and loss they carried. Yet even with our shared purpose, and with Anya and my daughters nearby, I felt lonely like at that grave.

Raven pulled me from my thoughts. "Could we have defeated those hunter-drones somehow?"

Garly said, "You can crumple them individually but can't sayonara the herd."

"That's why Zion uses them." I described to him how I cut into the floor to escape the initial attack. "I have a device concept that would've created the hole ten times faster, a rope-like accelerant."

After a few questions, Garly nodded. "I have the right trinkets. Shouldn't take long to clink a prototype."

Anya leaned forward. "We should go to the Department of Justice. They oversee The Agency, right? There has to be oversight."

"Don't bother," Jex said. "Zion would've replaced the top dogs with his people."

"So, what's the next step?"

The strain was clear on everyone's faces. If we fought with no direction, we'd lose.

Anya had been looking at me when she'd asked. I didn't tell her. I'd put her through enough.

* * *

An hour later, we finished moving our supplies and weapons into the top-floor loft. The vacated unit had a few provisions but was mostly bare, which meant the team would keep using sleeping bags.

Valor had helped Talia make a corner of the second bedroom her own, with a canopy so she could hack on her pad at night without disturbing others. Talia insisted on helping Valor make a spot of her own nearby.

Jex and Raven occupied the great room. They'd taken a break from inventorying weapons and sat close as light streamed in from the wall of windows behind them. Jex said something that evoked a smile. Briefly, I saw her as she had been, a college student rich with possibilities.

My eyes traveled over the others, taking in my new family forged from tragedy and desperation, now bonded by purpose and sacrifice.

I hoped they succeeded.

Before I could find Garly, Cole approached, signaling Jex to join us. "I need to update you." His voice was grim; he'd been furious he hadn't been with us when Britt attacked. "The rebel groups have started to waiver. I need your help convincing them to follow you."

"Later," I said. "Maybe."

"Not good enough. Lafontaine's been pushing on his end. He's using that sheriff's death against us."

Jex said, "The Agency pinned it on you, Dray. They've even shown videos. They're doctored but look real."

"We need to show you're still you. Help me get the fighters you need."

Before I could reject him, Nataly joined us. "The Agency's 3D network is getting closer. The terrain and denser populations slowed the rollout, but they're halfway across Ohio, Kentucky, and Tennessee. Should we leave?"

"Give me a day, then go," I said. "Jex, you're going on watch duty, correct? Keep an eye out for hoverbikes — and a helicopter painted in gold and silver. It's hideous-looking."

"Why? What's goin' on?"

I told them what I planned. I ignored their rising objections, until Cole grabbed me. "This is a worse idea than your chaos. You won't escape. And what if you do? You think you can get away clean?"

"I have to do this. If I fail, take over."

Jex said, "I gotta tell Raven. She'll go with ya."

"Not this time."

I started toward the main bedroom, taking Nataly with

me. "Convince those rebels to join us," I told Cole as I walked away. "Otherwise, we don't stand a chance."

With Fritz's help, Garly had turned the bedroom into his lab.

I signaled Fritz to leave, then got Garly up to speed. "I need you to make a lot more weapons—and I need you to finish those chaos items. There won't be much time."

"OK," he said, clearly unhappy. "I've already begun your burning rope—and I'm churning oodles of swarmbots. They saved you, my padre."

"Tell him to rest," Nataly said. She stroked his shoulder lovingly. "He's been working nonstop, trying to make everything you've asked for."

Garly rested his head against hers. "I'm good, chi'."

I said, "Take the night off and rest. But first, I need your help. Both of you."

"Ooh, both of us. Sounds juicy," Nataly said as Garly affectionately rubbed her back.

I removed the bracelet that tracked Raven and held up a pair of surgical pliers I'd stolen from Anya's stash. "You won't like it."

* * *

The restaurant I'd chosen was on the swankier side with exposed beams, white tile, subtle hologram accents, and chairs with noise-dampening backs that provided a level of privacy. The place was filled with many of Pittsburgh's dealmakers and influencers, corporate outfits competing with the latest fashions for dominance, each patron enjoying the discretion and exposure.

A fitting location to do this.

I followed the hostess, my jaw sore, my face unmasked—a huge risk. My modified shoe didn't feel any different.

I sat at the table I'd reserved, scooted close, then unzipped the inner lining of my jacket. A flash of silver hair told me I was already out of time. Kieran approached with equal parts grace and menace. If anything, he looked bigger, though there was something behind his eyes. Wariness? Disbelief? No matter.

He sat, silver hair catching the light, and leaned forward.

"Zion was all worked up about you."

"Don't be unmannered," I snapped. "Elbows off the table."

Amused, he did as I said, moving his arms under the table. "A final meal before I take you in? I'll even pay. He's expended a lot of resources to capture you. What's one more bill?" His smile dropped. "Britt wants payback even more than I do."

I heard it as it happened. Swarmbots I'd hidden in my jacket had crawled along the underside of the tabletop. They dropped down as a group and landed on Kieran's wrists.

He stood so fast his chair fell to the floor.

A set of handcuffs were wrapped around his wrists. Swarmbots nearly covered the magnetically-joined cuffs as they locked them, then dropped to the ground.

He glared at me, his face a mixture of astonishment and irritation, then looked at the floor and stomped on two of the 'bots. The others clicked in alarm as they scrambled back.

"Stop," I said. "Feel that jab? Sit down."

The needle from the cuff would've jabbed deep.

His expression morphed into fury.

I kept my voice level. "You don't sit, you'll be injected with venom from the Australian brown snake, which is strong enough to kill a thousand men. Think your enhancements can overcome that?"

Out of the corner of my eye, I spotted the tiny vial drop from the cuff. I hoped the swarmbots caught it.

Kieran sat. "What do you want?"

"Do you log in every time you access The Agency's network? Or is the access constant?"

He stared at me. "My access is constant, but it's tuned to my specific brainwave patterns, with a DNA confirmation every time it initiates. If anyone tries to remove my implant like that trick you pulled, the new one self-destructs, the blast strong enough to take out my attacker."

"Having explosives in your head doesn't bother you?"

"It protects The Agency."

"What you described isn't normal—and what you do isn't 'just.' Have you visited any of the towns Zion destroyed? Seen how many have been murdered?"

Kieran shifted uncomfortably.

Softly, I added, "Do you know how many kids have been killed? You've become what you despise: a terrorist."

I felt the slightest pressure along the side of my foot.

"Is this why you contacted me?"

Careful not to move, I recalled what Mina had said. "This isn't who you wanted to be."

"You're a shrink now?"

"Zion has brainwashed you. You can't even think for yourself."

Kieran grew quiet and darted his eyes past me. "He made Britt replace her whole leg. Said her injury made her weak," he murmured. "He's put a device in her head. If I don't deliver you, he'll end her."

"We can hide both of you. I can't remove your implants but can disable them, cut the strings he uses —"

"That's enough," Zion nearly yelled as he approached, leading Britt and two other Agents. She walked normal, but a flash of metal drew my gaze. Her right foot was metal now, which meant her entire leg was, the lack of skin covering an additional punishment.

I bolted for the rear exit.

Someone shouted as I ran — and Wraith emerged from the kitchen to step into my path. I tried to barrel past him, but he grabbed me and dragged me back to the table.

As Britt reached for Kieran's handcuffs, Zion punched me in the stomach, the blow so strong I couldn't breathe. "Once again, you're mine."

CHAPTER TWENTY-NINE

Britt hauled me down a nondescript hallway, away from the bustle of the office suite I'd been taken to, her gait uneven, her grip on my neck hard.

She forced me into a former storage room that contained a mat in a corner and dried blood on the concrete floor. "Raven made me lose a limb. I plan to return the favor."

I expected her to let go of me. Instead, she said, "Scan him."

Wraith entered with a multi-wave scanner. He ran the device over my chest, arms, and legs. "Clean."

He handed her the scanner as she let go, then punched me in the face.

I fell back into Britt, and she shoved me away.

Wraith swung again, aiming for my jaw. I jerked back but felt metal gouge into my gum as the blow drove me to the ground. I tasted blood.

Britt raised her metal leg to stomp on me when Zion entered the room. "Where the hell have you been?"

As Britt backed off, I sat up. "Hiding from someone I once considered a friend."

"You somehow evaded our sensors, but we're locked onto you now. No more escapes for you," he said. "Where's your team?"

"We split up."

"That's a lie. I would've taken you straight to D.C., but you wouldn't have strayed far from your kids. Your team's close."

"Pry it out of me—though you'll waste your time."

"Oh, I'm going to split you open, find out their location and all the nasty things you've been doing. And we'll figure out what Talia did to our system. Then I'll hang you in front of the world for your crimes."

"What about me helping you clean the air?"

"You lost your chance to be a hero, even an unsung one."

A younger male Agent entered the room. "We found the other clan."

Zion smiled at me. "I'm going to go watch another victory."

The four left and closed the door. The handle rattled as someone — I suspected Zion — made sure it was locked.

I'd helped him confirm Talia had altered their system. They would change how they searched for us. Dammit.

They'd taken me to an Agency regional office situated in a mid-rise office building in downtown Pittsburgh. I'd hoped to be taken somewhere with just one or two Agents, not over a dozen.

Zion, Kieran, and the others might become distracted by whatever "victory" Zion had mentioned — but they wouldn't be for long.

When Britt had forced me through the maze of offices, I'd spotted biometric readers on every office door. Though they looked like thumb scanners, that Agent in Ohio had indicated otherwise.

The door to this room, however, just had a standard lock.

I opened my mouth, reached in, and removed what looked like a caramel-colored molar from my lower jaw, though it was metal. The molar unfolded to reveal the small, transforming robot Garly gave me earlier. He hadn't been able to pull my tooth; Nataly had instead, so I'd had him connect a memory dot to the robot. I hoped I'd have a reason to use it.

I held the robot — which had tasted like metallic aspirin — to the door handle's keyhole and felt it shift. My heart rate accelerating, I twisted the robot, unlocking the door, and slipped into the hallway.

It was empty, though animated voices were ahead.

I headed forward, reached the first intersection, checked both ways to make sure they were clear, then entered the hallway to my left. Toward the voices.

I passed an empty conference room where the table had been pushed to one side. Three large objects took up most of the room, jagged, folded metal pieces similar to the riot robots. Next to them sat two robot dogs. They were powered down, but I eyed them warily.

The voices grew louder. Someone started chanting like they were watching a football game.

I approached a short corridor that curved out of sight, the voices distorted by the curve.

Moving cautiously, I followed the corridor to a large, round space forty feet in diameter. A bullpen dominated the space ahead, clusters of workstations with an open area in the center that contained a dozen vid screens. Glass-walled offices lined the walkway that surrounded the bullpen, some of which were occupied, though many weren't. Instead, those workers and others had gathered in the open area, focused on the vids.

Zion was there, as were Kieran, Britt, and Wraith. Kieran had his arm around Britt. As I watched, he whispered in her ear, and she smiled.

The offices surrounding the bullpen had desks with physical computers — which meant secured connections. But I'd be visible. If a single person spotted me, even the quickest of glances, I'd be busted.

The onlookers became more excited. The vids displayed armed Agency forces preparing for a raid of some sort. I couldn't tell where, someplace with tunnels, but I spotted Pierce onscreen.

I squatted and worked loose the piece of rubber that covered the hole in the sole of my shoe. After removing it, I used the robot to extract the tiny vial of Kieran's blood the swarmbots had hidden inside.

Holding the tiny vial, I took a breath, my heart pounding, and entered the open area.

The space felt too big, and I felt too exposed.

Forcing myself to move, I turned to my right and started along the walkway that followed the curving line of offices.

I didn't try to hide myself; instead, I walked as if I was meant to be here, though my hands shook.

The first office was occupied by a female Agent concentrating on a computer screen. I barely broke my stride before continuing on. I passed that office, then the next, the voices to my left dropping to an excited hush in anticipation of the raid that was about to commence.

I resisted looking. Instead, I approached the third office. It was empty.

As I neared the glass door, I knew I couldn't fumble this. If anything seemed awkward or unfamiliar, something in the Agents' training or electronics would warn them. Someone would glance back.

A small sensor, two inches by three inches with a depression the size of a thumb pad, had been attached to the glass wall next to the door. A tiny hole was just visible at the base of where a thumb would be placed.

I raised both hands, turned one hand upside down, and pressed my thumb against the top of the depression. As I'd anticipated, a needle jabbed out. I squeezed a drop of Kieran's blood onto the needle's tip. The needle retracted, and a second later, the door unlocked.

Fighting the urge to slip inside, I opened the door wide, walked to the desk in the utilitarian office, and sat. A small, oval-shaped device attached to the keyboard lit up. Did this one actually want a fingerprint? Then I realized. Zion would want Agents to pay a price every time. I gingerly placed my fingertips on either side of the scanner—and this time, a needle shot up from the middle of where the thumb would've been. I quickly dabbed another drop of blood, the needle retracted, and the computer illuminated. Kieran's name flashed on the screen, and the security unlocked.

Shouts of "Go, go, go," rang from the central area.

As I'd discovered in L.A., the software was similar to the system I'd created for my camera network, though it was massively more robust with so many redundancies that any modifications or sabotage I might try would take too long—and likely fail. I didn't have Talia's skills.

Instead, I pulled up the core architecture and searched for the design routes used for implant broadcasts. In less than a minute, I found it. The broadcasts issued from the former location of the Green Bank Observatory, which was situated within the National Radio Quiet Zone. The actual Observatory had shut down years ago, replaced with whatever Zion had constructed.

An eruption of cheers drew my attention. I let myself look. To not would've been suspicious.

Zion high-fived Wraith as Agents hooted and hollered at the vid screens, which showed Agency teams attacking people dressed in a range of clothing from survival gear to civilian outfits. Some were armed, but not all. The Agents made crude comments as bullets flew, some shouting with carnal excitement as the main vid showed Pierce snapping someone's arm in half.

"That's it," Zion cried as he grabbed Britt's shoulder. "We've taken out the second to last group of rebels."

"They were slippery," said an older Agent. "Just like the Colorado clan that acted like they were in *Red Dawn*. Remember that movie?"

Shouts issued from the vid screens, followed by explosions.

There was a flash of Lafontaine as gunshots rang out. This had been his clan.

Still gripping Britt's shoulder, Zion said to Kieran, "Britt outdid herself. Great intel."

Wraith's eyes flashed with data. "Sir, we've found the last group. Gave us their coordinates like the others."

"Dray's team? This is a day. After this, no one will be left to fight us. What the hell will we do then?" He let go of Britt and slapped Wraith on the back. "I'll let you do the honors."

I was devastated. Cole's efforts, our plans, were for nothing — and our group had been found. There was no one else.

The truth would die.

The future would be inescapable.

I remembered the salt mine where we'd hid, over six hundred citizens-turned-rebels filled with purpose and determination. Gone.

A vid showed a map with our loft highlighted. Cole's communications with other groups had to have been traps set by The Agency. I'd pushed Cole to recruit the fake rebels. He must've revealed our location.

I had to get to Talia, to Raven — but we needed the blueprints.

Fighting the urge to leave, I searched for blueprints of

the new Observatory complex. In seconds, schematics filled my screen—huge rooms, massive electrical wires, tubes exiting underground in all directions, and other images—but I didn't have time to analyze. I removed the robot from my pocket and pressed it against the USB-12 slot, where it shifted and then slid into the opening.

I directed the computer to download all blueprint files to the memory dot.

The information began to transfer.

Suddenly, an alarm erupted.

They'd discovered I'd escaped. Shouts erupted as Agents took off.

I hunched over as the files transferred. They would scan the building. I had seconds.

The download completed.

I removed the tiny robot. I wanted to trash the system, infect the software, something—but I had to go.

The open bullpen area had cleared out, though I could hear Agents shouting.

I left the office and continued along the curved walkway. I wasn't sure where to go; I hadn't pulled up the building's layout. I found an opening, hurried down the short hallway, and entered a longer hallway dotted with offices past a kitchenette.

As I passed the kitchenette, footsteps rose from a hallway farther ahead.

Three doors were spaced to either side of the hallway.

I quickly dabbed a drop of blood on the lock nearest me, slipped inside an empty office, and closed the door.

I tensed as the footsteps entered the hallway.

The footsteps rose, then receded.

I couldn't stay. I opened the door as two Agents disappeared around a corner behind me, exited, and dashed to the nearest intersection. An Agent darted past a farther intersection up ahead, so I took the one nearby and ran toward an exit at the far end.

"Dray," Kieran shouted behind me.

He was thirty yards away, his face red with anger — and eyes flickering with light from his feed.

I dashed to the stairwell, Kieran's footsteps growing louder, swung the door closed, and ran up the concrete steps of a narrow stairwell faster than I'd ever run before. Two flights up, I reached the top floor and flung open the door.

As I raced down the long hallway, an area extending off to the side appeared up ahead. Then a smell hit me: jet fuel.

Knowing I was risking capture, I slowed and ducked into the area. It contained a workshop space next to a stairwell that led to the roof. Metal shelves held a toolbox, small drums containing jet fuel, a fiberglass panel, and two dark matter spheres.

Whoever set this up worked on hoverbikes.

The stairwell door banged open at the end of the hallway, and Kieran sprinted toward me.

I snatched one of the spheres and ascended the stairs.

As shouts joined Kieran's footsteps, I burst through the door to the roof.

To my left, two hoverbikes sat ten yards away. To my right, Zion's gold-and-silver helicopter stood to the far side of the roof.

A man who'd been working on the helicopter spotted me. "*Hey*. No one's allowed up here."

I scurried toward the hoverbikes perched near the building's edge.

As the rooftop door crashed open behind me, I collided with one of the hoverbikes like I was back on Berkley's football field, shoving it toward the ledge.

The bike slid off the roof.

Behind me, I heard Kieran shout.

I lunged for the other bike as he thundered toward me.

The bike was more developed with gauges and an ignition switch. Thankfully no key.

As the first hoverbike hit the ground and exploded, I flipped the switch on my bike, grabbed the handlebars, and launched myself off the roof.

I gained altitude and glanced back. Kieran slid to a stop at the roof's edge, rage and frustration tightening his face.

I triggered my bike's rocket and shot off across the city.

CHAPTER THIRTY

I barely slowed as I approached our loft hideout.

I should've scouted the area, confirmed how many enemy forces had invaded, but my family was in danger.

Scanning the loft's large windows, I noted bodies lying on the wood floor while others crouched; Wraith pointed a gun at Nataly as she shielded a bloody Garly with her body, though Garly reached for her. I accelerated, raising my gun and aiming for Wraith. I fired repeatedly, then ducked as I crashed through the windows, the wire grid holding the panes giving way.

Falling among the broken wire and shards of glass, I landed to the side. My bike's fiberglass body shattered from the impact, and the frame broke apart when it slammed into the far wall.

Wraith smiled at me as I got to my feet, then shot Nataly, triggering cries of horror from Garly and others. She collapsed, dead.

"Welcome to the party," Wraith said. "Heard you escaped."

I scanned the room. Another Agent had invaded with Wraith but looked dead, Fritz and Cole appeared badly hurt, Raven held her side, Valor and Jex were tensed, and Anya was crouched near the door with Talia behind her back — though Talia had her fists up. Two machine guns were visible on the opposite side of the room but were too far away.

A broken rod from the destroyed hoverbike laid nearby.

As I scooped up the rod, Raven launched herself at Wraith. So did Valor, with Jex close behind. I ran forward, cocked my arms back, and neared as Wraith threw Raven off and raised his gun. I brought the rod down on his arm the instant before he fired, which made him miss.

He tried to grab the rod, but Valor hit him with more force than he'd anticipated. Jex tackled low a split-second later, nailing Wraith's knees and flipping him backward.

He landed on the shattered-glass-covered floor.

"Dray," Anya called and slid a scalpel toward me.

I scooped it up, flipped it to bring the blade end forward, and twisted my body. Valor, who had pulled Wraith's arms behind his back, wrenched him toward me as I brought the scalpel around. I drove it into his chest, burying it inches deep. Twisted it. "For Nataly," I said, and shoved the blade up his chest.

Valor let the Agent slump to the ground.

Garly was suddenly beside me. He dropped beside Wraith and bellowed as he pounded the scalpel deeper into his chest with a clenched fist.

Wraith spasmed, then died.

Garly hit the scalpel again. He raised his fist a third time.

I caught his fist, turned him to me, and wrapped my arms around him.

His body hitched as he began to cry.

I'd told Nataly about the implants. I'd been the reason she'd joined.

I pulled away after a few moments, aware more Agents would come, and Talia shoved at my chest. "Don't ghost me again. I don't care why. *Promise.*"

I wiped her tears. "I promise."

The group was reeling. Fritz bled from a head injury, Cole had been shot in the upper chest, everyone had been wounded — even Talia, who'd tried to fight — and the place had been wrecked.

They were also crushed they'd been beaten, and Nataly killed.

As Anya tended to Fritz and Cole, I made sure Raven's injury wasn't serious, pressed my forehead against hers, then briefly checked the place. Garly had been in the process of creating the glowing rope when Wraith attacked, others had been eating, and at least two people had been training, as sparring pads laid discarded in one of the bedrooms.

The swarmbot-making machines continued to run.

I shielded my implant, knowing it was a liability again, and returned to the others. Before I could warn them we needed to leave, the sound of multiple cars arriving rose from the street below. In the distance, sirens wailed.

"Agency forces," I said.

"Told you riggin' these was a good idea," Jex said to Cole. He limped over to a set of switches he'd screwed into the wall near the entrance. "Disruptors in each stairwell," he told me. "It'll buy us a few minutes."

While Anya helped Cole and Fritz to the elevator, the rest of the group hurried. Valor and Raven wheeled sections of Garly's lab into the service elevator while others grabbed weapons, bedding, and supplies. In less than three minutes, we had everything.

Jex triggered the disruptors, catching our enemy before they could reach us.

"What about Nataly?" Anya asked me.

"We can't. Garly, I wish we could."

Talia tried to pull him into the elevator with us, but he resisted. "I'll take her on the hoverbike." His voice was raw.

"It shattered when I crashed through the window."

"The Agents'. It's how they surprised us. They landed on the roof."

He scooped up Nataly's body and turned away.

* * *

Zion was arrested Sophomore year.

He'd developed a software that recast his favorite online game into a three-dimensional virtual reality when he was still in high school. His father prevented him from distributing the software, however, instead adopting it for business purposes and selling it to corporations across the globe.

Zion didn't receive a dime.

Sophmore year at UC-Berkley, he broke into his father's network, made a copy of his software, and modified it for a project. Even though it was his code, his father reported it stolen.

He languished in jail for two days before Nikolai, Tevin, Brocco, and I bailed him out.

His father later dropped the charges, but they never talked again.

He'd been a harsh, critical man. Zion looked almost exactly like him, so from what Zion admitted one night drunk on Grey Goose and Red Bull, his father had watched him to an uncomfortable degree to see when his "greatness" would kick in.

Apparently, it never did.

After the arrest, Zion changed in ways I could see and ways I couldn't. We all became like brothers, and though he was quick to anger and didn't always listen, we were the approval and validation he craved. Yet he never escaped his father's influence. He took the man's desire to manipulate people and decided to control them.

He'd even tried with us, risking our company for his factory project by executing agreements without approval or authority. We vetoed his plans and rolled back the agreements at considerable expense. That had led to the end of the Gang of Five. The end of our brotherhood.

* * *

I led Talia and Raven to the dark cabin, our group silently following. It was the off season, but the campground wasn't deserted.

We had to be careful. We were in no condition to fend off another attack.

I split our team between the cabin and one next door. No one complained. We all mourned.

During the trip here, they'd told me about the invasion. After the injury he'd sustained at the hospital, I had assumed Garly would've been hesitant to fight again. Yet he'd led the charge that killed the first Agent. Wraith tried to kill Garly in retaliation, but Nataly had shielded him.

"What if Garly can't find us?" Talia asked after we entered the cobwebbed cabin. We'd traveled nearly a hundred miles from Pittsburgh.

"I told him about this place," Valor said. "I stayed here after my eye surgery, back when we fled South Carolina."

Grief colored our voices.

Jex took charge of setting up our defenses. He became fanatical about it, with three remote-control gun sites and two drones that served as lookouts.

Raven fumed as he worked, having learned that he, Cole,

Nataly, and Garly had known of my plan yet none stopped me —
or told her. She probably felt betrayed, still not accepting that I
didn't have to answer to her.

As everyone else got settled, I finally let Anya tend to my
injuries. She removed the bits of glass and disinfected the cuts.
"I used the last of our nanobots on Fritz and Cole," she said as
she wrapped a protective band around my arm. "This will take
longer, but you'll heal. Serves you right for stealing my pliers."

I knew she was mad that I'd endangered myself.

I became aware of Talia sitting nearby. I worried how this
would scar her. "Energy level?"

Talia checked. "Thirty-seven."

"How are you mentally?"

She shrugged.

I replaced her battery, then asked Jex to gather the team.
When everyone arrived, I told them, "I need to show you what I
found."

I placed a hologram protector in the middle of the room,
plugged in the memory dot, and brought up the Observatory
plans.

A three-dimensional rendering of our target appeared
before us.

The Observatory's property had been transformed into
a nine-story complex nestled into a valley surrounded on three
sides by mountains, with more than half of the complex buried
underground.

Jex swore under his breath. "Sure we can't just hack the
place? It's enormous."

"The architecture is confusing," Raven said, her earlier
anger still sharp.

Huge shafts jutted into the ground in six different locations,
what I realized were heat sinks for the dozens of datatanks
they would've installed — which would've necessitated battery
storages to avoid any loss of power. Broadcast arrays and piping
were everywhere. The more I looked, the more it seemed like
a maze with shafts, conduits, and hallways snaking throughout
the structure.

A wide stairwell in the middle of the building plunged from the roof to the bottom floor.

I traced the stairwell with my finger. "I wonder if this was a central shaft they used when they'd built the place. The builders probably dug it first, then built outward as they removed portions of bedrock."

"Some rooms have labels: labs, conference arena, offices, generator rooms, and storage areas, but a lot aren't, and they don't make any sense," Raven said.

I pointed to an immense room six floors down, the room distinct as it was almost the height of two floors. "This doesn't have any support beams." Instead, angled braces distributed the weight of the upper floors to the exterior walls on three sides, which had been carved into the mountainsides.

"Why's it like that?" Jex asked.

"They didn't want any obstructions for some reason." The room's ceiling had wide, round openings in a grid-like pattern, each opening ten feet in diameter.

The bottom fourth of the room's outer walls, under the braces, appeared pockmarked.

Raven stepped even closer. "They must've added a subfloor of some sort. Look at the outlets. They're over five feet above the floor."

"We won't know until we get there."

"Are the plans incomplete?" Anya asked.

"They don't show everything." I brought up other plans, including one of the electrical layout. "The main thing missing is the equipment. Zion would've installed massive computing banks, datatanks, batteries, miles of wiring, and other things— including defenses."

I flipped back to the main layout and focused on the floors aboveground. There were only four, and only the top two had windows.

There was a single vehicle entrance with a reinforced gate, guard shack, and buried plates that could be raised to block entry.

Cole must have had the same thought I did. "We can't force our way inside," he said, his right arm in a sling, lucky the gunshot hadn't taken vital organs.

Fritz took a shaky step, his head draped in medwraps. "How about walking? To sneak inside? Would that work?"

The grounds appeared relatively benign, with gently-sloping hills that led to the facility, though someone walking to the nexus would be confronted with a ten-foot-high, solid wall, the outer wall of the building's wide third floor, the floors below it underground. But I doubted we could even reach the wall. When I zoomed in on the image, what looked like crazy random spider legs spread out from the complex in varying lengths, the longest stretching to the very edge of the property.

Jex leaned forward. "Those are conduit piping."

"Cameras," Cole said. "Of course they'd be hardwired. See any gaps in coverage?"

"Maybe one, but that'd be tight. We'd have'ta space it out enough we don't trip other sensors, which means we could get picked off one by one."

"They'd have motion sensor, sound, infrared, you name it," I said.

Cole looked at Jex. "How would you plan your attack?"

"We're better off not." He glanced around, then said, "I'd start by maskin' the sensors."

"How long would that take?"

Jex fell quiet.

I turned off the hologram. "There's a second issue. Agents have captured or killed every other rebel group. There's no one else. If we fail, the truth dies with us."

Raven gave me a confused look. "What about the teams Cole messaged? The attacks we've heard about in the news?"

"Lies created to capture us. It's how Wraith found the loft."

Cole looked like I'd sucker-punched him. "The Agency has been hunting everyone who survived the nodes."

I nodded. "We're the last ones. If we attack this place, it will just be us."

Fritz moaned in grief and loss. The others looked stunned.

Nine. Nine of us against The Agency.

* * *

Cole, Jex, and Valor took the RV to get rid of it.

Others went off on their own, cleaning up, resting, mostly contemplating what I'd said.

Cole grabbed my shoulder before he'd left. "Good job," he'd said, nodding to the hologram.

His compliment evoked an unwanted memory. A month before I'd left for UC-Berkley, I sought out my high school football coach and told him about my scholarship. I'd expected him to be proud. I was only the school's second running back to have won one. But he just turned away. "Your brains will get you farther."

I didn't have anyone to talk to about the sting of his disappointment. With Mom gone, I didn't have anyone.

I checked on my team. They were grieving and shellshocked, conflicted and uncertain. Garly hadn't returned, which added to the tension.

"Where are the 3D drones?" Anya asked. "Someone needs to check."

Nataly's pad was somewhere. It should still be hooked in.

Before I could search, Raven pulled me aside. "Ever since the Facility, I've had this fear that you'll die, and it'll be my fault. I know it's irrational, but I can't shake it."

"Do you want me to quit?"

"No. We need to finish this—but you can lead while staying safe. And no more lone-gunman stuff."

"We should stop. Leave the country."

"What about those who need us? Besides, you think Zion will stop hunting us?"

"There has to be somewhere we could hide." I hesitated. Forced the words out. "I feel I keep failing."

"After you tricked your way into The Agency's office and escaped with the plans?"

I ignored her question. "I don't know if Garly will fight, or Anya." With Talia mostly healed, even with our various injuries, Anya didn't have a reason to stay. Others did, but their reasons might not be enough to continue on. "I'm trying to be smart about all this."

"Thinking rationally? You need to stop that."

Three vehicles pulled up: a black Yukon, a gray Charger, and a faded-orange VW bus. Replacements for the RV.

I had our group assemble, though I avoided looking at my daughters. "We've confirmed the location of our goal, but there are still unknowns—and our task is extremely difficult. The farther east we go, the fewer places we'll have to hide. You need to decide if you're in. No hard feelings if—"

"I'm in," Talia said.

Cole smiled at her like a proud teacher, though his expression turned serious when he looked at me. "I've needed to atone for my mistakes. I'm not convinced about your plan, but you have my allegiance."

"I'm in," Jex said. "You're right about the surveillance. The last section of the country is gettin' software upgrades startin' next week. We do this, we gotta hustle."

Valor and Fritz nodded. They were in. "It's the right path," Valor added.

"We're not letting you take all the glory," Raven joked, which made Cole smirk.

"Make sure to keep your implants covered at all times. Now that we have a plan, we don't want Zion reading our thoughts. A single download could end us." I looked at Anya as she slipped her hand into mine. "Are you staying?"

"Why else would I have taken up sharpshooting?"

My relief was short-lived as a hoverbike landed outside.

Garly climbed off, eyes red, clothes coated in dirt. As I'd suspected, he'd buried his love.

Talia led him inside, where we consoled him. After, he looked at me. "Did you get what you trickstered for?"

I nodded.

"I didn't like your plan. Shouldn't have poked."

His words were deserved. I'd risked them—and was asking more.

"This is our chance," I said. I activated the hologram to reveal the blueprints. I then revealed we were the last rebels. "We do this, it's just us."

Cupping his ribcage, which he'd probably aggravated, Garly stared at the schematics, the blue light magnifying his paleness, his goatee in stark contrast.

"It's OK to walk away," I said.

He looked at the others, then me. "Nataly swooned for you. Swooned for the cause. And for me. I want to stomp every last silver-haired roach. We need to obliterate them."

As Jex gripped Garly's shoulder, Raven gave him a sad smile. "For Nataly," she said.

He made a noise, part sigh, part sob. "For Nataly."

CHAPTER THIRTY-ONE

Two days and seventy miles later, I sprayed Jex with the organic concoction we'd made, making sure to cover every inch of exposed skin.

"Close your mouth and eyes," I warned. I sprayed his face.

"Feels like I'm coated in plastic wrap."

"Good." The spray would hold his dead skin and hair in place. He'd leave little to any DNA. Yet it was still a risk.

The tiny robots crawled over his face and formed into the appearance of a tired-looking, middle-management-type male.

He planned to catch the new bullet train to Manhattan, the train's lines recently extended to encompass Pittsburgh — and was slated to link to Chicago if funding didn't run out.

"You won't stay in the city long, right?" I asked.

"Nope, two stops, the tunnel, then south." While Wall Street was the stock market's epicenter, all stock trades used lines that ran from Wall Street to New Jersey — which ran through the Holland Tunnel before splitting off in a dozen directions. The killswitch he'd install would cut off all trading when activated. As with our other killswitches, we didn't want permanent damage, just temporary blockage until we reclaimed the country. "Since there's a risk I'll be spotted, my 'switch has a surprise. Anyone tampers with it, it'll detonate, severin' the lines."

"You got enough cash for motels?"

"Yep."

As he started off, Raven appeared with a pack of her own.

"Where are you going?" I asked.

"To search for more towns." She took the spray bottle to coat her face.

"Babe, now's not the time," Jex said.

I agreed. "Your obsession has to wait."

"I want to protect people." She gave a cocky smile. "This goes against what you want, so Zion won't expect me to do it."

My frustration rose. "We have work to do."

"Saving people isn't part of that? Think of their lives and the lives of their children. We could be losing teachers, scientists, leaders that future generations will need. If I don't help them, no one will. I'll install the killswitches, but I'm doing this first. Otherwise, I'll never forgive myself. Our efforts will be hollow if we don't protect those we can." She gestured over her shoulder to where Anya sat, concentrating on a pad. "Don't forget why we're fighting."

She stepped out into the morning light, and Jex followed. Talia darted past me, hugged Raven hard, then hurried back.

I wanted to stop Raven but couldn't argue her actions risked her any less than mine did.

Besides, she was an adult.

An infuriating one.

We had relocated to a facility that had once housed a vocational school. It offered zero comforts, minimal heat, and lots of graffiti, but it had the space and power Garly required to expand his lab. Supply runs to three different stores had restocked him.

I joined Cole, Fritz, and Valor at the hologram.

"Not sure, sir," Fritz responded to Cole, scratching at one of his remaining bandages as the blueprints rotated before them. "It's so formidable."

Cole told me, "We're not seeing a way in—and even if we do, we won't win with so few fighters."

"Figure something out."

As he shook his head, Valor said, "Before he left, Jex checked his drones. Agents trashed the loft. Garly's place, too."

My fear for my daughters—especially with Raven off to God knew where—welled up, but I forced it back. Besides, with Nataly gone, we needed Talia.

I turned off the hologram. "Where are we with our chaos?"

Valor retrieved her pad. "We have the police network addressed—I'm assuming you can ravage your old system—traffic control software, the early warning systems, and all but one of the communications networks."

"Why not all of them?" Cole asked as Anya joined us.

Even with her fake eye, Valor's glare was impressive. "I'm getting to it." She swiped up on her pad. "The last one is tricky as they were too cheap to upgrade their security system. Instead, they layered three older security systems. Talia thinks she can break them, but she hasn't yet. Did you know she swears? A lot. Those words should not be coming out of that girl's mouth."

"I'll talk to her. What else?" I asked.

She went through the rest of the list. As we were relying on a child for our hacking—brilliant, skilled, apparently swearing, but still a child—we needed to help as much as possible, which included onsite software installs along with the killswitches.

But we were making headway.

"The electrical grids will be the most important," Cole said.

"And the hardest," Fritz agreed.

"The more systems we target, the better," I said. "Valor, focus on the grids. There are four in particular we have to take out. The one in northern Virginia will be the most heavily guarded, but it powers virtually all of D.C."

"Got 'em."

"Raven was supposed to focus on the currency markets."

"Jex gave her three killswitches, but Garly was still assembling the others when she left."

"I'll do it," Anya said. "Just tell me where to go."

I gave her the addresses. "Both of you, make sure each switch's remote is synched before you move on. You'll also need to install some software. Two of the electrical grids aren't controlled remotely, and Anya, your targets aren't, either. I have software that'll disable their redundancy backups." I paused. "This won't be easy. We need to take down multiple systems, each with different firewalls, security systems, software designs, and physical barriers. We'll need to coordinate our attack when we launch our chaos."

The group prepared to leave. We had other aspects to resolve, but there weren't enough of us.

Cole and Fritz left first. They carried a crate of weapons, Cole shouldering the weight on his end with his good arm, as they headed out. "We're meeting the arms dealer," he explained when he saw my confusion. "We're swapping these for remote devices and explosives. Four dozen machine guns don't help when there aren't enough fighters to use them."

"Wait, how's he operating if we're the only rebels left?"

"The rebellion was a small part of his volume. He mostly exports, though he also sells to gangs across across the country."

"You trust him?" When Cole nodded, I said, "We'll need more than explosives."

"I'll see what he has."

"Be careful. The 3D drones are close. They've reached Pennsylvania."

After they left, I prepared a bag for Valor, checking every killswitch.

She approached — and I was surprised to see her wearing her eyepatch again. "Couldn't stand the fake eye. The mask is bad enough," she said.

"Here," I said, handing her the bag.

"I should check the perimeter first. I know we created false trails on our way here, but The Agency could still find us."

"I'll handle it."

She triggered the robots, which covered her face to turn her into an older-looking Black woman.

After she left, I started for Garly's lab, but Anya pulled me into an empty room. "Before I go, Talia wants us to have some time alone."

"She said that?"

"She said you're happier when we do."

An ear-splitting sound suddenly assaulted us. Garly's sound machine. It would be a game-changer, crippling Agents due to the numerous implants in their skulls. But his timing sucked.

Covering our ears, we stumbled out of the room — and the sound ended.

Garly was visible in his lab down the hall, pacing and ranting. Talia, who'd taken to hanging out with him while she hacked targets, gave us an expression that this wasn't his first outburst.

She said something that calmed him. Yet I knew he felt the pressure. The injuries he'd sustained during her surgery slowed him. As did his grief.

"Watch her," Anya said. "She's so focused on helping him through Nataly's death, she's not dealing with her own emotions."

* * *

Hours later, I got the call.

The call didn't interrupt my work. The swarmbots did.

As I fine-tuned the foam wall expanders' release mechanism, a body formed before me, startling me. The body wasn't real, though. Swarmbots created it. Hundreds climbed on top of each other, forming legs, torso, arms, and head; as I watched, it raised an arm and waved at me.

They'd mimicked my body's size and shape.

I waved back, and they collapsed to settle at my feet, though a small group climbed onto the table to see what I was doing.

They'd modified themselves beyond the tiny speakers they'd installed. They were still lightweight but had added thin, metal plating for added protection. And their legs had been reshaped. They still ended in sharp points but now locked together when they created a form.

One of Garly's monitors chimed.

He lifted his head from his sound machine, hair sticking to his forehead, and checked the screen. "Zion has declared Raven and Talia are terrorists. Claims they're 'threats to society'."

"I'm putting that on a t-shirt with a picture of me doing this." Talia scrunched her face.

I didn't smile. Raven was out there alone.

Garly gave a chuckle, but his eyes remained sad.

I'd tried to comfort him, but Talia was better at that stuff, so I'd helped expand our available tech. We now had the rope device—with a Garly enhancement I hadn't considered—ear protectors for the sound machine, larger hand shields, and other items. I'd also fashioned the negation system for the dark matter sphere I'd stolen, the tiny force generators wrapped around the sphere.

Talia had encouraged him to work on the oscillating arrays for his supposed ice machine. He'd made progress, though the machine was still just a bunch of parts.

The call I hadn't expected went to my burner phone.

"I spotted Zion's ugly-ass helicopter," Jex said when I answered. "It landed on a skyscraper right on the east side of Central Park. I was heading to Midtown to rig up a data center when I saw it."

I searched online. Two residential buildings by the park had helicopter pads. He confirmed it was the one that also had balconies, a newer, high-end condominium tower. The multi-level penthouse, which offered three balconies, had been featured online, though the pictures didn't reveal anything about the owner.

I hacked into New York's property database, but the penthouse was owned by a private company, which was owned by another company with blank owner information. The state required it, yet none was listed.

It had to be Zion.

I retrieved the dark matter sphere. "I need the rope," I told Garly as I extracted a Glock, three clips, and a combat knife from a weapons crate.

"Why?"

"We found Zion's home."

"So you'll what, kidnap him? Kill him? I want him to fry for his crimes, but this is bigger than one dude. He's crafted a national network, wields Agents—"

"I take him out, it'll create a power vacuum. While D.C. fights over his office, we'll launch everything we have, bury them in problems, then invade the Observatory. End this for real."

My eyes sought Talia's. I also owed Zion for experimenting on her.

The lines of Garly's face became pronounced. "I'm coming with you."

CHAPTER THIRTY-TWO

I descended through the clouds on the hoverbike with Garly clinging to my back.

The clouds ended to reveal Manhattan stretched out below. High-rises reached for us while the streets churned with life, the millions unaware of the lies they'd accepted.

Zion's helicopter was parked on our target's roof, on a helicopter pad that dominated a corner of the rooftop.

His penthouse would have multiple defenses. I couldn't enter in a normal way.

I stopped a hundred yards above the penthouse, though the wind hammered us, pushing us back. I gave the engines a short boost, which propelled us past the high-rise. The street was sickeningly far below. "Go back to Talia," I yelled over the wind. We'd left her alone, which was dangerous. "I'll get back some other way."

I swung my leg over the side and leapt.

Gravity snatched me the moment I left the bike's influence.

As I plummeted, I triggered the small force generators wrapped around the dark matter sphere. The sphere negated gravity's pull—but made me helpless to the wind, which battered me as I fell.

The city grew closer.

At the last second, the wind shoved me back far enough that Zion's rooftop appeared under me. I disabled the sphere, dropped the last two feet, and stumbled onto the sealed surface.

Trying to shake my anxiety from the fall, I jogged to a spot far from the helicopter, removed what looked like a metal rope, and laid it on the roof in a circle. As soon as the two ends met, the device turned bright orange. The circle began to burn through the layers of sealant, steel, insulation, and ceiling drywall, creating an entrance as it descended—and multiple lasers, all aimed inward, sliced the rooftop into small pieces.

In seconds, the rope completed its boring and winked out

as it fell to the floor inside the building.

Using the sphere, I descended through the hole and landed inside an immense walk-in closet.

I slipped my sphere into my pack, removed my gun, picked up the rope—which was almost hot, though it was cooling—and brushed off bits of charred rooftop. I hooked the rope's end so it retained its circular shape, though I left a short portion sticking out to use as a handle. With the flick of my thumb, the handle would remain cool if I reactivated the rope.

I opened the closet's door. As I suspected, I was in the master bedroom suite. A hallway led to a bathroom larger than the RV in one direction. The other led to the bedroom, floor-to-ceiling windows revealing a sweeping view of the city along one wall, a massive bed with sleek furniture occupying another. A door led to one of the unit's balconies.

Remembering the layout I'd found online, I left the bedroom. The place was stunning, with servant's quarters, two full kitchens, weight room, balcony overlooking a two-story ballroom, and more space than any one man needed.

It smelled faintly of expensive aftershave and used sweat socks.

His decorations were strikingly different than the staged pictures. Many rooms had little furniture and nothing on the walls. Descending the stairs to the second level, though, the main areas were like the master bedroom: impressively laid out with sleek furniture and beautiful artwork, along with every home electronic available, including four multi-speaker sound systems. The artwork—paintings, photographs, and sculptures—was museum quality but didn't reflect any theme as far as I could tell; they sometimes went with the décor but sometimes not.

None of the photographs revealed his life.

My muscles tightened as I descended to the penthouse's first floor. There'd be guards by the entrance, if nothing else. I'd expected roaming drones or guards and other security.

Nothing.

It wasn't right.

A thin woman in a maid's outfit walked across the hallway

farther ahead near the large foyer. Even that didn't seem right.

Gripping the rope-like device, I scanned the hallway, which stretched from the far end of the penthouse to the front entrance. The penthouse was quiet.

I didn't trust it.

I stepped down the hallway away from the maid. If Zion was here, I knew where I'd find him.

The door at the end was closed. I pulled my gun, turned the knob, and entered the room, but nothing attacked.

I had breached his private office.

Built-in bookcases lining the back wall rose up behind an ornate wooden desk, more traditional than the rest of the house. Windows and the second balcony took up the wall to my left, while more bookshelves, a side door, and a dark walnut wet bar were to my right. A twenty-foot by twenty-foot rug laid before the desk. A leather couch occupied the wall behind me, beneath an oil painting of dogs chasing a fox across green fields.

The room contrasted with the rest of the penthouse because it wasn't Zion. It was his father. I'd visited Zion's childhood home once, a castle-like mansion with thick stone walls that kept everyone out. This office echoed his father's.

Maybe Zion had created it to seek a sense of comfort. His mother had lived a separate life, barely around, so his father's office could've been a place of solace. Then I noticed a torn portrait near the side door. The portrait's background was eerily similar to his father's portrait, though the tear covered the man's face.

I approached the bookshelves behind his desk. They contained hundreds of volumes, along with models of Zion's earliest ideas — and a photograph of the house he and I had rented at Berkley, the one he'd trashed in a fit of anger.

A metallic scrape came from behind me.

A robotic dog, the same model that had killed Monroe, stood in the doorway I'd used.

It stepped into the room and opened its mouth to reveal its razor teeth.

I aimed my gun, my other hand down by my side, gripping

the rope. I activated it, the heat almost immediately enveloping my arm.

I warily stepped out from behind the desk as it watched me, its gaze dropping to my legs—or, more accurately, the glowing rope. I kept the device behind me and advanced toward the robot. Every muscle was tense. If it jumped, I'd have almost no time to react.

Its eyes brightened.

I moved before it did, bringing my rope up and making a slashing motion as I threw myself to the left. At virtually the same time, it lunged. It tried to change course midair but couldn't; I felt a tug on the rope as I fell, the rope landing dangerously close to my leg. I jerked back, lifting the rope off the floor, and through the hanging noose, saw the robot sliced in half, its two halves glowing where it had been cut.

The two halves struck the desk, then fell to the floor.

As I laid on the carpet, the robot's upper half crawled toward me.

I brought the rope down on the creature, the metal burning at its head. It pulled back, then lunged again, its face partially damaged. I slapped at it again and again until both of its eyes were destroyed, its muzzle twisted. I then scrambled to my feet and hooked the rope around its neck. One heave and the head went flying into the dog painting.

Its torso fell forward, its neck components glowing.

The carpet smoldered in spots from where the rope had touched it.

I turned off the device, which had become nearly too hot to hold, and stomped out the tiny fires.

I heard something from the adjoining room.

I adjusted the pack on my back, then opened the side door and raised my gun.

The door led into the main living room which stretched the length of the building, floor-to-ceiling windows filling three sides with sweeping views to the west and south. The third balcony jutted from the long length of windows, though it was partly obscured by curtains on the near end that moved in the breeze from the open door behind them.

Artwork caught my attention first: a Franz West textured sculpture trapped behind glass, paintings by Lichtenstein and Warhol, an Octobong Nkanga segmented pit, and other sculptures.

Then I saw Zion among the artwork and couches and massive teleprojector. He sat on an oversized ottoman, seemingly meditating, legs crossed, eyes closed, hands on his knees.

I angled toward him and watched for a reaction. I noted a slight curvature to his body — a telltale sign. He was a hologram.

A body suddenly slammed into me from behind. A fist crashed down on my arm, knocking my gun away.

I caught my balance, shoved back, and turned. Zion stumbled backward from my shove, and I lunged. I struck him repeatedly, his hologram still visible in the corner of my eye.

He hit me in the stomach and then the face, which made me lose my rope device. As pain bloomed, I stepped back, then lunged forward and pile-drove him into a spun-glass sculpture which collapsed beneath him. I pounded at him, slamming into the same spot in his ribs to try to break them. He twisted and threw me so hard I stumbled back six feet, though I remained upright. I set my feet, pulled out my combat knife—

And Kieran grabbed my wrist.

He wrenched the knife from my hand, then shoved me into an armchair.

They knew I would find Zion's home. He'd probably used the damn helicopter as a beacon. And I'd fallen for it.

Predictable.

Zion smiled. "Always have a backup, like you taught me."

I told Kieran, "He would've let you die. If I'd injected you with that venom, he wouldn't have saved you."

Zion got to his feet. "It was a bluff." He gingerly touched the spot where I'd punched him. "Where's Talia? Recovering well?"

"Let me guess. I surrender, and you'll let her and Raven live."

"We're past threats." He motioned toward one of the

sculptures, steel and bronze curving in a way that was like emotion made real, hope and defiance reaching for the same goal. "See this? It's one of Valor's pieces. I got it to understand one of my enemies. I already understand you."

I forced myself out of the chair. "Then you know I've been torn between my kids and this fight. Not anymore."

"You'll fail. I won't kill Raven or Talia, though. They'll need reeducation. You warped them into rebelling against their homeland. But I won't hurt them. They'll live happy, *readjusted* lives."

"I won't let you touch them."

Zion waved Kieran away as if he were an overbearing butler.

As the Agent moved to a spot on the far side of the room, Zion admitted, "I worried you would somehow stop us from being able to read people's thoughts."

"So you can retain power."

"Dammit Dray, wake up. You could help me. Instead, you want to trigger anarchy. Do you realize how many people would get hurt?"

He took a calming breath. "The previous President brought me in to advise him. He wanted to recruit Nikolai to run the Department of Energy, to prepare the country for a future without oil. I convinced him we needed to mask the problem first. Every world leader feared their people would discover how royally screwed we all were — still are. We only have a year of oil left. I took over the NSA, secretly coordinated with other leaders to stretch the remaining supply and hid the results. Over time, they became dependent on me."

I could tell he felt he'd exceeded his father's "greatness." He had me to thank for it, to a degree. He'd known how my surveillance network overlapped information. He'd used the excuse of hiding D.C.'s sins to create a network of his own that had led to his encompassing, inescapable control.

I backed away, wanting to distance myself. "You could've made the world better."

"What would you have done? Let everyone know how

screwed we all are? Or give them peace while you tried to find a solution?"

"I wouldn't have taken over."

"Even if Congress wouldn't fix what they let happen?" When I didn't answer, he sighed. "I saved the world from imploding."

"The end justifies anything, doesn't it?"

"There are over ten billion people, and they all drain resources. Our planet can't support so many, even with the strides we've made to expand production and improve efficiencies. The bill's coming due, Dray. You're not a scientist, but you get it."

"The towns. You're killing everyone to reduce the population. You've slaughtered how many? Thousands?"

He walked toward the side window. "What should I do? Let everyone starve? Start a world war? That might slaughter millions but risked nuclear winter. Taking out population centers in weaker countries would also lead to war. My way makes the U.S. stronger."

I was so stunned I could barely think. I recalled the towns' lower-class homes. He would've justified his actions by targeting those who contributed the least to the economy.

I looked at Kieran, who stood off to my left. "And you do his dirty work for him."

"We follow orders, as we're trained to do."

"You told me Agents' kids are being enhanced. They'll become his puppets, too. You want that?"

There was a metallic snap as a gun was cocked—and Garly appeared in the doorway from the balcony. He'd used the curtains to hide his approach, the hoverbike a dozen feet past him.

He aimed his gun at Zion. Behind him, a long-range drone appeared on the balcony. I didn't know what it meant, but I knew what Kieran heading for Garly meant. I ran forward, scooped up the rope device I'd dropped while fighting Zion, and activated it.

"Kieran," I yelled.

I threw the rope as he strode toward Garly.

Kieran raised his left arm to block it—and the rope wrapped

around his entire arm, the end slapping into his shoulder.

He howled in pain and bent over as the glowing-orange device ignited his shirt and burned into him. Bending over, he struggled to pull off the rope, searing his fingers as he tore it from his flesh.

He ripped the front portion away, and the edge of the device grazed the carpet as it dangled from his arm. Fire bloomed.

I dashed forward as the fire spread and drove Garly out onto the balcony.

As Zion yelled behind us, we scrambled toward the hoverbike.

I looked back when we reached it. Kieran had untangled the glowing rope—half his shirt turned to ash to reveal third-degree burns, his arm and shoulder reddish-black—and stumbled out onto the balcony, his good arm cocked back.

I fired twice, both bullets striking his chest.

He faltered, his face already twisted in pain, then cocked his arm again.

Garly pulled me onto the hoverbike and launched us off the balcony, the rope Kieran threw just missing us.

* * *

Garly was still trembling when we returned to the shuttered school.

Talia rushed out of the building and punched me. "What did I blat about leaving me? You and Raven don't *listen*."

"It would've been too dangerous—"

"I could've been the secret sauce. I froze the elevators remotely so the shiny goons couldn't reach you."

She must've commandeered the drone I'd spotted to track us. I squatted before her. "You shut them down? Wait, where's Raven? Is she back?"

"No one is." Her eyes grew big. "The penthouse was a trap."

Realization hit me. "When I brought up the towns, Zion didn't react. He knew we'd found them. He could've set traps there, too."

I hurried inside and swiped my burner phone. "Did

THE PRICE OF FREEDOM

Raven take her phone with her?" Without waiting for an answer, I called her.

Talia said, "I know where she is. We zeroed a spot where a town should be but isn't, like someone smudged it."

Raven didn't answer.

I shot her a text, then texted the others that she might be in trouble—that they all might.

Garly, who had disappeared into our storage area, returned with machine guns.

"Where's the location?" I asked Talia as he stuffed the weapons in a duffel bag.

"I'll guide us there."

"No, you're staying here."

"Not if you want to know where she is."

CHAPTER THIRTY-THREE

I flew over the tree-covered hills, Garly clinging to me with one arm and holding a bag of weapons with the other. Talia pressed against my chest, wedging me between her and him, her hands on the inner part of the handlebars as I steered.

I'd resisted bringing her, but Garly had countered she would be in more danger alone.

The town was known as Youngsville, only about four hundred people.

I descended as we approached, its main roads making a "Y" through the downtown area. Near that intersection, a male Agent directed thousands of hunter-drones into transport containers. It was the only movement. No townspeople, no battle, no Raven.

I curved away to avoid being spotted and activated her tracker. The image that formed above my bracelet surprised me. It showed Raven—but not in town. Instead, the map showed her south of here.

I ignited the jets, triggering a muffled squeal from Talia.

The land wove beneath us, roads and towns appearing and disappearing.

We closed in on Raven's location.

A two-lane highway appeared below us as we descended, an unmarked tractor-trailer the only vehicle, though as we neared, Raven suddenly appeared on a motorcycle. She swerved into the left-hand side of the road and accelerated alongside the transport. She acted as if she wanted to take control of it, but it was automated. It didn't have a cab, no place to manually override its programming.

While the road was clear, she was approaching a town. There would be witnesses to whatever she was planning.

She neared the front of the multi-ton vehicle, let go of the handlebar with her right hand, and removed a curved object from behind her back. The next moment, laser light traced the edge of the object, which I recognized as the curved blade Garly had made her, the one I'd modified to betray her but didn't. With a swoop of her arm, she sliced a hole in the front edge of the semi, turned off the blade, then pointed—and fired a bolt of plasma from her fingers into the hole.

The vehicle's lights shorted out, and it started to slow.

The vehicle angled off the pavement, crashed through a row of bushes, and nearly slid into a ditch before stopping.

I landed near the side of the road to find Raven aiming her gun at us until she saw our faces. She then hurried to the transport's rear.

"What're you doing?" I asked her.

She worked the handles of the tall, double doors and swung them open.

Terrified men, women, and children filled the trailer, hundreds of them. Some were wounded. I spotted the telltale markings of laser fire.

"They're the townspeople," Raven told me. "Agents rounded them up. They were being taken somewhere—probably to be slaughtered."

* * *

As Garly tried to salvage data from the transport's computer, Talia and I helped Raven determine how many townspeople had been lost.

The survivors deferred to a man in an orange-and-red checkered shirt. He looked like an old farmer yet had an air about him. "Men with silver hair killed the sheriff, both deputies, the fire chief, and my successor," he told us. When I gave him a questioning look, he said, "I was mayor 'til last year. They shot a few others for no reason, Cassandra, Big Steve, and Marc, our country clerk. Made us watch. Then forced us in the truck."

I remembered the tread marks in the previous town Raven had found. I wondered if that town's entire population had been slaughtered and buried locally, but the process had taken too long, so Agents had set the town on fire.

Shipping townspeople to an Agency location for execution would be more controllable.

Their eyes glowed with readouts, their implants uncovered.

"We can't stay," I told Raven.

She faced the Youngsville citizens as they stared, any sense of safety utterly destroyed. "You have to hide. Those who did this will search for you. Stay with people you trust."

Talia added, "Don't let them look at you."

As Raven explained what Talia meant, Garly approached. "The trailer's computer is sizzled. I can't tell where silvers were shipping them. But I spotted a 3D drone disburser through the trees. It's close, maybe five miles away."

To the crowd, I said, "Everyone, go now. Stay away from roads if you can."

"And don't stick together," Talia added.

To the former mayor, Raven said, "She's right, but stay in touch with everyone. And let me have your number."

I shot her a look.

"We need to know who Zion's targeted," she said. "We have to figure out who else he's deemed unworthy of living."

* * *

Our nerves were on edge as we returned to the former school — and stayed that way over the next two days as we waited for the rest of our group to return from their assignments. Raven's statement haunted me. Zion could wipe out entire nationalities, interest groups, anyone he deemed undesirable.

Anya tried to reduce my anxiety by teaching me yoga. It distracted me but didn't soothe. Meditation only magnified my fears. Still, I valued our time together, my days divided between her, my girls, and helping Garly.

I flicked my eyes to Talia as she tracked Raven with her fists up. No parenting book could scratch the surface of what we had gone through.

"Come on, little stinker," Raven said. "Look for a weakness."

Talia took a couple of swings, then bounded back, her battery glowing green.

I wasn't sure I liked this, but she needed to learn to defend herself.

I also struggled with staying behind while my team risked

themselves, but Cole had insisted. "Lafontaine doesn't put himself out there," he'd said soon after swearing his allegiance to me. "You're the one everyone's relying on. Remember that."

Talia's cry pulled me from my thoughts. She laid on the ground, holding her leg.

"I got her in the knee. She didn't keep her guard up," Raven said as I hurried over.

"Too crafty," Talia said.

I wouldn't let her fight. She needed to be protected. Needed a normal goddamn life.

"You didn't expect me to come right at you." Raven helped her up, then said, "You lost the bet. Tell him."

Talia looked at me. "I told hackers about Zion's lies. Got 'em buzzing hard. They're gonna unleash digital demons."

My concern shifted to annoyance. "You should've asked before telling anyone about our plan. It could jeopardize everything."

"I trust my peeps." She took my hand, led me next door to Garly's lab, and grabbed a pad from the pile of motherboards, wave emitters, robot parts, and laser enhancers strewn across the main table. "I've been using Nataly's scribbles. I've cracked thirteen of our targets so far."

"Still doesn't make me happy about what you did."

"Garly will make you happy. Tell him about the sound machine."

Garly raised his head, his goatee sporting a few grays. "I've finito'd it. It's fugly but should sing." Though he still grieved, he'd worked nonstop, barely sleeping.

I knew the path he walked. I'd helped with his projects but couldn't ease his heartache.

Jex and Valor returned, the last of our group.

"How did it go?" I asked, relieved to see them.

"I'm exhausted and need a shower, but got every 'switch ready," he said.

I looked at Valor, who nodded wearily. "Everything's in place."

"Before you clean up, we need to plan our next steps," I

told them.

I steered them to the hologram projector, which sat on a stack of boxes in the middle of a former classroom where we'd stored most of our supplies. Raven was there as if she'd had my same thought, talking to Cole, Fritz, and Anya, the projected blueprints of the Observatory's new structure—Zion's communication nexus—the only light in the room.

"We could modify our masks to pose as staff members," Raven was saying. "That way, we could get inside undetected."

"In person, Agents see through our masks. Remember, at that jail?" I asked her.

"Not everyone at the Observatory is an Agent, are they?" Cole said. "We aren't sure, so we shouldn't try it—and our small size isn't an advantage."

"If you want more soldiers, we could tap into those I rescued."

I spoke up before he or Fritz could. "They're not trained, and we just saved them."

"They would fight if we asked."

"I don't like it either," Anya said as Valor and Fritz fist-bumped a hello.

Jex hugged Raven. Her annoyance with me muted her happiness for his return.

"Keep your implants covered at all times," he told the group. "People complained about theirs becomin' 'off.' The software upgrade is spreadin'. Remember, anyone gets it, you'll expose us all."

"So, what's your plan?" Cole asked me.

"Our chaos should distract Zion. As far as how we strike, that we need to decide but don't know what we're facing."

"Yes, we do," Fritz said. "The layout's here. Filled with Agents. So, let's fight."

I lifted Talia onto a weapons crate and sat beside her. "That's not enough. Our invasion needs to be meticulously worked out."

Talia scooted over so Anya could sit by me.

Valor said, "We should do broadcasts, set the narrative,

like Dray did in the beginning."

"No broadcasts. They alert Zion that we're going to act," I said.

"I can get more hackers to pitch in," Talia said. "Stir more madness."

As the group talked, Raven walked over. "You need to believe in me."

"I always have," I said.

Fritz thumped a stack of metal boxes. "We got ammo. Armor-piercing bullets. From the dealer. It changes things."

Valor straightened. "You did? They could overcome Agents' enhancements. A strike team could take down this whole mess."

"Bullets are just that: bullets. This is no ordinary target. They'll have dozens of Agents and heavy reinforcements. You realize they built a fortress?" Cole asked, pointing at the rotating hologram. "Without a goddamn army, we will lose."

As the group argued, I tried to come up with a solution. Warfare was Cole's specialty, but there had to be a way.

"Have some balls," Fritz snapped at Jex.

He shot back, "We go in guns blazin', they'll crush us."

Everyone's voices were rising.

Raven clenched her fists. "The people we rescued will help."

"You can't ask that of them," Valor said.

"They'll make a difference. You'll see."

"That's the challenge," I said loud enough to get their attention. "It's why Zion is so dangerous. He runs multiple plans so at least one succeeds. We only have enough resources to run one—and it *has* to succeed. That means not running in blindly or relying on unproven fighters. So, give me better options."

As the room quieted, Talia asked, "Whose phone is ringing?"

Her question surprised me. Then I heard it. I extracted my burner phone, which I'd forgotten to turn off, and answered cautiously. "Hello?"

* * *

An hour later, I pulled into an abandoned truck stop. Two partially-autonomous tractor-trailers were parked behind the building. I stopped near them, got out, and scanned the building. Any cameras that had guarded the area had been removed some time ago.

Cole, Raven, and Valor joined me, as did Talia, determined to stay close.

The cab door opened, and my former Director of Robotics, Amarjit, climbed down. "Dray — and the children! My eyes are so happy to gaze upon you."

He wasn't normally so profuse. "It's good to see you."

"Come, see what I've brought."

He proceeded to the first trailer and rolled up the rear door to reveal two rows of AG-M1300 robots from my old company's agriculture line. They were man-shaped, each over six feet tall with the ability to lift five hundred pounds or more.

Raven and Valor's eyes widened. They were both familiar with the robots, which were sheathed in layers of metal graphite. Raven and I had used them when we'd invaded the Facility; they were the same machine Valor had used when we'd broken out.

I was stunned. "Does Nikolai know you took these?"

"I don't think so," he said as Talia climbed up into the trailer. "I falsified invoices, then canceled the orders after the factory shipped them. I flew to Raleigh, met up with the trucks which I reprogrammed, and now stand here."

There were many ways Nikolai would discover what he'd done.

Amarjit seemed to read my thoughts. His bushy eyebrows lifted in worry. "Will I be fired?"

Talia called out from the far end of the trailer. "There's wicked stuff back here. Camo shields, parts, and extra batteries."

Amarjit said, "I've brought sixty robots total."

Cole grinned at Amarjit, who stepped back, startled by Cole's damaged face. "You said sixty?" When Amarjit nodded, the rebel colonel grabbed my shoulder. "*Now* we have ourselves an army."

CHAPTER THIRTY-FOUR

Days later, after we'd moved, hid, trained, and switched vehicles, we entered what looked like a junkyard, the lights from our vehicles sweeping over old objects: 2020 vehicles, original gen robots, ancient plasma TVs, pressure cookers, and other items.

My team and I parked and got out. Other than ambient light from a town in the distance, night coated the land.

We'd backtracked to southwestern Pennsylvania. Our last report showed The Agency's 3D drone network had spread to the north and east of us. It was risky being here, as we didn't know when they would reach this area.

A trainyard was visible past the mound to my left with multiple track lines. Three of those lines ran into and presumably through a rectangular building that stood silent in the darkness.

I used my pad to check my surveillance network. There were two cameras I could tap into, but neither showed movement, so I radioed Amarjit.

I watched with trepidation as he brought in both tractor-trailers. If we had to run, there was only one exit.

"Are we thinking straight?" I asked everyone.

"Hell no," Jex said, the others silent.

Anya had her sniper rifle but remained close. When it seemed no one was looking, her hand touched mine. "Will he come through?"

It had been three days since I'd called. "If he doesn't show soon, we'll leave."

Amarjit joined us, looking tense. "Whoever we are waiting for must be careful. My journey here, I encountered drone trackers, multi-wave scanners, and other devices that must be connected to The Agency. It's not just here. Public complaints swiftly fall silent. People disappear. It's unsettling."

News shows now had a missing persons segment, but there were so many, the faces became a blur.

Valor said, "If I somehow survive all this, I might go back

to Texas."

"To be with someone?" Or take Fritz with you, I didn't add.

"It's a quiet life. The work's hard, but I have time for my art. I found a source of materials for my sculptures—and got enough inspiration the last two months to fill a back forty."

"I hadn't thought about after, what I'd do. Didn't want to jinx it, I guess, or maybe too focused on all this. Keep raising my girls, of course. That never ends."

"And be with a special someone?"

"Does everyone know?" When she nodded, I allowed a small grin.

A small light, bright in the darkness, illuminated Talia's face.

Raven hissed at her. "Are you on your phone?"

Talia turned it off. "I was emoji'ing my hackers. It's OK, they have final-boss-level security. No way silvers can crack it." She looked at me. "My peeps have tricks ready to crackle."

I knelt before her. "Put it away. Is your battery charged? Is it secured?" After she nodded, I kissed her forehead.

Cole approached. "So far, the military hasn't bothered us because we haven't been a threat. Once we use robots to invade a government building, even a secret one like Zion's, they'll get involved."

I stood. "Should we contact them? Explain things?"

"Better to end this quickly, one way or another."

He wasn't wrong. I felt like we were on borrowed time. "You have family back home?"

"Haven't talked to them in sixteen years. My old man didn't believe in the cure for the OCB virus. Decreed the family wouldn't take it. He died from OCB, but my mom and siblings still followed his directive. Two are blind now."

"Why didn't he believe in the cure?"

"He thought the government would use it to control everyone. Bastard wasn't totally wrong."

With a rattle, a loading door on the side of the rectangular building rolled up. A figure appeared in the square light and jumped to the ground.

My team tracked the man with their guns as he approached.

"Dray," said the distinct voice.

Beside me, Raven smiled. "Uncle Tevin?"

I turned on a flashlight to reveal my former partner.

Tevin hugged her. "Glad you made it." He was disheveled but looked in his element, more than when he'd worked at Gen Omega.

I hadn't been sure he would even show. He'd made it clear he didn't want to get involved, not that it surprised me. He'd always been the most rigid of the Gang of Five. Still, I was glad for any help he gave.

Behind him, the sky reflected the first hints of the coming dawn.

"I have your transport," he said after Raven introduced him to the others. "Back your trucks in. The road continues around the side."

As Amarjit hurried to the tractor-trailers, Tevin led us to the building, which was designed for loading and unloading cargo. The structure was much longer than I'd realized, stretching into the distance.

"This is your ride," Tevin said, voice echoing as he indicated a sleek train. It was twelve cars in length, starting with a high-powered, electric engine car and two battery cars, the banks of batteries a quarter the height of the engine car.

To me, he said, "I got your stipulation about protecting the team. The car behind the batteries is armored. It's usually used by dignitaries in hostile countries. One of its modifications is space to hide bodyguards under the floor."

"Perfect."

Tevin gave a lopsided grin. "You planning to stick someone under there?"

I didn't answer, instead instructing my team to help Amarjit direct the robots into the train.

Jex took my arm. "This isn't the best move strategically."

Tevin said, "The route goes through the mountains rather than over them. It's a new track built over the last ten years, lower degree of ascent and straighter route so we can travel faster. I made sure the tracks will be clear for the next twelve hours, didn't put this train on any schedule. I didn't want to tip your hand to our old partner." When I didn't react, he added, "This won't get you to your destination, but it'll get you within a mile, and I have a place where you can lay up."

Jex said, "We can divide the robots into smaller groups, take the interstate."

"It's a single track, the trip is quicker than any interstate, and no one will see you."

Jex wasn't convinced, nor were the others. They didn't know Tevin. But I did. "Everyone, load up." I went to the pack of robots and pulled four away.

Minutes later, we were ready to go. I looked for Tevin to thank him. I was surprised to see him heading to the engine car. "You're driving us?"

"It's true I don't give a shit, but I'll get you to your destination. Besides, you might scratch my train." As he checked his watch, I noticed he'd covered his implant. "Time to go."

CHAPTER THIRTY-FIVE

Holding Anya's hand, I led her through the last train car as we started to ascend toward the mountains. The car contained supplies: food, water, clothes, a small box of explosives, two extra machine guns, and a cot next to a small bathroom. She raised her eyebrows when she saw the cot, but I continued past to the rear door, which opened to a small landing.

We found Jex staring at the dawn as our ride took us into West Virginia. Trees raced past as we churned southeast, the branches dark blurs.

"Get some rest," I told him. "I'll finish your shift."

He disappeared inside.

Anya turned to me and slipped her arms around my shoulders.

I wasn't sure how long we kissed, but she was the first to pull back. "You just bring me here to make out?"

"We rarely get time alone." The first hour of our journey had been quiet, so I'd thought we could risk it.

"Tell me something I need to know."

"I'm scared. Scared of how our fight will end, how we'll be able to build what I hope becomes a long-term relationship — assuming we survive. It's been decades since I've dated anyone."

"The fact you're sharing these thoughts tells me we have a good chance." She shifted her focus, looking past my shoulder — and her eyes widened.

I followed her gaze.

A hoverbike kept pace with the train, the rider's silver hair just visible. Britt. She flew sharply upward as a deep roar grew in volume, followed by darkness as we entered a tunnel.

Our route took us through a series of tunnels punched through the undulating mountains, each tunnel progressively longer.

When we emerged from the tunnel, I searched the skies. Britt reappeared behind us, though she hung back. As if guarding the rear. Or coordinating.

I stepped to the side of the landing and looked around the edge of the car. A row of mountains approached, our tracks plunging into the one directly ahead. I could just make out movement on either side of the tunnel entrance. Agents, dressed in black.

Oh god.

I pulled Anya into the car and told her what I saw.

There was a series of thuds, followed by fast footsteps. From the sounds, two Agents must've leapt from the mountainside like goddamn fleas to land on our train. I grabbed the machine guns and handed her one. "Warn the others."

She dashed to the next car as I scrambled back outside. I climbed the ladder imbedded in the cab's end and raised my machine gun when I reached the top. I caught a flash of silver as someone slipped down between the cars, leaving the roof empty.

The mountain neared.

Another hoverbike approached but I ignored it, instead dropping down and hurrying back inside as the train plunged into the tunnel.

The tunnel's racing darkness filled the windows as I ran for the next car. It was a storage car; robots stood immobile, each one in SLEEP mode. I tapped the chests of the two closest, and their eyes lit up. I pointed toward the last car. "Defend."

I hurried past the others, exited the car, and entered another storage car, which contained most of the rest of the robots. Two Agents stood among them, staring with stunned looks. I raised my gun, shot them — the bullets enough to knock them down — and sprinted forward. I touched the chests of four robots near the Agents. "Attack."

They swarmed the Agents.

The two men tried to fight back, but though they were enhanced, they were still flesh and blood. The robots weren't, and in the enclosed space, the Agents were ruthlessly dispatched.

As the robots straightened, I activated others. More Agents would come. I directed one group of robots to defend the rear of the train, kept the four that had killed the Agents in this car, and activated eight past them. "Come with me."

The four that remained in the car would block the door, but it would only slow Agents, forcing them to the roof to advance.

I entered the next car, the sleeper car. Anya must've roused the group as it was empty. I directed two robots to create an obstacle when thuds warned me Agents were landing on the roofs of different cars along the line as we exited the tunnel.

I scurried back outside, the coupling that linked the sleeper and storage cars squeaking over the sound of the wind, and climbed the imbedded ladder to peer over the top.

Agents stood on multiple roofs, though not on the armored car. Not where Talia was.

I dropped down and plunged back inside the sleeper car. The eight robots huddled close in the tight space, eyes glowing reddish-yellow. "If we encounter anyone with silver hair," I said, pointing at my head, "attack them."

They nodded.

Gunfire erupted both ahead and behind me.

I ran forward, exited the car, stepped over the next coupling, and entered the kitchen car, the robots following. The car, which smelled of cooked meat and onions, was also empty. As I moved past the ovens and prep area, gunfire erupted from overhead as an Agent fired down into the car, bullets striking a metal worktop, the floor, and two of the robots. I dove to the side and fired at the ceiling, but that triggered gunfire from a second location overhead. I pressed myself against a dishwasher as bullets pierced the air where I'd been.

One of the robots leapt and punched through the ceiling. I heard a cry as the Agent sailed off the train, his cry fading.

I rolled onto my back, focused on where I thought the second gunman stood, and opened fire. There was a thud, then a blur as a body fell past the windows.

As I stood, gunfire and shouts rang outside.

I gathered my robots, exited the kitchen car — and spotted Agents swooping down toward our train on three hoverbikes, each bike holding two Agents.

The sharp crack of high-powered gunshots punctured the

air. The lead bike's flyer jerked back, and the bike veered sharply to the side, angling down into the valley. Another crack, and the second bike exploded.

The flyer of the third bike steered close to the train. As soon as they got close enough, both the pilot and passenger leapt onto the kitchen car behind me, the hoverbike falling out of sight.

Two of my robots disappeared back into the kitchen car as I climbed to the roof. The Agents were already gone, having dropped down on the far side of the car—though as I watched, one of them sailed out into the valley, a robot wrapped around him.

Two hoverbikes flew past on the other side, flying level with the train, the Agents raking our transport with gunfire.

Closer shots drew me to the next car, the dining car.

A fight raged among the narrow tables and small booths, Cole and Amarjit against a male and female Agent. Cole was bloody, and Amarjit looked terrified. They were being driven toward the front as they exchanged gunfire with the Agents, Amarjit using a small table as a shield while Cole fired.

I yelled to get the Agents' attention.

They turned—then ignored me as my squad of six remaining robots surged toward them. The Agents fought, managing to disable the first robot, but gave their lives in the process.

A deep roar built ahead as we approached the next tunnel.

A wrenching sound erupted behind us.

I went to the windows. The train trembled under my feet as four hoverbikes appeared overhead, jets blasting, with ropes stretching from each bike down to the train. I raised my gun but was too late as the hoverbikes pulled the last two train cars off the tracks.

The cars plummeted toward the valley floor as the tunnel enveloped us, the next train car—still connected to the falling cars—starting to tip. A boom thundered a second later, the train jerking as it slowed, bounded, and then sped back up. The tunnel must've kept the third car from following the first two, the car colliding with the tunnel's opening and breaking the coupling between it and the falling car before resettling on the tracks.

"Damn you," Amarjit yelled. "That was half our army."

Amidst the noise from the train plunging through the tunnel, more gunshots rang.

I hurried to the next car, one of two lounger cars, to find Fritz fighting two Agents, both sides using chairs and shields to block the others' gunfire.

My robots surged forward, though the Agents must have been warned, for the closest one fired at the robots' heads, dropping one to my surprise.

The far door opened.

Raven dove into the car, Jex right behind. As he fired at the Agent closest to me, she struck the other one in the head with a metal bar, taking him out with a swing perfected from years of softball. Jex continued to shoot at the other Agent, the bullets sparking as they ricocheted off the Agent's implants.

Fritz leapt at the silver-haired enemy, blocked his gun with a shield, and fired point blank, killing the larger man. Then he ducked down as my robots swarmed close.

"Get up, soldier," Cole said as he approached.

The redhead shook his head. "My implant's exposed. Cover got knocked. I got upgraded."

I worried about what Zion would learn from him, but that had to wait. "We need to get to Talia."

Sweat and pain coating his face, Jex said, "There's more Agents in the next car."

"Two of them," Raven said, swapping her bar for a pistol. "Garly's fighting them. He told us to find you — he stacked hand-shields to hold them back. We gotta help him."

I feared he wasn't the only one in trouble.

We'd originally had twelve cars, though the last two had been pulled off the tracks. That left the engine car, two battery-cars, the armored car where I'd put Talia, the first lounger car where Garly was, and the second where we were, followed by the kitchen and our remaining storage car.

Agents were probably in the cars behind us — and were definitely ahead.

"Use the robots," I said as the train cleared the tunnel. We were down to four 'bots, plus two we'd stationed near the engine. Six versus who knew how many Agents.

I led my team outside and heard gunfire from the next car.

As Raven's group prepared to enter the car where Garly had set up shop, I ascended the ladder, my machine gun in one hand.

Wind buffeted me when I reached the roof. One mountain range rolled away from me and another approached, the valley between layered with trees.

The roofs were empty, though four hoverbikes descended into the valley with three more in the distance.

I scrambled along the roof of the lounger car, multiple gunshots—high-powered sniper shots, rapid machine gun rounds, and an occasional pistol—just audible over the wind.

I reached the front of the car as the engine plunged into the next tunnel. I strapped my gun across my body as the tunnel's entrance swallowed the first battery car and lunged for the roof's edge as the tunnel swallowed the second, swung down—and the tunnel shot overhead to deafening sound.

I dropped onto the narrow platform attached to Talia's car.

As the gunfight continued in the car behind me—faint over the roar of the tunnel—I raised my gun and reached for the door. It was partly open; the lock had been busted.

I threw myself inside.

The interior was fit for a diplomat with velvet-covered chairs, polished-wood ceiling, and multi-hued finishes, walls tastefully decorated. Past a mini lounge area and wet bar, three Agents stood in an open area, their backs to me. Talia stood on the far side, facing them defiantly, seemingly unfazed by their weapons or strength. She'd tied one of the curtains around her neck like a cape and held a curtain rod as if it was a scepter or sword.

"Kneel before me," she cried.

A metal arm broke through the floor under the middle Agent, grabbed his knee, and wrenched him down. He fell forward, caught unprepared. A second arm burst through the floor, grabbed his neck, and broke it.

The next Agent, a tall woman, yelled, "Look out," but an arm grabbed her leg before she could move.

The last Agent, a much smaller man, jumped forward, landing right in front of Talia.

She stumbled back as he swatted away her curtain rod.

I aimed and fired, clipping the top of the Agent's head.

He spun with a hand to his head—and was pulled down by another robot.

I hurried forward, but the robots dispatched the Agents before I reached them.

I swept Talia into my arms. "You OK?"

"Yeah, I smote them."

Our train exited the tunnel, and morning sunlight streamed in from the window she'd stripped off the curtain.

The Agents must've been too confused by her cape and rod to immediately shoot her—or had been ordered to take her alive.

As I set her down, Raven led the others into the car, a stream of blood lining her cheek. After I assured them Talia was safe, I confirmed Garly had been rescued, the Agents destroyed. "Tell Garly to get his sound machine ready."

Jex and Fritz exited the armored car.

"What about when we attack the Observatory? They'll know about the weapon," Raven said.

"If Agents keep coming, we won't have a choice."

I unlocked the door behind Talia and opened it. Valor stood on the other side, buffeted by the wind as she stood guard. Past her, Anya laid on the battery car closest to the engine car, tracking one of the hoverbikes.

"Get Talia to the engine," I yelled over the wind.

Valor scooped her up and stepped onto the first battery car.

I directed Raven, Cole, and our robots to follow.

As I climbed onto the batteries, two Agents appeared on the roof of the armored car. Three hoverbikes flew up to drop off their passengers on the roof behind them. Then Britt dropped off Kieran before flying away. Unlike the five Agents who wore black tactical outfits, he wore a white Oxford shirt with the sleeves partly rolled up and dark slacks.

I scrambled toward my family.

Gun raised, Raven waited for me near the end of the first battery car.

Past her, Valor set Talia down by Anya, Cole, and Amarjit at the far end. My four robots joined the other two to create a barrier between them and the Agents.

I stopped beside Raven and faced the Agents.

Anya, perched near the engine control room, picked off the one farthest to the left. The Agent flew back, the bullet's momentum, the wind, and the smooth roof throwing him out of sight.

Kieran and the others jumped down onto the battery car as the wind changed.

Another tunnel approached.

Raven and I shot at the Agents as the tunnel swallowed our train, though the sudden change to near darkness interfered with my vision. My eyes adapted but not as quickly as I needed. Kieran returned fire and would've hit me, but Raven protected me with her shield.

Our team stood by the engine car with their guns raised but didn't shoot, either blocked by the robots or afraid they'd hit us.

"You're never going to win," Kieran shouted over the echo of the tunnel. "Surrender. I'll let Talia walk. Let Raven live out her days in a protected facility."

Past me, I heard Talia yell, "Off with their heads." Probably holding her curtain-rod scepter high.

"Go to hell," I shouted.

A male Agent with the physique of a professional runner leapt and landed near me. Before I could shoot, he ripped away my machine gun, threw it off the train, and wrapped an arm around my throat.

Talia yelled at the robots to help me as Cole and Valor

tried to get past them, but I told the robots, "Keep protecting them, priority one."

Raven alternated training her gun on the Agent who'd grabbed me and the others as they approached. She fired as one neared, and though she hit him, he lunged fast enough she only got off a second, grazing shot before he disarmed her.

The one who'd captured me dragged me to the side of the battery car, lifted me into the air, and swung me out over the edge of the car.

The ground beneath my feet was a blur.

The door to the armored car busted open, and a circular device appeared.

Recognizing the device, I thrashed against the Agent, causing him to take a step back —

And Garly's sound machine erupted.

A horrific sound — one that Raven, Valor, and I had experienced at Brocco's house — assaulted me, a high-pitched, throbbing shriek that echoed against the tunnel walls. The first time I heard it, the sound made my bones vibrate and pain flood my body. This time, the tunnel magnified the sound, the rising echoes nearly lethal.

The Agent holding me collapsed from the audial assault, and I fell with him, my feet just catching the edge of the car. The man was physically pulsing from the onslaught; he gripped his head, though I knew it didn't help. With his multiple implants, he was vulnerable in a way we weren't.

My team was down. Everyone was down except for the robots. The earplugs we'd fashioned to protect ourselves were packed away somewhere, so we suffered from the magnified assault as well.

The Agent who had grabbed Raven laid near her, his mouth locked in a scream, though I couldn't hear anything other than Garly's shrieking machine. Beside him, Raven was on her knees, struggling to stand as tears coated her cheeks.

I had to act before the sound stopped.

I grabbed the Agent who had nearly thrown me off, channeled my anger, and heaved. I swung his body out over the edge of the train car, nearly tipped over after him, and let go. The Agent fell away and disappeared.

A second Agent nearby was on his hands and knees.

I headed for him, lowered my shoulder, and hit him as hard as I could toward the other side. He managed to catch himself before he fell off the battery car, but I barreled into him again, driving him off the train.

Raven kicked her assailant, making him fall between the car and the next.

The train car jostled as he fell under the wheels.

The fourth Agent laid unmoving on rows of batteries, the blood seeping from multiple implants tinting his silver hair pink.

Kieran was still alive—and was moving, crawling toward the armored car. Toward the sound machine.

Before I'd taken two steps, morning sunlight filled the tunnel, then surrounded us as we exited the tunnel.

The sound burst forth, no longer confined by the tunnel, blasting at the hillside where more Agents awaited. Anya later told me the sound threw back the Agents who had crouched there waiting for us, the wave so powerful it ripped leaves from trees.

With the sound no longer magnified, Kieran lunged for the device and punched it with the arm I'd burned—which now had what looked like darker streaks just visible under his white shirt, as if he'd tattooed his arm.

The blow dented the machine's domed top. The sound frequency changed, still painful but not as debilitating.

I charged toward him.

Kieran laced his hands together and raised his arms to crush the device—revealing the edge of what looked like metal embedded in his wounded arm—but I crashed into him before he could. I slammed him into the doorframe, then collided with the sound machine, driving it back into the armored car.

Kieran grabbed me—and that's when I saw the extent of his injuries. Blood seeped from multiple implants, his face was gaunt, and a blood vessel in his left eye had popped. Yet he gathered his strength and punched me.

The blow threw me back, and I landed on the battery car, the grooves from the battery packs digging into my spine.

A high-powered gunshot rang out. Anya, firing from the engine car and between two of the robots.

The shot drove Kieran back against the lounger car.

I forced myself to get up, my head ringing from both his blow and the sound machine.

The largest mountain in our track's path rose ahead of us, dominating the land, its tunnel over a mile long — as more Agents swooped toward us, a dozen reinforcements we couldn't defeat.

Kieran pulled his gun, stepped onto the battery car, and aimed at my family.

The robots shifted their stance, overlapping to prevent him from getting a clean shot.

As the Agents neared on their hoverbikes, Raven activated her shield and fired at Kieran.

He flinched from the shots, his shirt spotting with more blood, but he remained standing. He aimed low to avoid her shield and shot her in the calf. She collapsed — and her shield went out.

I was unarmed and unprotected but went for Kieran anyway.

A red blur got between us as Fritz appeared and charged the Agent, grabbing his right arm and shoving it upward to deflect Kieran's gun. "Here you are," the Irishman cried. Blood from his infrared implants framed his face, and he had what I realized was one of Talia's spare slings hooked over his neck. The sling held a rounded object.

Kieran twisted out of Fritz's grasp and shot him.

The bullet ripped through the former soldier's stomach.

With an effort, Fritz raised a metal tool Garly used to bend steel and slammed it against the side of Kieran's head.

The Agent, already bloody from the sound machine, stumbled back.

Behind them, Agents landed on the armored car's rooftop.

I reached for Fritz to help him, but he shook me off. "Go separate us."

I didn't understand. Then, I recognized the object in his sling.

As Fritz went after Kieran, Garly and Jex emerged from the armored car, weighed down by two large bags and the sound machine slung over Garly's shoulder.

I hurried across the batteries, dropped, and shoved my arm between the two battery cars. As Garly and Jex stepped across to the front battery car, I uncoupled it and the engine from the rest of the cars and unplugged the secondary batteries. Then I helped Raven get up and onto the front car.

We pulled away, first by six inches, then twelve.

Kieran knocked Fritz's weapon from his hand and threw him back.

Unburdened by the weight of the other cars, we picked up speed.

The mile-long tunnel approached, the sound growing.

Kieran took a step toward me, already healing, Agents jumping onto the battery car behind him, when Fritz yelled. "Hey silver freak." He removed the rounded device, one of Garly's web expanders, and tossed it past Kieran, where it rolled toward the front of the slowly-receding battery car.

Valor cried out, "*No.*"

The other Agents didn't recognize it, but Kieran did. Fritz had rolled one of Garly's web-expanders, the device Garly had used to block off Kieran's team at the hospital.

Kieran launched himself as the device triggered, the whitish-gray webbing exploding outward — and he'd moved so fast, he got in front of the webbing. The device formed into a wall thirty feet wide and fifteen high, the bottom edge adhering to the batteries. His momentum threw him forward, reaching for us —

Then was jerked short. He fell, his chest hitting the front edge of the slowing battery car.

He hadn't been fast enough after all. The webbing had snared his right foot.

The next instant, we entered the mountain, and the webbed wall smashed into the tunnels' entrance with a thunderous boom, followed by metal tearing and concrete webs snapping. Kieran disappeared in the darkness, the sounds of the crash adding to the cacophony as the tunnel swallowed us.

CHAPTER THIRTY-SIX

Four hours later, after our incinerators scorched the engine and battery car to burn any evidence we'd left behind, we limped into Tevin's safe house. The Agency had found out about the train, so they could've discovered the house, though Tevin insisted it was clean.

"We won't stay long," I assured Jex, who didn't look convinced by any of Tevin's many assurances. Neither did the others.

The hideout was a faded Colonial with a gravel drive leading to a warehouse behind the house, the remnants of a failed business, the warehouse big enough to store the two semis Tevin had arranged to transport the robots we no longer had.

We all had injuries, even Talia. Anya had patched us up as well as she could on the train, including Raven's gunshot wound, but we needed supplies. And rest.

We brought in what little we had, our weapons and the tech Garly had salvaged. We'd lost so much. All we still owned had been grabbed during the fight or stashed in the engine car.

"I'll ditch our ride," Valor murmured with a nod toward the extended-cab truck we'd used to transport our sad little team, the third vehicle Teven had arranged.

"Get somethin' inconspicuous," Jex said.

She nodded and left with tears in her eyes.

We were badly shaken from the fight and devastated by Fritz's death, her and Cole most of all.

Cole went to leave, possibly to set up a perimeter, but before he did, he squatted in front of Talia. "Remember what you said about me fighting because I'm sad? You're right. But it's more than that. I want better for others. I need to, to make our losses worth it." His face twisted, which made his scar more pronounced.

They were the first words he'd said since Fritz died.

Talia traced his damaged jaw. "I'm sorry."

"We lost most of our 'bots and the element of surprise," Jex said as I watched Cole leave. "Garly thinks he can rebuild his sound machine, but Agents know 'bout it now."

Amarjit entered the house, his face downcast. We only had six of his robots left. "The 1300s are operational. One suffered damage to its optical sensors, but I can fix it." He hesitated. "You're disappointed. I can reinforce the robots' armor, but I can't get any more, not without many risks."

After I assured him I wasn't upset, Tevin came over, looking haggard. "I don't know how they knew about the train."

"How well did you hide your arrangements?" I asked.

"Damn well. I handled virtually all of the logistics myself."

Amarjit said, "I'm worried I led the enemy to you with my robots."

"I could've as well," Tevin muttered as he scratched his stubble.

"Any of us could have," I said. A bad thought struck me. "Zion could've read your mind. You're part of our old group — and stopped being a fan of his years ago. He could've tracked you without your knowledge."

Tevin dropped his gaze, his fists clenched, then looked at me. "I stopped caring when I was at Gen Omega. I can't do that again, especially if he's in my goddamn head. I'll fight with you."

He'd probably been upgraded — but didn't know our plans. We would shield him, make sure he didn't become a liability.

"Good to have you," I told him. I faced the group. "Rest up. We'll leave soon."

As the others walked off, Anya approached and made a show of checking my injuries. "Maybe we need to stop making out," she murmured.

"Never."

Jex cleared his throat. I hadn't realized he'd stayed.

"That attack, Talia had been the target," he drawled. "We all were, but her 'specially."

I remembered how Zion had asked about her at his penthouse. She was more of a threat to him than I'd realized.

As if she knew we were talking about her, Talia appeared. "I have two bips of scatt to tell you. First is one of my hacker groups left messages. You got a call on the dark web. I can link it without spiders tracing you."

"You know who that is," Anya said.

"Zion. Not interested," I said. "It'd be more justification. I can hear it now. 'The political squabbling wasn't getting us anywhere. We need a single focus, one person who can fix things.'"

"And he's that 'one person'," Jex said.

"Of course. He's like his father—though his father wasn't a murderer."

I contemplated our next step. We were close to our destination, only a few miles from the Observatory, but it wasn't easy terrain—and there would be layered surveillance. We also had the 3D drones to worry about. We'd lost Nataly's pad, so we no longer knew their progress.

I feared I was missing something.

I took in my team. Anya had led Jex to a nearby window and was tending to him. Raven sat in a corner with a burner phone and a pad, though she seemed dazed, her injured leg propped up, the nanobots hopefully already rebuilding tissue. Even though Garly had aggravated his ribs during the train attack, he was busy working on a strange-looking weapon, a mixture of a Gatling gun, an industrial-grade chemical compressor, and a gamma ray emitter. It was his ice machine, which I doubted would be effective if it ever worked.

Then I remembered Talia's words.

She wore a guilty expression as I refocused on her, a look she rarely had. "What was the other 'scatt' you had to tell me?"

"I did something you won't like."

* * *

Hours later, I was still simmering.

"I am not happy with you," I told Talia for the fourth time as I parked the car. Raven sat beside me, stiff with anger and a host of other feelings that needed professional therapy to work through.

Talia knew better than to speak. The last time she had, we'd both snapped at her. Instead, she tapped her battery pack and gave a thumbs up.

I turned off the engine and stared at our destination. Skylar's was a small diner, the wavy metal exterior painted in bright pastels, the property well maintained. It looked like a place locals loved, though at 2:15 on a Tuesday, it was nearly empty, as promised.

Mina sat alone in a booth. She no longer looked polished; she wore makeup and had composed herself, but she'd lost weight and had let her hair grow out.

Talia hugged her.

Raven slid into the booth across from them, having struggled to hide her limp, and I sat next to her as Talia took the spot next to Mina.

Somewhere, a radio played "Tracks of My Tears".

"Thank you for coming," Mina said. She spoke quietly, though we were the only patrons in the diner—a good thing, since Talia had insisted we not be masked. "I have important information. And, well, I wanted to say goodbye to the girls."

"What?" Talia asked in bewilderment.

To me, Mina said, "The members of Congress are gathering for a private banquet. They're spinning it as an ultra-exclusive holiday party, but that's a front."

"People in D.C. have parties all the time."

"Not with every single member of Congress. Attendance is mandatory. No donors, no staff, just Congress. It's for Zion to flex his power. He wants to celebrate the end of all rebellion. His national surveillance programs will be in place, which they expect will reveal any last rebels."

She was referring to the 3D drones. Between them and his mind-reading technology, no one would ever be able to rise up against him. "An event like that will have heavy protection."

"That's why I wanted to tell you. Zion will pull Agents from other areas to protect his puppets. The target you've been looking for will be vulnerable."

She meant the Observatory. "Are you suggesting we

attack the target during the event?"

She nodded. "The party is in eleven days, at the Grande Salle de Bal. It's a new venue they built by the Potomac, in a former baseball park just south of the Roosevelt Memorial. This could be a way to end everything."

"Has she been upgraded?" Raven asked me. "We'd be sitting ducks."

"I've been careful," Mina said. "I wouldn't risk you like that."

"How did you learn about the party?" I asked.

"I used connections I've built over the years. There are still good people in D.C. They want this to end."

Raven spoke to her for the first time. "Ever hear of towns disappearing?"

Mina's face showed her surprise — and hope. "No, but I could look into —"

"Don't bother."

I studied Mina as she gazed longingly at Raven, not sure I believed her. I wanted to. I saw her struggling, wanting her family back but unable to feel our embrace any longer, instead helping our fight, though she hadn't chosen it.

I slid out of the booth. "Raven, Talia, give us a minute."

Raven got out, but Talia lingered. "What will you do after all this?"

Mina stroked her hair. "I'll try to help people in some way." She hugged Talia. "Goodbye, sweetheart. Raven."

Raven took Talia's hand, and they walked out.

I sat back down, the radio now playing "Mr. Sandman." I'd shared nearly half my life with Mina. I hadn't had a family growing up except for Mom, and none after she died. Mina and the girls became my family, along with Nikolai and the guys.

So much had changed.

"Zion has put targets on their heads," she said. "I hope you know what you're doing."

"You've seen Zion's operation from the inside. Is anyone *not* monitored and manipulated?" When she shook her head, I got up to leave.

"I'm sorry for what I did."

I forced my voice to be gentle. "Being sorry and providing intel, while appreciated, doesn't make up for everything."

"I don't think anything will. I'll have to live with that." She searched my face. "Keep them safe."

"I'll try."

I could tell she wanted redemption but didn't know how to get it. "After this is over, file for divorce. I won't fight you. It seems kind of small in light of everything, doesn't it? The end of a marriage?"

I'd had things to say to her, but they no longer needed to be said.

I started for the door.

"My news helps, doesn't it?" she asked.

"I think so. Thanks, Mina."

* * *

Twenty-eight hours later, I grabbed at the fractured rock and dirt as I climbed the last few feet up the wind-scoured terrain.

The mountain should have been covered in trees. But those would have provided cover. The Agency had removed all vegetation on this and nearby summits, exposing the ground and any potential trespassers.

We'd hiked our way here, catching a few hours of sleep before ascending the mountain's highest peak. We were dressed like hikers as much as we could pull off with hiking shoes and loose clothes, though our shirts were muted greens and browns. And we were armed.

I'd picked this path as it was the hardest to reach, different than Omura's act-like-a-lost-hiker approach, and the one least likely to be patrolled. At least we didn't have drones to contend with. The quiet zone negated all communications, a double-edged sword.

Jex, Cole, and I pressed our chests against the rock as we cautiously crested the mountain and peered down the other side.

The facility Zion had built on the former Observatory's site dominated the valley below.

I'd assumed his center of power would look like a sleek

building half-buried in the ground. Instead, it looked like a stronghold. The top two floors were the only ones with windows from what I could see, a rooftop door the highest part of the building; the third and fourth floors were solid concrete. Only two doors led into the building, both near the parking area. The fifth floor stretched outward across a third of the valley floor.

The vehicular entrance and parking area had been placed on the roof of the vast fifth floor. A road rose up to reach the entrance, with just enough room for a single car to stop in front of the gate.

Four cars were parked near the building's front door.

The plans had revealed that the roof of the fifth floor was reinforced with thick steel. It could withstand numerous blasts. Besides, the important levels were buried underground.

Kieran's 3D drone net would soon reach this area. Though it wouldn't work inside the zone, we couldn't risk being discovered when we rejoined our team.

"How the hell we gettin' in?" Jex asked. "Can't sneak in from the ground. Even if we get across the valley undetected, that road's what, a dozen feet up? Don't see anythin' to hook onto to get up to the drive."

I said, "The road is heavily guarded." So was the building. I could just make out a couple of Agents guarding the facility, but there would be more.

Cole said, "The quiet zone would blind them, so they would've hardwired hundreds of cameras. They'll have defenses: collapsible walls, robot dogs, and the Agents themselves. Did you create any countermeasures for the dogs?"

"I'll get with Garly, see if he has any ideas."

Jex ducked below the summit and fixed me with a hard stare. "Are we really relyin' on Mina's intel? Thought you stopped believin' her."

"Lying to me would endanger our girls."

Cole sighed. "Right now, this may be our best shot."

Jex said, "Raven suggested we attack a few days 'fore the event Mina told you about. I agree. They'd be off-kilter, busy movin' Agents from here to D.C. 'Sides, if we attack the night of, every Agent will be on high alert. Do it while they're still preppin'."

I said, "It doesn't give us much time."

Jex peeked over the edge again. "The place is designed for a frontal assault. So we should give it to 'em."

Cole grunted. "I was thinking the same thing."

"Let's use armored cars, the kind banks like."

"We wouldn't reach the gate. We need to surprise them. But I think I know how to get us inside."

"What do you have in mind?" I asked.

His expression hardened. "Can you actually trust Mina? After you rejected her, how do you know she told you the truth?"

I wanted to assure him that she would never help Zion again, but no words came.

CHAPTER THIRTY-SEVEN

Cole drove through the night, taking us east.

The next morning, as Jex and I woke, he pulled into a shipping yard that had been converted into some sort of manufacturing facility, though it was heavily guarded with a military feel. Jex gave me a mystified look, but I could only shrug.

"Grab your bag," Cole told me. He'd had me bring a duffel bag full of swarmbots, which we'd left in the car during our hike.

I did as he instructed, though they weighed me down, and we approached the yard.

"Anyone see us, what do we say? We're lost hikers?" Jex asked Cole.

"Act like you belong."

He led us away from the main entrance, which had guards and surveillance, to a supply warehouse that bustled with activity. We slipped inside the hangar-sized warehouse, keeping our distance from the men unloading a fleet of trucks, and walked the length of the building as voices echoed.

We stepped out of the warehouse into the yard, then wove our way across the complex. I glimpsed workers and what looked like guards periodically, but Cole didn't slow as he steered us through the former yard, his posture the only indication he was coiled for an attack.

The buildings of downtown Baltimore were visible past the complex; we were closer to Washington than I wanted.

The yard had shipping containers, though they appeared to serve the role of sectioning off areas. I spotted large structures being constructed within each area, though we moved too briskly to get a good look.

Cole had us hide inside a nook created by a shipping container and a stack of crates, then disappeared.

Jex removed a drone broadcaster and flew it to the container's roof.

"How many have you placed?" I asked.

"Forty or so. They're shielded from most interference, so Silvers shouldn't be able to screw with 'em."

Cole returned. "Our destination is on the other side." He opened his pack, withdrew two ion blades, and handed one to each of us.

I was glad to have one again, but I frowned. "How long have you been planning this?"

"Online attacks and broadcasts might give Zion a headache, but the Observatory will be braced for an assault. Our approach has to be unexpected. I've been tracking these, figured out where they're built and stored."

"What're you talkin' about?" Jex asked.

Cole said to me. "It's the most idiotic thing I thought to do." He stepped out of the nook, took the corner, and motioned. "We're taking this for our assault."

A floating platform filled the workspace.

The sixty-by-forty-foot craft wasn't floating. Its multidirectional engines were off, the curved-edge structure tied down by four ropes, the platform's left and right sides touching the ground. Those sides curved as if the architect had remembered the contraption was supposed to fly, so had added stubby wings.

A two-story control tower stood in the front left corner.

As I stared at the platform, stunned, Cole asked Jex, "You get why, don't you?"

"It's not dumb."

Two guards emerged from the tower and started off in different directions.

"This part will be," Cole said.

The swarmbots shifted in my bag as he raced forward, staying low until he reached the platform, then leapt up onto it.

Jex followed, pulling his gun. I did as well, though I was slowed by my bag.

Jex leapt onto the platform as Cole dashed toward the tower.

I reached the platform, climbed on, and ran for one of the guards as Jex charged the other.

The platform's surface was unique. The floating weapon

held dozens of panels that it dropped onto people; the tops of those panels stuck up above the deck, creating rows of exposed metal, the deck curving up to cover most of the panels' tops.

The guards shouted as they went for their guns.

I was farther from my target than Jex was from his. I wouldn't make it before my guard opened fire, so I threw the duffel bag at him.

After the motel attack, we'd learned. The bag didn't have a zipper. It had Velcro, which the swarmbots could undo.

They burst from the bag and enveloped the guard.

He collapsed as I approached, writhing from the 'bots. I brought the handle of my pistol down, the swarmbots creating a clear spot on his head, and I knocked him out.

Beside me, gunshots made me jerk back. Jex's guard collapsed.

The swarmbots picked up the body of my guard.

"Cut the ropes," Jex hollered.

I hurried across the undulating deck as shouts rose. A guard appeared from around the edge of the containers and fired as I reached one of the ropes binding the platform. I dropped to the deck as he boarded the platform, his gun trained on me. Then he paused as swarmbots carried the downed guard toward him. He stepped back—and cried out as 'bots began climbing his legs.

I pulled my ion blade, activated it, and cut the rope.

As the man fought the 'bots, I dashed to the other rope.

Footsteps rose, punctuated by more shouts, as I severed the binding, freeing us.

Jex had cut the ropes on his side, but we weren't rising.

More guards appeared and ran toward us.

Returning my blade to my pocket, I hurried toward Jex. Neither of us had hand shields.

Guards neared, the closest two leaping for the platform—when the craft suddenly lurched and rose.

Jex and I were thrown on our backs.

We climbed to our feet as the platform rose, though we had to grab the tops of two panels as whoever was piloting—I assumed Cole—tilted the platform and accelerated, the guards we'd incapacitated sliding off the side, the swarmbots letting go to cling to the ship.

The guards who had tried to board fell away, but gunshots from the captain's bridge alerted us that we weren't out of the woods.

The ship leveled, though it began to tilt in the other direction.

Jex and I hurried into the control tower.

The narrow building contained a small storage area behind a set of stairs leading to the second-story bridge.

We charged up the stairs.

Control panels and displays filled much of the small bridge, some of which had blood splatters. Two guards laid on the ground while a third fought Cole, both men bloodied.

Jex ran forward to help.

As the three fought, I went to the main control panel and stabilized the ship.

Cole administered a blow that took out their opponent.

While Jex tied up the guards, I scanned the control panel. Among the steering controls and release buttons, I found an interface that allowed for remote control of the platform's entire operations. I disconnected the interface to make sure no one could stop us.

Cole took control and sent us higher. "We'll have visitors. Find the cloaking device. It's our only chance."

Floating platforms had an integrated cloaking mechanism that was key to their effectiveness. They were too slow to approach enemies and too slow to flee an attack. Even now, with the engines at full speed, we were barely past the shipping yard.

As I scoured the controls, Jex searched the first-floor supply area for weapons. He returned with a box of dark matter spheres, extras for the platform's flotation system. "Think these'll help?"

A hoverbike approached.

Before Cole could evade the threat, Kieran landed near the center of the platform, once again in white Oxford and dark slacks, and climbed off. He was hobbled and looked like he hadn't fully recovered from the train crash, but he was still dangerous.

"Fly us out of here," Cole told me. "I'm going to throw this guy off."

"I'm going with you." I pointed to the box in Jex's hands. "If a gunshot hits a sphere, the explosion could take the entire ship."

"No, stay here. Have your little robots help me."

He left.

"Keep the engines maxed and find that cloaking mechanism," I told Jex, then hurried outside, aware more Agents could arrive any second.

My swarmbots had clustered toward the far side of the platform. When they saw me, they began to stir.

Cole had moved to a spot a dozen feet past the tower, facing the Agent like a lone cowboy.

Kieran stood beside his hoverbike. "You claim you're good guys, yet everything you do is a crime."

"Says the man who's slaughtered entire towns," I said as I stepped out from behind the tower.

"I was going to be reasonable with you. Not anymore."

The swarmbots scurried over, tiny legs scraping on the platform's undulating surface, pooled in a spot a dozen feet past Cole, and fixed their gazes on him.

"Remember them?" I asked.

He pulled his gun. "I do. I remember they're keyed to you."

As the swarmbots charged toward him, chittering and hooting, he aimed at me and fired.

Cole crashed into me and wrapped his arms around me, the swarmbots squealing. I expected to feel pain from the gunshot, but there was none.

Cole had taken the bullet.

The swarmbots paused as if conflicted between protecting me and getting Kieran.

The Agent fired two more times, Cole taking both shots.

I gripped him as his legs gave out, his weight pulling me down.

"...good death..." Cole said. He shuddered, then died.

Fury and grief gripped me as I gently laid his body on the platform's surface.

Kieran kept his gun aimed at me. "I'll honor his memory by killing you quickly."

Two gunshots rang out from almost above me. Jex, having emerged from the control tower, fired a third time as he drove Kieran back.

The first two shots struck Kieran, though his protected skin reduced the damage.

Jex ran at him. The swarmbots were also heading for him, though they were slower.

I stood, pulled my gun, and raced forward, angling outward to get a clean shot. I fired as Kieran aimed at Jex, distracting the Agent, my shot nailing his shoulder. There was blood, but Kieran seemed only marginally hurt — though as he ducked to the side to avoid my next shot, his right foot, the one that had been caught in the webbing, almost gave out.

Jex neared him as I fired again, then lunged with his blade. He sliced Kieran's gun apart, taking most of the barrel.

I ran faster but was too far.

Kieran grabbed Jex's wrist with one hand, his hair with the other, and swung him toward the front edge of the platform, pivoting on his good foot.

Jex sailed out, hit the deck close to the edge, and kept sliding. He jabbed his blade into the carbon polymer surface, but his momentum was stronger.

I shouted, "*No*," and threw my hand out. The swarmbots surged past Kieran to try to reach Jex, most of them disappearing as they followed him over the curve and out of sight, the ones I could see jabbing into the surface to brace themselves.

I reached Kieran and launched myself.

Kieran grabbed me, but I twisted in his grasp and nailed his chin. He stumbled toward the edge, limping on his injured foot. I swung again to take advantage, but he avoided the blow, then threw me to the deck.

Before I could move, he grabbed my neck and began to

squeeze, his expression revealing that his offer for a quick death had been revoked.

I punched his arms, his chest, but he didn't flinch.

His primary implant stuck out farther than a normal one. I'd noticed it before, figuring it stuck out because he'd had it replaced—due to me. I reached up, grabbed it, and wrenched it as hard as I could.

Kieran jerked back, cupping the implant, and stood, his face creased with worry. Blood appeared beneath his hand.

There was a tap on my thigh. A swarmbot.

I got an idea.

I swung my feet under me, launched forward, and shoved Kieran as hard as I could.

The blow was so strong it threw me back—but it pushed Kieran near the edge.

"You're on the losing side," I told him as he regained his balance.

His face hardened. "You think you can win?" He grabbed his shirt and ripped it from his body. His left arm and shoulder, formerly scarred by my rope device, had sections that were now no longer human. Actuators—rotational, linear, and revolving—had been implanted into his arm and shoulder, layered between sections of unburnt skin. "I'm stronger than ever."

Zion had deemed his burns a weakness.

"I never should've let you escape." He set his feet to go after me, then looked down. Swarmbots had covered both of his shoes and locked themselves together.

As he wrenched his bad foot free, I ran forward and kicked him with both feet square in the chest.

The swarmbots let go as I struck—and he sailed out over the edge.

I scrambled forward and leaned out over the platform to watch Kieran fall. The Agent didn't cry out as he plummeted eighty feet to a wooded area. He disappeared through the trees and triggered a large concussion wave when he hit the ground.

My satisfaction was short-lived as I couldn't see Jex. I called his name.

A tired voice spoke. "Wanna help?"

With a grunt, a leg appeared. I grabbed it, and appearing out of a haze, Jex rolled up into view using my hold—and the swarmbots. The group that hadn't helped me with Kieran had held onto Jex. He must've been dangling over the side, masked from view.

I pulled him away from the edge. "You activated the cloaking device."

"Yeah. Glad you beat him. I was almost a goner."

He winced as I helped him stand.

We went to Cole.

"We need to change course," I said, but neither of us moved.

CHAPTER THIRTY-EIGHT

As the sun's last rays painted the side of the Smoky Mountain I'd selected, I set a slab of rock close to where Cole's head rested, creating a kind of tombstone.

Jex had asked to help, but I'd dropped him near a residential area to return to the others. I wanted him to start using the drone broadcasters he'd hid to spread the truth to everyone who would listen.

Besides, I needed to do this alone. Cole had become a mentor to Jex, but he'd been my military mind as well as my friend. Without him, my doubt grew about our success.

I felt responsible, though if I'd stayed back as Cole asked, he still would've been killed. What happened might have been the only way we could've defeated Kieran.

I recalled the first time Cole and I had met on Free Isle. He'd been dismissive and suspicious, already coated in the self-incrimination that haunted him.

I stared at the mound. "This probably wasn't the redemption you envisioned. But you'd already redeemed yourself."

I stepped away from the packed dirt but paused.

"I'll try to end this. Try to make your sacrifice worth it."

* * *

When I arrived at our newest hideout, a former manufacturing facility with bars on the windows and broken pallets scattered in the yard, my team was grieving Cole's death.

Anya hugged me. "I'm glad you're OK."

"Where did you bury him?" Jex asked.

I described the location. "He would've hated it."

Jex's brave face cracked. "Oh god." He turned and wiped his eyes. I put a hand on his shoulder but stepped back as Raven hugged him.

She held him until he composed himself, then frowned at me. "I told you, you need to be careful. Kieran nearly killed all of you."

Talia said, "I'm protecting Dads from now on. He's not leaving my side."

I assured her it was my job to protect her, then took in my crew. They looked lost without our gruff colonel.

Valor settled beside me. "Lots of signs not to fight. Fewer left to do it."

"If nothing else, we could do some damage with Cole's platform."

"And hurt Zion."

"Do you want to quit? I wouldn't judge you."

She sighed. "I'd judge me. And dear lord, I do hate that man."

Anya told me, "I know what you're thinking. We're committed, so don't ask again. I called in a favor while you were out and got twenty syringes' worth of nanobots and synthetic stem cells, if that tells you."

I nodded and took a breath, aware Cole hadn't sacrificed for the platform. He'd sacrificed for the cause. "Then it's time. Jex, Tevin, and I will work on our invasion. The rest, we're initiating our plans. Today."

Talia gasped. "Time for chaos?"

I nodded. "The radder, the better."

"Don't try to hipster," she said, grinning.

My people hurried off, Talia calling out orders like she was in command. Maybe she was.

The former factory was two stories high; the machines left behind had once made brooms, brushes, and other items. I followed after Tevin to what had previously been the main shop floor and took in the hologram of the former Observatory with fresh eyes.

"We're outnumbered and invading the Agents' turf," Tevin said. "But his platform does help."

"And his armor-piercin' bullets," Jex added.

I stared at the hologram. "We could use the main entrance to distract the Agents."

"I've been thinkin' 'bout that," Jex said. He indicated a stack of plasma guns as well as Gatlin guns Cole had obtained from the arms dealer, though braces had been welded to these weapons. He explained his idea, adding, "Talia helped increase the power of the plasma guns."

"I'm not happy with her handling weapons."

"I made sure she was safe. I installed electronics to trigger them remotely—"

"The Observatory blocks all signals."

"They're line-of-sight. Tevin suggested it."

"Dray, his plan is good," Tevin said.

I nodded, glad that Jex's head was in the game.

We called in Garly to discuss what we needed.

"I got the perfect puzzle piece," Garly said, absently holding his ribcage. "Tech was already crinkled as a rescue system for miners. Just need some mods to it." He took measurements using the schematics and, after Tevin offered to help, promised he'd have it ready in the next few hours.

Before they left, Tevin leaned in my ear. "It's ready for her."

When we were alone, Jex said, "I'm worried 'bout that huge subfloor, the one that's so tall. Somethin' ain't right about it. I'm gonna bring sledgehammers."

"That's a lot of weight to carry." His back seemed healed, but this could aggravate it—and make him vulnerable.

"Upper floors feed to that room. Whatever's there is key. They could've hidden somethin' in the floor. Sledgehammers will trump anythin' they tried to hide."

He took me to Amarjit who was working on the robots, surrounded by more abandoned manufacturing equipment. Amarjit showed us how he'd enhanced the robots, making some heavily shielded with thicker steel and camo shields strapped to their chest and others lighter to move faster.

I complimented him, then asked Jex, "Do you know how you want to use them?"

"All part of the plan."

I directed them to keep working and went to find Talia.

I could feel the excitement as I entered the command center she'd created in the factory's former offices. She, Valor, and Anya sat at stations they'd fashioned out of dented metal desks, each with media rods that projected readouts and software commands. Talia sat in the middle, directing the growing attack. Vid screens off to one side displayed multiple news programs, most of which showed images of airports and train stations.

"We've zapped the software that wizards all flights, trains, and subways," Talia said. "I used the FAA's system to warn airports to land every bird. Gave 'em twenty minutes."

"The scope of this is insane," Anya told me. "Did she tell you about the websites?"

Before I could respond, Valor said, "Talia changed every major airline's website, along with transit and AMTRAK. Each one now plays videos on how to block their implants, how to fight — and warning that the government is lying to everyone."

"It's where they'd turn," Talia said. "I wanted to hook eyeballs."

I glanced over at the vid screens and noticed two of the stations were playing the videos she'd mentioned. *"You've been enslaved,"* scrolled across the black screen. *"This is what it feels like: no information, no direction, just confusion."*

When I returned my gaze to Talia's screen, I realized she'd hooked into my police network. Feeds from across the country showed crowds of various sizes. In each, people were getting anxious.

She pulled up an ancient-looking software system and executed a program. "I just iced every ATM," she said.

Anya looked at me for an explanation. "There's a little-known software in every ATM. If there's an invasion, the government wanted a way to prevent the invading country from stealing U.S. dollars."

Talia had been monitoring a second screen that displayed every plane in the air. The sky cleared as planes landed at major and regional airports, military strips, wherever they could find. "Time to shut all transit."

On her signal, Valor and Anya executed commands. Within seconds, the news channels showed airplanes stacked at airports, subway trains unmoving at stations, passenger and commuter trains stopped on tracks. Images showed patrons starting to panic.

"OK, do the face hack," Talia said.

Valor initiated a program she'd had ready.

On Talia's screen, my face began to appear at random locations.

"What the?" I asked, severely bothered.

"It's to make coppers dance," Talia said. "The software alerts police across the country that you've been spotted. They'll goose chase everywhere."

I watched, stunned, as my face appeared in spots among the growing chaos in multiple cities where the streets had been cut off, and the subways weren't running.

"What's that?" Anya asked Talia, pointing at a program she'd pulled up.

"GPS." She initiated her hack, and alarms erupted in the distance. I looked out the closest window in time to see police and other drones in the distance faltering. Without guidance, their programs couldn't determine where to fly.

Talia switched one of her screens to the NYSE's live feed. The traders on the floor seemed wary, unsure of what was going on. She grabbed a burner phone and hit the call button, the number already entered. "Ready?"

"Been ready," Raven replied over speaker.

To Valor, Talia said, "See those switches over there? Trigger them." She leaned toward the phone. "You too, Raven."

Valor got up, flipped the switches to three remote detonators—and the stock price data scrolling along the bottom of the feed winked out.

Raven said, "I triggered Jex's killswitches. They severed everything."

"The trader peeps are going crazy," Talia said.

Anya pointed at a financial news show. "Not just them. The currency and commodity exchanges are gone, too. Investors have to be going nuts."

The financial advisor onscreen claimed the missing market figures were just a "glitch" but looked terrified.

Talia said, "Cole insisted we don't wipe any data. It'll all be there so longs as their IT peeps reset things the right way."

I feared we'd missed something. Or that this wouldn't be enough.

"I tried to figure out how to trigger every car alarm in the country, but it'd take too long," Talia said. She switched her vid screens to various websites—YouTube, Zappos, and Instagram—and kept typing.

"I'm heading to the next spot," Raven said and hung up.

"You going to cut the power to everyone?" Valor asked Talia.

"Soon. Still have a few trickeries."

I asked, "Do you have access to traffic signals?"

Talia said, "My hackers should send it over. They've been ripping it! They've rewritten the automated playlists on streaming platforms to play the video messages, have caused havoc with banking software, and other gizmos. They'll be doinked when we kill the power. They like the messes they've spilled."

I sensed Anya's concern and touched her shoulder. I suspected she was worried about how many innocents would get hurt from our efforts. I worried, too, though we couldn't stop.

The scenes on the various screens revealed the rising chaos, the crowds and the overwhelmed police, talking heads criticizing the government, and various Senators calling for people to remain calm.

Talia nodded with an expression beyond her years. "That'll teach you to hunt us." She brightened. "Dad, the software now shows you in Atlanta."

The news programs displayed drawbridges lifting, forcing people to abandon their vehicles and scramble off the bridges; gaming software freezing with texts scrolling across the screen, warning players they were being watched; and automated buses frozen on streets, blocking traffic, though there were more people in the streets than vehicles at this point.

The things everyone expected to operate no longer did.

Talia keyed more commands—and the websites she'd had pulled up suddenly presented the same video. It was one of ours, black screen with white letters, warning of the government and their control. "Now any website someone tries to access, they'll just see our vids."

"You hacked every website?" I asked. She wasn't prone to exaggeration.

"I hacked the system that converts names to IP addresses. No matter what site you type in, you'll only see this."

I motioned to Valor and Anya. "I need you to grab every drone we have that can carry a discharger. We'll need cover for when we leave."

As they hurried off, the news broadcasts switched to a live press conference. The Treasury Secretary approached the podium, looking frazzled and irritated. "We want everyone to know your money is safe. Whatever glitches we are experiencing, every bank account will have the same funds as when this started."

"So that's where Zion reacts, the financial markets," I said. "He must have a fortune at stake."

Raven called Talia's phone. "I'm ready," she announced.

"Kick it," Talia said.

"See you soon." There was a high-pitched buzz, then the line went dead.

On a number of television screens, interviews were interrupted. In the streets, the chaos seemed to multiply.

"The cell towers?" I asked. Talia bobbed her head, excited that she and her sister had just infected every phone tower in the eastern half of the country with software that spun in endless loops, blocking all cell communication.

On the vids, Chicago, Birmingham, and Boston descended into violence.

"The drones are ready," Valor said, rejoining us. "None too soon. Cops pulled up to our building but then drove away. Someone might've spotted us."

"Or the 3D network has reached us. Suit up. We're leaving in one hour." I squatted beside Talia. "I need to show you something."

* * *

I took her to what had been the building's receiving area.

The minivan sat inside the high-ceiling space, its modifications barely noticeable from the outside.

I opened the sliding door and stepped aside.

Talia took in the two monitors that Tevin and Garly had attached to the interior, along with the satellite comms equipment, tiny desk, and bank of batteries. "What's this?"

"You're not going to the Observatory. You'll help us from afar. This equipment boosts your access and will give you a chance to intercept and hopefully block any communication between Agents. You can have fun with them, like you did sending fake images of me to the police."

"The area's a blackout. I won't be able to talk to you."

"You'll help by protecting our backs. There will be drones you can send —"

"I'm going with you."

"Not this time."

Tears formed, and from her expression, I could tell she hated that they had. "I can't lose you. I won't."

CHAPTER THIRTY-NINE

As dusk slowly surrendered the sky, Tevin and Jex launched the dozen drones Valor and Anya had prepared. The drones rose gracefully, each carrying an electrostatic discharger, and flew off in different directions. The last slowed after only a few yards, its predetermined spot one that would give us our initial cover. The next moment, the discharger activated with a throaty buzz. If there were any surveillance drones in the area, 3D or otherwise, the discharger would've fried them.

I keyed our comms, which we'd shielded. "Go."

Our caravan set off for Maryland, speed and caution warring for dominance. Valor took the lead in her Charger. Amarjit drove Talia and me in the modified minivan—which smelled a little musty—the Yukon behind us towing a covered trailer.

Talia had the electrical grid killswitches ready. The final step—which would be the first reversed after this was over. We weren't knocking out everything. That would endanger more lives and take longer to fix, so we'd focused on the Eastern third of the country.

She was quiet from her seat in the back, one of her screens tuned to a broadcast that showed the worsening chaos as people were forced from the systems and resources they'd fashioned their lives around.

"Talia, do you have the traffic controls ready?" I asked.

She reluctantly typed on the keyboard. "Don't assume I'm giddy using this lame setup."

"I think it's nice," Amarjit said.

She let out a forced sigh. "Take a left."

I radioed ahead, and Valor turned left. We followed, and the traffic lights before us switched to green, triggering honks from other drivers at the abrupt light change.

I nodded my thanks to Talia, though before she could utter whatever quip she'd planned, gunshots rang out. We passed a street filled with protestors, then another with looters. She stared wide-eyed, her fingers motionless.

* * *

Three hours later, after night had fallen, we ascended a dirt road, the minivan bouncing as we followed Valor's car.

The road curved up the hill before terminating at a ledge that looked out over a valley.

We parked and headed for the ledge. Scattered towns were visible, along with light from a larger city in the distance. What we couldn't see was our ride.

As we approached the steep drop-off, the towns turned fuzzy. I reached out, and my hand seemed to disappear.

I raised my foot, angled forward as if I was going to fall over the ledge, and instead stepped onto the rear of the platform. My presence interfered with the cloaking shield, revealing the back edge of the craft to the others.

Raven stepped onto the platform next, gun drawn, and moved past me to make sure the ship was empty.

The others climbed on, moving weapons, supplies, and tech we needed for our assault.

Talia joined us as we worked, though she was mesmerized by the cloaking shield, waving her arm through it and watching it disappear.

Anya pulled me aside. "I need you to wear this." She held up a protective body vest. I started to protest, pointing out that none of the others had one, but she cut me off. "They have shields of various kinds. I know you gave Raven your hand shields, so you need this."

She helped me put it on. When she extended the front part down so it covered my crotch, I said, "If I have to run in this, I'm not sure I'll be able to."

"You'll thank me if we decide to have kids." She then blushed. Even in the darkness, I could see it. "No. Table it. Later."

"But you...?"

Jex approached, saving her from responding. "The cargo van will reach the Observatory's entrance in forty-five minutes," he said as she stepped away.

I could tell he was nervous. "We have this. We've timed it." I waved Tevin over. "Go to the control tower. Prepare to leave in…"

"Two minutes," Jex said.

As Tevin headed to the tower, I asked, "How's your back?"

"Doc shot it with magic."

I was concerned but let it drop. I went to Talia instead, moving a little awkwardly in the protective gear, and found her scoping the front of the ship. "You need to trigger the final chaos."

She pulled out her pad, accessed the program she'd written that would remotely activate the killswitches, and tapped the button.

The streetlights of a nearby town went out, followed by lights in homes and businesses. A transformer blew. The town disappeared as the damage to the region's electrical grid spread, followed by other towns, one after another going dark.

I squatted before her. "I'm proud of you. You're going to be a force when you grow up."

"Already am." She avoided my gaze. "Too much schmaltz."

I hugged her anyway. "I love you, my lioness. Go with Amarjit. He'll protect you." I waved him over, and the robotics expert took her hand to lead her away.

I was surprised she didn't resist.

I watched the two head to the ledge but lost her in the cloaking shield. Past them, the robots climbed onto the platform, which I wanted clustered in the center.

Wanting one last look, I tried to spot the minivan driving away but couldn't.

"No no," Garly cried as he struggled with the ten-foot long, five-foot in diameter wrapped-webbing-and-multi-metal-rod contraption he and Valor had brought on board. It started to unravel, the first two rods tilting outward. I hurried over and helped them regain control. We set the contraption near the front of the platform, the device too heavy for one person. Once we laid it down, Garly grabbed his ribcage. "I think I cracked something."

"Stand clear," Tevin called from the tower.

More areas darkened as we rose into the sky, with key grid points exploding and power stations blowing across the states. Only a few needed to be detonated. The rest, over forty substations, had been disabled remotely, severing electricity to over one hundred million people.

As the darkness spread, the landscape black except for moving cars and a rare generator powering lights, I stood before my group. Jex and Raven were gearing up the robots, Garly was booting up some of his tech, and others were preparing their weapons and shields, yet they all paused. It felt like the last time we'd be together.

We hugged, said words of endearment, took in the moment.

"I wish Nataly was here," Garly whispered.

After we comforted him, the others resumed their preparations. Before Jex and Raven could do the same, I pulled them aside. "When we get to the Observatory, I want you two to stay on the platform."

"Gonna shoot me if I don't?" Jex joked. To Raven, he said, "Told ya he'd do this."

Raven frowned at me. "You're asking me to go against my nature."

"I couldn't live with myself," he added. "B'sides, you need us."

I would've begged them to keep them safe. Yet I had to accept the risk, no matter how it hurt.

"If it helps, Talia magnified my fingers," Raven told me. "She turned them into greater weapons."

"Those cartridges can only handle so much pressure. If they crack, they'll cycle up and explode —"

"They're already charged. Nothing happened."

As I nodded in surrender, Amarjit rushed up, surprising me. "I'm so sorry. I lost her before we left."

I stiffened. "Talia," I shouted.

She seemingly appeared from thin air, stepping forward from a spot to one side.

She'd hid in the cloaking shield.

"*Goddammit*," I said.

She spoke fast. "You're not zippy enough to handle computer stuff. I'll do it so you can focus on chopping." She made a karate-chop move.

"This is too dangerous. Damn it, Talia." Risking the team was one thing, but with the way Zion acted, he would immediately target her.

I went to the bag that held the dark matter spheres Jex had found on the floating platform. She'd glide down to the surface. "Garly, do you have a regulator?"

"Don'ts send me away," Talia said.

Jex took my arm before I could pull out a sphere. "Dray, don't."

Raven joined us. "She'd be all alone."

I felt my struggle, sharper than before—and I couldn't stop what I'd set in motion.

I glared at Talia. She looked properly chastised, but I could tell she was excited.

I took in the team as I went to her. "Let's end this," I said as I gripped her shoulder hard.

"Ow," she said.

I squatted before her. "You stay on this ship. You get off when we land, you're grounded until you're fifty."

"That's ancient."

With numb lips, I asked, "Energy level?"

"Really high." Then she saw I wasn't in a joking mood. "It's good. I'm good."

As we rose, darkness consumed the land as far as I could see, our chaos running free.

Chapter Forty

A glow appeared in the distance.

Other than a random vehicle weaving along a mountain road, it was the only light we'd seen in the last hour. The glow increased as we headed for it, metamorphosing into the valley that contained the former Observatory.

Seeing they still had electricity increased our anxiety, though we'd expected it.

As we entered the valley, I made out our target: The Agency building, the modern fortress that dominated the far end. Then I spotted two roaming Agents, with two more manning the gate.

We stayed silent and didn't move, our implants covered, to try to avoid being detected. We didn't think Agents could pick up our engines' heat signature, as they'd been built inside the structure to mask them, but we weren't sure.

A box truck approached the main entrance, which drew the Agents' attention.

More Agents exited the building, most heading to the truck, a couple rushing over and triggering intense spotlights they aimed at the arrival. Within moments, the vehicle was virtually surrounded.

Cole's plan to drop in from the sky might've been our only chance.

The Agents suddenly retreated. They must've read that there weren't any lifeforms, fearing a bomb.

Jex aimed his line-of-sight transmitter at the truck and pressed the button.

Plasma bolts and gunfire lit up the night, the blasts and bullets erupting from the truck and spraying the fleeing Agents.

They dove behind cars or past the edge of the building, the spraying blast pulverizing the cars and carving grooves in the building.

Three didn't reach safety.

As the silver-haired men and women regrouped, we

silently drifted downward.

Tevin steered us, slowing our descent, and stopped with the front edge nearly touching the rooftop of the Observatory's top floor, the rest of the platform hovering over the side opposite the drive. Our cloaking shield fuzzed out along the edge where the roof interfered with it.

Without a word, we stepped off the platform onto the roof, light from the truck's plasma blasts and Agents' returning plasma fire flickering like a light show, the far side of the roof blocking our view of the battle. I kept an eye on that edge as we signaled our robots off the platform, and Valor helped Garly carry his huge contraption.

Gunshots, shouts, and cries from the Agents below filled the air.

I opened a duffel bag and released swarmbots. I directed them to cover the building's edge, then ducked down as Agents blew up the box truck, the explosion lighting up the grounds below. The bag over my shoulder contained the dark matter spheres Jex had found. If Agents managed to reach us, and a bullet hit the bag, we'd all be killed. But we needed their properties.

Smoke from the explosion washed over us.

I backed away from the ledge and spotted Talia on the edge of the platform.

I waved at her to stay on the platform, but she typed on her pad and showed it to me. *A hoverbike could show up and grab me!*

Letting her travel with us was one thing. Going inside Zion's hellhole was another.

Yet she wasn't wrong.

As I wrestled with myself, Raven used Garly's tiny robot to unlock the rooftop door.

The last of my resistance gave way. My team needed me present. Focused. Regardless of the cost.

I waved Talia off the platform, my glare inefficient to negate her excited and nervous expression.

Raven opened the door, and we headed inside: five men, three women, five robots, and a young girl. We carried packs, bags, and as many weapons as possible.

Jex left one of the AG-M1300 robots behind, set to DEFEND the roof.

We'd see if it was enough.

The concrete stairwell descended nine stories and was forty by forty feet in width, the remnant of the immense shaft used to drill into the surrounding mountains. Simple fixtures lit the chasm.

Garly and Valor carried his contraption through the doorway and set it upright in the stairwell's top corner, Garly wincing in pain from the weight.

As they prepped the device, I spoke softly to the rest of the team. "Be as silent as possible and stick together. Comms don't work here. We *have* to stay close."

They nodded.

Jex carried Garly's sound machine to the scientist and held onto the mine tunnel tech while Garly strapped the sound machine to his back, then looked at me.

When I gave the signal, he pressed a button, and a pole extended from the back edge of the accordion-like device to the ceiling in order to brace itself.

Jex backed away, as did Valor.

She pulled her weapons—two Glock 19s with patterns etched into their barrels—and Garly pressed a second button to activate the mine tunnel tech.

The contraption rolled forward and started down the stairs, the massive cluster of webbing and poles unspooling itself and leaving bands of black, reinforced-polymer webbing along the wall. It followed the measurements Garly had made, reaching the end of the wall, bracing a pole at the corner, then taking a ninety-degree turn and following the stairs down to the next corner.

The thick material stretched out along each wall as the device unrolled.

On each floor—which had a large landing and a door that led into the interior—thicker bracing cords extended from the corner pole to a hexagon-shaped device that the webbing placed against the door.

The device activated as soon as the mine tunnel tech planted the next corner pole.

Talia whispered to Raven that Garly had upgraded the tech—and figured out how to briefly mimic outer space. The stairwell door and jam were both painted, but the locking pin that held each door closed, and the plate it rested against, weren't. With each activation, the exposed metal in the pin fused with the metal plate as if they were in space—essentially becoming one piece. Even Agents wouldn't be able to break through.

Her description was close, but before I could correct her, Amarjit inhaled sharply. "Agents are coming."

He gripped a pad that tracked thermal readings. Agents were displayed, heading to the stairwell three stories down. "The sealer won't reach the door in time."

Raven and Valor hurried down the stairs, Raven starting to limp from her prior gunshot injury after the second landing.

The rest of us raced after them—including the robots, the larger ones lagging behind due to their slower pace—except for Jex. He grabbed a rope, hooked it to the railing, and leapt into the open stairwell.

Even weighted down with packs and weapons, we moved fast, but Jex had the two sledgehammers strapped to his back. He dropped like a stone.

He used a fast-grip to slow his rapid descent when he reached the sixth floor—the third from the top—arriving right as Agents cracked open the door. He straightened his legs as he swung into the landing and slammed into the door, throwing them back as he barked in pain.

We rounded the stairs across from him. The webbing device was the next section ahead of us, whirling as it took the corner.

Jex unhooked himself from the rope and lunged for the door as it started to open again, managed to close it, then lurched back as the webbing spun past and covered the door.

We reached him as the webbing disappeared down the next flight—but the hexagonal device moved. The Agents had opened the door just enough to prevent it from sealing. We shoved at the door, but the Agents blocked us from closing it.

Amarjit and I exchanged glances. It was a weak spot. The webbing would hold them back, but I didn't know for how long.

I led the team and robots down to the third floor. The device had avoided this door, instead angling the webbing up and over it before continuing its trek in order to seal the floors below us.

As we gathered in front of the door, Raven handing Garly his large bag, I was reminded of when she and I had invaded the Facility. I glanced at her. She smiled, though I saw her anxiety.

Our three larger robots finally joined us.

Amarjit scanned the corridor through the door with his thermal reader. Four Agents waited for us, probably scanning us with their thermals.

I held up four fingers, signaled to Garly, and had Talia move to the side.

Garly approached the door, reached back with a wince, and triggered the sound machine.

The sound echoed harshly in the concrete shaft, assaulting us from every direction.

Jex opened the door, and I fired at the Agents inside, clipping one and missing another.

Two of the Agents were on their knees, gripping their heads, one bleeding where I'd shot him, but the others seemed unaffected by the sound. The unaffected ones returned fire. I stepped back as the robots entered the hallway and fanned out to create a moving wall. Raven and Jex followed in lockstep, firing at the Agents as they proceeded into the depths of the Agency stronghold, taking out the two on their knees.

The hallways were light gray, industrial, with white floors and black trim, stylish in its own oppressive-state kind of way, and the recycled air smelled faintly like bad breath.

Though two Agents were down, the other two continued to fight, joined by three others, the sound machine wailing as Amarjit, Anya, and I followed Raven and Jex, the rest behind me. The sound was so loud, I could barely hear the Agents' gunshots, bullets pinging off the robots' metallic skin. We reached a side hallway, and our two fast robots darted to either side, taking out one Agent and hurting another, Anya activating a shield as we fired at the remaining Agent.

Chips of drywall and bits of shattered light fixtures gouged my arms, neck, and face.

A grenade was lobbed at us.

Amarjit raised his hand shield to deflect the blast, though the explosion threw the robots and us back, and both Tevin and Anya suffered minor injuries. My body vest took a portion of the explosion.

As I struggled to my feet, Jex threw a flasher ball at advancing Agents, the light blinding when it detonated.

Valor and Raven took them out.

Garly reached into his large bag, pulled out two web expanders, and tossed them into the side hallways as the two smaller robots hurried back to us. The expanders triggered, the white substance filling each passageway with white webbing and hardened. Garly had strengthened them, but there was a risk Agents could break their way through.

We hurried forward and reached a "T" intersection.

Agents waited on both sides. Before we even stepped into the hallway, shots were fired.

Garly tossed another expander, sealing the hallway to our left, then we entered and went to the right, bullets flying, robots progressing, our shields holding as we drove the Agents back. Jex suffered a shot to the shoulder, having turned his shield to deflect a second Agent's gunfire and leaving himself exposed. I fired between two of the robots and took down the Agent, who looked surprised that a couple of bullets could take him down.

They hadn't anticipated armor-piercing bullets.

As Anya swiftly patched Jex, gunfire erupted behind us. Two Agents had appeared and launched a rear attack. Tevin and Valor reacted in time, blocking with their shields and firing back, Talia screaming as more gunshots filled the air. The two Agents, a man and woman, paused in confusion at seeing a kid. They wore helmet-like coverings, which must have dampened the sound machine's assault—which was why they weren't affected. I fired at their heads, managing to shatter one of the helmets. The Agent collapsed, the other backing away as she fired at us, her bullets wide.

Jex, wielding the plasma gun Talia had enhanced, took out two Agents.

My vest absorbed three shots, though each strike was excruciating.

Garly unstrapped the sound machine and held it over everyone's heads as more Agents appeared. We aimed at the helmets of those who wore them, the others wearing earplugs that offered some protection.

Jex led us forward, though at times, even just a few steps were hard won, another grenade deflected, though a third grenade damaged one of the robots.

I alternated between shooting at the Agents, shielding the dark matter spheres, and keeping an eye on Talia.

"Hey," Valor shouted at me over the near-deafening sound. "I've got her."

Nodding my thanks, I helped Garly seal off two more corridors—both with Agents racing toward us, though too slow to stop the sealants—and continued forward.

We didn't pass many doors. The route we chose had the fewest offices, instead containing supply rooms, chillers, backup generators, and other equipment. It made for a longer journey, but we'd have fewer surprises.

Following cable lines that hung from the ceiling, we passed a programming room, the chairs empty this time of night—or the programmers were hiding from the war we'd brought—then down a short flight of stairs to the left.

A dozen Agents waited for us.

They opened fire, plasma fire and gunshots assaulting the robots and our shields. My team and I returned fire, pushing forward, Jex launching a grenade that took down two Agents and filled the air with acrid smoke.

The robots were the only things keeping us in the fight with this level of onslaught, though they took hits. A second became damaged, both it and another still able to move though with difficulty.

With our armor-piercing bullets, we took down most of the Agents. Two backed away, seeming to realize that their enhanced skin no longer provided enough protection. They scrambled to the next intersection and hid around the corner, using the wall as a shield to occasionally return fire.

Anya took out one of them when the man appeared from around the corner to shoot at us.

We hurried to the intersection, but the other Agent had run off.

We progressed another dozen yards and turned the corner to an empty area. An elevator was just ahead. Garly carried his bag to the elevator, as we needed to secure it—when six robot dogs appeared from a side hallway past the elevators.

He was exposed. And we didn't have anywhere to hide.

CHAPTER FORTY-ONE

The robot dogs' eyes glowed as they fanned out. Two hung back while the other four advanced.

I imagined them growling, though if they were, I couldn't hear them over Garly's machine.

Talia held out her pad like a shield.

Our robots started for the dogs—which attacked them, moving nearly too fast to track. The two sides fought ruthlessly, tearing out parts, one robot slamming a dog down onto the ground while another dog went for one of our robot's faces.

Raven started forward to help, but I stopped her. The two dogs that had held back were circling past the fight. Beside me, Valor switched clips.

As I gauged the dogs, Garly reached the elevator and pulled out a rod that would've kept the elevator doors open. Then Talia screamed a warning as one of the dogs stepped toward him, her voice barely audible over the sound machine.

The robot was no more than a dozen feet away.

Before he could react, the elevator doors opened to reveal a car packed with Agents who flinched at the audial assault.

I ran forward, firing at the dog and yelling at Garly, though I doubted he heard me. "*Seal the door.*"

My bullets drove the dog to the side, the mechanized weapon focusing on me and preparing to launch—when there was a sudden plasma blast. Raven. The built-up charge from her fingers slammed the dog into the wall.

With the robot neutralized, I spun and fired at the lead Agents as they started to exit the elevator, backing them up that one additional second.

Garly dropped the rod, pulled out a web expander, and tossed it to the closest Agent, who reflexively caught it—and the device triggered.

The web-like sealant filled the elevator.

Jex lobbed his second to last grenade at the remaining dog

as Valor fired to distract it. The explosion sheared off the forward part of its body, and it collapsed.

Our robots had destroyed the other dogs, but The Agency's robots had taken down three of ours in the process. We were down to one of the fast, less-shielded robots and an injured shielded one.

The sealed elevator had been our backup getaway in case we couldn't return to the central stairwell.

Talia looked shellshocked, the others only marginally better.

Nursing our wounds, we continued forward. We had to reach our destination. Agents would keep coming.

We sealed off another stairwell, proceeded forward, then encountered three more silver-haired enemies. As they opened fire, Valor tackled Talia while Tevin protected me with the other enhanced plasma gun—but not before a square-jawed female Agent shot me, clipping my leg. Raven fired more plasma shots, then huddled behind Jex as she switched cartridges in her fingers. He took down one Agent, and Anya took down the other two.

Garly had one last sealer.

He used it to cover an adjoining hallway as Anya wrapped a self-sealing bandage around my leg and injected nanobots, then approached the command room.

Though the doors were double-bolted, Raven used Garly's shifting robot to unlock them. The doors opened to reveal banks of control equipment laid out in a U-shaped pattern. Like the programmers' room, it was empty.

Tevin and Amarjit entered first.

As Tevin extracted two large cylinders from his bag, Amarjit used his machine gun to smash the control screens. Tevin followed, pouring nanotech particles into the exposed electronics. The particles would crawl deep into the systems and dissolve the technology from the inside.

Satisfied, I limped to the set of double doors that opened onto the mysterious room that was our destination, Talia and the others behind me.

The room was immense, filled with dozens of towers that

stretched half a football field in length.

The floor wasn't lower as we'd expected; it was the same as any other floor, covered in a black rubber coating designed in a grid pattern.

The towers were optical data processors, each the size of a walk-in closet with a level of computing power and speed unheard of a decade ago. Each processing tower pulled from datatanks situated on floors above with the tanks' waterlines hanging down from overhead.

Garly gave Amarjit the sound machine before joining us among the towers, leaving him and the robots to watch our backs.

While we could still hear the painful sound, we could at least talk to each other, though my ears rang.

As we walked among the towers, we found that they touched the floor. Brilliant white light glowed from where they touched.

"Think you can install a virus or something?" Valor asked Talia, gesturing with one of her etched pistols.

"No. Their system will be stacked with armies of anti-viral spiders."

She faltered.

"What is it?" Valor asked as I knelt before Talia, my knee sinking into the rubber floor.

I checked her chest. "The electronics are interfering with your battery. Go back to the command room."

"I'm sorry," she said.

As she left, we began to disburse the explosives and dark matter spheres we'd brought. I directed my team to position the explosions to try to create a cascading effect. My eyes kept going to the base of the towers. There was something about the white light. I traced the pattern in the floor around me, and that's when it struck me. The flooring wasn't a single piece. It consisted of rubber mats laid tight together.

I found the corner of a mat, lifted it — and was blinded by rapid flashes of brilliant light.

I cried out as I stumbled back, my lenses darkening to protect my retina a second too late.

The others ran over, but I waved them back. "Shield your eyes." I then threw two of the mats back completely. Intense, flickering light burst forth.

The center of the web, a blinding orchestra of lies.

My team pulled more and more mats aside. Everywhere they looked, flickering light filled the space beneath them — which descended a number of feet.

"My god, the floor is one gigantic piece of glass," I said. As my eyes adjusted, I began to make out more detail. "The plans make sense now. Look. Light signals, each one a packet of information, are emitted by the towers down into the glass. Tiny angled bits were embedded in the glass under each tower. They don't interfere with other signals but deflect the ones they receive out to the outer walls. Remember what looked like receptors along the bottom portion of the walls? That's what they are. The signals are sent to those receptors and then out to every part of the country."

Tevin shook his head. "This thing is a feat of engineering. I wouldn't even know where to start creating something like this."

"The floor had to have been formed in place. That's why there aren't any support beams." I took in the room with fresh eyes. "We could take down the towers, but those can be rebuilt. This five-foot-thick sheet of glass can't, not without a tremendous amount of time and effort."

"We need to shatter the glass," Raven said.

I yelled to Talia. "Send the robots back in."

Valor touched my arm. "I'll go protect her."

As the others gathered up the spheres and bombs they'd laid, Jex and I directed the robots to different spots in the room. We positioned them where we thought they'd do the most damage, then gave each a sledgehammer.

"Told ya we'd need 'em," he said.

The robots raised their sledgehammers, slammed them down, and repeated their assault. Shards of glass flew as they deepened their holes.

Talia opened one of the doors. "Agents are coming," she yelled over the sound machine. "They're digging through what looks like duct work between floors."

Raven hurried to the command room.

I had Garly, Anya, and Jex stay behind and sent the rest to join Raven. Together, the four of us tied the explosives together with dark matter spheres.

Gunshots rang out from the command room — and Garly's sound machine cut off.

I wanted to go to Raven and Talia but couldn't. Not yet.

I snapped at Anya and Jex to take their sets to the hole closest to the door, then led Garly to the other hole. Light bathed the hammering robot, the distorted rays flickering over its body. I commanded the robot to stop and sent it to the command room to fight.

The ground crunched under our feet from the layer of glass shards, the air throbbing with distorted light. The hole, which was nearly four feet deep, had to be interfering with thousands if not millions of signals, but they were just a fraction of the data being transmitted to the receptors that lined the walls under the glass, the signals sent out to Zion's national network of drones.

I leaned into the hole, forced to put a hand against the jagged side in order to lean down far enough to place my dark matter bomb. I got it into position, then called out. "Set your timer for one minute on my mark."

Jex shouted he heard, and we set the timers.

Garly and I stood and scrambled toward the exit, our feet slipping until we reached one of the rubber mats, my wounded leg flaring. Pockets of brilliant light painted the tanks and ceiling where the glass had been uncovered.

I silently counted in my head as we hurried.

Anya and Jex had already disappeared into the command room. I didn't hear gunshots, but I didn't know if that was a good sign.

I drew my gun and opened one of the doors to the command room.

Fear shot through me as bodies laid scattered. Four had silver hair, two didn't. Valor and Jex were both down.

A muscular Agent covered in blood stood near the center

of the room. His face was either grimacing, smiling, or a strange mixture of both as he towered over Anya, who crouched with her hands up. I fired at him, the bullet tearing into his chest. He staggered back, then raised his gun to return fire—when Garly tackled me.

He'd kept count.

The explosion was so powerful it lifted us off the floor and threw us a dozen feet as it shook the entire complex.

The Agent was blown back from the blast and slammed into the far wall. He collapsed to the floor as the doors to the data room flew over our heads and crashed against one of the consoles.

The boom was followed by high-pitched cracking.

The air filled with vaporized glass particles.

Covering my mouth, I rose unsteadily on my knees, made sure the Agent was dead, then went to Anya, who had been thrown on top of Jex. She was shaken but OK.

Jex opened his eyes, his expression dazed. "There's an Agent," he warned.

Anya did a quick examination. He had a dislocated shoulder, cracked rib, hyper-extended knee, and multiple bruises.

As she and Garly popped his shoulder back into place, I went to Valor, who was bloody. She insisted she was fine, but I administered some of Anya's nanobots in three spots.

I searched the others. None were badly injured. They'd hidden behind the consoles and had prepared to rush the Agent when the bombs detonated.

But Garly's sound machine had been destroyed.

Talia, who brandished a broken piece of metal she'd found, approached the doorway. "Epic sauce," she said in wonder.

The massive data room had been decimated. Some glass remained intact around the edge of the room, but it didn't matter. The floor had been destroyed—and with the glass no longer supporting them, the towers had fallen. Water poured from ripped data lines, while sparks flickered in the dust and smoke.

"Let's get out of here," Anya said.

We found the two robots in the hallway outside the

command room. They had defeated another Agent, though the heavier robot was badly damaged.

We retraced our steps, moving as fast as our hurt group could manage. We'd all suffered at least some cuts, even Talia. Valor seemed to regain her strength as she walked, though Jex and I limped badly, which prompted more nanobots. I only had one more clip for my machine gun; others were running low, too. We were out of wall expanders and only had one grenade left.

Alarms rang throughout the complex, as if anyone didn't already know we were here.

Jex had left his sledgehammers behind, but Garly carried his broken sound machine.

We reached the remains of the robot battle and passed the elevator, the doors of which were still open. Though the web sealant held, Agents were breaking it apart on their side. In another minute, their hole would be big enough to climb through. As I thought this, a hand appeared.

"Move," I whispered.

We took the corner, the damaged robot's joint grinding as it walked.

We reached a cluster of Agents we'd defeated. There were over a dozen, yet they were only a fraction of Zion's army.

We proceeded up the short flight of stairs, slipped past the programming room, and continued our tense journey.

Though adrenaline coursed through me, I struggled to keep up as we approached the "T" intersection.

Agents fired at us through the wall we'd used to seal the other hallway.

I scooped up Talia and shielded her as we scrambled back to the last intersection, gunfire striking our shields and two hitting my body vest.

We regrouped around the corner but couldn't stay. Agents would come—yet if we wanted to reach the stairwell, we'd have to walk right up to the seal in order to reach the next hallway. Agents had created three head-sized holes in the wall.

Jex removed his last grenade. "We should use this."

"It could pulverize the wall," I warned.

"Give it to me," Valor said. "I'll use the robots and shields to get close."

"I got it," Jex said. "Your shield is dimmer."

Garly said, "They've all weakened. They'll fail soon. I can't Nostradamus when."

"Be ready to run," Jex said as Talia looked at him with huge eyes. He sent the robots back around the corner, which drew a few gunshots, and activated his shield, which looked dimmer. Then he disappeared around the corner.

We followed, Valor and I in the lead, our shields at max power, streaks of blood magnifying her hatch-mark tattoos.

Gunfire erupted, bullets sparking off of the robots. The injured robot moved too slowly for Jex, so he took a position behind the smaller one and pushed it faster. Gunfire increased from all three spots. Jex struggled to keep up with the faster robot, his limp more pronounced. When they neared, he pulled the pin on the grenade, shoved the robot into the side hallway, and went up to the wall.

Our group ran to join him, to help somehow, though we wouldn't reach him. Valor fired as she ran.

Jex shoved the grenade through one of the holes, then pressed his hand shield against the hole as an Agent thrust their arm out of a different hole and aimed at him.

The grenade exploded.

Jex was thrown back as the wall collapsed, smoke and pulverized webbing filling the air. We were thrown back as well.

I got to my feet and forced myself forward.

Two of the three Agents appeared dead, the third holding his stomach as he laid on the ground, their augmented bodies unable to withstand a blast that close. I climbed over the debris, knocked the gun away from the Agent, then went to Jex, but Raven was already helping him up.

She slung his arm over her shoulder.

He could barely walk, so Amarjit helped, slinging Jex's other arm over his shoulder. Anya wanted to inspect Jex, and Talia wanted to comfort him, but there was no time.

Raven and Amarjit led the way to the central stairwell.

Tevin moved past them, opened the door—and quickly shut it. "We have company."

Amarjit checked his thermal reader. "Three Agents."

I couldn't call the robot down from the roof—no comms—the sound machine was broken, and we only had one fully functioning robot with us.

I directed the heavily damaged robot, which just now reached us, to defend our flank, then signaled the smaller, faster robot forward. I flipped open its cover, which showed it was in ATTACK mode, and connected that mode to a base command: CORRAL CATTLE.

"One last push," I said, then opened the door.

The robot darted out as gunfire erupted.

It raced to the nearest Agent, grabbed her as she fired at it, and threw her over the railing. The other two Agents stopped firing as she fell, her cries echoing before they cut short.

Beside me, Talia gasped.

I entered the stairwell as the robot bounded up the stairs to the next Agent, a man with bodybuilder-sized muscles. Behind him, the third Agent, another woman, backed up the stairs, her face reflecting her fear of the robot.

The male Agent lunged as the robot approached, grabbed its arms, and began to wrestle it.

My team joined me on the stairs. We had to get to the roof. Every second we stayed, the greater the chance of being killed.

Valor stepped past me and fired at the third Agent.

The male Agent ripped an arm off the robot, sparks flying, but the robot spun around the man, hooked its remaining arm around his neck, and took him with it as it went over the railing.

That move surprised me—though the Agent had probably been more so.

We started up the stairs, Valor driving the remaining Agent back, and reached the fourth, then fifth floor. The woman scrambled to the sixth-floor door and started to shout as she disappeared inside. That explained why there weren't more Agents: they couldn't use comms.

Together, my wounded and bleeding team reached the

sixth floor. Valor trained her gun on the unsealed door as we hurried past, the black webbing torn, and then followed us up.

Agents beat at the metal doors on the seventh and eighth floors to try to break through. At both levels, the metal bowed outward but held.

As we reached the rooftop door, we heard an explosion.

Clinging to my side and gripping her piece of metal, Talia said, "It's not safe."

"We're almost there, little stinker," Raven said as she and Amarjit continued to support Jex.

"What does your scan show?" I asked Amarjit.

He extracted his reader. "The roof's clear, but Agents are trying to climb up."

I cautiously opened the door.

Our last robot swiveled to us, though a scan assured him we were the ones to defend.

Agents were trying to climb the building onto the roof, their efforts punctured by shouts and occasional gunfire, but when they reached for the top, they found the edge covered with swarmbots that broke apart, stealing their grip. I suspected a number of Agents had fallen as a result.

Shouts rose as more Agents poured out of the building at ground level.

I directed my team onto the floating platform. Raven and Amarjit went first, helping Jex on, followed by Talia.

Tevin climbed on and hurried to the command tower.

"Dad, look out," Talia cried as Garly and Anya climbed onto the platform.

I ducked as a mighty boom erupted and part of the roof sheared off. A ten-foot-wide gap had been carved in the roof, the leading edge stopping only a few feet from me. When I straightened, I spotted three Agents on the main drive holding a concussion cannon. The soundwave took out part of the roof — and allowed them to see what we were doing.

"Move the ship," I yelled.

I fired down at the Agents as the cannon cycled up again.

I took out one Agent, causing the others to struggle with

the cannon's weight, but two others ran to help while others shot at us.

Valor fired beside me.

"More are coming up the stairwell," Amarjit called as he stared at his thermal reader.

Valor pulled me back as the cannon cycled.

We hurried to the platform, which was already starting to rotate. I reached for the edge, and the cannon fired.

The blast sheared away part of the roof to our right—and struck the edge of the platform.

Tevin fought for control as the platform was thrown backward, my team knocked off their feet, though he managed to stop them from crashing into the complex.

Metal pings rang behind me. The robot had stepped between us and Agents to block their gunfire.

Tevin was bringing the platform back toward us, but it was still ten feet away.

As it approached, I said to Valor. "You ready?"

She followed my lead as I bent down into a runner's stance, then burst forward, taking the two, three steps, leapt—

And landed on the platform.

Valor landed beside me, and I shouted at the command tower. "*Go.*"

Tevin used the platform's momentum to continue its swing, rotating to face away from the complex, angled us up, and floored the engines.

The craft shook. It had been damaged.

Tevin pivoted to the left, using as much of the building for cover as we slowly ascended. I helped Talia stay in place as everyone laid down on the deck, holding onto the tops of panels as Tevin banked hard, part of the complex and the valley appearing below us. The cloaking device remained activated, which helped our odds, though we weren't safe yet.

The platform straightened as we climbed and slowly gained speed, heading for the mountains that rose before us.

I felt elation as I stood. We'd done it. We'd destroyed Zion's grip.

Smiles formed all around, though they faded as a hoverbike approached.

The hoverbike swooped down and nearly hit Amarjit as it landed, its underbelly scratching the deck—

And Britt leapt off the bike.

CHAPTER FORTY-TWO

The female Agent came at us like an assassin in a black dress and knee-high boots, slicing Garly across the chest, cutting Valor's arm with her knife, and kicking Jex in the back, the exposed part of her robotic leg catching the faint light as she moved with ruthless grace.

I was furious. This should have been a celebration, not another goddamn fight.

Britt smiled at me as her silver hair swayed in the breeze. "So many people, did you really think you could hide?"

She'd spotted our body heat.

I aimed at her and pulled the trigger—but was out of bullets.

Talia raised her piece of metal and started for Britt until Anya snatched her.

"Get off this ship," Valor cried, machine gun raised, arm bleeding.

Britt's smile faded as the closest mountain neared, which we would just clear. "Blowing up this place isn't enough, Quintero. We'll keep up the charade. It's all part of Zion's sick ploy. He even confided in me, as if spilling his dirty secret would make up for what he did to me.

"But you," she went on. "He'll reward me for you."

She headed for me, undaunted by our guns. I reloaded, raised my pistol—when Raven slammed into her, knocking her knife away. She punched the Agent, chopped her in the neck, and reached for the Glock tucked in her belt when Britt snatched her to use her as a shield.

We held our fire and stepped back when the Agent advanced. She forced Raven to move with her as she pinned Raven's arm behind her.

Raven struggled, but Britt held her, then shoved her to the side and sprang at me. She tackled me—and we sailed off the back of the platform, the Agent giggling just before we landed on the backside of the mountain we'd just flown over.

I rolled down the fractured rocks.

I tried to stop my fall but slid on my stomach fifty feet before I could, the rocks slicing my calloused hands.

Britt had arrested her fall quicker than I had. She stood thirty feet farther up the mountain and brushed her hair from her face. "Having fun?"

My feet shifted under me as I stood — but I'd held onto my gun. Hiding it behind me, I waited until she neared, then fired.

She stumbled and grabbed her side with an almost comical expression of surprise. Blood seeped through her fingers. "You cheat. Armor-piercing."

Distant gunfire drew my attention. Two hoverbikes had approached the platform, but Anya shot them down.

"And you have a sharpshooter," Britt said.

She lunged at me.

Even though she was hurt, she moved too fast. I fired again but missed — and she knocked my gun away.

I swung, aiming for her wound, but she danced out of reach.

Though I still wore my body vest, she could hurt me in a number of ways.

As if reading my thoughts, she ducked forward and punched me in the shoulder, striking an open wound, then kicked me in the jaw.

I stumbled back, sliding farther down the hill and barely keeping my balance.

Britt walked toward me, unconcerned.

A hoverbike appeared behind her, heading toward us. At first, I assumed it was another Agent, but the driver's hair was golden-brown.

I locked eyes with Britt. "Stop this. It's over."

"You have to pay for Kieran."

I ground my foot into the rocks to make noise as she approached. "Let's talk about this."

She frowned and cocked her head.

Raven neared.

"Listen to me," I shouted, startling Britt, then dove to the side.

She spun—and Raven smashed into her.

The Agent sailed fifty or more feet before she fell to the ground and rolled nearly twice as far.

As I stood, Raven landed the damaged hoverbike by the Agent. I started jogging toward them.

Raven climbed off the hoverbike and charged Britt, gun in one hand and hand shield in the other.

I broke into a run.

The two fought, Raven shooting at Britt, the Agent able to avoid one shot but taking a bullet to the arm. Blood dripping from her wounds, she knocked Raven's gun away, then ripped the shield emitter from Raven's hand.

I shouted at them as I made it halfway to them, running faster.

Raven pointed her right hand at Britt, but the Agent must've known about the finger weapons. She grabbed Raven's hand, bent back her metal index and middle fingers, ripped them away—triggering a cry—and broke the plasma cartridges.

Britt let them fall from her hand.

Raven snatched the cartridges, which were sparking, and jammed them down Britt's shirt. She then spun around the surprised Agent, grabbed both arms, and pulled them back.

Britt swung her arms forward, throwing Raven a dozen feet away, and glared at her. But Raven's move had been a stall tactic. Light flickered inside Britt's shirt. The cartridges would be vibrating as the sparks intensified.

Britt dug into her shirt as Raven ducked and covered her head.

The next moment, the cartridges exploded in a flash of blue-white light.

Britt was thrown backwards, her body no longer moving as it hit the ground and slid down the rock and dirt.

I reached Raven, who nearly cried when she looked at me.

* * *

We used Britt's hoverbike to rejoin the team and headed

back to the abandoned factory, the team exhausted and hurt, relieved but overwhelmed by the battle we'd endured.

With Zion's nexus destroyed, we didn't have to worry about the 3D drones—or anything anymore.

We reached our cars after sunrise.

During our return to the factory, electricity came back in spots. The start of the recovery.

Once inside our base, I helped Anya attend to everyone. No one got away unscathed, not even her, all of us having run on adrenaline and desperation during the fight.

After our triage, we commandeered one of Talia's vid screens to see how the public was reacting to the coup we'd unveiled.

The news channel flashed scenes of multiple arrests, riots, and destruction. After a few seconds, the screen switched to the news anchor. "Everyone can see the smog, the brown skies," he said in a grave voice.

"Oh yeah, that makes sense," Valor said. "It's new to them."

"Let's hear from a White House official." The screen changed—and projected Zion's face.

He announced, "Your implants have been hacked by the traitor Dray Quintero. He and his team are warping what you see, which is why the skies look brown. We are doing everything we can to fix what he's done and bring him to justice."

To our surprise, the screen then changed to a live feed of Senators Dixon, Malatone, and others grouped in front of a cluster of microphones on the Capitol steps.

"Were you aware of the damage to our skies?" a reporter asked.

Malatone ignored the question. "We call for the capture of Dray Quintero. This is an attack on the entire country."

An Agent I didn't recognize stood close behind him.

"What the hell?" Raven asked as Malatone ranted about me. "How are the Senators still masked?"

I was just as confused.

I switched to C-Span, which showed the House Chamber

where two Representatives demanded an inquiry into how everyone's implants had been hacked.

Agents stood in the Chamber's corners.

"I can't believe nothing's changed," Anya said.

"Zion has to have a backup system," Tevin said.

"Where?" Raven asked.

"Inside the Capitol?" Anya asked.

Tevin said, "Possibly. It wouldn't be as sophisticated as what we destroyed, but it could be enough until they rebuild their nexus."

I thought about what Britt had said. They would keep up the charade.

A horrible idea struck me.

I focused on the Agents. They didn't need to be there. The Capitol had an army of guards. No one would attack the Chamber.

Realization took hold. "Agents are the broadcasters. It's why they have so many implants, to act as a backup to hide Congresspeople's identities. It wouldn't be enough to have a mini broadcaster hidden in the Capitol. That could be found, and the Senators and Representatives need coverage outside the Capitol, outside Washington, hell everywhere."

The group fell silent, their despair mingling with their pain.

"We're never gonna be free," Jex said.

Raven agreed. "Not unless we destroy every damn Agent."

CHAPTER FORTY-THREE

I was in a daze. I had been for the past twenty-four hours, since we'd discovered Agents were walking broadcast towers. They were the perfect backup, nearly indestructible and able to scatter or fight as needed.

I wasn't the only one stunned. The whole team was. They'd kept to themselves, nursing their injuries, since the news broadcast.

We couldn't stay. Zion would be gunning for us. We had to pay for the destruction we'd wrought.

I wandered the first floor of the old factory, oddly comforted by the abandoned machinery, all examples of mechanical engineering. A thought had been nagging me, and I finally gave in, pulling out my burner phone.

I dialed a familiar number.

When Nikolai heard my voice, he shouted. "You have some nerve. Your acolyte stole millions of dollars in assets."

"Consider it part of my severance."

"You don't get a severance."

"You didn't have a company without me."

"I fired you. Tell Amarjit he's fired, too."

I knew this conversation wouldn't go smoothly. "We need tech, armor, transportation, and funds to get settled."

His voice calmed. "What are you talking about?"

"I have to create some sort of life in Zion's world."

He paused. "I didn't think you gave up on things."

"I need fake implant codes as well, ones I can graft onto a thin cover. With your contacts, you can get them. And I need a job, something to hide behind."

"Why should I do anything for you?"

"Because you haven't once expressed alarm that Zion is behind everything. How long have you known? His Agents pilot hoverbikes—*our* hoverbikes."

"You got the robots Amarjit stole. My gift is I won't press

charges."

"They've been destroyed." The last one had been left at the Observatory. "My girls and I need help, Nikolai."

"Is that why you want to hide, because you're out of robots?"

"He'd already won."

I waited for him to react, but he didn't.

I sighed. "Do what you can."

"And how will you pay me?"

I squeezed the phone. "You're building fusion reactors but can't light them." I explained how I'd lit the first one, the damaged robot that angled the pressure. "Use the maintenance vids to confirm the robot's position. That should light the other cores."

I could hear the conflict in his voice. "I'll think about it."

* * *

I hung up, bothered. Then I heard the tapping of metal from the receiving area.

I found Talia installing two of Jex's data pads to the inside of the van. The wail of police sirens outside rose then faded, a near constant sound the past day. "What's all this?"

Talia didn't look up. "You and doc together now?"

"Does that upset you?"

She shrugged. "She's smarter than you. Graduated tops at John Hopkins."

"School indicates intelligence?"

"You get shot at. She doesn't. She's smarter."

I smiled at her joke. "What are you doing?"

"I needs a boss command center."

"We're not fighting anymore."

"Not fighting *yet*. You need to get crackin'. Chop chop."

"Talia..."

She lowered her screwdriver and faced me. "I fear the Silvers learned from me, and I made their protections stronger. We can't let them podium."

As gently as I could, I said, "We lost before we even started."

"I have a plan. I need you to install something that interacts with multiple systems at once. You're wizardly with hardware."

"The war is over."

She booted up her screens and pointed to one that showed a cluster of Agency drones. "They haven't found us yet, but they will. And when I went outside—"

"You *what*?"

"I had to glean the chaos. Things are rebooting. We're losing ticks of the clock."

She had a hand to her chest as if it was hurting, but when I asked, she said, "Stop wrinkling about me. You have bigger guppies. First, I want you to install your gizmo in the corner here."

I inspected the inside of the van. She'd taken the components Tevin and Garly installed, and either she or Jex had added multi-band broadcasters, intercept systems, computer cores, and other hardware. She might claim hardware wasn't her specialty, but she'd installed enough processing power to coordinate tens of thousands of pieces of tech.

Then it hit me. She was accepting what I'd asked her to do: play a supporting role. It was a huge step, as that wasn't her personality.

"If they capture us, it'll be a horror movie," she said. "I can't live spooked."

* * *

I was irritable the next day and barely slept that night, an idea flicking at me like an annoying pest.

"What are we doin'?" Jex asked.

"Investigating," I said.

He'd mostly rebounded from his injuries, aided by sleep and nanobots, though he still had ugly bruises, a concussion, and two cracked ribs.

I led him and Tevin among the expanding chaos to do a quick recon near D.C.

Shouts, cries, gunshots, and breaking glass drifted to us from different spots.

"Your drones are still broadcasting, aren't they?" Tevin

asked Jex, his voice tense.

"Yeah, not that anyone's listenin'. Were you able to cover up the train attack?"

"Hell no. The tracks are impassable. God knows how I'll convince the insurance company to rebuild them."

We were cloaked in mini-bot masks and fake implant codes, yet we were pushing it being this close, five miles from the center of it all.

The area had devolved into lawlessness. Restaurants were empty, stores were closed, yet there were people on the streets, looking for trouble or guidance. The rest hid.

"Wasn't this what you wanted?" Tevin asked me. "To take everything down?"

I started to protest, then the realization hit. "Zion isn't trying to stop the chaos," I said. "He could've sent forces to quell all of this. He's letting cities tear themselves apart."

"If we're gonna do somethin', gotta do it soon," Jex said.

Tevin scoffed. "What can—"

I grabbed him and Jex and yanked them back.

They protested until they followed my gaze. Hundreds of drones adhered to the brick wall of a two-story building. As we watched, a drone launched itself and followed someone in a hoodie the next block up.

More drones would follow if the first one determined he was a risk.

It was a glimpse of our future.

* * *

Hours later, I pulled into the factory's receiving area and triggered the remote to close the door.

We got out and undid our masks, the tiny robots freeing our faces. Glad to get the sweaty thing off, I wiped my forehead.

Light flickered from inside Talia's van. I considered going to her when I heard Raven's voice—and what sounded like people. Lots of them. And, of all things, the air smelled of baked goods.

With rising alarm, I followed the noise to the building's main factory area.

The old machinery had been pushed against the walls, and fifty or more strangers filled the space, standing in formation before Raven. Boxes with store-bought pastries and muffins laid open on a side table.

I interrupted her giving some sort of instructions. "What the hell's going on?"

"They're my recruits. They want to fight," she said with pride.

I was horrified.

"Nice job," Jex said.

Tevin agreed. "You are a force, Raven."

I pulled her away from her "recruits." "Bringing in strangers is beyond dangerous. It exposes us."

"I covered their implants. Besides, the government showed it doesn't care about them. They deserve a chance to make their own fate."

"Are they the ones we rescued?"

"Yes, and the next of kin from the town in Ohio. I found them using the tax rolls. More are coming, over a hundred."

The strangers were watching us—and I remembered I was unmasked. I tensed, though some nodded at me. None seemed angry or hostile.

She watched my reaction. "They know the claims against us are lies."

"I don't want to risk any innocents."

"No one's innocent anymore. We opened their eyes."

"Dammit, Raven."

She jerked her arm from my grasp. "This is their battle, too. Whether we use them or not, they're going to fight for their families, their friends, and their towns."

Behind her, many recruits nodded in agreement, though I ignored them, my irritation rising. "This is wrong."

"Dad, they want this."

I walked away.

Voices followed me as I ascended to the second floor, calling out that they were ready to fight.

I'd surrendered the war, to some relief if I was honest with myself, though I'd felt a growing pressure in my mind, and this didn't help. Neither had the trip to D.C.

I recalled something Nataly had said. She'd told me to recruit people not to risk their lives but to rescue them. Yet Raven's recruits would be at risk. We all would.

Anything we tried now would have a terrible price.

Anya found me in the hallway outside the office area. "I see you're not the only Quintero with groupies," she teased.

"I wish that's all they were."

"Think Talia will get some as well?"

"She already does. Hackers around the globe do anything she asks."

She stroked my cheek. "I'd thought things had gotten real before. Now with these new faces, everyone determined yet inexperienced—"

"When does it end?"

"Does it end?"

"It has to. One way or the other." I kissed her, then pulled back as I heard a car drive off. "At least someone came to their senses."

She looked out a nearby window. "I think that's Jex."

I pulled out my burner phone, turned it on, and dialed him. "Where are you going?"

"Snatchin' armored vehicles with A and V." He meant Amarjit and Valor. "We doin' this, we need better rides."

I growled as I hung up. "I feel like I'm being pushed."

"Then avoid Garly. He's been busy making weapons. He told me he's 'going epic this time'."

My phone vibrated.

I answered it, expecting to hear Jex's voice, but it was a robo recording. I realized who had commissioned it. "Remember the town you planned to retire in?" the voice asked. "There is a warehouse south of there. Look for a familiar name."

* * *

The journey had been perilous.

The 3D drone network could have reached this far, definitely would have if not for our chaos, and could have been synched with Zion's systems. Even if not, there were DNA scanners, the police, searcher drones, and my surveillance network all on high alert. Even with my mask, I could be detained. Questioned. Discovered.

The chaos we'd unleashed, though settling in some areas, continued in Mt. Airy, a larger town just over the border in North Carolina. People protested while fires dined on evacuated government buildings.

I'd visited the area years ago when we'd considered an acquisition. I'd passed on the business but fell in love with the town.

It took longer to find what the voice had alluded to than I cared to admit, the warehouse unremarkable except for the sign proclaiming who owned it: Ravendell Corp.

I approached the rust-streaked building.

There were no windows, just a large roll-up door and a side entrance. Both were locked, though a finger scanner had been installed next to the entrance. I mentally shrugged and pressed my finger to the scanner.

The bolt turned.

There was just one interior light, which pierced the darkness to reveal a large box truck parked inside the warehouse.

I extracted a flashlight and searched the warehouse, but the truck was all it held.

A faint ringing drew me to the truck's cab. A scrambler phone had been left inside.

I answered but didn't speak.

"I'm not going to fight," Nikolai said after a moment. "I don't do that. Look in the back. It's the best I can do."

I eyed the truck.

"The combo is your ID number." He paused. "You're a lot of things but not a traitor. That was asinine."

He hung up, and I went to the back. I punched in my Gen Omega number on the digital pad, then raised the rear doors.

My flashlight's beam was reflected back to me from multiple angles.

The reflections were from the metal that made up robots.

Ten of them. Eight were the large, eight-foot-tall digger robots Amarjit had designed and built, with broad shoulders, flattened faces, short legs, and long arms, their fingers consisting of foot-long blades, each one wielding five times the strength of the models we'd used to invade the Observatory. The other two were four feet high, built on all-terrain frames with balloon tires, our carrier robots, what Amarjit had called "clean-up" robots designed to scoop and transport dirt and other objects.

I climbed into the truck.

The digger robots had been reinforced with metal plates across their face, chest, and legs. Nikolai knew the purpose they'd serve.

The feeling of being pushed intensified.

My broadcast had started this.

I feared I'd fall short again. Even with these, we'd been outgunned and outmanned. We couldn't match The Agency's power.

And yet.

CHAPTER FORTY-FOUR

I drove the box truck into the receiving area, parked near Talia's van, and shut the rolling door.

Raven was giving instructions to her recruits as Jex armed them.

Talia scurried past with a fistful of wires, her battery pack strapped to her chest. She was the key. Maybe always had been — though Raven was integral as well.

Watching Raven in control, handling her recruits, I saw the woman she'd become.

I felt my need to protect them, though I recognized now where it came from. I wanted to be the father I'd never had, the supporter and protector. That was why I fought. I'd learned to set aside my wants to help Raven after she joined the rebels, though my need had driven me to abandon the rebellion to find Talia. It's why I tried to stop Raven from fighting at the Observatory, why I could never stop trying to protect them and shield them from this brutal world.

I wanted to be the father they deserved.

Now, I had to let them go.

I'd made that decision before, but not to this degree. I had to. No holding back. No matter how much it hurt.

To have a chance, we had to use every resource we had. Every person we had.

Anya approached. "I can read your face. I've already been practicing with my sniper rifle." She touched my cheek. "I'll gather everyone."

The group, including Jex, Amarjit, and Valor, who had returned before I did, assembled by Nikolai's truck.

I looked at them and announced, "I think we should try one more time to take it all down." With a smile, I added, "I'm definitely not thinking straight."

Talia clapped, excited.

"What changed?" Valor asked.

"My perspective, helped by Raven and the army she's raised. But there's something else." I led them to the truck's hold and showed them the robots.

The team was shocked—and Amarjit was thrilled. "You want me to program them."

I nodded. They were the last critical piece, along with Raven's volunteers.

"We have one shot," I told my team. "It's not to fight Agents, though we will. We need to expose the members of Congress."

Tevin said, "Dray, the Observatory was bad enough. Agents will protect Congresspeople with their lives—and not just them. Police, the FBI, the goddamn Army."

"It's our only chance. Their event is tomorrow. Let the chaos end. Let Zion think he's won."

They objected over letting the chaos end, but I was insistent. "If we don't, he'll know we're planning something. When we strike, we'll trigger some distractions, but they're not our focus anymore." I gazed at each in turn. "I won't be able to protect all of you. Maybe none of you."

"So we're all a part of the battle?" Raven asked.

"Even your recruits."

"I'm so in," Talia said, which made Raven look worried.

I leaned toward my older daughter. "You have to let her go. As do I."

Her worried eyes swept over me, but before she could say whatever she was thinking, I squatted down to Talia's level. "You'll be in your command center, so we'll make sure you have what you need."

Jex said, "I can keep helpin' with that."

"I need you to focus on something else instead. Plan our invasion." I gave a few other instructions, then looked at each one. "Get some rest tonight. We leave before dawn."

The group disbanded, and I followed Talia to her van. "I have to check your broadcast arrays. You're going to use drones."

When I described what I wanted, she smiled. "I already noggined to use drones."

"What for?"

"I got surprises." Her smile faded. "Tomorrow, if I'm danger-zoned, will you keep fighting or try to save me?"

My mouth grew dry.

I memorized her face, wanting to cherish every moment we had.

* * *

Early the next morning, our headquarters clamored with activity as the teams made their final preparations.

Anya was one of the few not running around. At the moment, as Raven watched, Anya leaned over one of Raven's recruits and carefully burned a hole in the older man's lens. She'd wanted everyone to have the same advantage we did. The man was the last one. Now, none of our fighters could be blinded by The Agency.

By my direction, she'd also implanted our core team with mics and earpieces. My daughters had been thrilled.

Once Anya finished, I motioned Raven over. She frowned at me when I grabbed a scalpel and directed her to sit. I then took her arm and placed it on the table.

"You know what you're doing?"

"This time I do." I covered the area with iodine, then a numbing agent. I made a small incision, and with the tip of the scalpel, carefully fished out the tracker I'd installed. I handed it to her and pressed gauze against the cut.

She studied the tracker, then raised her gaze. "I'm going to marry Jex. We're not going to have kids right away. I have ideas on how to help those who lost their towns."

I grabbed the suture glue to close the wound. "You need help with those ideas?"

"No, but you'll want to get involved when you hear them. You aren't upset about me marrying Jex?"

"I expected it." He'd told me he planned to propose—but since she wasn't wearing a ring, he must not have popped the question yet.

Once again, I was struck by her maturity. Her recruits would be in great hands. I felt proud, though she'd grown up with less help from me than I'd anticipated.

I glued her skin closed.

"You should have extra protection. I can't shake my premonition. Dumb, I know," she said.

"I have the swarmbots and a vest." I cleaned her forearm, then removed the bracelet I'd worn and set it on the table.

She touched my hand. "Please be careful."

"I was going to say the same thing."

She was called away, so I went to Jex, who was reviewing his plan, something he'd done a dozen times. "You ready?"

He nodded. "Got the blueprints for the event center from Talia. I figured out the schedule based on an afterparty two Senators are throwin'."

I scanned the notations he'd made. "Cole would've been impressed."

"If Agents counter our armor-piercin' bullets, we'll be screwed. They're how we survived the Observatory."

"We ran out during our escape. Maybe they'll assume we don't have anymore."

"We don't have as much as I'd like."

I left to join the final stages of preparation.

A group of recruits loading two of the armored vehicles wore patches on their sleeves with an emblem they'd created: a hammer striking a mirror. Along with their various weapons, each carried a pouch Anya had distributed, which held tiny medkits and syringes with nanobots. She'd distributed nearly all of her supply, though with the numbers we had, each recruit only received a small amount.

Garly stood near the front of one of the armored cars with Valor and Tevin, his modified Kevlar vest a hardened shell to give his ribs extra support, a firehose slung over his shoulder. He would control the armored cars remotely.

"Where'd you get that thing?" Valor asked, motioning to the hose as robots stomped past.

"The fire station a town over." He saw their expressions. "Don't fret. I left two hundred clams."

"Is that how much one costs?" I asked.

"No clue."

Tevin asked, "Why a hose?"

He pointed to a cannon-type device encased in white with a jagged-looking collar and two wide handles. "Do you know what X-12 ice is?"

I said, "Get into it later."

Tevin lifted the sound machine, which he'd repaired. "They'll probably be ready for this, but I wanted Brocco represented."

I nodded and glanced at Nikolai's robots.

Talia approached, enthusiastic. "I'm 100% charged. The bus and I are rarin'."

I flashed back to last night when I'd asked Valor to protect Talia. It was the only concession I allowed myself. "You're more important than being a guardian, but it's the most important role to me."

"I was already planning to," she told me.

"If I don't make it, I want you to raise her."

Talia pulled me from my thoughts. "Three protests are planned for today, all near where we'll be. Those fuming peeps will be its own chaos."

"I'm OK with that." I faced the group and raised my voice. "Thinking straight?"

"Hell no," was the reply.

My team gathered close, and we did a group hug. A last bond.

As they pulled back, Tevin asked, "Think people will understand what we went through to save everyone?"

Jex said, "Not even if we win."

Raven gripped her machine gun, strong and fierce. "But we will."

Chapter Forty-Five

Zion's party was already underway when we approached Grande Salle de Bal, the event center located in what had been West Potomac Park in Washington, D.C.

As clouds shielded the late-afternoon sun, tiny lights flickered in an expanding cascade across the sky, the poppers we'd disbursed destroying the 3D drones in the area.

Talia's voice issued from the speaker implanted in my ear. "I'm starting to mess with the police network." Her hackers had created a way to disrupt what I'd built.

Amarjit drove me in the lead car down Ohio Drive SW toward the event center with Valor right behind in Talia's yellow van. The rest of our caravan, three armored cars, the box truck, and a string of random vehicles, waited six hundred yards back.

The four-lane road was otherwise empty.

"To confirm, you're up and running?" I asked.

"Oh yeah, fingers a-fire and trouble is a comin'."

"That's why you couldn't drive," Valor told her from her driver's seat, her voice as clear as Talia's. "You're too distracted."

Raven's voice came next. "And because she's twelve."

"Don't label me," Talia said. She sounded as tense as I felt. They all did.

The cascading lights spread across the horizon as they destroyed more 3D drones.

"My hackers are rebroadcasting the truth online, parroting Jex's drones," she reported.

Seconds later, Valor spoke again. "We're in position." I spotted her in the rearview mirror pulling over at the edge of the event center's property.

I glanced at Amarjit. "Go time."

With a nervous expression, he signaled though no cars were nearby, slowed, and turned left into the entrance fashioned within the ten-foot-tall steel fence that surrounded the large property.

The Grande Salle de Bal stood perched on what was now a landscaped hill in the center of the grounds. The building was a modern-looking, country-club-type event center, its exterior a mix of concrete and steel with windows along the front. The roof contained angled skylights and a glass dome in the center.

Six columns supported a wide portico that covered the building's entrance.

A drive led from the portico, in one direction curving past the building to a parking garage in the rear, while the other direction stretched past a fire hydrant and through the well-manicured lawn down to the entrance gate where two muscular guards stood, their machine guns half-raised as Amarjit stopped our SUV before them.

They and the gate arm weren't the only impediment to the building. Temporary concrete barriers blocked the drive twenty yards from the entrance.

Close to the event center, which stood a hundred yards past the barriers, was a black, military-type vehicle.

I suspected the two guards were Agents, though their helmets covered their hair.

Amarjit rolled down his window as the man closest to the guard shack approached. "We're late, I'm afraid."

We both wore fake-identity masks and were unarmed.

The man looked confused. "You in the right place?"

"Yes, certainly." Amarjit grabbed a satchel from the back seat and started to dig through it.

The guards, even if they weren't Agents, would've already scanned us for weapons. As the lead guard hovered near Amarjit's window, the second guard approached my door.

He motioned me to lower my window. "Your face has never been seen before. How is that possible?" The Agent—he had to be—raised his machine gun. He didn't aim it, yet, but he would.

"You have our invitation?" I asked Amarjit.

The guard at his window said, "Produce it or leave."

Amarjit dug through his bag more frantically, causing synth papers to fall out. "I have it somewhere. Here, hold this."

He tossed the man what looked like a silver ball about the size of a softball.

The man caught it reflexively. As soon as he did, the energy absorber activated.

Anya, who'd taken a rooftop position across the river, spoke in my ear. "Get your guy to back up."

I let out a huge fake sneeze, aimed right at the second guard.

He stepped back, then stiffened as his colleague collapsed. He aimed his machine gun—

The armor-piercing sniper round took him down.

We'd drawn first blood.

I jumped out of the car and lifted the gate. Amarjit drove forward, followed by our armored cars, the box truck, and the array of vehicles crammed full of Raven's recruits. The last few vehicles parked in front of the entrance instead of driving through to block potential reinforcements.

Inside the gate, Tevin peeled away in his armored car and took a side road that followed the property's edge before looping around to the back. A tarp draped across his roof flapped as he drove; sunlight flashed off of one of the mirror-smooth claws just visible under the tarp.

I hurried toward my group, which parked up ahead.

Our two other armored cars and the truck parked near Amarjit; as soon as the truck stopped, our digger robots climbed out, two of which carried the carrier 'bots.

Jex exited the passenger side of the first armored car wearing the protective body vest Anya had given me. It was my other concession.

I wore a standard Kevlar vest and hand shield.

Before I reached our team, the event center's front doors opened, and Agents rushed out.

Jex jogged to the rear of his armored car, threw open the doors, and stepped aside as recruits climbed down. After they exited, he lunged inside.

I reached him as he dragged a large box toward the truck's edge. Together, we opened the box, and my swarmbots poured out. Jex then handed me my bag. As he retrieved weapons from his own bag and my swarmbots pooled beside me, I grabbed a Smith & Wesson pistol, shoved extra clips into various pockets, spotted my ion blade handle and slipped it into my back pocket, then added a backup pistol before grabbing my machine gun.

Raven's recruits scrambled out of the collection of vehicles that had been parked haphazardly and joined us, as did the lead digger robots.

Talia's voice burst from our implanted speakers. 'Ready to get crackin'?"

I envisioned her in her command center with multiple screens and bands to oversee the operations and whatever else she'd cooked up, the center boosting her signal to give her vision to so many cameras.

With only Valor—who still limped—to protect her.

Jex yelled so everyone could hear him. "We need to get inside fast, or we're dead."

We didn't have the numbers, and not all of us had hand shields. Everyone wore Kevlar vests, but that didn't guarantee any would survive. Nor did our shields.

I removed my mask and extracted the posts from my mouth. No more hiding. "Ready?"

Garly climbed out of the second armored vehicle and unfolded his lanky frame. "There's the hydrant I need." It stood between our location and the building.

"No time."

Shouts rose from the event center as Agents continued to exit the building.

More of Raven's recruits scrambled to join us from cars parked farther back.

Amarjit directed his team a few dozen yards over, urging them to hurry, while Jex directed two robots to move the concrete barriers out of the way.

Weapons were checked, safeties flipped off.

Agency forces continued to exit the center, silver-haired fighters as well as non-enhanced Agency soldiers, some erecting mobile, military-grade barricades while others aimed at us. Over a hundred defenders in total came out, at least thirty of which were Agents along with twenty Secret Service men.

Zion's forces took positions in multiple rows in front of the covered entrance, some holding semi-opaque, gray-and-black riot shields that extended their defensive barricades.

They'd expected we would attack. Of course. It was predictable.

With the concrete barriers out of the way, recruits drove the two armored vehicles through the gap, then waited for us. We moved into position behind the vehicles, and those of us with hand shields activated them.

"You doing OK, Talia?" I asked.

"I replaced the police network feeds with pics of a wolfhound named Harry. They're freaking out."

We started to advance, the armored vehicles taking the lead to shield us.

As soon as we began to move, The Agency's forces opened fire.

Bullets filled the air. Most clanged off the cars' metal frames. Others zipped past.

The last of Raven's forces hurried to join us. Some were cut down, while others used the concrete barriers as cover. Many of those hit were protected by their Kevlar vest, but a few were shot in exposed areas. Three died.

Garly raised his rebuilt sound machine, his long arms lifting it higher than the armored vehicles, and activated it. The deafening sound burst forward.

From my spot near the bumper of the lead vehicle, I saw a few Agents collapse, but the non-Agents helped them don insulated helmets to block the sound.

Jex signaled to Garly, who turned off his machine. "Leave it. It's no good n'more."

We continued forward, though not as fast as I wanted.

As we advanced, two more robots hurried through our growing crowd to join us at the vehicles.

We'd installed shields under the armored vehicles, so we were safe behind them, but once we stepped out, I didn't know if our hand shields and Kevlar vests would be enough against the onslaught.

The gunfire fell off as some of the shots changed in pitch. I looked to my left to see Amarjit starting forward with his team, his hand shield activated, a reinforced digger robot taking point with a dozen recruits behind.

Jex had listened to me, attacking at an angle to force the Agents to split their focus.

I signaled to my right. My swarmbots rose up and created a rippling wall that also advanced. Bullets took out individual 'bots, but they absorbed most of the bullet's force, and other 'bots took the place of the ones destroyed.

Other swarms of the tiny 'bots stayed in reserve inside the armored cars.

We proceeded twenty yards, then another ten.

A group of Agents began heading toward us, concentrating fire as they proceeded in a slow, coordinated fashion.

I didn't hear the gunshot behind me but saw the results. An Agent leading their advance team collapsed, followed by a second.

The other Agents paused, and a few retreated as they scanned the area.

A third gunshot alerted the survivors as another Agent dropped. Not only did we have a sniper, her armor-piercing bullets were lethal.

The troops clustered together and lifted their shields to protect their heads. They prepared to continue their advance as we moved closer — but then looked up.

As did we.

Drones approached, dozens of them from all directions, large delivery drones, smaller personal drones, corporate advertising drones, news channels' drones, police, weather monitoring, surveillance, medical, and many others. They filled the sky overhead, the dozens turning into hundreds, then thousands to shield us from overhead attack. More joined, the collective, buzzing machines stretching outward to create a protective dome over the park and surrounding area, the bottom edge reaching down to the basin to the east and the Potomac to the southwest. There were so many, hovering within feet of each other, they dimmed the sunlight.

"Talia, did you do this?" Raven asked in amazement.

"No one thought about air control. You digs?"

"You outdid yourself."

Talia had modified my software and used its multi-system core to pull the drones from cities across the Eastern seaboard.

We progressed toward the building, passing the fire hydrant. On Jex's command, two additional robots came in from the side, the last digger robot held back to protect our flank.

The sky darkened further as the floating platform uncloaked itself.

Garly had steered it remotely, flying it over the river slow enough to avoid stirring the water, then up over the land. He must've coordinated with Talia to fly it in before she closed her dome. He walked slowly as he focused on flying it, using a joystick-type controller attached to a motherboard that also contained a series of buttons and the specialized transmitter.

Since nobody was onboard, there hadn't been any body heat to expose the platform before it uncloaked.

The Agency's gunfire decreased again, this time due to the platform gliding over them toward the event center's north end.

We continued east toward the building, the main entrance now sixty yards away.

Agents shot at the platform, but their bullets were ineffective.

The platform stopped at the north end, rotated, and dropped a metal plate.

Agents flinched in surprise. It only took them a moment to realize the plate had sealed the north exit door.

The platform's propulsion engines pushed it forward, heading to the event center's rear doors.

An older Agent near the main entrance shouted at his comrades to refocus as the platform glided out of view.

I triggered my mic. "Tevin, where are you?"

"We've engaged the enemy," he yelled over the sound

of gunfire. He'd taken a dozen fighters and a robot to prevent a possible mass exodus from the building. "Agents are coming out the back."

"That door needs to be closed," Jex said.

"On it."

The platform glided to a stop but paused.

"OK, drop it," Tevin yelled.

Garly hit a button on his motherboard, and a metal plate dropped, disappearing from view.

"Back door's blocked," Tevin reported.

Garly started the platform toward the south end of the event center, the underside low enough that it almost touched the building's glass dome.

Once Garly sealed the south doors, the main entrance would be the only way in or out. Zion's puppets wouldn't be able to flee.

We reached the halfway point in our advance. Another fifty yards to the entrance — which meant we needed to execute our next step.

I exchanged glances with Raven, Jex, and Garly. "Let's do it."

With a yell, I led our forces out from behind the armored cars.

Gunfire once again filled the air as we fanned out from behind the armored cars.

Bullets embedded themselves as they struck my enhanced hand shields, while others sparked off the armored cars or shot past. An occasional plasma bolt deflected off my shield.

Fighters spread out as they followed me, some with shields, others ducking low. All returned fire. Gun smoke tinged the air on both sides, the smell acrid.

Raven and Jex led their teams from the other side of the armored cars, further splitting the Agency's focus as their teams opened fire.

Garly stayed behind the armored vehicle to continue piloting the platform.

Three digger robots emerged from behind our vehicles, two

with Gatling guns and the third with a plasma cannon. All three had their hands modified to hold and fire the weapons. Before Agents could adjust, the robots rose behind us and unleashed their weapons, taking out multiple forces, including six Agents.

I signaled to one of our two carrier robots.

The low-riding robot zipped up the drive, bullets pinging off its front grill, and drove past us toward The Agency's forces.

Agents adjusted their fire to try to stop the robot, which carried a modified energy emitter in its carrier bay. Bullets shredded its grill and blew out both front tires, but the Gen Omega robot kept coming, propped up by secondary, solid-core inner tires. It entered The Agency's midst, which forced soldiers to dive out of the way, and stopped.

A black-clad soldier dashed toward the robot with an unpinned grenade—but before he reached the robot, the emitter activated.

A magnified electrical charge burst forth, the sphere of energy expanding outward thirty feet, the electricity carrying shrapnel with it. The metal shrapnel expanded past the sphere, slowed, and hovered. The shrapnel then rotated a few degrees and collapsed inward, following the sphere as it shrunk.

The device took out every soldier in its range, bodies falling as the sphere collapsed inward, along with a dozen Agents.

The unpinned grenade exploded, its handler already dead. The blast took out most of their mobile barricades and the building's portico.

The attack threw the Agents' efforts in disarray.

We used their confusion to gain another five yards, then five more.

The floating platform overhead sealed the south exit with another panel, then started toward the covered entrance.

Two Agency soldiers ran toward the military-type vehicle. Raven's recruits fired at them, but the soldiers reached the vehicle and ducked around its far side.

Before we could send recruits after them, The Agency's surviving forces unleashed layers of gunfire while more men exited the building to join the fight.

The sudden onslaught slowed us. We returned fire, my ears ringing from the barrage from my machine gun and the others around me, but Agents repulsed our efforts with more barriers, along with cannon blasts. They interlaced their gunfire with grenades, which eliminated a number of our forces.

I wanted to shout in anger and grief every time one of our recruits went down.

We advanced a few more feet, the attack intensifying.

Amarjit's team got even closer—and was met with a salvo of concentrated gunfire that forced him to drop his robot to its knees and activate its own shields.

The platform appeared over the Agents' heads, which caused some to look up.

The older Agent yelled into his wrist mic as the platform glided over him. Two regular gunshots struck him—we'd only had enough armor-piercing bullets for a few fighters—but he seemed unaffected.

A metal plate dropped from the platform and slammed into the ground next to the walkway that led to the front doors, the vertical plate nearly hitting one of the soldiers. A second plate followed, then a third, the three lined in a row.

I was surprised. Garly was supposed to fly the platform away. Instead, he'd created a twelve-foot-long wall.

"Keep pushin'," Jex yelled, urging our forces forward.

A rebel next to him was suddenly shot in the head and went down. A second followed moments later.

"Shooters on the roof," Talia shouted.

Jex raised his shield just in time to stop a sniper round meant for him.

I spread the word to my team and kept my shield high. Past Jex, Raven lifted her shield.

"I'll find him," Anya said.

Jex spoke next. "Dray, snag the rest of your swarmbots. Everyone, we're a hundred feet from our goal. Get ready for a final push—and protect your heads."

I ran back to the first armored car and opened its rear doors. Tens of thousands of swarmbots poured out.

As I dashed to the second car, where Garly hid, Talia's shout filled my ear. "A scrum on the roof's got a *rocket*."

Garly looked at me wide-eyed.

"Get the platform out of here," I said.

He peeked around the side of the armored car as he engaged the joystick.

I threw open the doors to the second car to release more swarmbots, then started back to rejoin the others.

As I ran out into the open, bullets still flying, the platform tilted and began to rise. Then movement caught my attention. One of the soldiers at the military-style vehicle had been taken down, but the other still stood—and had a rocket launcher.

I raised my machine gun too late.

The soldier triggered his weapon.

The rocket streaked upwards and exploded against the side of the platform, lifting it—then a second rocket, launched from the roof, struck the platform, exploded, and ignited the fuel tanks.

The resulting explosion was ten times greater than the rockets. The floating platform shattered, sending metal plates, shrapnel, and debris in every direction.

CHAPTER FORTY-SIX

Our teams scattered as the floating platform exploded overhead.

Metal panels slammed into the ground in random patterns. Some collapsed while others pinwheeled across the landscaped lawn and crushed fighters on both sides. The platform itself followed, burning sections of the formerly airborne vehicle striking the ground in different spots. Smoke, debris, and death blanketed the battlefield.

Talia yelled in my ear, but she was drowned out by the destruction as the decimated ship crashed around us.

A rocket suddenly launched from the event center's roof, struck one of the armored cars, and detonated. The car rose into the air, then crashed on its side.

I ran for the other car, shouting in my mic to Anya, but she was shouting back. "I can't get a clean shot."

Garly was crouched behind the second car.

I tackled him, throwing us both out from behind the vehicle. The next moment, a rocket exploded into the vehicle.

The armored car flipped into the air and smashed down where Garly had been hiding.

"Tell me you're OK," Anya called.

I used my hand shield to protect us as I pulled Garly to a section of platform wreckage that blocked the Agency's fire, then assured her we weren't injured.

"I can't see anything in the smoke," she said.

"Keep tryin'," Jex said. "We need that guy neutralized."

Our forces were in disarray, fighters scattered, many dead and others injured, our momentum gone. There was a shriek as another rocket launched and took out the box truck, which we'd left as a backup.

As I scanned the battlefield through the thick smoke, a recruit dragged his companion behind a downed plate.

Raven was just visible to my left, her golden-brown hair helping me identify her. She and Jex reconnected, both wearing med patches to cover minor wounds, but before I could go to them, shapes appeared out of the smoke a dozen feet before me. One leapt onto a pile of smoldering debris, five others emerged next to it, and two more jumped onto the platform's fallen command tower: Agency robot attack dogs.

"Jex, Raven," I yelled. "I need reinforcements."

They scrambled to find help.

I stepped back cautiously, eyeing the robotic dogs, though they could move faster than I could react.

They crouched as they tracked me, though one suddenly spotted a recruit, leapt at her, and took her down as she cried out.

Heavy footsteps came from my left—one of the digger robots, marred by bullets and shrapnel but moving fast as it charged toward me. It was Amarjit's, who struggled to keep up. The digger thundered past me toward the Agency's robots, its bladed fingers missing me by inches.

Three dogs leapt at it.

The digger took out the first one, but the other two clung to it and dug into the metal plates that protected its hydraulics and circuits.

Three other dogs focused on us.

I darted forward as one charged Amarjit, the unsteady tower of debris it leapt from robbing it of its normal quickness. I shoved my arm outward and deflected the creature with my shield, then brought my weapon up to shoot it. Amarjit fired as well, though the robot's plating deflected our bullets.

The creature got to its feet and bared its teeth.

Before it could attack, a flash of plasma blasted its side. Raven ran forward and shot it a second time with her rifle to fry its circuits.

"You good?" she asked.

Before I answered, she spun and deflected a leaping dog with her shield. Its momentum sent it into the tower debris. She rushed forward, pinned it with her shield, jammed her hand under the shield, and fired.

Stepping back, she yelled to her team. "Shield wearers, use them to take out the dogs."

Amarjit's digger robot destroyed the two dogs that clung to it, but others were still out there. Through the smoke, I discovered they'd dismantled a different digger robot.

Three recruits, working together, took out one of the robot dogs with armor-piercing bullets.

Raven, Amarjit, and I split up to look for the last two.

I stepped around a fallen plate, which protruded from the ground at an angle, and squinted as I tried to see through the smoke. There were two smaller piles of debris and what looked like the body of a fallen recruit, but that was it.

Something jumped down behind me.

I spun to find one of the dogs five feet away.

It paused when it identified me, then ran off.

Zion wanted me alive.

The dog ran toward a recruit.

Before it reached him, Amarjit opened fire. The bullets drove it to the side, then his digger robot appeared out of the smoke, snatched the dog, and severed its head.

The last dog vaulted onto its back and dug into the digger's neck. It would incapacitate it in seconds.

I dashed forward and helped the digger pull the dog from its back. The dog froze when it saw me — and the digger crushed its head.

"You're OK. I must return," Amarjit said. He gestured to his robot, and the two ran back to his team.

A collision sounded overhead. A hoverbike spun as it sailed toward the ground, a fragmented police drone falling with it, and crashed near the military-style vehicle. An Agent must have tried to break through Talia's dome.

Farther away, barely visible in the smoke, a digger robot fought four Agents, its huge size making it seem invincible — though as I watched, the Agents ripped off the arm wielding a Gatlin gun, forced the robot to its knees, and destroyed it.

Exhaustion gripped me as the battle continued. Shouts and cries assaulted my ears, Jex's voice joining the cacophony as he shouted orders to his team. The robot must have been his.

Plasma fire flashed in the smoke as Agents and recruits

fought.

"Agents are heading for Dad and Garly," Talia said. "Who's in the area?"

I switched my magazine, then started forward, gun raised. Garly would be nearby.

Wind pushed at the smoke but wasn't strong enough to clear it.

Gunfire warned me as I approached a blocked-off area. The Agents Talia must've spotted fought a cluster of rebels who used stacks of wreckage as shields. I crouched near a plate embedded in the lawn, lined up my shot, and took out an Agent. The other Agent swiveled her gunfire from the rebels to me and clipped the edge of my Kevlar vest as I ducked behind the debris.

I glanced to my side and spotted Garly on his knees near one of the damaged armored cars, focused on a case he'd pulled from the wreckage. Before I could warn him of the Agent's presence, he opened the case to unleash modified hunter drones. The two dozen drones rose into the air, targeted the Agent, swarmed her, and ignited their lasers. Within seconds, they took her down, though they were too late to save the three recruits she'd killed.

The drones wouldn't be enough to turn the tide in our favor. I wasn't sure any of this would.

As fighters cried out in pain, their voices cutting through the smoke, I called my swarmbots.

Within thirty seconds, they'd gathered in a semi-circle, a mass of over two hundred thousand. I placed one against my implant to make sure they received my intent, then dropped it and started forward.

Gunshots drew my attention, and I spotted Agents firing at five recruits who were pinned down.

I sent two clusters of swarmbots forward. They scurried across the lawn and rose up, connecting together to take the form of a man. The illusion wasn't perfect, but in the smoke and haze of battle, it distracted the two Agents. They fired at the swarmbots, but the swarmbots kept "running" toward them before crashing into them and attacking.

As the Agents cried out, Talia keyed her mic. "Dad, Agents are heading toward Amarjit's group."

I sent more swarmbots, which helped Amarjit eliminate them. He was more proficient with his robot than anyone else, and it showed in how he dispatched three Agents while my swarmbots took out a fourth.

I sent more 'bots to take down Agents, but Zion's forces pushed back. We lost ground, our losses mounting. I counted thirty-one recruits dead—not counting however many Tevin might have lost—and another ten injured. Yet there were still more than two dozen Agents and multiple squads coming at us.

"More baddies are exiting the center," Talia said. "Some are pushing the wreckage aside to make paths."

"How's Tevin doing?" I asked.

He responded before she did. "Got my hands full."

"Know the feelin'," Jex said. He and Raven joined me near the concrete barriers. He keyed his mic. "We gotta get inside that center. Everyone assigned to Raven and me, regroup by the armored cars. Amarjit, hang back 'til we advance. Tevin, try to get over to this side. By attackin' at once, we'll have a better chance of overwhelmin' 'em."

Anya spoke, her voice relieved. "I took out the men on the roof."

"Good job."

"I'm out of plasma," said Raven. "Anyone have extra cartridges?"

"Take this." I ignored her objections as I handed over my machine gun. I extracted my pistol and keyed my mic. "Garly, how many diggers are operational?"

"Four, counting Amarjit's."

We'd lost more than I'd realized.

To Jex and Raven, I said, "I'll take one. Take the other two but be careful. Use the wreckage as cover. I'll use my digger and the swarmbots to take out as many Agents as I can."

Raven gave me a look to be safe, then took off, as did Jex.

I hurried to the digger robot that had protected our rear flank, pulled datarings from my pocket, slid one on each middle finger, and synched with the large machine.

When that was done, I started forward, the digger following, and summoned my swarmbots. I sensed them crawling over the shredded battlefield as they headed for me.

A male figure appeared in the smoke ahead, walking stiffly toward me like a goddamn nightmare.

It couldn't be.

The smoke cleared enough to see his face.

Kieran.

Chapter Forty-Seven

My sweaty skin turned cold as Kieran approached in his white Oxford and dark slacks. I'd thought he'd died after falling off the floating platform. He couldn't still be goddamned alive.

He stopped fifteen feet from me.

Smoke drifted between us. "Look what you've wrought," he said. "You're not freedom fighters. You're murderers and anarchists."

Talia's voice erupted. "Kieran's with Dad."

Anya said, "I can't see through the smoke."

"I'll find him," Raven said.

I keyed my mic. "Stay away. Stick to the plan." I turned down the volume on my speaker and noted the Glock in his hand, the way he held himself. The fall had hurt him, but I still couldn't beat him muscle-for-muscle.

He didn't have his exposed implant anymore. He'd gotten rid of that weakness.

A large portion of my swarmbots neared.

"I was going to leave all this," he said. "I'd nearly convinced Sari to go with me, had a way to get Zion to release her. Then you attacked our nexus. Revealed yourself. And with your help, Raven killed her."

Sari. Britt's first name. I'd forgotten. "More death won't fix what happened."

His anguish was evident. "I was going to make you a deal. Have you live out your days as a consultant for The Agency, your daughters as free as anyone can be. Zion would've let us go."

The fighting continued past him, gunshots and shouting, drones flying and flashes of plasma.

"Sari attacked us. We were leaving," I said.

He raised his pistol. "I never should've let you escape."

I activated my shield as I raised my Smith & Wesson — but he fired first, three shots.

My shield caught two of the bullets, the third hitting my

side and causing a burst of pain, though my Kevlar vest protected me. I returned fire. My bullets carved two holes in his chest, but nothing deep. Unlike my machine gun, they weren't armor-piercing.

I triggered the swarmbots, which rose up to either side of him.

Aggravation flickered across his face. "I knew you'd use those damn things." He extracted a device from his pocket and pressed a button.

The swarmbots collapsed.

I sent a command for them to get up, but they didn't respond.

"I had our scientists study copies you left at the Facility. This jams their comms, so they no longer act like a swarm. Now they're just helpless little robots." He crushed a few with his foot, then fired at me again.

I deflected the shot and fired back to little effect.

He charged.

I shifted my stance as he rushed me, then swung my left arm, using the edge of the hand shield to nail him in the jaw. I brought my gun up to shoot him as he stumbled to a halt, but he wrenched it from my grasp. As he threw it aside, I hammered my shield's edge into his hand, knocking his own gun away, then caught him by surprise by punching him in the throat so hard it would've killed a normal man.

Kieran staggered back as he struggled a little to breathe.

I kicked his pistol into a pile of wreckage twenty feet away.

We circled each other.

"How many crimes have you committed for Zion? Have you kept count?"

He raised his fists.

"Hey, remember this guy?" I asked.

I'd maneuvered Kieran to stop in front of the robot I'd synched to. With a jerk of my arm, I brought the digger robot forward.

The robot charged, its foot-long blades flashing.

Kieran lunged to the side but hadn't reacted quick

enough. The robot's blades caught his rebuilt arm and shredded it, triggering blood and sparks as it gouged his shoulder, triceps, and elbow.

Kieran hissed in pain as he grabbed his injured arm, though he had to jump back to avoid another blow.

I commanded the robot to change its attack by throwing out my left hand. The robot immediately responded. Blade-tips sliced Kieran's clothes and gouged his skin, followed by a killing shot—but even injured, Kieran moved too fast. He ducked under the robot's swing, then sprang at me. He ripped off the dataring on my left hand before I could react.

Desperate, I gestured the robot to lunge forward with my remaining ring.

Kieran blocked my arm with his bloody one, grabbed my right hand—and crushed the ring on my finger, breaking the bone in the process as he jerked back. I shouted as I cupped my injured hand.

The blades of the now-frozen robot splayed where Kieran had stood a moment before. The robot, positioned between us, stretched outward like a fencing athlete and was now balanced on its forward leg, one arm extended.

The Agent grabbed me with his good hand and pulled me toward the blades. My Kevlar vest protected me, but the blades cut into the fabric, weakening my protection.

My right hand was nearly unusable, but I continued to fight. I punched his new, smaller main implant with my left hand, which triggered another burst of pain—though it hurt Kieran more. As he stiffened, I grabbed a fistful of silver hair, pivoted, and used my weight to swing him into the robot's head.

The blow stunned him.

I hurried around the robot. I needed to get to the disruptor and smash it.

I closed within ten feet of the device when Kieran shot me twice in the back, the quick shots dropping me to the ground.

As I rolled onto my back, he approached, blinking as he recovered from the blow to the head. "Your vest protects you, but those bullets still hurt, don't they?" he asked. He fired twice more, both close to where he'd cut my vest, the pain enough to take my breath.

My gun was nowhere close, so I activated my shield, climbed to my feet, and launched myself. I deflected a shot, spun, and nailed him in the jaw with the edge of my semi-transparent shield.

Before I could take another swing, he pulled me close, pinning my left arm against my chest. The hand shield vibrated against us. "We know some of your people have armor-piercing bullets. We're leveling the playing field."

He fired his Glock into my stomach, below my hand shield. The vest stopped the bullet, though the pain was excruciating.

He was going to kill me. Our previous battles, he'd held back. But this was to the death.

With a bloody arm around my neck, he used his free hand to push his pistol lower, found the bottom edge of my vest, and began to work the gun underneath my protection.

I reached behind me with my right hand. I tried not to jostle my broken finger as I dug into my back pocket.

The scorching-hot barrel slipped underneath my vest.

In a haze of pain, I stomped on his bad foot—then turned off the hand shield.

The shield collapsed, freeing my left arm.

I shoved downward, pushing the barrel of his gun away from my vest as our chests came together, then reactivated the shield.

It was just the distraction I needed.

As he fought to get his gun around my shield, I brought my right hand up behind him, triggered my ion blade, and rammed it into the back of his head.

Kieran's body went rigid.

My right hand throbbing with agony, I managed to twist the blade. Then I turned off the knife.

Kieran collapsed at my feet, dead.

He'd had a code of honor, warped as it had been. Yet he'd violated Raven, scarred me, manipulated Mina, and imprisoned Talia.

He would never hurt my family again.

The battle seemed to crash back in. Explosions rocked the earth, gunfire stuttered the air, and a small fireball appeared overhead where an Agent had tried to pierce Talia's dome.

I left to search for my team.

The smoke cleared as I headed up the lawn to reveal more bodies, both ours and theirs. I spotted the digger robots Jex and Raven had commandeered. Both had been destroyed, dead Agents lying around each. Farther away, I glimpsed Amarjit's. The robot was missing an arm and its head was dented, but it continued to protect him and a squad of recruits.

I turned up the volume on my communications to find both Talia and Anya yelling for me. "I'm here," I said.

"You OK?" Talia asked.

I assured her I was and straightened in case she spotted me with her drones. "Report."

"Tevin popped out from behind the building and whizzled three Agents, but more goons are coming from their headquarters. Dozens more. Maybe a hundred."

Kieran had been a delay tactic.

I was about to ask where the others were when a tall female Agent ran toward me. I raised my shield but didn't have a way to fight back.

Gunfire erupted to the side, and the Agent fell to Raven's recruits, two of whom rose up from behind a pile of debris.

My daughter appeared moments later. "Where's Kieran?"

"I killed him—for sure this time."

"Did you make him suffer?"

"He's dead. That's what matters."

She led me toward Jex's location. "Agents pushed us back, then most of their forces retreated and are fortifying their defenses." In a lower voice, she added, "Talia's dome is holding, which is about the only bright spot."

Jex had relocated to one of the destroyed armored vehicles. Thirty or so recruits hid behind various pieces of wreckage nearby, and Garly hunkered beside him.

The lanky scientist looked as tired as I felt. "I've been

launching my tech armada," he told me.

"It's helped, but we gotta get in that buildin'," Jex said.

I gestured to the fighters. "Did you split up your teams?"

"The ones you see are all that's left."

"We've made some progress," Garly said when he saw my concern. "Tevin and Amarjit have positions near the entrance."

I said, "The Agency's reinforcements have armor-piercing bullets. Kieran told me. They'll shred our forces." And Talia's van.

"Any weapons you haven't used?" Raven asked Garly.

"Just the ice machine."

I keyed my mic. "Talia, where's the fire hydrant?" After she told us, I said, "Garly, grab your weapon and meet us there."

The scientist handed Jex a multi-tool, then ran off.

Talia spoke up again. "The D.C. Police are on their way."

Raven raised her eyebrows. "Is that a good thing?"

"The smoke and drones must've alerted them," Jex said. He keyed his mic. "Tevin, Amarjit, make a distraction. Don't let Agents see what we're doin'." Then to us, he said, "Let's go."

Six of the recruits followed as Jex led us across the shredded battlefield, where the smoke continued to thin.

I wasn't sure whether it would be better to force my broken finger down and wrap my hand or leave it. No time.

Raven toggled her mic. "Talia, we can't see the hydrant."

Talia used her drones to track us and guided us through the maze of blood and destruction. Suddenly, she yelled, "Stay away from her, shiny." Two drones swooped down, flew over our heads, and collided with a younger Agent who had charged toward Raven. I hadn't spotted him until Talia took him out.

Gunfire erupted as we stepped past a large pile of wreckage and into the open. Our team returned fire and took out the soldiers who had hidden nearby, but one of the recruits fell to the soldiers' bullets. More sacrifice.

We hurried forward.

"OK, you're there," Talia said when we reached a long stretch of wreckage. "It's the second mound. Hurry. Vans stuffed with Agents are pulling into the rear entrance."

"We'll cover you," Raven told Jex and me. Then, she addressed two of her fighters. "Find Garly. He needs to get here at all costs."

Jex and I picked up and tossed aside the scorched, mangled, and broken pieces of the floating platform. It took us seconds we didn't have to clear away the mound, the hydrant slowly becoming visible as we removed the wreckage.

As I revealed more of the hydrant, Jex brushed aside the soot and pulverized material to get to the side valve.

I glanced up as five unmarked vans stopped near the edge of the debris field. Dozens of armed Agents climbed out, each clad in tactical outfits. Man-sized Agency robots exited a transport vehicle, adding to the threat.

Two Agents jogged to our right, heading to the entrance gate. They were going after Talia.

"Hey," Jex snapped. "Help me."

I fought the urge to chase the two Agents. Instead, I cleared more of the debris as he unscrewed the cap on the side opposite the valve.

"Stay focused. You got this," Raven told her people. She handed her youngest fighter, a sixteen-year-old boy, one of her hand shields. "Protect these two."

It took me a second to absorb her instructions.

Before I could protest, she hurried around one of the floating platform's mangled engines and ran toward the horde of Agents. She yelled as she fired my machine gun strapped to her right arm, left arm holding her remaining hand shield, her last two recruits a step behind.

The boy activated the shield she'd given him and positioned himself in front of us.

Agents returned fire, and multiple bullets lodged themselves in Raven's shield.

I reached across my body to grab my pistol with my good hand when Garly arrived with the other carrier robot, his two escorts nowhere to be seen. Lying in the robot's scoop was his unproven ice machine, along with the fire hose.

Agents took down one of Raven's fighters, the man's

Kevlar vest unable to protect him from the Agent's armor-piercing bullets.

Talia's voice came over our comms, her fear audible. "Raven?"

"Focus on Dad," Raven said.

I was about to run after Raven, who had stopped fifty feet from us, but Garly handed me the firehose. "Normally, it takes three or more people to control a hose, but you two will have to manage."

His weapon could help her.

I attached the hose as Jex readied the multi-tool to turn on the water.

Drones shot over us and headed toward Raven. She stood alone, the second recruit at her feet, as over two dozen Agents ran toward her, her golden-brown hair flashing in the intermittent sunlight, her machine gun chugging.

The drones flew past her, across the closing gap, and into the Agents. The heavier drones hit with such force that they knocked down the lead Agents, but the other drones only slowed the rest.

An Agent collapsed suddenly, which told me Anya was firing at them to help protect Raven.

I feared it wouldn't be enough.

There was a hiss as water filled the hose from the hydrant — and the large brass nozzle nearly flew out of my hand from the sudden water pressure.

Garly hiked his ice machine, which reflected a row of lights that turned blue.

Jex stood, reached behind his back, and grimaced as his torso jerked straight. I realized he'd locked his spinal brace to take the weight of the spray.

He took the nozzle from my hands with gritted teeth. "Save her."

I should've objected, told him his ribs wouldn't be able to handle the strain. Instead, I pulled my gun, scrambled past the debris that blocked my path, and ran.

Raven continued to fire at the Agents. She took out a

number of them, and Talia's drones took down more, but they couldn't stop the Agents—and the newer group carried shields. They were different than our hand shields, translucent semi-spheres of energy that deflected Raven's bullets. Pierce emerged from the crowd, taking the lead, and fired at her as his shield flashed from deflecting her shots.

Out of bullets, Raven dropped the machine gun and grabbed one of two pistols jammed behind her back.

Talia sent more drones, though Agents shot them down as they advanced.

I could fire at the Agents, though I feared hitting Raven in my haste, so I focused on running.

I was twenty-five feet from her when Pierce changed tactics. Instead of firing at her body, where she neutralized his bullets with her shield, he lowered his aim and shot her in the thigh, similar to when Kieran had shot her on the train.

She cried out as she dropped to her knee, her left hand coming down, her shield digging into the grass.

She forced herself up as he and I raced toward her from different directions, but instead of raising her shield, she turned it off to reach behind her, pulled her other pistol, and fired both.

I yelled out, but was too late.

Pierce opened fire.

Bullets pierced her Kevlar vest as they threw her back.

She fell to the ground.

My vision seemed to fracture.

I fired at Pierce, but my bullets were wide.

Shouts flooded my ear. I was vaguely aware Talia and Anya, along with Jex, were shouting my name, telling me to get down, but I had to reach Raven.

Something slammed into my back, knocking me to the lawn.

I lifted my head in time to see a police drone—which Talia had used to knock me down—explode in a spray of Agency bullets.

Jex unleashed a column of high-pressure water that arched over my head. The water took out the flaming remains of the drone and struck the Agents swarming toward me and my fallen daughter—when Garly triggered his device.

The spray instantly hardened, separating and widening as the water turned into jagged, barbed fragments of diamond-hard ice, the edges reflecting the sunlight that pierced the clouds. A weird, angry-vibrating sound scratched at my eardrums, the X-12 ice zinging as it flew over me—and slammed into the Agents. Pierce was first, a plume of blood the only indication in the fraction of a second before he disappeared from the onslaught. The rest of the Agents disappeared after him.

Yelling as he held onto the twisting hose, Jex sprayed the area to annihilate the forces that had arrived, a handful able to duck behind debris or fallen plates in time, though the ice pierced much of the debris as well.

The smell was unique, like a strange mix of ozone and dry ice, mixed with pulverized meat.

The sound stopped as the water turned off.

I scrambled to Raven.

Four bullets had pierced her vest, two in the chest, two in the stomach. I ignored the blood that trickled from her mouth. Ignored what it meant. "I'll get you to a hospital," I told her.

Anya spoke. "How extensive is the damage?"

"You have to hold on," I said to Raven. "Talia needs you." I needed her.

But it was too late.

She was already gone.

CHAPTER FORTY-EIGHT

I felt myself falling into the numbness of despair that had gripped me when Adem died, when I'd thought Talia had.

There was an occasional gunshot in the distance, but the battlefield near us fell quiet.

I knew I should worry about the Agents who'd escaped the ice onslaught, about the fight and the war, but I couldn't concentrate.

Raven had been the one who'd pushed me, challenged me, her heart too big for this world. Those she died trying to help would never know her caring spirit, her smile that could melt the coldest heart, her passion and determination and altruism.

I fought my emotions as they continued down the well-worn path. I had to let go, to be there for Talia, who needed me now more than ever.

Jex and Garly joined me, Jex stiff with his locked spine, and crouched beside Raven. He looked gutted, and Garly looked lost. In my ear, Talia wept, her devastated moan further gutting me.

Raven had wanted to be part of something great. She hadn't realized she'd already been great. She'd been my inspiration her entire life.

Anya directed Talia to give a status report, as much for us as it was for Talia.

After a few moments, Talia spoke, her voice broken. "The teams are fighting but all three, Amarjit's, Tevin's, and the rest of R-Raven's, are losing ground." She turned off her mic.

Tevin spoke up. "The D.C. Police are at the rear entrance with two SWAT teams. They're moving the metal plate to get into the center. Dray, they could evacuate the building."

Amarjit's voice came next. "Agents have reinforced their defenses. They'll attack again. I do not know how long we will hold them. Many of my team are injured, and my digger's energy is at twenty percent."

Valor said, "Agents are approaching. They found our van."

Not only would the Agents' armor-piercing bullets punch through her vest, they'd shred Talia's van.

Talia keyed her mic again. Through her sobs, she said, "We gotta finish this, Dad. Do it for Raven."

I felt a stab at the echo of our old battle cry. I'd beaten Kieran but lost Raven. I hadn't sacrificed for her — but she wouldn't have wanted me to. She'd already told me what she wanted, what she'd started those months ago. Regardless of the cost.

She, Cole, Nataly, and so many others. All lost for this damn cause.

I stood, a rage growing inside of me. "Jex, Garly, prepare to clear a path."

I looked down at Raven. I knew I'd have to surrender Talia as well, had known when I'd started this — but I wouldn't leave her vulnerable.

I ran back the way I came, past the hydrant and through the maze of destruction to where I'd fought Kieran. An occasional bullet whizzed past, but I didn't care. Kieran laid where I'd left him, but I didn't focus on him. I approached the digger robot, its arm still outstretched.

I squatted and flipped open a small panel near its side. A screen brightened to reflect rows of faces. My team. My family. I had set up the program as a backup. I selected Talia's face, then Valor's. At the bottom, I hit the word DEFEND.

I stepped back as the robot rose and scanned me. I pointed toward Talia's van, and the robot ran off.

I felt the pull to go with it but fought against my need. Instead, I strode over to Kieran's disruptor and crushed it with my heel.

As the swarmbots stirred, I grabbed one and attached it to my implant. The sync took seconds. In that time, the swarmbots rose up, rippling as they reconnected.

At my command, they encircled me to create a wall of protection. They chittered as more joined, tens of thousands of them. They created additional walls, seven in total, the robots hooking together as they rose up in rippling black curtains and began to rotate.

I would find out if they were enough.

I started forward, and the rotating swarmbots moved with me.

Talia asked, "Dad, what're you doing?"

Our fight was for my family — those who still lived.

My voice thick, I said, "Jex, Garly, hit it."

There were shouts, followed by gunfire.

I picked up speed, and the gunfire increased. A swarmbot suddenly disappeared from the wall with a squeal, shattered by a bullet, the force briefly bowing the wall inward. As the wall straightened, robots above shifted to fill the hole.

The swarmbot wall steered me around a pile of wreckage. Past it was a path to the building's entrance, though Agents and soldiers stood in my way, the enemy just visible through the swarmbots' undulating walls.

More shouts rose after ten yards, the shouts growing louder — and gunfire erupted from both sides.

Bits of robots and bullets filled the air as I ran, the swarmbots struggling to keep pace. I activated my hand shield to protect my face from the onslaught, but shrapnel sliced my hands, arms, and cheeks.

I couldn't see much of the area around me, just flashes through the rotating black curtains of swarmbots, the 'bots absorbing the brunt of bullets and plasma but dwindling in the process. The seven circular walls reduced to six, then five.

Shouts and gunfire filled my ears.

There was a whoosh as X-12 ice cut across my path and took out Agents ahead of me. The light from the ice cast the swarmbots in strange patterns, the edge of the X-12 blast clipping some of them and forcing them to pull in tighter.

Men and women cried out as the ice cut through their ranks.

Jex and Garly were giving as much help as possible, but they'd only be able to do so much.

Something moved directly ahead.

By unspoken coordination, I lowered my hand shield, raised my pistol—and the swarmbots in front of me dropped down. An older Agent stood a dozen yards before me. I fired, catching him by surprise, and the swarmbots rose back up as he fell from the head shot. The next moment, more gunfire, retaliatory strikes, erupted, the gunfire closer. More swarmbots exploded, absorbing the bullets meant for me, the leg of one imbedding itself in my neck.

The walls around me thinned from the onslaught. As I watched, one merged with another to reinforce it, though it left four layers.

Talia keyed the comms. "You're over halfway there, Dad." As she spoke, Valor shouted in the background.

"OK, be ready," I said.

I passed the destroyed armored cars and entered a section that, while littered with some wreckage, was more open than other areas of the battlefield.

The gunfire increased, further reducing my defenses, but through the swarmbot attached to my implant, I knew help was coming. Tens of thousands of additional swarmbots, which I'd sent earlier to distract and attack Agents, scurried toward me. They joined the others to fashion two more walls.

"People are coming," Talia yelled. "I've been streaming the battle. They're coming to fight on our side."

By the time anyone got here, Zion's Congresspeople would be gone. They'd continue to rule.

The gunfire seemed to double.

As I ran, I breathed the acrid smell of gunpowder and shattered metal, the bits of broken swarmbots and deflected bullets before me so dense my vision grew murky. I kept my shield up as shrapnel cut nearly every inch of my exposed skin. Blood leaked from larger cuts.

My walls began to thin again. I was still forty yards away.

More X-12 ice burst across the landscape, but I was running out of protection. Snatches of silver hair appeared on both sides, each a lethal threat.

A sudden gunshot dropped a silver-haired target.

This was followed by a collective cry to my right. Raven's remaining recruits were just visible through the rotating swarmbot-walls as they charged forward and fired at Agency forces. Overlapping buzzing sounds came from my left as Talia flew drones toward Agency positions, adding to the assault.

I reached the last hundred feet.

Even with the recruits and drones, the gunfire intensified. More swarmbots dropped as Agents tried to stop me. Many of the Agents were entrenched defenders, and the sheer volume of their attack slowed me.

Gaps appeared in my defenses as another wall fell. Three left.

Talia sent additional drones to smash into our enemies. Her dome shrunk in size as she pulled more and more pieces to help.

I forced myself to go faster, though I had to squint so much from the spray of broken and shattered swarmbots I could barely see. To the side, I spotted not just Raven's team but Amarjit leading more fighters with our last digger robot. And Garly's X-12 ice flashed again.

Though my team advanced with me, my protection shrunk, my reinforcements spent, two walls left.

I reached the wall of metal plates Garly had dropped earlier.

As soon as I did, I directed the swarmbots away from that side to shore up the protection to my other sides.

I slowed as I approached the entrance, the area littered with bodies, abandoned mobile barriers, and the remains of the collapsed portico. The event center's wall, windows, and front door were scarred from gunfire and jagged ice, which reverted to water as soon as Garly aimed his machine elsewhere.

I hurried up the wet stairs onto the raised entranceway, the swarmbots before me sliding to my right as I walked past the last metal plate—though a portion surged forward as a blood-streaked female Agent appeared before me and fired.

I'd already had my hand shield in front of my face, which

is what saved me. The bullets stopped in front of my eyes — then a cluster of my remaining swarmbots grabbed her. As she fought them, a thick drone smashed into her from the side and threw her off the entranceway.

Gunfire continued to assault my swarmbots, which were down to a few hundred.

I rushed past the downed Agent, opened the door, and ducked inside the building.

CHAPTER FORTY-NINE

Intermittent sunlight caught the four massive chandeliers that hung from the event center's two-story foyer, the chandeliers glittering in the light. Platinum-etched wallpaper and crown moldings decorated the walls, while the far side contained three sets of double doors amidst replicas of famous Greek statues.

The glitz bellied the war outside, PowerBar wrappers and a couple of helmets abandoned on the luxurious, patterned carpet the only indication something was amiss — along with the boxes of ammunition visible in the room to the right, the doors left open to where Zion's forces had waited for our arrival.

At least we hadn't disappointed.

The other doors stood closed.

Someone shouted outside. "Keep Agents back. Give Dray time."

My hand shield flickered, the device worn down from the onslaught I'd just endured.

As the battle raged, I focused on the entrance doors. My remaining swarmbots crawled up the doors, fashioned a brace, and locked their joints together to seal them. But they wouldn't hold Agents back for long, and Zion's people could destroy the thick windows — many were already damaged — to get inside.

I had to hurry.

I wasn't sure where to go, but the double doors in the middle of the far wall seemed the logical choice.

I started for them when my hand shield flickered again, then went out.

While I still wore my torn Kevlar, I felt defenseless.

I approached the doors, raised my gun in my left hand, and carefully opened one of the doors with the thumb and index finger of my right hand.

I entered a grand ballroom two stories high with walls that were gilded in a modern style, sleek and lustrous. Stairs rose to a balcony that ran the length of the back wall, which was illuminated by the sunlight streaming in from the glass dome overhead. Two rows of skylights let in additional light.

Round tables took up much of the floor space, though there were open areas directly in front of me and along the left-hand side. A stage rose against the far wall to my left, perpendicular to the balcony, the hologram-projected orchestra paused.

Clustered in the center of the room were the country's Senators and Representatives.

I didn't know that because I recognized any of them other than the former Senator who had taken Dixon's persona. My implant was blocked by a swarmbot. Instead, I identified them by the large, ropelike necklaces draped over their shoulders. They no longer wore the headbands I'd previously seen but wore a dot on each of their cheeks, which, along with their necklaces, helped Zion's software accurately project each Congressperson's fake identity onto people's lenses to mask their coup.

Many of the men and women glared at me, fearful yet defiant, the rest wary.

Two Secret Service men stood between us, their guns drawn.

"My beef isn't with you," I told them.

A voice spoke from somewhere to my right. "This is beyond a 'beef,' wouldn't you say?"

Zion. He stood with four of his Agents, each armed.

He aimed his pistol at me. "You're going to hang for what you've done."

"I'm here to reveal what *you've* done, old 'friend.' Your secret dictatorship is over."

One of the Secret Service agents asked, "What are you talking about?"

"Don't listen to him. He's delusional," Zion snarled. To me, he said, "Drop your weapon."

"He's got a knife, too," the female Agent in the group said.

I gauged my odds. If I flinched, Zion or the Secret Service men would shoot.

I tossed both weapons aside.

Zion approached and forced me to my knees. "Your attack

on my communication center will cost billions to fix. I'd make you oversee the rebuild, but you'd sabotage it every chance you got." He grabbed the swarmbot leg sticking out of my neck and twisted it, the metal scraping my muscle. "I knew you'd come and that you'd come alone. Such an aversion to risking others, including your daughters. How'd that work out for you?"

Talia keyed her mic. "OK Dad—" She squealed as something thudded against the side of her van. "Keep him yappin'. Ten seconds."

Zion waved the Secret Service men back, moved to where they'd stood, and gestured to his Agents. "If it's any consolation, you figured out they were my secret weapon."

The sunlight flickered in the skylight behind him, which made me smile. "You saved mine."

Talia landed a drone on one of the skylights—and detonated the grenade I'd given her, the sharp boom echoing throughout the large space.

The Senators and Representatives scattered from the center of the room, some dashing toward the far side to huddle near a minibar forty feet away while others scrambled toward a door across from me on this end of the room.

The grenade damaged the thick pane of glass but didn't break it.

A delivery drone slammed into the glass, followed by a second, a third, then a fourth, heavy drones that further weakened it.

As soon as the drones started slamming into the skylight, I got to my feet and propelled myself toward the Congresspeople by the minibar.

They scurried backwards.

Before I'd taken a dozen steps, a hand grabbed my collar and forced me to my hands and knees.

Zion. He'd caught me faster than he should've.

"I knew you were enhanced," I said.

The cracked pane of glass shattered.

Damaged drones fell to the ballroom floor, prompting cries from some Congresspeople, followed by two undamaged

THE PRICE OF FREEDOM

drones that followed the falling cluster before veering off and flying across the room.

I got my feet under me to leap up—but Zion was ready, his gun trained on my head. "You need to stand trial, but if you move, I'll shoot. We'll convict you posthumously."

More drones hit the shattered glass pane, widening it, as the Congresspeople huddled together. Then, five larger news drones flew in and spread out.

Silence settled over the room, disturbed only by the buzzing of the drones and faint shouts and gunfire from outside.

From the shouts, I feared my team was retreating.

Though Talia had done her job, we'd failed. I'd failed. The Senators were so close, only twenty feet away. Too far now.

Zion motioned to the drones. "Shoot them down."

Before his Agents opened fire, the doors on the far side of the ballroom opened, and a dozen D.C. police officers entered.

My despair grew.

"What's going on here?" the lead cop demanded. His frown deepened when he saw Congresspeople clustered nearby, the rest on the far end. I doubted he'd expected the nation's leaders at the heart of this mayhem. He addressed a gaunt-looking woman with a tight bun, who stood nearby. "Ms. Speaker, are you harmed?"

Her image must've been that of Sanchez-Riaz, the Speaker of the House.

"They're fine. You can go," Zion called out. "Members of Congress, stay where you are."

I suddenly realized I could use the cops. "Grab the Speaker's shoulder. She and the others are wearing tech that hides their real identities. She's fake. Every member of Congress is fake," I told them. "You can't see the necklaces they're wearing, but they're there."

While I could see the low-slung necklaces, the cops couldn't.

They exchanged confused glances as more drones flew in from the broken skylight, smaller ones that filled the air over the orchestra. The news drones remained stationary, watching as the

MICHAEL C. BLAND

cops approached the Speaker and other Representatives. I didn't catch what they said, but after a moment, the Representatives seemed to relax. Shit.

Agents rushed in from outside, some bloodied, but they paused when they spotted the cops.

"Ignore his claims," Zion told the police. "He's trying to confuse everyone to destroy this country."

"Try any of them," I shouted. "Just reach for their shoulders."

A female cop raised her hand as she took a step toward Sanchez-Riaz.

"Don't," Zion bellowed, swiveling his gun away from me to point it at her.

It was the opening I needed.

I slammed into his chest under his outstretched arm, just like Cole had taught me.

As Zion hit the ground, I ran toward the Congresspeople. I zeroed in on two in particular: the one I suspected was Senate Majority Leader Malatone and the fake Senator Dixon. The old man and woman moved slower, especially Dixon. I'd discovered months earlier that she was decades older than she appeared, a former Senator who'd "retired" then got elected under the Dixon persona.

Drones swooped down and flew past me as I ran.

I glanced over my shoulder and saw Zion chasing me — until a drone slammed into him. Other drones slammed into the other Agents who had switched their attention to me, though they were too far back. Zion avoided a second drone and came for me, though a larger drone dropped him to a knee.

I narrowed the distance to the Senators when pain erupted in my back as a gunshot rang out. A second bullet sliced my left arm, then a third pierced my right leg.

I stumbled and fell. Glanced back. Zion was on a knee, his gun trained on me.

Senator Dixon had stopped backing up, seemingly mesmerized, only seven feet away.

Marshaling my rage, I lunged for her — the gunshot to

my thigh nearly robbing that leg of function—though I was shot again in the back. As I stumbled, I managed to hook her necklace and pulled the thing off her body to reveal her true identity.

She gasped as I turned to the cops. I later learned a faint image of Dixon's fake face remained visible to them, though it was distorted as the device hung from my grasp, the eyes empty, the real person stunned.

Blood from my arm dripped through the holographed face.

"That was a trick," Zion proclaimed. He pointed his gun at the cops. "Everyone out—and if you say a word, I'll make you disappear."

Though I was losing strength, I lurched over to the one I suspected was Malatone and grabbed his necklace as his fellow conspirators skittered away instead of helping him. He fought me, but I ripped off his mask. "These aren't our leaders," I yelled as I held up the necklace.

The female cop reached for Sanchez-Riaz and pulled off her necklace.

The remaining Congresspeople erupted, yelling at me and the cops to stay back, to not touch them, the Agents yelling at the cops to leave immediately. "We have jurisdiction," the lead cop yelled back. "And you have some serious explaining to do."

More cops entered the ballroom.

A fight broke out as the fake Congresspeople tried to flee. None were recognizable other than the former Senator, disciples of Zion who could slip into obscurity if they escaped.

The cops grabbed some and had to tackle a few others to keep them in the room, though many fled through the doors I'd used.

The men and women in blue pulled their guns and aimed at the Agents.

"Wait, we're the good guys," the female Agent said.

Three gunshots cut through the noise, Zion's arm held high. "No one's leaving," he shouted. He swiveled his gun to me. "Starting with you."

"You're done," I said. "You and your whole damn

Agency."

"We'll sweep this away. You did nothing."

Talia's voice erupted overhead. "Did you forget about me?"

Zion lifted his gaze as the news drones glided toward him. They were from a range of agencies, one a conservative network, one a liberal, the rest somewhere in between. "I've been broadcasting this live across the country. There's oodles of people heading this way to fight you. Oooh, you should see the looks on your Agents' faces."

He looked at me in horror. "You've ruined everything."

"Zion Calloway," Dizziness washed over me from my multiple injuries, but I forced out the words, "In the name of the United States, you're under arrest for treason."

A handful of swarmbots I hadn't noticed crawled up his legs, wrapped around his wrists, and locked themselves in place.

CHAPTER FIFTY

The D.C. Police spent the next two hours searching the event center to find the fake Senators and Representatives who ran and hid, bringing each one back with their necklace, the circular device like a trophy. At first, the cops had been sickened by the deceit. That turned into disgust.

After paramedics bandaged me up, injected me with nanobots and painkillers, and put a splint on my broken finger, I helped the search with the aid of a crutch.

I returned to the ballroom as Tevin and his team appeared with a half-dozen Agents; each silver-haired fighter had swarmbots cuffing their wrists. "Where'd you get the limp?" I asked, which was nearly as bad as my own.

"Gunshot." He motioned to his hip.

"Nice haul with those Agents."

His voice dropped. "They had us. We were finished. Then more cops arrived and demanded they stop, which confused them."

"They considered themselves patriots, so their fight wasn't with the police."

"Until they decide it is."

The Agents had been freed from Zion's control. They could run. Yet he had put trackers in them. Brocco had shown me. We could help the authorities find them. They'd be tried for their crimes.

I thought to tell Tevin, but exhaustion gripped me, drained by my injuries and my grief over Raven's death.

I'd tell him soon. Besides, he and the others should enjoy their victory.

I started for the exit when Garly walked in.

"Get some rest," I told him. "I need to deal with Raven's body."

He placed his huge hands on my shoulders. "She's on her journey home, the first of many from this dark day. Jex is with her. He needs time to traverse." He sighed. "I don't know if Nataly would've anointed me for my actions."

"We couldn't have won without you."

Raven's recruits came in. They were a living legacy to her efforts, a reflection of all she'd accomplished. They trained their weapons on the Agents, but their eyes darted to the person cuffed and bleeding: Zion.

A bruised Amarjit kept guard over him, as did three cops, while two police captains argued over how to handle him.

Talia rushed in and hugged me tight. I squeezed almost as hard. I made sure she was OK as Anya and Valor approached. I then hugged each, though Anya warned me to be gentle with Valor, who clutched her side.

"I got shot up," Valor said. She looked visibly drained. Bandages covered part of her hatch-marks, and dried blood stained her clothes.

"I took out two Agency snipers, the guy with the rocket launcher, three Agents, and some fighters, but that's nothing compared to Valor. Tell him," Anya said.

Valor fixed her eye on me. "I protected Talia. As promised."

I was about to prompt her when Talia spoke up. "She was a sizzle machine. She took down *seven* Agents."

"Twelve ended up attacking. They must've figured out we were a major threat. The robot you sent helped. It took out a bunch before they destroyed it," Valor said.

"Seven were yours. I saw the torch marks," Talia said.

I frowned. "Torch marks?"

Valor visibly struggled with her emotions. "Raven gave me her curved blades. Said if I ran out of bullets, they'd fend off anything that came for her sister."

Anya added, "Valor suffered three gunshots, all armor-piercing, but even with her injuries, she didn't let anyone get to Talia."

Valor grumbled. "The last Agent nearly got me, but Anya stopped him."

"I extracted the bullets and injected all of my remaining nanobots, but she should be hospitalized."

"I feel them sloshing."

"Thank you," I said to Anya, then faced Valor. "I don't know how to repay you."

She looked over at Talia, who was hugging Garly. "She was worth it."

My relief over Talia, over Anya and Valor and the others, was a balm to my sorrow, if only temporarily.

I noticed most of the drones Talia had commandeered were gone, though two news drones remained. I suspected they were being used by the news agencies that owned them — or Talia was recording everything.

Anya touched my arm. "Raven would've been proud of you."

"This was her dream, freeing everyone."

The female cop who had listened to me about the necklaces approached. "We're transferring the fake Congresspeople to federal custody. We've been in contact with the Department of Justice. They're dropping everything to focus on this."

"And the Agents?"

"They're traitors, whether they realize it or not. The Feds will handle them. A ton of people are on their way here, including the military's top brass. They all want to speak to you."

Talia came over, holding her pad. "Not just them. People are stunned-like. I've been tracking news feeds. Regular peeps are statues."

I said, "They need reassurance."

She tapped her pad, and one of the remaining news drones swiveled to focus on me. "Good call. We go live in thirty seconds."

"That's not what I meant."

Before I knew it, my face was streamed online, which I later learned was almost instantly picked up by the major news outlets.

I forced myself to speak. "My daughter Raven died to expose the truth," I said and struggled with the emotions that threatened to overwhelm me. "My friends fought and died too. America was fooled, its leaders overthrown. Today starts the process of undoing what was done. Every police station across the country, I need you to check your elected officials. The D.C. Police will explain how. If an official is legitimate, they're who they appear to be, protect them at all costs. Arrest those who aren't.

"My fellow citizens, new elections have to be held shortly. I'll do what I can to help, if it's wanted.

"To our foreign allies, the U.S. remains strong. Those who wish to attack us, our military will defend us. And we will come out of this better than before." A thought struck me. "Now, my companions and I are going to go visit the President. I suspect he's not who he claims to be."

EPILOGUE

The next six months passed in a flurry of activity that bordered on anarchy at times, layered with grief.

President Holland had been fake, though he'd been smarter than most. When my group arrived at the Oval Office, my broadcast granting us the ability to walk right into the famous room, his necklace laid abandoned on the wooden desk, the hologram the ghost of a man Americans thought they'd elected. The person who'd worn the mask was gone, the Agent assigned to him and the First Lady gone as well. They must've used whatever connections they'd built to sneak out of the White House undetected.

They hadn't been the only imposters.

The Supreme Court Justices had been fake, along with every major ambassador, trainees for the next generation. While all but one of the Joint Chiefs had been legitimate, the heads of the FBI, CIA, and Homeland Security had been fake, along with others in key roles.

It took nearly this entire time to root out every person Zion had installed. A few bodies had been found as well.

With Congress scrapped for now, the federal government was being run by the governors of the five most populous states after I confirmed they were legit. They would only hold that level of power for the next few months until elections were held.

I'd helped with those efforts, along with calming the financial markets.

In exchange, all charges against me and the surviving rebels had been dropped.

The amount of attention cast upon us was beyond anything I'd ever experienced. We were the most recognized people in the country. What didn't help were the news conferences. At the request of the temporary Governor-core, I'd reassured the country numerous times that the government was in good hands and the damage from Zion's coup would be fixed.

Before I did that, though, I'd demanded that each citizen have the right to have their eyes replaced, one with a computer screen and one with a clear lens, neither of which contained a camera. That way, no one could be blinded from the truth, at least not against their will. And none would lose their privacy.

Talia, though, asked for a number of things in "payment" for us freeing everyone.

"…and I want Garly made head scientist of everybody. I want unlimited access to all Top-Secret files, I wanna know about the aliens in Area 51, and I want one of the states to be renamed in Raven's honor."

"Which one?" I asked as I worked the new, smaller battery pack into place.

"Duh. Ravenfornia. Be happy I've only asked for eight things."

"Ten."

"Semantics."

I finished attaching the pack to her heart machine.

"The battery is charged by kinetic energy," I told her as she inspected it. "So you can't just sit on your computer all day."

"Is this your way of making me exercise?"

"There's a Bluetooth in it, which monitors the battery level. We'll both get a warning if the battery drops below a certain level."

"I'm totally hacking it." She looked up. "Instead of a battery, I want a tiny fusion reactor to power my heart."

"Sounds like you have a project to work on."

She narrowed her eyes.

While she didn't have any visible scars from the battle, her heart was permanently damaged, though that didn't slow her down. If anything, it seemed to galvanize her.

"Get your shoes on," I said. "The car is arriving in ten minutes."

She stopped me before I reached the door. "Dad? What happens if I cry? If people see?"

"Grief is a reflection of your love. Don't ever feel you need to hide that."

Anya waited in the hallway. She hugged me, then walked with me to the foyer. "The nanobots in her system have stimulated muscle growth in her heart's ventricles. It's preliminary, but if the growth continues, we may be able to remove the patches one day."

"How risky would that be?"

"Some, but I've been contacted by the top surgeons in the country. They'd be thrilled to help her. She has a bigger following than you."

Ten minutes later, we left the house where they'd put us and climbed into the limousine. Jex, Garly, and Valor were already inside. We were dressed formally, a drastic change from six months ago.

As the limo exited the neighborhood, I leaned toward Jex. "You going to make it through this?"

He nodded, though his face was drawn. "I wouldn't be anywhere else."

He and I had mourned Raven's death. We all had, but he'd helped me with the pain, many nights sobbing or storytelling or drinking, and I'd helped him. Helped Talia, too, though she'd been stronger than I'd expected.

"What new news?" Garly asked. He'd been lost at first without his love. Though he and I had talked about forming a company together, which would become a competitor to Gen Omega, I suspected he'd never be as light as he'd once been.

Anya leaned forward. "We've decided it's too risky to surgically remove the Agents' implants. There are simply too many holes. They wouldn't survive."

"Don't let that stop you."

"I say try it," Jex agreed.

"We've fried their transmitters and will remove the electronics," I said. "Basically, they've been neutered. Nearly all will get jail time, and many face murder charges."

The others shifted, unhappy. "So, they could be brought back," Garly said.

He understood new transmitters could be installed. "There's no leader. Zion is gone, Kieran, Britt, all of their upper brass." Zion's end had been particularly gruesome. The guards at the federal prison had taken it upon themselves to teach him a lesson. When they'd learned he was enhanced, they'd gone to an extreme, one he hadn't survived.

Valor broke her silence. "There's lots of talk of dismantling the government," she said as she fidgeted nervously.

"Good or bad, it's this country's glue," Garly said.

I agreed. "We're stronger together. But we're going to make changes, starting with Raven's Act." That was the law that gave everyone the right to change their lenses—and decreed The Agency be dismantled, the implants in every Agent's head emptied of their tech. That had been my other demand.

Jex smirked at me. "How deep have they pulled you into runnin' the country?"

"More and more every day, it seems. I'm glad elections are almost here."

"I hear people wanna write in your name for President."

"God no. Besides, the two candidates are better qualified."

"May not have a choice."

He held himself stiffly. Even with Anya's efforts, he hadn't fully healed from his injuries. None of us had. Probably never would.

The limo slowed to a stop as we arrived at our destination.

We climbed out and once again stepped onto the grounds of the Grande Salle de Bal event center.

It was eerie being back here. The skylight Talia had destroyed had been covered in plywood, but other than that and the removal of the bodies, the battlefield remained untouched. There was talk of leaving it as it was, a shrine to those who'd perished—and a reminder never to let ourselves become blinded again.

Though the late-Spring air was warm, the Potomac was darker and more foreboding than the shores of the Pacific.

Along with the temperature, there was another difference from that fateful day: a twenty-foot-tall covered statue now dominated the front of the property. A temporary stage had been erected beside it, placed in front of a dozen rows of folding chairs, the invited guests already seated.

Past the ceremony area, rope lines held back throngs of people.

A cheer rose when we emerged from the limo, though it was muted as befit such a somber occasion.

This soon after the battle, it was disconcerting to see people clustered here like this was some big event. Which it was, in a way.

Applause encouraged us as we headed to our seats on the stage.

The white tarp covering the statue flapped loudly in the breeze.

I thought back to the miniature sun I'd ignited the night Raven's call had started this, the warmth and light I'd created. The last few months had felt the same, a new sun, a new beginning, one big enough to encompass the entire country—a sense of community, at least for the moment. With that spirit, ten of my fusion reactors had come online, with more to follow. Though the new Congress hadn't been elected yet, this was important enough that we hadn't waited.

I gripped my notes as the ceremony began. I struggled to face why we were here, undaunted by the exposure or those who sat in the rows of chairs before us: the Governor-core, the two Presidential nominees, dignitaries and celebrities, and Raven's recruits.

I'd wanted to return to Los Angeles like Amarjit had, but there was more work here. The damage to our sky was my top priority. It wouldn't be an easy fix, but I'd work with whoever was elected, I thought as Anya slipped her hand into mine. I needed to clean the air for future generations—including the child that was on the way.

With Garly's help, I'd built a prototype that cleaned the air more efficiently than what Zion had wanted to construct. We'd need hundreds of massive filters. Removing the additives from the oil supply would be harder, causing seismic shifts in nearly every aspect of everyday life. But we didn't have a choice.

When it was my turn, I spoke at the podium, words I'd

poured over, feelings and accolades and indications of hope that now felt inadequate to capture what this moment meant. What Raven had meant.

I hadn't been sure I could give my speech, to say my words of love—and farewell. But her sacrifice had been her choice, which both cut and soothed.

There would always be a hole inside of me. She'd been a major focus of my life since the day she was born and had been by my side throughout this fight.

As the workers prepared to unveil the statue, Talia tugged on my jacket. "Do I get a statue for being your secret weapon?" she whispered.

"Yes, but you won't get to see it."

"Why not?"

"It's a secret."

Her expression pulled a smile from me, though that faded when the tarp fell to reveal a statue of Raven with flowing, wavy hair, the face a perfect likeness of her. Her jaw was thrust forward, full of confidence and beauty and might. She was in mid-action, pulling off a blindfold with her left hand, her right hand outstretched, her index and middle finger glowing from the plasma cartridges Garly had installed. They'd glow for a hundred years. Maybe longer.

A part of me was aware of applause from the crowd, though the sound seemed muffled.

I hoped this was all a projection, another Agency lie cast onto my lenses. Then maybe it wouldn't hurt so much. The governors had even suggested a hologram, but though it magnified my pain, I'd insisted on a physical one.

I'd had enough with illusions.

My fingers touched the marble, felt its fine grit and the curve of its shape, the sacrifice it signified, the loss I suffered.

Valor had dived into the project. She'd claimed she was rusty, but she'd captured Raven's strength and vibrancy.

I hugged Valor. "It's exceptional. She would have loved it."

She blinked back a tear and avoided my gaze, uncomfortable

with my compliment. "If you get the White House, I want to be the czar of the Arts. I got time to make up."

After, I shook the hands of those who approached, accepted kind words, all a blur except for Raven's recruits. Every fighter hugged me, each gesture both wounding and lifting me. They'd become crucial these past few months. Many citizens had resisted the truth, too comfortable in their delusion or unwilling to accept that they'd been deceived. Yet Raven's recruits had recounted The Agency's atrocities, shared their losses, their pain too great to ignore.

They'd also created a grass-roots movement, campaigning for politicians who said and did the right things, the recruits' small-town determination a force to be reckoned with.

I heard some planned to start hunting the Agents who'd avoided capture.

Raven would've been proud—though it wasn't just Agents we had to address. We had to decide about their enhanced kids.

I thought of Adem, who'd died so young. He would've been proud of his sister. Of both of them.

The onlookers and attendees left, everyone except for my group, each of us wrestling in our own way.

I touched Raven's statue once more, then spotted Mina past the barricade, gripping her jacket tight. She was free to live her life now, not only due to Zion's downfall. Our divorce had finalized last week.

We shared a sad smile before she turned away.

Unaware of her mother's presence, Talia answered the call she received. After a moment, she told me, "It's for you. Why don't you carry a phone anymore?"

I saw the dried tears on her cheeks. "I've had enough tech."

"They say they're ready for you."

As she, Valor, Anya, and I turned to leave, Jex stood close to the statue, wiping his eyes as he gazed up at Raven's face. He saw us preparing to leave, touched her hand goodbye, and started toward us.

Garly went to him and hooked a long arm around his stooped shoulders.

"I made notes for your meeting with the governors," Talia told me. "I'll zip 'em to you."

"Shouldn't you be running around in a field somewhere, celebrating your freedom?"

"Why do I have to run in a field? Besides, we have work. Raven would've wanted it."

I gently said, "She would've wanted you to live your life."

She put her hand in mine. "I will. After we fix everything."

Acknowledgements

Dray's sprawling adventure started with a two-paragraph blurb. It was a concept pitch, one of many ideas I threw out to see which one caught people's attention. At the time, I had no idea it would turn into a best-selling, multi-award-winning trilogy.

My characters have been taken on a long, painful journey, and while I'm sadder to see them go than I would admit out loud, they've completed their story, and my god, they've earned their rest. I feel I do, too—during this journey, I've lost people dear to me, yet also gained new family members, both two legged and four.

While writing can be solitary, with characters and subplots and twists being expanded or cast aside in my mind as I pretend to be engaged in the real world, the creation and release of a story, especially a trilogy, takes many skilled, talented, and patient people. I want to thank those who helped me and acknowledge their efforts.

I want to thank my wife Janelle for your love, encouragement, unwavering support—and for how strongly you felt about the characters. It meant so much. Thank you to Dad and Debby for your support and enthusiasm. It was a thrill to see and hear your reactions when you read the rough draft. Thank you to my sister Lisa for your exceptional editing, insightful notes, and your heart. You've shown to so many what I've known since I was little: how strong and fierce you are. Thank you to Jeremy and the rest of my family for putting up with my writing quirks. I love you all very much.

Thank you to my other Beta readers: Sarah Greenwell, Nancy Broudo, Dorothy Mason, and Judy Sachs. I particularly want to thank my writing brother, Robert Kerbeck for your support, keen insight, and fantastic notes.

To Dorothy Mason for the incredible cover. You are truly gifted. To Karen Fuller and everyone at World Castle Publishing, thank you for your support.

Lastly, I thank you, dear Reader, for sticking with me through Dray's journey. I truly hope you enjoyed *The Price of Freedom*, as well as the overall trilogy. None of this means anything without you.

Follow me on social media and sign up for my newsletter at www.mcbland.com to hear about future novels. And please leave reviews on Amazon, Goodreads, etc. They mean so much.

Michael C. Bland

Michael is a founding member and the secretary of BookPod, an invitation-only online group of professional writers. He pens the monthly BookPod newsletter, where he celebrates the success of their members, which include award-winning writers, filmmakers, journalists, and bestselling authors.

One of Michael's short stories, "Elizabeth," won Honorable Mention in Writer's Digest 2015 Popular Fiction Awards contest. Three of the short stories he edited have been nominated for the Pushcart Prize. Another story he edited was adapted into an award-winning film.

He also had three superhero-themed poems published on *The Daily Palette*.

Michael currently lives in Florida with his wife Janelle and their dogs Nobu and Pico.

His novel, *The Price of Freedom*, is the final installment in The Price Of trilogy.